The Tombstone
Imperative

The Tombstone Imperative

The Truth About Air Safety

Andrew Weir

SIMON & SCHUSTER
A VIACOM COMPANY

First published in Great Britain by Simon & Schuster UK Ltd, 1999
A Viacom Company

1 3 5 7 9 10 8 6 4 2

Simon & Schuster UK Ltd
Africa House
64-78 Kingsway
London WC2B 6AH

Simon & Schuster Australia
Sydney

A CIP catalogue record for this book is available
from the British Library

ISBN 0-684-81993-7

Typeset in Sabon by SX Composing DTP, Rayleigh, Essex
Printed and bound in Great Britain by
Butler & Tanner Ltd, Frome and London

Acknowledgements

Thanks first to Alex, my partner, and our children Esther and Helen for their patience with my absences – in spirit if not in person – while writing the book. It was Roger Houghton, my agent, who persuaded me it was doable and worth doing, and whose constant encouragement was indispensable.

In the aviation safety community I will single out CO "Chuck" Miller, Eddie Trimble, and Frank Taylor, director of the Cranfield Aviation Safety Centre, from many inspiring figures. Ira Rimson gave me invaluable help by critically reading my manuscript and making wise comments. Other investigators and advocates of greater aviation safety I am grateful to include Eric Newton, Doug Dreifus and Bill Tench. Pete Mellor was especially helpful in regard to the material on software. Other writers on the subject to whom I am indebted include Macarthur Job and Byron Acohido. David Daslow and John Smithson were kind enough to allow me to quote from some interviews we did for Channel Four's Black Box, and it was while working for them that I formed my interest in this subject. For their determination to see aviation safety improve and their example to others I also want to thank the following campaigners, lawyers and survivors: William and Linda Beckett, Noel Crymble, Pamela Dix, Jean-Noel Chatre, Hubert de Gaullier, Guy-Michel Ney and Gerald C Sterns. Other thanks and citations appear in the text. None of the above, however, bear any responsibility for what I have written, nor can any of them necessarily be associated with my views.

Andrew Weir
April 1999

Contents

Introduction

THE TOMBSTONE IMPERATIVE was not originally a thriller novel's title. It was used as a chapter heading in a book quoting Barry Sweedler, one of the senior officials of the National Transportation Safety Board, which supervises aircraft safety in the USA.

In a moment of gallows humour, for which accident investigators are notorious, he said, "We regulate by counting tombstones". This was both a sad acknowledgement of the way in which the world works and a perfectly accurate statement. In the main, changes to the safety of modern aircraft are only made when a cost-benefit analysis has been done in which the cost of the new safety measure is balanced against a notional figure for the monetary value of a life. If the cost of the measure exceeds the "value" of the lives saved, then it won't be implemented.

The broad theme of this book is that there ought to be a better way of implementing safety measures than simply counting tombstones. We can prevent tombstones too, and the means are well within our power. You will also see that the vast majority of crashes are preventable, and that none of them is "just one of those things". We are encouraged by the aviation business to think about all this in a schizophrenic way. On the one hand, they want us to be fatalistic about air crashes: "there are risks in everything". On the other hand, they tell us that no method of travel is safer. This is untrue.

Generations of air travellers have been brought up on the idea that commercial aviation is as safe as can be, that no effort is spared to make it safer, and that other forms of transport are more risky.[1] This is, as we shall see, not the case. Statistics have been yoked to all sorts of purposes, and forced to support all sorts of statements, but few question those used by the aviation business, even when it leads them into absurdities.

A case in point arose in 1996 when one of the US FAA's top personnel, Tony Broderick, admitted in public that he was happy not to compel US airlines to carry safety seats for children under the age of two. The logic he used was that compelling the airlines to do this would increase the cost of air travel. Therefore, he said, poorer families would travel by road, and because road travel is more dangerous, more children would be killed. Mr Broderick thus managed to deflect an initiative that would have improved airline safety and which airlines were resisting strongly. Using Mr Broderick's argument, they elegantly saved money and claimed to save lives, while simultaneously failing to improve airline safety. This kind of deft sophistry has characterised the airline industry's view of safety for a long time.

In fact, as I shall show, air travel is more dangerous when calculated on a per-journey, rather than per-mile, basis than car travel. Mr Broderick's argument also followed another time-honoured industry practice, that of pointedly asking the safety critic whether he or she "really" wants to raise the cost of a ticket by x-hundred dollars by introducing such and such a safety measure. Somehow, the same question never gets put when the airline is contemplating a multi-million-dollar advertising campaign.

The aviation industry persistently resists new safety measures, but when such attitudes look like attracting widespread criticism it commissions research. The research takes years, sometimes over a decade, and yet definitive results never seem to emerge. "More research" always seems to be required. When they are obliged to get off the fence the cost-benefit analysis is used. The reason why nothing can be done then becomes, "nice idea, but not worthwhile in terms of the number of lives saved". For misleading uses of statistics, the airline industry is the place to go.

Perhaps it has something to do with reassurance in the face of one of modern society's greatest fears. While most of us do not worry about death by drowning at the seaside, or being killed in a car crash on the way to the superstore, many of us experience a special fear when being propelled six miles up in the air in a noisy, cramped aluminium tube which is travelling at 500 mph. Anyone would need reassurance in such a situation, but airlines have over-reached themselves in doling it out.

They have certainly gone too far in saying that air travel is the safest mode of transport. It is a mantra of the industry and has been said so often by so many professionals in the field that they have probably forgotten what the statement is based on. However, in making this claim, they use only one measure for comparing air travel with other forms of transport.

If you plot the number of fatal accidents against distance travelled, air travel is indeed the safest mode of transport, registering about 0.03 fatalities per 100 million kms, compared with 0.10 fatalities per 100 million kms for rail travel – a rate over three times higher. These are the figures usually used by the airline industry when blowing its own trumpet.

Closer examination shows that the other transport modes are not competing with air travel on a level playing field here. Typically, aircraft travel huge distances – much greater than most of the competing transport modes – and while the risk of having a fatal accident in those other transport modes is distributed more or less evenly throughout the journey, it is not so with planes. The risk of an aircraft accident is heavily concentrated on take-off and landing, which represent only 4 per cent of journey-time, and 70 per cent of all aircraft accidents take place at this time.[2]

If you plot fatalities against distances, you effectively dilute the accident rate for aircraft – which could be why the airline industry uses that method of analysis. A better measure for safety comparisons is to plot the number of fatalities against the time travelled, i.e. quantifying the rate for fatal accidents per 100 million hours of journey time. This is a fairer means of comparison, since many car, bus, train and ship journeys are of similar duration to plane journeys.

Even if you use this measure, you still face the same problem: that of the risk to aircraft being concentrated in the first and last phases of flight, while the risk to the other modes is more even throughout the time of the journey. This way of measuring accidents has been particularly kind, for example, to Qantas, the Australian airline, which has not had a fatal accident since 1968. This is, obviously, a creditable record, but it tells us very little. The vast majority of Qantas flights are international and very long in duration. As a result, they fly a comparatively large number of hours per journey, and thus are less exposed to the risk of crashes than another airline that might fly the same number of hours, but over a much larger number of flights.

The best way, therefore, of comparing the different modes of travel thus becomes to quantify the rate of fatal accidents against the number of journeys made. Indeed, this is the method used by Boeing in its annual compilation of accident statistics.[3]

As a tool of analysis, this makes much better sense because the priority to the individual is the journey, not how long it took or how far it went. By that measure, air travel takes on a different complexion entirely. Fatalities per 100 million passenger journeys are, on average, 55 for aircraft, against 4.5 for cars, and 2.7 for trains. Only motorbikes, at 100 fatalities per 100 million passenger journeys, count as more risky than aircraft on a per-journey basis.[4]

Does this mean we are in greater danger when we fly than we thought? For most of us, no. As any insurance expert will tell you, your risk depends on your exposure. Journey for journey, it is much safer to travel by train than by car, but if you don't own a car and usually travel by train, your risk of death in a train is higher. If, for example, you are a business traveller who rarely drives but uses airlines twice a week in the course of your work, your chances of being killed in an air accident are much greater than when using the road.

It is also worth bearing in mind that risk on the roads is very different from risk in the air. A newly qualified male teenage driver is a poor risk, and his insurance rates will reflect the huge difference between the probability of him being responsible for a crash and, say, the chance of the same thing happening to a middle-aged woman with twenty-five years behind the wheel. Both, however, are in the same situation when it comes to travelling in an aeroplane. So, if you are in a very low-risk category for road travel, air travel might be even riskier for you.

Whatever projections are made for the different modes of transport, and however you quantify safety in the air, at least the situation is not getting any worse. The rate at which air accidents occur has now virtually stabilised. In 1947 approximately 600 people were killed in air crashes. Despite an exponential increase in the numbers of flights and passengers carried, the average deaths per year is now only about double that figure. If the same proportion of passengers and crew were being killed now as fifty years ago, there could be 50,000 deaths in a typical year. In essence, air travel progressively became safer at the same time as it grew in popularity.

There are many reasons why safety managed to grow in tandem with the rise in the amount of traffic. Although those safety improvements should be hailed, and have been most welcome, it is depressing to note that the improvement in the figures has come about as a by-product of technological change, not as a result of conscious efforts to lower the death toll.

In the 1950s scheduled passenger aircraft services began to replace piston engines with jet engines. This provided the biggest leap in safety the air industry has ever known. Piston engines were being made as reliable as possible, but, as any engineer will tell you, a mechanical system that involves parts pushing forwards and backwards, as in the motions of the internal combustion engine, is inherently prone to greater wear and greater possibility of failure.

The beauty of the jet engine is that all its parts rotate in one direction and as a result it is much less prone to failure than a piston engine. Although the jet engine was introduced to passenger aircraft to improve travel time and economy it had the unintended but happy by-product of increasing the safety of air travel. No other single change to aircraft design and construction has had such a dramatic effect.

Over the years new aircraft systems – including air traffic control by radar, automated systems for landing in bad weather, better airports and weather radar – have improved safety on board. As a result, the accident rate of aircraft kept falling through the 1960s and 1970s. Interestingly, the measures being brought in to lower costs and improve operational performance such as more sophisticated autopilots, flight simulators and more efficient navigational systems, also increased safety, albeit only serendipitously, rarely by design.

The serendipity no longer applies. Innovations continue apace, but overall they are not making flying any safer, only more cost-effective. The probability of a fatal accident has now levelled off at between 1.5 and 2 per million departures. That amounts to an average of about 1,500 deaths per year world-wide, the former Soviet Union excepted.[5]

While the accident rate has stabilised, air travel has not. The year-on-year increase in commercial air travel is now estimated at 7 per cent world-wide. The vagaries of the business cycle means there will be fluctuations, as in the downturn of the Asian economies in the middle of 1998, but that figure is generally accepted as an average. On that basis, and with the accident rate no longer falling, the number of crashes is going to increase in total every year unless the accident rate starts to fall once again. Ten years from now, on present traffic growth rates, twice as many people will be killed in air crashes as today. To maintain approximately the same number of crashes and fatalities as we experience now, air travel would have to become about three times safer over the next twenty years.[6]

This is where perceptions come into play. The sight on a news bulletin of the burning wreckage of yet another airliner, the bizarre news jargon of "rescuers" and the knowledge that another 200 people have died in one of the most terrifying ways imaginable may be shocking to many but has been accepted as a "fact of life". If the same bulletins were being broadcast weekly, which is on average what could be happening ten years from now, the public would be unlikely to take it in its stride. Given the nearly random occurrence of such tragedies, their distribution would be uneven, so that there could be, say, three jumbo jet crashes with all on board perishing in the space of a week, followed by a month or more of no accidents. A bad year could see over 3,000 dying in air crashes.

Stuart Matthews, the president of the Flight Safety Foundation, probably the most prominent international body in air safety, is one of many who have spoken out on the danger this poses to the industry: ". . . political and public tolerance of the current number of accidents, let alone any further increase, has probably reached its limit".[7]

Congressman Norman Mineta also addressed the problem when he made his opening remarks to the US National Civil Aviation Review Committee in October 1997: "It is also clear that the anticipated growth in aviation coupled with the current accident rate [will mean that] the frequency of accidents in the future will become wholly unacceptable. The accident rate, which has been low but flat for the past twenty-five years, must somehow be reduced dramatically if people are going to retain their confidence in the safety of air travel."[8]

People's perception of risk is not always rational, not least because most of us are not statisticians or mathematicians. The probability of a shark attack did not increase following the release of *Jaws!* in 1978, but it still emptied beaches all over the world that summer. Take another example of the vagaries of risk perception. In the UK nearly 95 per cent of the eligible population has bought a ticket for the National Lottery, despite the odds of winning a jackpot being about one in 14 million. The odds of being killed in a plane crash every time you buy an airline ticket are some ten times better than that. Understandably, we do not view the risk in the same way.

Nevertheless, the aviation industry is playing a dangerous game by peddling misleading information about safety statistics and resisting or failing to enforce better safety procedures and equipment. They could find that, for rational reasons or not, the public gradually begins to distrust air travel and looks for safer alternatives.

In this context it is worth bearing in mind that the aircraft manufacturing industry's two remaining giants, Airbus and Boeing, are laying out designs for airliners that will carry over 600 passengers. However unlikely the crash of such a plane may be, it is improbable that the travelling public would remain quite so serene about air travel after one of those has spread itself all over a mountainside.

In other modes of transport, especially road vehicles, safety has been improving year after year in the industrialised world for over thirty years, ever since governments decided to take a hand in improving the situation. The travelling public is entitled to demand the same of aviation. For too long the aviation industry has been operating on the assumption that it is "safe enough".

However, aircraft manufacturers in particular have to take a long view of developments, and they are well aware of the potential dangers. Although they have often been those most anxious to reassure, and have sometimes shied away from safety recommendations, they are, ultimately, the losers if the travelling public chooses other ways of getting around.

The International Air Transport Association, which represents the world's airlines, voiced such concerns for the first time at its AGM in November 1997. IATA director-general Pierre Jeanniot set a target of halving the hull-loss accident rate by 2004 "as an interim measure".[9] However, he did not specify how this could be achieved, nor offer to organise any reporting system on how airlines could monitor their progress. Since the linkage between making airline operations more efficient and safer no longer applies, it is unclear how airlines can be expected to fund the safety improvements. He was suggesting, more or less, that everyone in the industry all holds hands and prays, as well as exchanges information. There were no concrete measures. Exhortation alone has never improved safety in any line of business, and there is no reason to suppose aviation is any different.

Unfortunately, Mr Jeanniot, like the UN organisation which

supposedly governs international civil aviation, ICAO, has no power to force airlines to follow safer practices. In China, for example, which has the worst aviation safety record of any nation, up to twenty times worse than Western industrialised countries, aviation is run by the state and there is no impetus for change. Until Chinese aircraft are forbidden to fly abroad, or measures are taken to force or embarrass the authorities into action, no improvement can realistically be expected. Much the same is true of Africa, whose aviation record is nearly as frightening.

Lest we imagine it is a Third World problem, here are a couple of examples from closer to home. Airbus Industrie blamed pilots for several fatal crashes, and yet made changes to the aircraft after each accident. Despite the fact that toxic smoke and fire are the second-biggest killers of air travellers, the US FAA steadfastly refuses to implement smoke-protection or water-sprinkler systems. Since 1988 the FAA had vigorously resisted the idea of having smoke detectors and automatic fire-extinguishers installed in all cargo holds. However, when a ValuJet DC-9 crashed in May 1996, due to a cargo-hold fire, they decided to accede to the requested changes.

If IATA, ICAO and the national regulatory authorities are to get anywhere they will have to "name and shame" nations and airlines that are falling short of best practices. Aviation authorities, for example, should be allowed to ground foreign aircraft that their inspectors judge to be in an unsafe condition. Currently, ICAO rules do not allow them to do this.

In many countries accident investigation is so slow as to be practically useless, and in others it is secret. Some reports have still not been filed on crashes that happened more than ten years ago. Singapore Airlines, for example, is typical of the secretive organisations. When its Silk Air 737 crashed in January 1998, the company announced that this was its first fatal accident. All the pilots in the region knew that, in fact, the airline had lost a Lear jet and its crew beforehand. Singapore Airlines justified excluding that crash from the statistics because the plane in question was not "in revenue operation". A fatal crash, most people think, is a fatal crash whichever way you cut it.

Since efforts to improve aviation safety are currently confined to urgings of one kind or another, they are doomed to failure. A particularly stark example is the CFIT Task Force, which was set up by the Flight Safety Foundation and ICAO in 1992 with the aim of halving the number of controlled flight into terrain (CFIT) crashes by 1998. (CFIT, pronounced "See-fit", is a euphemism for flying into a hillside.) The first couple of years showed a decline, but CFIT crashes went up in 1996, and 1997 proved to be the worst year ever for total CFIT crashes and fatalities.

To be generous it could be said that international organisations start by recommending, move to urging, and then take enforcement measures. If this is so, the pace is so leisurely that it is extremely unlikely to catch up with the increase in fatalities arising from increased air travel in general. It should also be noted that none of these organisations has made any proposals on improving the currently poor standard of crashworthiness in aircraft design. While the rate at which fatal accidents occur fell, before stabilising over the last twenty years, the number of fatalities per crash has barely changed at all. Operationally, the modern airliner is as efficient as any top-of-the-range Mercedes, Volvo or BMW. In terms of crashworthiness, though, it is a Model T.

It is frequently said by airline representatives that nobody is interested in having a poor safety record because it will drive away customers. "We", the airline representative will say, "put safety at the top of our priorities." This, frankly, is a lie. An airline's first priority is to earn revenue because, without it, it would not exist. Profits are the *raison d'être* of airlines and without them you don't have safety, because without them you don't have air travel. There is nothing wrong with profits or maximising revenue, but the airlines always attempt to give the impression that they are doing more than the minimum. In fact, very few of them do.

Unnecessary costs are the enemy of profits, and safety measures increase costs without increasing revenue. It is therefore obvious that safety measures that involve considerable expenditure will be hotly debated in the airlines where they are proposed. Essentially, this means that no airline will spend money on safety unless it is obliged to, for the simple reason that by increasing its costs it would be putting itself at a competitive disadvantage to other airlines.

Let us take one example of the way in which the industry is pulled both ways. On the one hand, the major airlines and manufacturers participate in the various initiatives now being developed to improve safety. They are, however, reducing the amount they spend on training pilots, thanks to the enormous work-capacity of modern cockpit automation, a trend that is growing in the most competitive airlines. There are important dangers here because many of the automated systems in modern cockpits, while saving pilots' time in normal flying operation, succeed in *increasing* pilot workload when the situation deviates even slightly from normal (*see* Chapter 6).

Also, in the drive to cut costs, an ever-increasing number of airlines are contracting out their airliner maintenance work to competitive tender. This is a trend the US NTSB, among others, has warned against on the basis that, at the very least, maintenance workers outside the airline cannot have the same loyalty and commitment as those within the company. They add that a direct line-management route of accountability from maintenance department to flight operations is broken. Although, legally, a maintenance error that led to a crash or other financial loss would ultimately also be the responsibility of the airline, it is simple common sense to realise that the supervision cannot be as great as if the maintenance were being performed in-house.

Contracting out maintenance in this way cannot be good for safety overall, and maintenance-related accidents have increased as a proportion of all crashes, especially in the last ten years. Equally serious, moreover, is the worry that safety may have been compromised within the maintenance company, so that it could enter a bid low enough to win a contract through competitive tender. Several startling examples (*see* Chapter 7) illustrate the current trend of increasing maintenance errors.

The fact that being safe and being profitable do not have the same status within an airline means that an enormous responsibility is placed on the regulatory authorities to supervise and enforce safety practices. Unfortunately, the regulators usually share the same broad philosophy as the airlines and are unwilling to require safety measures that cost airlines money unless they cannot be avoided. Indeed, many regulatory authorities have responsibility to promote and/or protect the aviation industry written into their charters. Changes in auto safety, in contrast, were initiated by governments and the improvements in the statistics began to be felt almost immediately. Once that had taken hold, manufacturers then began to market cars on the basis of their safety features.

The individual air traveller, however, does not buy aircraft, and has no influence on the industry. The passenger is too often looked upon as, in the pilots' jargon, "self-loading cargo". The all-important customer is the airline, for whom many aircraft are specifically designed, and with whom the manufacturers consult endlessly. As a result, the push for greater safety is unlikely to come from the manufacturers, even though they are the experts. They, however, have a longer-term interest in safety than the airlines, because the investment required for major new airliners may only be recouped over a period of twenty years or more. They are thus more able, as Boeing has done, to comment on the coming increase in air-crash numbers and say that something should be done about it. The airlines and the regulators are the ones who will force changes, if they exert enough pressure.

The safety of planes has another aspect. Although the passenger may desert an airline perceived as unsafe, and this often happens to an airline in the immediate aftermath of a serious crash, most passengers have few real choices. In the highly competitive US market, ValuJet achieved notoriety for its May 1996 crash in which 110 people died, and subsequently lost huge amounts of business – up to 50 per cent, according to some sources. Soon afterwards it acquired another carrier, AirTran, and thereafter used that name instead of ValuJet. British Midland, however, suffered very little loss of business after the Kegworth crash in January 1989, because competition on its route to Belfast was minimal.

If you want to go from Manchester to Tenerife on holiday,

sailing there is not a realistic option. With transatlantic travel it is the same. However, if jumbos are falling out of the sky once a week, how soon will it be before the ocean-cruise liners set themselves up for regular passenger services, as in the days before air travel? The railway service between London and various French and Belgian destinations has proved competitive with the airlines, as have high-speed trains throughout Europe. How soon before more such lines spring up, especially in the United States, which has no high-speed railways at all – yet?

The travelling public has much less of a voice in air safety than in other transport modes, and has been excluded by the industry, which does far too much self-policing. If we are to demand to be heard we should be better informed, and this book will help provide strong arguments against the industry's view that safety in the air is none of the travelling public's concern.

The main theme of this book is that the travelling public has a right to better safety in the air, and to a continually improving safety picture across the board. As air accident investigator Eddie Trimble puts it, "The reason the industry is so leery of safety improvements is because passengers are not properly represented."[10] If they were, the pressure for change would be far greater.

CHAPTER 1

Why planes crash

PLANES CRASH BECAUSE somebody screwed up. However far down the line it may have occurred, human error must always be the reason, from the drafting of a poor regulation, to an error by air traffic control, bad design, slips during maintenance or manufacture, or the bad judgement of a pilot. Since aircraft are made and operated by humans it could not be any other way even if, in the final analysis, the error was not perceived at the time, or not perceived as having any significance. To blame the weather for a crash, for example, is absurd. If the weather is too dangerous for flight, aircraft ought not to be flying.

Take-off, as one wag put it, is optional: landing is compulsory. In the world of those who study car crashes, the word "accident" has fallen into disuse. The word tends to absolve humans from responsibility, and implies that these are things that "just happen". "Crash" leaves less to the imagination, and is more accurate.

There are very few crashes where the precise "why" is not known. Cockpit voice recorders (CVRs) have been compulsory on all large jets flying internationally since 1974, and many were fitted with them long before that. These record the last thirty minutes of flight-deck conversation and cockpit noise on a loop tape so that when power is lost, as it would be during a crash, the tape stops and the last thirty minutes are preserved. Flight data recorders (FDRs) have been around longer, recording basic data about the heading, attitude, altitude and time, although modern models now record up to 500 aspects of what the plane is doing.

These "black boxes" are not the be-all and end-all of accident investigation but they are the main reasons why the number of inexplicable crashes has fallen to a tiny proportion of the whole. Nevertheless, although there are fewer gaps in our knowledge nowadays about why planes crash, the reasons have changed little over the last thirty to forty years. Of the crashes with known causes, over 70 per cent were caused by the crew, about 11 per cent by a defect in the aircraft itself and between 4 and 6 per cent by poor maintenance, weather, air traffic control, and miscellaneous factors.[1]

The only significant change in these proportions has been the number of accidents caused by flight-crew. Pilots are not becoming more incompetent; indeed, they are more highly trained now than ever. It is simply that as the aircraft have become more reliable, particularly with regard to the difference made by the jet engine, the proportion of accident-causation that belongs to the flight-crew inevitably increases.[2]

It is worth considering a few examples of widely differing types of crash, illustrating the sometimes bizarre coincidence of extremely unusual circumstances which is the hallmark of most of them. Modern airliners and their operating environment are what computer specialists call "tightly coupled systems". The interdependence of many different aspects of the operation is so complete that a glitch in one small area can cause a set of dominoes to fall, a "cascade" as it is sometimes called. Many crashes follow the pattern: for want of a nail, the horse was lost, for want of a horse, the king was lost, and so on.

Other accidents, on the other hand, albeit a minority of them, had single causes. Nevertheless, every type of crash has this much in common: nobody could perceive the conspiracy of events that would lead to disaster; second, they were all preventable.

One of the best examples of an almost bizarre conspiracy of

coincidences resulted in the world's worst air disaster, when a KLM 747 collided with a PanAm 747 at Los Rodeos Airport on Tenerife in March 1977. There were five vital conditions for the crash, the absence of any one of which would have prevented it. One of them was the Dutch captain's failure to ask permission to take off. That was the only preventable factor, and so that is why, rightly, he was held accountable for causing the disaster.

In giving an account of what happened, the odd circumstances can be seen to build up. First came the fact that these two heavily laden 747s were diverted, along with a number of other aircraft, from Las Palmas airport on Gran Canaria to Tenerife airport. Canary Island separatists had set off a bomb in the Las Palmas departure lounge and the authorities had to inspect the airport before clearing it to resume business.

Tenerife airport, which only had one runway, was therefore unusually crowded and some imaginative shuffling was going to be required for the officials to manage all the departures.[3] After they heard that Las Palmas airport was once again clear for landings, the captain of the PanAm 747 decided to leave, but the KLM plane was in the middle of refuelling and it stood between the PanAm plane and the runway, meaning the Americans had to wait.

Eventually, the tower instructed the KLM plane to taxi down the runway, turn itself around and wait for permission to take off. While it was doing this, the PanAm plane was also instructed by the tower to taxi down the runway, to leave at the third taxiway, and report when it was clear of the runway.

This is where the weather came in. Lying at 2000 feet, nearly at the foot of the gigantic inland volcano that dominates the island, the airport is situated at the precise point where clouds form. The clouds tend rapidly to form and dissipate, lift up and come down, all in an unpredictable way. Just such a cloud began to lower visibility as the KLM plane turned around at the end of the runway.

In the gathering gloom the crew of the PanAm plane could not find the taxiway they had been told to go to, but they spotted the next one along and were just about to take it when they saw the

KLM plane accelerating towards them. They desperately pushed the throttle levers forward in an effort to get off the runway. Having seen the PanAm plane at the last moment, the KLM captain tried to lift his plane over it. The jumbo got off the ground but part of one engine and the central undercarriage gouged into the roof of the PanAm 747. The KLM plane flew on for a few seconds, pancaked on to the runway and burst into a series of explosions which killed everyone on board.

Many of the PanAm plane's passengers were elderly and had difficulty getting away, although there were some sixty survivors. With the roof of the 747 having been ripped away like a tent blown away by a gale, many of them simply stepped over the remains of the cabin wall directly on to the wing before jumping off. The fire quickly gathered in intensity and the fuel tanks soon blew up, killing all who remained on board. In total the disaster claimed 586 lives.

The last, but most vital, part of the unusual circumstances in this tragedy, was the Dutch captain's failure to request permission to take off, one of the grossest mistakes it is possible to make. There were circumstances which indicated the possibility of confusion about this permission, but none that mitigated this cardinal error. There was a terrible conspiracy of odd circumstances – the bomb, PanAm having to wait for the KLM plane, PanAm's failure to find the taxiway – the absence of any one of which would have been enough not only to prevent the crash, but probably to leave everyone unaware that disaster had been narrowly averted. Of all the circumstances, however, only one was the result of negligence, and that was the KLM captain's failure to request permission to take off.

The investigation of this tragedy began with speculation that faulty instructions from the tower had caused the crash, but the CVR tapes and the FDR data dispelled that view immediately. Listening to the conversation in the KLM cockpit, the investigators found they were listening to an overbearing and impatient captain who was not communicating or interacting particularly well with his crew. Captain Jacob Van Zanten was an outstanding pilot of unparalleled prestige in the Netherlands. He was KLM's chief training pilot on the 747 and his good looks adorned KLM's magazine advertising.

However, the Dutch government had recently brought in new regulations restricting the amount of time pilots were allowed to spend on duty, along with heavy sanctions for breaking the new rules. If the KLM 747 was to reach Las Palmas, and still make it back to Amsterdam before the duty restrictions came in, the captain knew they would have to hurry up.

The KLM co-pilot that day was relatively new to the 747 and had been approved for flying 747s by Van Zanten himself. This was later believed by the investigators to have been the crucial element at work in the cockpit: a junior officer intimidated by his superior to such an extent that he did not feel able to contradict him, even when the captain was doing something wrong.

In fact the co-pilot did assert himself; once, anyway. As they were waiting at the end of the runway, the captain started to advance the throttles. The co-pilot piped up, "Wait, we do not have clearance." Irritably, the captain said, "Yes, I know. Request it." The co-pilot then radioed for and received the air traffic control clearance, which tells the crew what path to follow after take-off, but does not constitute permission to take off. After the captain said, "We go," the co-pilot blurted out, in an anxious and highly stressed voice, "We are uh . . . taking off," an odd pronouncement not called for by the procedures.[4] A few seconds later the KLM flight engineer heard the PanAm crew tell the tower that they would report when clear of the runway. He then said, "Is he not clear then, the Pan American?" and the captain responded, "Of course." A few seconds later the plane smashed into the PanAm aircraft.

Bob Bragg, who was the co-pilot of the PanAm 747, gives his account of what happened.

Since the ramp was completely congested all traffic had to taxi back down the runway. We followed KLM – we were directly in back of him – taxiing down the runway . . . As we were taxiing down KLM got his Air Traffic Control clearance.

As he was getting his clearance a fog bank came down on to the runway. The visibility went from unlimited to 500 metres. At the same time the tower told us the centreline lights were out of service . . . we needed at least 750 metres' visibility before we could take off. So we thought the airport was closed . . .

Everyone was in a big hurry to get out of here. The KLM captain had called numerous times trying to get information on when he could leave. He was probably very irritated, as all of us were.

We were taxiing down the runway very slowly due to the low visibility. We were just beginning to see the turnoff we were supposed to take, and we looked up and saw the KLM airplane's lights, which didn't bother us too much because we knew he was down there. He was supposed to go down the end, make a turn and wait for us to get off the runway. At that time the tower gave him his Air Traffic Control clearance, which basically gave him the routing to take from Tenerife to Las Palmas.

As soon as the KLM airplane read his clearance back the tower asked us, "Pan Am, have you cleared the runway?" I said "Negative. We will report when clear of the runway." About that time we looked up again and there the KLM airplane was and the lights were beginning to shake and I made the comment, "I think he's moving," and about that time it was obvious he was moving. He was coming down the runway straight at us. So I started saying, "Get off, get off," and the captain had already gone to full throttle on the engines. We were only going three knots so the airplane was moving very slowly. I reached over and tried to help him but he had already pushed the throttles to full power. We got the airplane turned. I looked up through the right window and the KLM airplane was right close to us, had lifted off and I could see his rotating beacon underneath the belly of the airplane.

As we were turning I closed my eyes and ducked and then the airplane hit us. I didn't think he had hurt us because it was just a very slight shudder with very little noise associated with it. When I looked up it was obvious he had done us a lot of damage, the windows were completely gone.

I looked out to the right; the right wing was on fire. I looked back to the left. We had twenty-eight people in the upstairs lounge and the lounge was no longer there. In fact I could look right to the tail of the airplane. It was like someone had taken a big knife and cut the entire top off the airplane.

At that time I reached down and tried to shut down all the four engines. Nothing happened. I guess all the controls were severed. I looked up to get the fire control handles which shut down all of the engines and that's when I discovered there was no top to the airplane at all. I stood up, there was only a foot of the console left, there was no side of the airplane left. I stood up and elected to jump over the left side of the airplane. Which was about forty-eight feet . . . I hit on the grass and rolled.[5]

Bragg, who later went to fly as a 747 captain for another airline after PanAm went bust in 1989, survived with a broken arm.

The KLM plane had caused a disaster mainly because of poor communication and crew co-ordination, and the disaster spawned a new industry which goes by the name of cockpit resource management. Some airlines give it different names, but the idea is the same: to overthrow the old concept of the domineering, all-knowing captain. CRM training is meant to encourage the senior crew members to listen to what their juniors are saying, to persuade junior officers to speak up when they feel something is wrong, and to foster all-round collective effort.[6]

CRM and associated activities by psychologists encouraging the best possible working atmosphere in the cockpit have become a sizeable industry in the last twenty years, although crashes where poor CRM bears some responsibility still occur with depressing regularity. Under the general title of "human factors", armies of psychologists analyse crashes to see what went wrong. They often end up with training recommendations that call, more or less, for the elimination of human error, an impossible task. Some pilots distrust the idea of warm, fuzzy cockpits with caring and sharing crews.

Aircraft designers and maintenance engineers are not subjected to the same amount of CRM exhortation as aircrew, even though

their failures to listen or consider alternatives have serious implications for safety. And while CRM teaches pilots important
lessons about co-operation, when an emergency arises person-
alities very often revert to instinctive type.

The aviation world is lagging behind the automotive world in
this respect. Before all manner of safety devices were installed on
cars it was assumed that the only way of reducing the death toll
on the roads was to educate the driver. This is sometimes known
as primary safety, i.e. stopping crashes from happening. Later, we
realised that drivers would, whatever happened, sometimes do the
wrong thing, and for maximum safety you had to assume that the
worst could happen. This led to secondary safety measures, i.e.
seat-belts, airbags, and so on. The aviation industry has yet to take
account of this and remains stuck on primary safety.

The way in which seemingly innocent circumstances can con-
spire the way they did at Tenerife has long been recognised.
"Murphy's law" states that if something can go wrong, it will.
Most crashes consist of a combination of Murphy's law and a
human error or two thrown in. There are occasions, however,
when a single mistake, possibly a conceptual error, can spell
disaster.

The human element in a disaster is usually only one part, and
not always a large part of the circumstances leading to tragedy.
Illustrative though it is of how critical the human component can
be, the Tenerife disaster is not typical of the type of crash that
causes the most casualties. Even if no crash can really be
considered typical, runway collisions have not yet resulted in a
death toll even a quarter as large as that at Tenerife.

The most lethal of the crashes in which the human element has
been regarded as decisive go by the strangely antiseptic name of
CFIT. This covers incidents when the pilots did not know where
they were, and found out too late to do anything about it.
Formally, CFIT is defined as an accident "in which an otherwise
serviceable aircraft, under the control of the crew, is flown
unintentionally into terrain, obstacles or water, with no prior
awareness on the part of the crew of the impending collision".[7]

CFIT crashes are highest on the world aviation community's list of things to prevent. In the ten years to the end of 1996, there were on average four commercial-jet CFIT crashes a year, causing up to 500 deaths, nearly half the total fatalities in that period.[8]

At the end of 1992 the Flight Safety Foundation, in conjunction with the UN body governing international aviation, the International Civil Aviation Organisation (ICAO), set the industry a target of reducing CFIT crashes by 50 per cent in the next five years. It was an extraordinary target for the industry to set itself, especially as trends in air safety can take ten years or more to demonstrate themselves statistically, and shows that serious consideration of safety issues is new ground for the industry.

The CFIT Task Force produced few concrete proposals. Despite involving some 150 representatives from twenty-four airlines, five aerospace manufacturers and "a host of key aviation organisations", the best it could manage was to circulate training aids, videos and other material.[9] It did not recommend simulator-based training for escape manoeuvres, nor has it tackled the serious lack of modern navigational and landing aids at many airports. Laudable and useful though its training aids and videos might be, it is clear that stronger suggestions – effective ones – were not made because they involve expense.

Meanwhile, "more training" is uttered like a mantra. As the magazine *Flight International* commented in relation to the Task Force's efforts, "You can, it seems, lead a pilot to the best practice, but you can't always make him follow it."[10] The advantage to the industry of calling for more training is that it perpetuates the half-truth that all CFITs are down to stupid piloting, and ducks the much more difficult questions involving airport infrastructure, the availability of simulator-training, pressures on pilots to fly when they do not think it advisable, improving escape manoeuvres, and even the crashworthiness of aircraft. Industry organisations cannot grapple with such questions because they involve spending money.

The sorry fact is that the CFIT Task Force campaign has been a miserable failure. In 1997, 640 people died in CFIT crashes, the highest figure ever. There was a greater number of crashes, too.

However, the Flight Safety Foundation offered no comment whatever on the failure to meet the CFIT reduction target.

Flight International, in its Comment section in the issue reporting the 1997 accident statistics, mentioned the CFIT Task Force's goal of reducing CFITs by half over the period that had just ended. The FSF and ICAO, it said, "were rewarded with a dramatic drop [in the number of CFITs] in the first two years, but the rate has risen, especially for jet airliners. Instead of celebrating success in 1997, the industry is looking at over 600 CFIT-related deaths in a year."

Despite the facts, however, "celebrating success" is exactly what the FSF did. Faced with failure, they trumpeted success, perhaps hoping no one would notice. A press release from the Flight Safety Foundation announced on 27 February 1998, "The FSF CFIT Task Force reached its primary goal in 1996, when the number of CFIT accidents involving large commercial jets had declined from seven in 1992 to three in 1996 and in 1997 the number was two."[11] Not a single mention was made that more people had died in CFIT crashes in 1997 than ever before.

According to the annual review of 1997's air safety by *Flight International*, the FSF's figures were wrong. The magazine's safety editor, David Learmount, wrote, "CFIT, which has consistently killed more passengers and crew than any other accident category, killed more in 1997 than ever before." He went on, discussing the CFIT Task Force,

> the FSF posted the objective of halving the CFIT accident-rate within five years: i.e. by 1997. It is arguable that, in terms of rates, the graph has begun moving in that direction, but the target has proved wildly optimistic. Although small carriers and non-passenger operations tend, in most years, to account for the majority of the CFIT accidents, major carriers are manifestly still vulnerable. Four of 1997's total of seven CFIT accidents involved large jet-powered passenger aircraft.[12]

According to the FSF, as was mentioned earlier, 1997 only saw two large-jet CFIT crashes. This demonstrates another feature of the aviation industry: using statistics flexibly and selectively. It appears that the CFIT Task Force managed its sleight of hand by only including "large commercial jets".

As if to confirm the somewhat cavalier attitudes of industry organisations to these vital safety issues, and the status of much of the aviation world as a mutual admiration society, *Flight International* ignored its own criticism of the FSF's "wildly optimistic" targets and went on to award the Flight Safety Foundation the "1998 *Flight International* Aerospace Industry Award for Training and Safety" at the Asian Aerospace air show at Singapore on 26 February 1998. At the ceremony, the FSF president, Stuart Matthews, said, "Receiving this recognition is an immense source of pride for FSF, as it should be for the many organisations and individuals whose hard-earned efforts have made this campaign a success because lives have been saved."

Nobody, least of all the aviation press or the transport correspondents, asked Mr Matthews how he squared that statement with the fact that more people died in CFIT crashes in 1997 than any other year in recorded history. The industry specialises in this kind of exercise. Why is it, for example, that only large jets are included in their statistics? Be it in a thirty-seater or a 300-seater, a CFIT usually spells death for all on board and happens in the same way. Furthermore, the CFIT reduction campaign was not launched in 1992 with the statement that only wide-bodied commercial jets would be counted. Yet that was how it calculated the figures, and even then they used a category that gave it figures 50 per cent lower than those of *Flight International*, which bases its figures on its own research as well as on data from the leading airline insurance organisation, Airclaims, and the UK's CAA.

A CFIT in point

One CFIT tragedy that has much in common with other crashes of this type befell the crew and all but four of the passengers on an American Airlines Boeing 757 flight from Miami to Cali, Colombia, on 20 December 1995. Again, although human error is not the whole story, its intractability is well illustrated here. The post-crash analysis, too, illustrates that radical measures will be necessary if any future task force is to make a serious dent in the CFIT casualty statistics.

American Airlines was a relative newcomer to international flights when the crash occurred, but until then had experienced no significant problems in its new operations, for which it had prepared assiduously. The captain and first officer on the plane were exemplary pilots with immense experience, men who had received numerous commendations for their leadership qualities and their courtesy towards passengers. The airline was well aware of the new hazards its pilots would encounter flying in the unfamiliar environment of South America. Accordingly, these pilots, like others, had been trained specifically for Latin American operations.

The courses they attended had titles such as: "Warning! Arrivals May Be Hazardous", or "They'll [air traffic control] Forget About You!" and "Know Where You Are". These pilots had even been fully briefed by the airline, during another CRM course, about the crash of a Thai Airways Airbus A-310, which ploughed into a mountain in Nepal in July 1992 while pilot and co-pilot fiddled about with their flight-computer, trying to find out where they were.[13] In Colombia it seems the pilots forgot all they had been told.

That December night, the flight was uneventful until the aircraft started to approach Cali and the crew contacted approach control, which is the airport-based part of air traffic control concerned with shepherding the plane on to the ground. The crew had instructions to contact Cali control once they passed a radio beacon called Tulua. All navigational radio beacons have unique names, and provide a vital means of navigation for aircraft. The aircraft's equipment shows where the beacon is and when they are overhead. The crew passed the relevant beacon but without getting any indication that they had done so, leaving them uncertain as to where they were.

The reason they did not register passing the Tulua beacon was because they had reprogrammed the flight management system.

The FMS is the brains of the aircraft's autopilot. Once upon a time, the autopilot was simply a device for keeping the aircraft on a particular heading. Now, however, it is capable of taking an aircraft from take-off to touchdown with virtually no input from the pilots, giving commands to the control surfaces and engines in order to follow courses that have been programmed into the computer. Pilots can still "hand-fly" the aircraft, and they must do so from time to time to maintain their flying skills. But the FMS is a potent aid, and an extremely reliable one. Many pilots nowadays fly the computer while the computer flies the plane.

Because they offer so many cost savings, these computers have become increasingly common and no modern large jet is built without one. Most of the time they ease the flight-crew's task, economise on fuel consumption and smooth out the flight for maximum passenger comfort. It is easy, however, to take them for granted, and one of the peculiarities of the modern computerised systems is that pilots can unwittingly set them off on the path to disaster without being aware of it.

In Miami the crew had programmed the FMS with the data for the approach they expected the plane to make into Cali, using the runway American Airlines planes normally used there. But while the plane was descending, the air traffic controller offered its captain the option of coming "straight in", in which case a different runway would be used, obviating the need to circle the airport before coming in to land.

The captain, who as the non-flying pilot was managing radio communications, wanted to compensate for a two-hour delay in their take-off at Miami by speeding up the approach to Cali. So he was pleased to take advantage of the controller's offer and therefore keyed a new approach to the airport into the FMS.

Should the captain have accepted the approach controller's offer? The official report into the crash says the flight-crew simply did not have enough time to go through all the correct procedures for the new approach. It listed the tasks they had to perform, including fetching a paper chart from its folder, reviewing headings, altitudes, distances, radio frequencies, entering new data in the FMS, double-checking each procedure, and carrying out a variety of other tasks while communicating with approach control. "Consequently, several necessary steps were performed improperly or not at all," the report states. In other words, like the KLM crew in Tenerife, they were cutting corners because they were in a hurry.

When the captain keyed a new approach into the FMS, the computer deleted the previous flight plan, and with it the reference to the Tulua beacon. According to the system's logic, reference to Tulua was no longer necessary, which was why the displays did not show it when the plane passed overhead. The crew, however, had forgotten this, or did not know it, and were expecting the Tulua beacon to show up. The CVR recorded the captain's annoyance at having missed Tulua: "It's that [****ing] Tulua I'm not getting for some reason . . . Tulua's [****ed] up."

This problem did not bother the crew much. The first officer, who was flying the aircraft, suggested they fly to the beacon near the end of the airport runway, called Rozo. The captain agreed, got approach control's permission to do this and then entered the co-ordinates for the Rozo beacon by typing the letter "R" for Rozo on the keyboard of the FMS. In theory the aircraft would now find its own way there, suitably monitored by the crew.

Unfortunately, the letter "R" was not the correct designation for the Rozo beacon. "R" stood for another beacon, the Romeo beacon, which was close to Bogota airport, 130 miles to the northeast. To get the Rozo beacon, the captain should have entered "Rozo" in full. He was hardly to be criticised for this, since his paper chart of the approach marked Rozo as "R", so that was what he programmed into the FMS. Unfortunately, the approach charts and the FMS abbreviations are not standardised, so the beacon's name on the paper chart was different from its name in the FMS computer.

By now, descending at a rapid but normal rate for the approach to Cali, they were flying down a corridor of mountains that rise to around 10,000 feet but which they could not see. After the wrong beacon was entered in the FMS, the aircraft did what it was told and turned to adopt a course for the Romeo beacon 130 miles away while the descent continued. The computer, of course, could not know that a 9000-foot mountain lay between its current position and the beacon it was now heading for. The CVR contains the damning evidence that the crew did not know exactly what was going on. Less than three minutes before the crash the first officer asks, "Uh, where are we?" and nine seconds later, he says, "Where [are] we headed?" The captain responds, "I don't know . . . what happened here?"[14]

The situation they were in is familiar to pilots, especially those flying computerised planes. They were "following" the aircraft. Instead of being in command and being clear about where the plane was heading they were programming it, and just hoping that it was doing what they wanted it to.

It was, in fact, behaving precisely as instructed and that is why it was making straight for a mountain. What happened next was that one of the failsafe systems designed to prevent CFITs did its job. The ground proximity warning system announced in its mechanical voice, "Terrain, terrain", followed by a *whoop*, *whoop* alarm and the exhortation "Pull up, pull up". The captain swore as they disconnected the autopilot, pulled the nose up as far as it would go and pushed the throttles to maximum. The alarm calls continued as the captain added his words of encouragement, "Baby, pull up."

They pulled up the plane as steeply as it would go, eased off slightly when the stall warning sounded, and then pulled it up again. About twelve seconds after the GPWS starting to sound, the tail of the plane hit trees on the eastern slope of El Deluvio mountain. The rest of plane cut a swathe through the trees. It had been so close to clearing the mountain that the main part of the wreckage breasted the ridge and came to rest on the western slope. When the wreck was spotted by a rescue helicopter at first light, five people were found to be still alive. One later died in hospital. All other passengers and crew, 159 people, were killed in the impact.[15]

Of all the things that had gone wrong, yet again the most crucial had proved to be the human errors. Worst of all had been a fault that many pilots greatly fear: failure to observe the first rule of piloting, "Fly the plane." This may sound like a banality of the first order, but it emphasises to pilots that whatever else may be going on, however preoccupying, one person must be in charge of the aircraft and deciding where it is going to go. The pilots did not fall back on radio navigation, regain a safe altitude and abandon the FMS, which they were trained to do and perfectly capable of doing. Instead of leading the computer into what they wanted it to do, they allowed themselves to be led by its logic.

According to other pilots, this crew may also have been victims of complacency. In the United States, air traffic controllers watch out for pilots to a much greater extent. Captain Wally Roberts, in *Airline Pilots Magazine*, wrote:

> *A generation of [US] pilots have become hooked on letting the controller take responsibility for long-range radar steers, direct routings, and repairing of programming problems in flight management routing systems. Most of this occurs with pilots' absolute trust that controllers will infallibly ensure terrain clearance and assist pilots with navigation.*[16]

Near Cali the pilots may have been relying on the controller to provide them with the same kind of service, and a safety net that they would have become accustomed to in the United States, where both pilots had flown almost their entire careers.

All these were sins of omission, not commission, but in the air these can be the worst kind. The crew were steering 162 souls on a large aircraft at over 200 knots at night without being certain where they were, in the middle of a highly mountainous region, and descending at 1500 feet per minute. Despite this apparent recklessness, the aircraft could still have been saved and it took one further error to complete the ingredients for a catastrophe.

The ground proximity warning system was introduced with CFIT in mind from the start. It is a warning system which uses one of the aircraft's altimeters to assess the ground beneath the aircraft. If the ground is approaching at too rapid a rate, it issues warnings in an artificial voice and emits an alarm signal with increasing frequency. GPWS is made to international specifications and has been an ICAO-recommended (not mandatory) installation on all international jet transports since 1979.[17]

Despite the increasing popularity of GPWS on airliners, they were dogged by a high proportion of false alarms, especially in their early days. It has been a difficult problem for the GPWS', designers because most CFIT crashes happen during the descent and final approach phase of the flight. During that phase of flight the pilots are expecting to encounter the ground. The system has had trouble differentiating between ground you are expecting to see (the runway) and ground you don't want to see (a mountain).

In mountainous areas in particular GPWS gave many false alarms. Originally, airlines ordered crews to observe every GPWS warning and engage in escape manoeuvres, but they became so frequent that many airlines briefed crews to ignore the GPWS warning at certain airports. This, however, mitigated the effectiveness of the system. In one study Dutch researchers found that in one-third of jets which had a CFIT crash and were equipped with GPWS, a GPWS alert had been given and ignored.[18]

British Airways contributed data to a study on GPWS warnings in its own fleet which showed that in the twelve months from September 1991, there had been 301 GPWS warnings, of which 13 per cent were genuine. However, despite the fact that the BA pilots' rule was that all GPWS "pull-up" warnings – the most drastic of the system's warnings – had to be obeyed with immediate action, only 81 per cent of the genuine warnings were acted upon.[19] Why this should be so is unclear, but if one of the world's leading and safest airlines was prepared to admit to it, the idea that safety is uppermost is clearly wrong.

It was only in November 1996 that the Flight Safety Foundation issued a "safety alert". "When a GPWS warning occurs," it said, "pilots should immediately and without hesitating to evaluate the warning execute the pull-up action recommended in the company procedure manual." It commented, "Of those CFIT accidents in which aircraft were equipped with a properly operating GPWS, an alarming number of flight crews did not follow recommended pull-up procedures in response to GPWS warnings."[20] There was nothing new in this; they were simply repeating something they believed pilots and airlines already knew but were obviously forgetting or ignoring.

The CFIT Task Force had already realised this and warned airlines to operate policies of obeying all GPWS "pull-up" warnings. Standard operating procedures of most airlines repeat this instruction, and yet the warnings are still ignored. The inescapable conclusion has to be that, at least informally, airlines are telling crews to ignore GPWS at certain airports, and the reason is operational pressure to be on time. This is just one of a number of examples where operational pressures compromise the safety of the passengers. They also have the insidious effect of laying the blame on the pilot should a crash result.

The gap between how pilots actually respond to GPWS warnings and the theory that they are always supposed to take immediate action is probably explained by the grey area of operational pressure. It is well within the realms of technology, and has been for many years, to correct the problem by auto-matically linking the GPWS to the flight control system. Once the warning sounds, the aircraft could be made to perform the escape manoeuvre instantly.[21] One suspects, however, that the reason this has not been done before is that airlines do not want the grey area cleared up.

Neither operational pressure nor GPWS false warnings applied in the case of the 757 at Cali, however. GPWS has been through a large number of modifications, many increasing its reliability, and the Cali-bound 757 crew trusted the GPWS they had absolutely, reacting to its warnings within two seconds. Unfortunately, they had already deployed speed-brakes to aid the aircraft's descent to the airport. These are large flat panels which extend from the top of the wing perpendicular to the airflow to slow the plane down. On this occasion, the speed-brakes remained extended throughout the crew's attempt to fly out of the encounter with the mountain – they must have forgotten about them too.

Most CFIT crashes take place within 200 feet of the summit of the obstacle, and this aircraft came so close to clearing the ridge altogether that the crash investigators concluded that if they had stowed the speed-brakes at the same time as beginning the escape manoeuvre the plane could have been saved. The pilot also failed to fly the plane at as steep an angle as was possible.[22]

It was, in many respects, a typical CFIT crash. The crew had lost what the trade calls "situational awareness" (knowing where you are and where you are going), and when responding to the GPWS warning had not carried out the optimal manoeuvre for escape. And yet, their airline had given them numerous reminders and training sessions about losing situational awareness, CRM, Latin American hazards, mountainous terrain, and so on, all in excess of what the law or regulations required. It is hard to imagine what more the airline could have done.

Ultimately, the accident investigators simply commented that well-trained, experienced and intelligent professionals sometimes cut corners when they are under stress and in a hurry. Put another way, it could have happened to anyone.

It is interesting to compare what the investigators recommended to prevent a recurrence of such a tragedy with the action of the CFIT Task Force. The former specifically recommended simulator-based training in avoidance manoeuvres. The CFIT Task Force showed how such simulator-based training in avoidance manoeuvres could be done, but fell short of saying that everyone ought to do it. Simulators are very useful, but very expensive. Although not as expensive as training in real aircraft or learning from crashes.

However, is more training the answer? At Tenerife a cata-strophic error was made by one of Europe's most acclaimed, skilled and experienced pilots. At Cali the errors were made by a crew which in every other respect was a model of professionalism. They had been fully trained and amply briefed, well beyond the call of the regulations, in the hazards of their flights. And yet all became victims. Perhaps, rather than believing practice makes perfect pilots, we should accept that fallibility needs to be accepted and accounted for.

Both the investigators of the Cali crash and the CFIT Task Force have recommended the installation of enhanced GPWS on all aircraft carrying more than nine people, and the biggest airlines are now either installing or evaluating it. EGPWS is the latest and best, by far, of the GPWS systems because it uses the technology of the global positioning system for the first time.[23]

GPS is a remarkable navigation system which operates by triangulating your position, taking readings from satellites transmitting signals from their orbit around the earth. It is capable of amazing accuracy, and although it was developed for the US military, civilian versions have long been in use. Sailors, because of the featureless nature of the ocean, have found it particularly helpful.

If the GPS system "knows" exactly where the aircraft is at all times, it can then correlate that to a contour map of the world, stored in its memory. Since it is comparing the aircraft's current location, including altitude, speed and heading, to a relief map of the world, it can "see" if high terrain lies in the flight-path. EGPWS can give the crew a sixty-second warning of an imminent mountain, compared with just ten seconds in some circumstances with the older system.[24]

EGPWS has immense potential to reduce CFIT crashes in the future, but it may be some considerable time before all aircraft are equipped with it. In the meantime, the industry holds its breath. With a technical fix on the horizon, it fails to address the other issues involved in the cause of CFITs, meaning that no improvement in the CFIT situation can realistically be expected for a long time.

Neither the Cali crash investigators nor the CFIT Task Force pointed out that the majority of CFIT crashes occur on what are called non-precision approaches. Most airports operate instrument landing systems (ILS), whereby the aircraft flies down two radio beams, one extending in a straight line from the centre-line of the runway, telling the aircraft when it is left or right of the centre-line, the other operating in the other axis, letting the plane know if it is above or below the glide-slope, as it is called.

Cockpit instruments show the position of the plane relative to the beams, and the landing pilot has to keep the plane as close to both of them until he or she reaches a point where the runway can be seen. There are many different kinds of non-precision approach, and different airports are capable of different kinds of ILS. The most highly specified type of ILS is the Category IIIa, under which an aircraft, and a suitably qualified pilot, can land when it is not possible to see the runway at all.

If one of these beams is not working, landing is still possible, but it is less accurate and different rules need to be followed. It then becomes a non-precision approach. There is a bewildering number of different types of non-precision approach, but in the final analysis they all have one thing in common: they are not as safe as full ILS. However, the CFIT Task Force, while recommending EGPWS and better training, has not called for non-precision approaches to be abandoned, at least for passenger-carrying jets. This would be too expensive.

Captain Wally Roberts, who commented on the complacency US pilots can experience if they are assuming they will be getting the same level of service from controllers abroad as they do at home, added, "Non-precision approaches should be outlawed for use by large transport-category aircraft."[25] Basically, the equipment used for NPAs is not as accurate as it should be to ensure safety. This is also the position of the largest US airline pilots' trade union, ALPA.

As if to vindicate Captain Roberts's words, a Korean Airlines 747 crashed short of the runway at Agana airport, on the Pacific island of Guam, in August 1997, despite having the latest-version GPWS system, and a further safety system. This flight was making a non-precision approach to the airport at night and in rain and it was receiving GPWS warnings as it came in. The crew did not pay attention to them, presumably because they were in the process of landing and they may have expected a GPWS warning for a normal landing.

A special feature of the Guam tragedy was a relatively new safety system called MSAW, minimum safe altitude warning. This simple and useful device is installed at Agana airport. It monitors the track of approaching aircraft by radar and if they drift below the minimum safe altitude, it alerts the controller in the tower who can then tell the pilots. A minimum safe altitude is exactly what it says, a formal statement by an aviation authority that no aircraft may descend below such and such an altitude in a certain area. Unfortunately, it was only discovered after the crash that a software fault had made the warning system inoperative on the runway the airliner was using.

However, that cannot be considered a contribution towards the crash because the system must not be relied upon entirely by the pilots – it just adds another layer of safety by introducing an additional alerting system into the equation. If the pilots of the Korean 747 had been depending on it, they should not have been.

Not only was the MSAW not functioning on the Guam runway the Korean flight was planning to use, but MSAW is only used in the US (Guam is an overseas US territory and thus under the authority of the FAA) and Israel. Despite the fact that it is a software-based system that interacts with the airport's existing radar, and is thus cheap and easy to install, hardly anyone uses it. The CFIT Task Force called for MSAW's world-wide implementation following the Guam crash. The Flight Safety Foundation's director of technical projects, Robert Vandel, said, "MSAW is not experimental or speculative technology . . . Any airport with approach radar that fails to include MSAW capability is missing a golden opportunity to make flying safe. Unfortunately, missing that opportunity is exactly what most of the world's airports are doing."[26]

If safety were the prime concern of airlines, they would have banned non-precision approaches.[27] Unfortunately, the balance of profit versus safety has not permitted this to be done yet. Forbidding non-precision approaches would restrict the number of airports planes could be operated into and out of, meaning less service by the airlines, and if the approach remained legal any airline which banned non-precision approaches would lose out to its competition.

If the industry were really serious about getting rid of CFIT crashes, this would be done. However, it is an unwritten and unspoken assumption that whatever is done for safety reasons must also involve virtually no financial penalties. Cali, Guam and Tenerife all show that operational pressures on pilots can result in all that fancy training being thrown out of the window. And yet, when such a disaster does occur, nobody addresses what is variously called "hurry-up syndrome" or "get-there-itis", but merely calls for more training in areas where the crew were already extremely well trained.

If the Tenerife and Cali disasters show what can result from pilots' errors, under operational pressure in particular, there are many crashes which have resulted from poor design or maintenance procedures which left the pilots no option whatever for recovery. Once again, the circumstances also open the regulators to charges of not putting safety first.

A failure in maintenance

One of the worst examples of maintenance failings, combined with design shortcomings and failings by the regulator, was the destruction of an American Airlines DC-10 at Chicago's O'Hare Airport on 25 May 1979, which claimed the lives of all 271 people on board.[28] The failure sequence started with an engine pylon, and thus is fairly representative of the kind of mechanical failures which make up the next largest category of crash causation after pilot error. Spectacularly captured by an alert photographer was the image of the plane stalling to the left, moments before it struck the ground and disintegrated in a fireball.[29]

Just before take-off parts of the left-engine mounting began to separate from the wing, falling on the runway. As the aircraft began to unstick and the thrust was nearly at maximum, the pylon attaching the engine to the left wing broke free. The thrust of the engine now threw it back over the top of the wing, along with the still-attached engine pylon and a three-foot length of the leading edge of the wing.

The loss of the engine did not directly lead to the crash. As usual, it took more than one simple factor to turn a crisis into a disaster. Pilots continually rehearse having to persist with take-off, despite losing one engine, because a point is reached, called V1, at which there is not enough runway left for the aircraft to stop safely. All jet transports therefore have to be able to continue with take-off, despite losing any one engine. The DC-10 had just gone past this point of no return and normally it would have continued, climbed and requested permission to return for an emergency landing.

Unfortunately for the investigators the separation of the engine took away power to the CVR, and the last word heard on it was the captain's "damn" as he realised he was losing the engine. Its absence, however, was not to prove an obstacle to the investigation.

Following standard operating procedures, the crew completed the take-off, and slackened off their speed slightly once they were clear of the ground. By slowing down, however, even though the reduction in speed was small, they were unwittingly putting the plane in danger. It gradually began to veer to the left, and about thirty seconds after it took off the roll to the left had nearly turned the aircraft upside-down. The left wing struck the ground, pivoting the nose round to impact with a trailer park, killing two on the ground as well as all on board as the heavily laden and fuelled aircraft burst into a colossal explosion.

All the pilots had known was that they had lost the left engine. They probably did not even know that it had left the aircraft, since the engines, as on most passenger jets, are not visible from the cockpit. Only exhaustive analysis after the crash managed to reveal the precise sequence of events, which began with the fact that when the engine, pylon and leading edge separated, one of the hydraulic systems and one electrical system were also knocked out.

The result of these failures was that the leading edge slats on the left wing retracted. The slats are devices which extend forward from the leading edge of the wing, just as flaps extend from the trailing edge of the wing. Between them, they increase the surface area of the wing, enabling it to generate more lift at lower speeds. When the aircraft is travelling faster it needs less lift, or a smaller wing, so the slats and flaps are pulled in. At low speeds extended slats are absolutely critical; without them the wing will stall. In a stall the flow of air over the wing is interrupted, thereby killing its lift, and at a low altitude this can result in hitting the ground before recovery. It is one of the most vital contingencies to guard against; stalls at low altitude have claimed many aircraft.

Unfortunately for the people on this aircraft, the warning system that told the pilots the slats were retracting was powered by the electrical system that had been disabled. There was no back-up warning system. However, the absence of this key warning was still not enough to cause disaster. Two other safeguards should have come into play, but neither was available on the DC-10. The first safeguard was the stick-shaker. When the aircraft detects an imminent stall, an electric motor vigorously shakes the control column to tell the pilot to lower the nose of the plane, and thus increase speed, which would normally get the plane out of the stall. The electric motor powering the stick-shaker was fed by the electrical system which the engine had severed. Again, no back-up.

The second safeguard should have been what is called a mechanical lock-out on the slats. This simply means that if hydraulic power to the slats is lost, a mechanical link prevents them from retracting. However, McDonnell Douglas showed the certification authorities that even if hydraulic power were lost, there was still easily enough power from the engines – even from just two engines – to increase speed and take the aircraft out of the stall. What nobody had anticipated was the possibility that the pilots might not know that the slats had retracted, and with the warning system inoperative would not know they were in a stall. McDonnell Douglas attracted considerable criticism for allegedly making short cuts in its determination to get the DC-10 into the marketplace ahead of rivals. All of the alleged short cuts, however, were approved by the FAA when it certified the aircraft as safe to carry passengers.

If the crew had known the slats had retracted they would have increased speed and thus stayed out of the stall. However, as the stall began, with the left wing dropping, the pilots attempted to compensate by trying to lift the nose, the investigators believed. Given another minute or two they probably would have worked out what was going on, but they did not have that luxury.

This remains the United States' worst-ever airline disaster and it attracted dozens of aviation officials, who took part in an exhaustive inquiry. They soon found that the fault that started the disastrous sequence of events lay with the maintenance department of American Airlines. In common with Continental Airlines, the engineers had found what they thought to be a more efficient way of removing wing-mounted engines from the DC-10 than that recommended by the manufacturer. Instead of removing the engine from the pylon, and then removing the pylon, they placed a fork-lift truck under the engine to bear its weight while pylon and engine were removed together.

The problem with this approach was that it placed undue stress on the parts that held the pylon to the wing. Maintenance engineers had worked on the engine which separated from the crashed plane, and when all the crash debris was assembled and labelled it was clear where the fatigue cracks had appeared and how they had been caused. The NTSB, however, still criticised the FAA very heavily for major failings, two of which consisted of the kind of mistakes that most bureaucracies can suffer from at one time or another, and one which exposed a serious philosophical failing which has yet to be seriously addressed if the accident rate is to be greatly improved.

The first of these was that, although Continental engineers had obtained approval for their way of changing the wing engines from their local FAA inspector, he did not consult McDonnell Douglas about the new procedure. When McDonnell Douglas engineers came to Continental they immediately stopped the practice, but the information about this maintenance method was not shared between airlines or reported centrally to the FAA. In other words, a communications failure resulted.

The philosophical failure arose in relation to the absence of mechanical lock-outs for the slats. Other aircraft had to have them, but McDonnell Douglas did not because they had showed the FAA, by mathematical formula, that the likelihood of the slats retracting *and* the engine failing at the same time was so remote as to be not worth guarding against. It did not seem to occur to anyone that the pylon could fail along with the engine and thus cause the slats to retract. The system was not, therefore, failsafe. One fault – in this case the pylon separating from the wing – could lead to a chain of events that would claim the aircraft. As is so often the case, however, the manufacturers had cited the mathematical improbability of a catastrophic event as a way of avoiding having to make the system failsafe.

The improbability of disastrous events is a leitmotif of the story of air safety. The number of times an extremely improbable event, often in combination with another, has resulted in disaster is relatively great. Usually, it has not been the "extremely remote" event which has caused the crash but its causation of other failures in the aircraft system, a disastrous domino effect. The linking of events towards catastrophe should receive, critics say, as much attention as the sheer improbability of the first event in the sequence.

In the case of the Tenerife disaster a gross human error combined with smaller errors to produce a catastrophe. At Chicago in 1979 the chain of events was mechanical in character. What both had in common was the absence of a single cause and the fact that they were preventable.

The Tenerife disaster is an illustration of the human element conspiring with other factors to cause a disaster, and thus belongs to the 70 per cent of crashes involving actions by the flight-crew mentioned earlier. The Chicago tragedy was the result of mechanical failings beyond the ability of the crew to rectify, and was representative of the next largest category of crashes.

And Cali represents the grim toll of CFIT. Why aircraft crash has, basically, a banal answer – because someone screwed up – as well as a complex one – which error combined with which other error, whether sequentially or not. What is surprising is that there are very few unknown errors that lead to crashes; there is nothing new under the sun. It is the will to anticipate them correctly that is the important factor – and what is currently missing.

CHAPTER 2

What happens to a plane in a crash

EVERY SPEED AT which aircraft travel, from walking pace while taxiing to twice the speed of sound in the case of Concorde, is strictly guided by where it is, the air temperature, the elevation of the airfield, wind direction, loading and more. Unlike car drivers, pilots cannot simply "open it up" when they feel like it. The pilots have charts on which to calculate their take-off and landing speeds and must adhere to them strictly. On rare occasions, even going five knots too slow could cause a crash.

If an aircraft overshoots the runway on landing, or does so because the pilot decided to abort the take-off, the plane can be travelling between 100 and 150 knots. Aircraft are not particularly well designed for braking. Most of the braking effort comes from the wheels (anti-lock brakes were designed for aircraft long before cars), and most aircraft improve the braking action considerably with the spoilers, panels that come up into the airstream from the top of the wing and help kill the aircraft's lift, thus assisting it to settle on the undercarriage. They also use reverse thrust, whereby panels come out of the engines near the exhaust and redirect the blast forwards.

There are times, however, when the aircraft cannot stop. If that is the case it will, sooner or later, hit something. It is not worth considering the effects of an aircraft hurtling to the ground at 500 knots, because no structure could conceivably survive such an impact. Cases where aircraft disintegrate in mid-air due to a bomb, or where extreme turbulence or corrosion has caused a piece of the tailplane or wing to part company with the plane, are not only almost unbelievably rare, but cannot be taken into consideration when assessing crashworthiness.

In fact, about 80 per cent of all airliner crashes are at impact velocities survivable by the human frame, which makes the crash-worthiness of the aircraft well worth examining. In addition, most crashes take place on landing or take-off, and the extreme speeds and heights that jet planes are capable of do not apply there.

First of all, however, we need to consider the runway itself. How long does a runway need to be? Philosophies of which comes first, the performance of the aircraft or the runway, have differed over time and so the development of runway length has been haphazard. When Vickers launched the VC-10 aircraft in the mid-1960s, it was generally assumed that it would be difficult to have runways lengthened. As a result, the VC-10 was designed to operate efficiently from short fields.

However, runways *were* soon lengthened to accommodate the equally new 747, against the expectations of BOAC, the VC-10's launch customer, and the manufacturers. Because the extra power needed for short take-offs, particularly in Africa, had com-promised the VC-10's payload, an otherwise excellent aircraft was condemned to a future of British military and VIP duties, because it was no longer an economic proposition.

From the start of the 747 project, on the other hand, Boeing knew that runways would have to be lengthened to accommodate it. Equally, because so many airlines would want to operate the jet, Boeing's executives knew the job would be done. And so it proved. Airports all over the world lengthened their runways to accommodate the new giant jet at a rate far in excess of what the forecasters had thought possible. The VC-10 was a victim, in a sense, of the 747's success. This essentially commercial story concerning runways leads us neatly into a discussion of how the length of runways also has safety implications.

Nobody has ever made a hard and fast rule about how long a runway ought to be, despite the fact that more crashes take place on or near them than anywhere else. ICAO specifies the minimum lengths of runways, and all airports are supposed to adhere to them. When airports lengthened runways to accommodate the 747s, they did so because any that did not would lose the business of the airliners operating them. A commercial, not safety, imperative was at work. By happenstance, which is the usual way safety is improved in the aviation industry, the extra length of the runways added a margin of safety for the planes that did not need as much ground as the jumbo. It would be a sobering exercise to work out how many smaller jets have been involved in emergencies that involved using the extra length of the runway – a runway that would not have been there had it not been for the requirements of the 747.

How long a runway should be depends on how much of it an aircraft needs for landing and taking off. All commercial jets have two critical speeds during take-off. The first is called V1, which varies according to the weight of the aircraft, atmospheric conditions and runway length, and is the speed at which the pilot flying the plane has to decide whether to abort the take-off. After V1 there is not enough runway left for the aircraft to stop. Once the non-flying pilot has sung out, "V-one," and the pilot has decided to go on, they must do so, even if one of the engines loses all power. (All large passenger jets must prove, at certification stage, their ability to continue take-off despite losing one engine.) They then quickly reach VR, which is the speed at which the aircraft "rotates", that is, begins to leave the runway by lifting the nosewheel off the ground.

Not surprisingly, pilots sometimes wish they could abort a take-off after V1 has passed. Confidence in the equipment notwithstanding, it is understandable that a pilot should want to stay on the ground just after hearing a loud explosion from one of the engines. However, in this situation discipline and training are expected to overcome instincts and the take-off must be continued.

Pilots are regularly trained in this procedure. Even airlines

which have been criticised for the minimal time their pilots get in
the simulator practise this kind of exercise. If a pilot does abort a
take-off after V1 he or she could face strong criticism if they
survived, although the authorities are beginning to show some
flexibility on this question.

On 13 June 1996, for example, the right engine of a DC-10
operated by Garuda, Indonesia's national carrier, failed noisily
just as it was taking off from Fukuoka airport in Japan. When it
came back down it overran the end of the runway, collided with
obstacles and caught fire. Three people were killed and many were
injured during the fire and the subsequent evacuation.

The Japanese investigating authorities blamed the pilot for
aborting the take-off, saying, perfectly correctly, that the other
two engines could easily have coped. Which element of the pilot's
training failed him that day can only be imagined, but perhaps an
image of the American Airlines DC-10 at Chicago in 1979 flashed
through his mind as he made his split-second decision and
desperately regained the ground.[1]

A highly experienced captain of a Canadian Airlines
International DC-10 faced a similar situation at Vancouver
International airport on 19 October 1995. His aircraft was taking
off normally on the 11,000-foot runway. It reached V1, which
was 164 knots, and two seconds later there was a loud and
startling bang, shuddering and much vibration. Just over one
second after the bang, and before the aircraft had left the ground,
the captain called for a rejected take-off and pulled back the
throttles, while the second officer deployed the spoilers, which
commanded the automatic braking system to activate. The plane
ran off the end of the runway but suffered no serious structural
damage and there were no major injuries.[2]

Although the V1 rule is supposed to be inviolable there are
exceptions and complications, not least of which are the instincts
of the pilot. The official report said that the Canadian captain,
based on his understanding of the provisions in the DC-10's flight
manual, and also on a fatal DC-8 crash he had witnessed, "had
developed a mental rule to not take an aircraft into the air if he
suspected that there was an aircraft structural failure". The rules,

indeed, state that you may reject a take-off after V1 if you believe the plane will not fly. (It is one of those truism regulations – "if the plane won't fly, don't fly".)

Presumably, his thought process was that since the noise he heard was totally unfamiliar it could have been a structural problem and so he decided not to take off. As it happened, the official report commented, because of the captain's flight-deck colleague's prompt action in selecting the spoilers and ABS, the plane only left the runway at a speed of 40 knots. Had they reacted more slowly, and had they opted for manual rather than automatic braking, as suggested in many DC-10 manuals, they could have left the runway at 80 knots and suffered considerably more serious consequences.

This fifty-five-year-old captain had over 16,000 flying hours, nearly 4000 of which had been on DC-10s, and had received top marks on an assessment flight about a month earlier. Engine failure on take-off is something pilots may be trained for, but a pilot can go through a thirty-five-year career without experiencing one. When something this alarming did happen it was hardly surprising he chose the ground in preference to the air. In fact, the noise was an engine compressor stall, an alarming but not necessarily safety-critical event.

Boeing has conducted a study of such events, where the engine failure proved not to be critical and where the crew rejected the take-off, in their term, "inappropriately". They found that in most cases, loud noises, shuddering and severe vibration had been influential in persuading the crew to do what "the book" calls the wrong thing, namely aborting the take-off. It would be a bold pilot, however, who could confidently claim the ability to identify alarming noises instantly and categorise them into ones that demand an immediate abort and those that do not. Determining which is which can, unfortunately, probably only be made with hindsight.

Unlike the Japanese authorities' response to the Garuda DC-10 overrun, Canada's Transportation Safety Board seemed reluctant to criticise the CAI DC-10 captain. They recommended that crews be better trained in recognising compressor stalls and engine failures and that the dangers of rejecting take-off be emphasised.[3]

It is hard to escape the conclusion that the Canadian pilot escaped sanction because nobody was injured, while the Garuda captain was facing the possibility of criminal charges because deaths and injuries occurred in his case. The problem arises from runways not being long enough to permit a more flexible approach to this question.

Aviation safety specialist Robert O. Besco has emphasised the dangers, particularly for heavily loaded planes departing from what are termed "balanced field length runways". These are runways where the aircraft's take-off weight has to be carefully balanced against the amount of runway available. In such circumstances the aircraft may have to unload passengers or cargo simply to meet the limits of V1. Dr Besco writes:

> When a heavily loaded aircraft attempts a take-off from a balanced field length runway, the margins of safety are narrower than in any other phase of aircraft operations. A problem at or near V1 requires an almost instantaneous response from the crew, and that response may be based on data that are misleading, incomplete or simply overwhelming. The first take-off that a pilot makes when his aircraft's weight is limited by runway length is an eye opener. To the pilot who is inexperienced with a balanced field length take-off, V1 speed occurs when the far end of the runway is apparently directly beneath the nose of the airplane. Every pilot is convinced that it would be impossible to stop the airplane on the remaining runway. Fortunately, most take-offs have excess runway length.[4]

In an error-tolerant system, hopefully one would leave aircrew a larger margin in which to make such decisions – which they now have to do in an instant. If runways cannot be made much longer, then at least, perhaps, they could have long, flat and obstacle-free overrun areas where the plane would suffer minimal damage and where no large structure would turn the overrun into an aviation disaster. Such moves are very unlikely, however, in the present climate. Many airports, furthermore, simply have no space beyond the end of the runway for adequate overrun.

V1 has long been a bone of contention between pilots, on the one hand, and the airlines and manufacturers, on the other. Pilots, especially US airline pilots grouped in the Air Line Pilots' Association trade union, argue that V1 has become increasingly unrealistic and that the Federal Aviation Administration has been leaning over backwards to accommodate the industry.

The problem is simple. Jet aircraft have become longer and heavier as engine performance has improved. The more an aircraft can carry in cargo, passengers and fuel, the better the operating profits of the airline. The heavier the aircraft, however, the more runway it needs to accelerate to become airborne. If V1 were set conservatively then many aircraft would not be able to operate to their capacity limits, especially at smaller airports, and that would affect profits all round. As a result, experts from ALPA argue, the FAA has been succumbing to pressure and is not realistic when conducting the aborted-take-off tests that all new aircraft are obliged to conform to in order to be granted their airworthiness certificate.[5]

A US airline pilot quoted in Ralph Nader and Wesley Smith's *Collision Course* said, "The tests that tell us when it is safe to abort are not accurate. First, the pilot knows the test is going to happen. In a real abort, it takes longer to react. Second, they use brand new planes, with new engines and unused brakes. That plane will stop faster during the test than it ever will again. Third, they begin with wheels at the edge of the runway. ALPA ran a test on the issue and discovered that it takes 130 per cent of the length of plane to line up for take-off under real conditions."[6] In other words, operational aircraft do not leave the taxiway for the runway and then reverse so they can get their wheels right at the end of the tarmac.

The official tests not only certify to the aviation regulators that the aircraft can abort a take-off in time, but also set the V1 speed for that aircraft. In reality, therefore, an everyday, operational aircraft filled with passengers and cargo and being operated not by a test pilot knowing what is going to happen, but by a line pilot expecting nothing out of the ordinary, is extremely unlikely to be able to stop in the same space as the test aircraft. The biggest danger, of course, is that when aborting at V1 the aircraft would still run off the end of the runway, with consequences that vary from airport to airport.

Perhaps the most serious indication of the lack of commitment on the part of the industry in tackling this problem is the fact that until very recently in North America the authorities did not require airlines and manufacturers to recalculate V1 speeds for wet runways. As with cars on the road, a wet runway is much harder to stop on; not least at Vancouver where, in the Canadian Airlines International DC-10 incident mentioned above, it was calculated by the investigators that if it had been raining, the aircraft could not have stopped on the runway even if the command to abort the take-off had been taken at the authorised time, at V1. (The UK's CAA does require that data for wet runways be provided by the manufacturers.)

In response to the ALPA's concerns, the FAA ordered that, for the V1 tests, a two-second gap be inserted between the "event" calling for the take-off to be aborted and the abort itself, so as to mimic the delay in decision-making for a pilot not anticipating the event. The rule, passed in the late 1970s, did not, however, include the main aircraft then in development and which now carry a huge proportion of air travellers – the Boeing 757 and 767.

After further pressure from the ALPA the FAA was ordered to draft a new rule making the V1 tests more realistic. However, according to ALPA president J. Randolph Babbitt, the proposal went to the public expenditure body, the Office for the Management of the Budget, who killed the rule on the grounds that it would be too costly to the airlines. (It would have reduced permissible loads, especially from certain airports.[7]) Here is a crystal-clear case of operating costs overruling safety concerns. The latest chapter of this saga unfolded in February 1998 when the FAA adjusted the meaning of V1, to encompass many of the objections of the ALPA and others. The airworthiness regulations were changed so that V1 calculations had to account for the possibility of worn brakes and wet runways. This will take decades to become effective since it only applies to new aircraft designs. Newly manufactured aircraft of older designs will not be obliged to meet the new standard.[8]

If a runway is not long enough, that, logically, has the same consequences as an aircraft not being powerful enough, either in terms of taking off or braking on landing. Short runways cannot cause accidents in themselves, but like so many other aspects of commercial aviation they represent an increased risk when compared with longer runways.

Investigators looking into crashes that involve runway overruns rarely direct attention to the length of the runway itself. One example was the case of USAir flight 405 on 22 March 1992, a Fokker F-28, one of the smaller passenger jets, with fifty people on board. The plane was experiencing delays on an unseasonably cold day at LaGuardia Airport, New York City's domestic airport. LaGuardia has remained a local airport, leaving the big jets and the long-distance international flights to John F. Kennedy Airport, further out of town, near Jamaica, New York. LaGuardia is more conveniently situated for access to the city, but it has remained small because its runways were built out over water, and the New York City authorities decided it would be too costly to extend them, given the amount of land reclamation necessary.

Flight 405 had been de-iced as it waited for permission to take-off. De-icing is crucial to the performance of aircraft. Many modern jets, the McDonnell Douglas DC-9, Fokker F-28 and Boeing 737 in particular, start to misbehave quite radically with only a small quantity of ice or snow sticking to the wing. The design of the wings is matched so closely to the speeds at which the aircraft is designed to be flown in its various configurations that ice can throw out all those calculations. The captain of the F-28 was aware of the problem and decided to ask for a further de-icing of the plane while they suffered another delay. So the de-icing truck visited the aircraft again and sprayed its glycol mixture, similar to the anti-freeze used in cars, over the wings and departed.

The F-28 had to wait a further thirty minutes before it got permission to take off, but, unbeknown to the captain, ice had re-formed on the wing because of this new delay. When the plane began its take-off run down the snowy runway the captain was using the wrong reference speed for take-off and was not corrected by his co-pilot.[9]

Going at just five knots below the correct speed and with an imperceptible film of glycol and ice affecting the lift of the wings, the plane could not make it into the air for more than a few seconds. The aircraft drifted back down to the end of the runway, hit the end and ploughed into a lighting structure, before breaking into three pieces upside-down in the water, which was about five feet deep. The captain, one cabin crew member and twenty-five passengers died, about half of them killed by the impact and most of the others drowning.

Survivor Richard Lawson gave a passenger's-eye view of what happened: "I was underwater in my seat, upside-down. I swallowed jet fuel and I had trouble breathing. I tried to accept this reality of dying. Then I had an overpowering feeling to overcome this. My spirit did not let me accept dying." He undid his seat-belt and swam up to an air-pocket. He could see a hole in the fuselage above him but there was no way he could reach it. "A guy up on top reached down and pulled me up through the hole. I got on top of the plane with him. We jumped into the water because we thought the plane was going to explode. We discovered how shallow it was and we made it to shore."[10]

The inquiry focused on important matters, as they always do. The NTSB was highly critical of the fact that, despite the harsh winters that occur in the United States, there is no rule on how long an aircraft can wait on the apron before it needs another de-icing. The airline had no such rules either, and the testimony of the co-pilot made it clear the captain checked for contamination of the wing many times before starting his take-off run.

The investigators' recommendations covered procedures for improving rescue services, airline de-icing practices, revising the aircraft manufacturer's advice on which speeds should be used for take-off in such conditions, and other factors. Nowhere, however, was it remarked that if the runway had been 1000 feet longer, the aircraft would, in all probability, have descended back to it and not crashed.

There was a further irony to this crash. Although his death meant that no one could be sure about it, the captain, the investigators believed, had selected a slightly lower than normal take-off speed because he feared that if he needed to abort the take-off on such a short runway, especially when it was covered in snow, he would not have enough room to stop. He was heard on the CVR saying at one point, "It's a short runway when you're going that fast." Unfortunately, this decision itself may have played a part in the aircraft's failure to get into the air.

Contributory causes like this are not usually addressed in crash investigations because they are too obvious, despite the fact that if the goal of the investigation is to help prevent a recurrence, it seems such factors should be mentioned. Simple solutions are often anathema in high-tech industries. "There is a strong tendency in aviation", says Robert Besco, "to employ our most elegant and sophisticated technology to solve simple problems. There seems to be an intrinsic reward for engineers to implement the most complex systems available to arrive at a solution."[11]

The New York authorities had had a chance to do something to prevent this crash by extending the runway. It is a disturbing fact that another USAir jet, this time a B737-400, had already crashed into the water at LaGuardia during a rejected take-off only three years before. Indeed, that crash, on 20 September 1989, when two passengers were killed, may well have been preying on the mind of the captain of the F-28 when he made his remark about the shortness of the runway. Since it belonged to the same airline, which was in the middle of a bad spell of fatal accidents, all the pilots would have analysed it carefully.[12] The NTSB offered no comment on the shortness of the runway in either crash – which seems odd given the similarity of the circumstances.

The earlier crash threw up other lessons about air safety, this time in relation to the different ways in which survivors can react. This event may have seemed fairly minor in terms of its effects, but for two passengers, it changed their lives entirely.

The account of the following survivor, who must remain anonymous, shows that doom, gloom and post-traumatic stress are not necessarily the outcomes of every narrow squeak. She was sixty years old at the time of the accident.[13]

> *I felt the plane vibrate . . . I could hear the brakes being applied, but we were not stopping . . . finally we stopped. I was alert and awake, my head was resting on my knees, my hands were dangling beside me. I was unable to speak, but I heard what was going on around me. I think I was trapped in the airplane for 90 minutes. I heard the rescue people saying, "We've got three DOAs [dead-on-arrivals]". I could tell that the two people in front of me were probably who they were talking about . . . and me. I could not speak up to tell them I was alive. It became very warm in the airplane, although I do not remember being afraid. I could not understand why no one was helping me escape. I could not see the water seeping in. Finally, the rescue workers pulled me from the airplane. It could not have been more than five minutes before the airplane sank.*

She was treated for injuries to her arm and sustained permanent nerve damage to her wrist. Far from feeling resentful towards the airline she thought they gave her much more money than she needed when they contributed towards buying new clothes and personal items.

She continued to be happy with her treatment from the airline thereafter. Family, friends and work colleagues were extremely supportive, despite the fact she could not work for two and a half months. She appeared on TV as a celebrity, kept in touch with the worker who rescued her, and when the airline paid her compensation she was able to buy a house for the first time. Asked if she thought anything positive had come from the crash, she answered, "Yes. I bought a new house, I'm financially better off and I've made new friends."

The experience of another survivor of the same crash, a forty-one-year-old man, could hardly have been more different.

> *It felt like a normal take-off. We went up to take-off speed when suddenly there was a sound of deceleration, the sound of*

the engines decreased. Within a few seconds, brakes were applied . . . the reverse thrusters were thrown. He [the pilot] went down the runway trying to stop the plane. I assumed we would abort take-off, circle around and try again. Then I became concerned.

I heard elevated voices from the cockpit, even though the door was closed. By virtue of where I was sitting, I could hear, "We're going off . . . We're not gonna make it!"

We could hear the noise of the floor of the plane ripping out beneath us — it did not rip open, but you could feel it. The plane had made a horrible impact.

The stewardess in front got on the intercom telling everyone to keep their heads and shoulders down. There was a lot of screaming and commotion . . . I remember sitting there thinking, "Gee whiz, what's it gonna feel like to die? This is real, you can't get out of it." I knew, where I was sitting, the odds of surviving were not good.

The plane came to rest. There was an eerie moment of silence. The lights were out. The emergency floor lights came on. It was a surreal surrounding . . . like something out of a horror movie. There was a light smoke coming up from the floor of the plane.

The plane had broken into three parts. As I looked back I saw fog rising up behind us where the plane had broken directly behind where we were sitting. I could not see behind this because of the lights and fog. After the plane came to rest, it seemed like an eternity. A stewardess in the front started to shout, "Get out, get out." She reached over and threw the door open. That's where we really got into trouble. I remember standing in the doorway looking for a split second at the person in front of me looking down the chute. You could not see . . . it was pitch black.

All of your senses said that you were still over land. When we hit bottom we found ourselves in the middle of the river . . . a total shock. We were in water, jet fuel! We sucked in jet fuel when we hit the water!

The water was very cold . . . The rain was coming down,

there were no lights. I was looking back up at the image of the plane and treading water.

Again, fate or whatever, a part of the timber structure from the trestle had broken off at impact and as I was treading water, this telephone pole comes up and I put my arms around it. We got it stable in the water and hung on to it.

Two women came down behind us – one of them could not swim. She was panicked. Her daughter was with her. The daughter screamed, "Mother cannot swim! Please help her!" Horrible screams, not only from them, but others as well. I was closest to her, so I went and grabbed her. She grabbed my arm and came over my back. I still had one hand on the trestle. I wound up being pulled underwater.

It seemed like an eternity I spent under the water. I remember struggling to try to get back to the surface. My lungs felt like they would break. Someone else took her off of me. I was able to break . . . to the surface. That was as bad as the plane crash!

The current was unbelievably strong. The tide was going out at the time. It was pushing us away from the plane. We thought that was wonderful. We still thought the plane would blow up. The water was covered with jet fuel . . .

Strange, some of the thoughts that go through your head. Someone said they were afraid of sharks and asked if they might be eaten by sharks. One guy said sharks or anything else could not live in this river!

Panic thoughts go through your head. This was my first real exposure to panic. I believe that panic is defined as a sudden unreasonably overwhelming fear. That's what I felt.

We drifted back on the river. At that point rescue crews were showing up on the river above the plane. We were able to get the people's attention on the tarmac or runway. They put the searchlight on us – they said that a boat was coming to pick us up.

We were within sight of a bridge within several hundred yards when a boat came by and [the boat operator] pulled up beside us and threw a big raft to us with the instructions,

"Don't try to get in." He told us to hold on to the side and said, "I will pull you around to the back of the boat and I will give you instructions on how to get in."

I remember starting to shiver uncontrollably at this point because of being in the water 45 minutes. My clothing felt like dead weight.

He pulled us around to the back of the boat. As luck would have it, the raft came around to the back. On the back was a catwalk. I was in back of the boat and he asked me to hang on to the metal ramp and the raft. A gentleman across from me was holding on to the rope that he had used to pull us around and with the other hand he was holding on to the ramp. The Port Authority officer was explaining to us how to get on the boat step.

We were moving the women around so they could get in first. That moment someone started the engines and the boat stared to move forward. The result was that we were pulled under the boat. I had let go of the raft.

There was a lot of screaming and panic. The man across from me let out the most blood-curdling scream I've ever heard and I hope I'll never hear again. All that was out of the water was his hand. He was under the boat. My hands were slippery. I couldn't hold on. I got drawn underneath the boat. I had visions — my gosh I've survived a plane crash, been under the water, now what a horrible way to die — going under the propellers. I don't want to die this way in engine propellers.

In a split second, while I was under the boat, the engines were shut off. I came up on the front right-hand side of the boat. I was able to hold on to the [spray] rail. It was slick, slimy from barnacles. I could hardly hold on, but I knew that if I let go I would be sucked away. I worked my way to the back of the boat.

When they pulled me on to the back of the boat I was completely in shock. They took us to the terminal building. My wife was at the airport in the other city waiting for me. I called home and talked to my older son. I told him that the plane had crashed and they had pulled me out of the water. At that time I did not know how many people had died. I told him to call the airline, not to take no for an answer, to tell someone at the airline to find my wife and tell her I was alive. He did.

My wife was the first one to find out there were any survivors at all. She said they [the airline] had them upstairs at the conference room at the airport. They had told them that the plane had crashed and they did not know if there were any survivors. She said a girl walked in and asked for her [my wife] and said, "I have very good news. Your husband called and he said they are pulling people out of the river."

Today, sometimes, I wake up and smell jet fuel. For weeks after [the accident] I felt like I reeked of jet fuel. The taste of jet fuel is still with me.

Dr Coarsey-Rader, the psychologist who recorded this testimony as part of a study of survivors, followed up and found that all this was but the beginning of this unlucky man's troubles. After being taken to the hospital, he sat ignored for several hours in wet clothes and with no shoes or socks. After being examined, he was told by an airline official to take a cab to a hotel to clean up, where he made arrangements to get home.

In place of his wet clothes the airline gave him a sweatshirt and some oversized trousers, but no socks or shoes. Shunted around by the airline and still in shock, he was eventually helped by some USAir pilots, whose briefing room he had stumbled into, who gave him some shoes, socks and trousers that fitted him. Eventually, after getting on the wrong plane and being challenged by security because he had no ID, which had been lost in the crash, he got home but collapsed soon afterwards.

He underwent psychiatric care but remained scared of flying, so much so he had to give up his job as an international marketing executive. His medical bills were only paid for one year, and because he had seen a psychiatrist, he was refused subsequent medical insurance. His income dropped massively, and he suffered from nightmares, flashbacks and depression.[14]

Myopia regarding runway length has been seen in regard to other crashes. In October 1979 a Swissair McDonnell Douglas DC-8

overran the runway on landing at Athens airport. All would have
been well but for the fact that a sunken road four metres deep runs
perpendicular to the end of that runway. When the plane reached
the road it fell into the gully and broke up, catching fire and killing
14 of the 154 people on board.

More than two years later, however, the Greek authorities
found the flight-crew entirely responsible for the crash. Judicial
proceedings followed at great length and complexity, and
although they were never imprisoned, captain and co-pilot were
sentenced to terms of imprisonment more than once. The piloting
community believed that the pilots were charged and tried to draw
attention away from the unsafe condition of Athens airport,
which regularly attracts criticism both for lack of safety on the
ground and for air traffic control problems.

Similarly, when a Lufthansa Airbus A-320 crashed at Warsaw
airport on 14 September 1993, killing the co-pilot and one
passenger, the investigators concentrated on the piloting and the
computerised aircraft's behaviour to the exclusion of all else. This
flight was approaching Warsaw in driving rain, and the pilots
decided to add a little extra speed, a precautionary measure in case
of adverse winds.

However, they landed relatively far down the runway, and the
slipperiness of the surface had a disastrous effect on the plane's
automated systems. The computers governing many of the plane's
functions do not allow safety-critical systems like the spoilers (air-
braking devices) or the reverse thrust to operate until it "knows"
it is on terra firma. If reverse thrust were deployed in mid-air the
plane could well crash and kill all on board.

The aircraft "knows" it is on the ground when two switches,
one on each main landing gear leg, are thrown by the weight of
the aircraft settling on the ground. However, the Warsaw runway
was so slippery that it took a critical nine seconds before the
switches activated and the crew could use the wheel-brakes, air-
brakes and reverse thrust. By then they were already too far down
the runway and could not avoid running off the end. The pilot
tried to swerve but could not avoid the massive earth embankment
near the perimeter fence. The plane hit the embankment, the

fuselage broke behind the nose and fires started. The co-pilot was killed in the impact, along with one unconscious passenger who was not noticed during the emergency evacuation and died of smoke inhalation. Nowhere in the accident report was it mentioned that removing the embankment might be a good idea.[15] It is still there.

London City Airport shares some of LaGuardia's problems, being a small, inner-city airport designed for smaller jets and with relatively short runways. Unlike LaGuardia, though, London City has only been operational for less than ten years, having been built over the derelict docks of east London. Being of such recent construction, it might be assumed that it would avoid the kind of problems that LaGuardia and older airports suffers from. Not so.[16]

The shortness of the runway became clear to the crew of a British Aerospace 146, carrying forty-seven passengers, on 18 November 1996. They suffered a technical problem similar to the one that claimed the A-320 in Warsaw. As the aircraft touched down between one-third and halfway down the runway the captain selected the spoilers, which aid braking by speeding the aircraft's descent on to the wheels, and the brakes. Meanwhile, the tower controller, seeing how far down the runway the touchdown had been, pushed the crash button to alert the fire-tenders to the crash he thought was about to happen.

The pilot realised the spoilers were not working. He felt that the plane was "skating on glass". It is believed that the plane had bounced and was floating when the pilot tried to deploy the spoilers. Because of the "float", the landing gear switches were not depressed. Both pilots confirmed there were no brakes, and the captain tried the spoiler lever once again. This time it worked, and braking took effect as the spoilers deployed. However, they had lost valuable seconds and by the time they came to a complete halt the plane had gone beyond the official landing distance. It came to rest on a seventy-five-metre extension of the runway, designed for aircraft to queue for take-off.

Nobody was hurt and the aircraft was undamaged, but the AAIB investigated the incident because of the obvious implica-

tions of a longer overrun. It emerged that under certain circumstances the pilots can be unaware that the aircraft is floating and
the effect this has on the landing gear switches.

A longer runway is not an option at London City because the
surrounding buildings are too close. This means there is no formal
remedy for the "floating" effect. And if the plane looks like
touching down too far down the 4000-foot runway, then
according to the rules the pilots must start a go-around – the
problem is that they cannot do it after landing. British Aerospace,
the manufacturer, looked into the possibility of initiating a go-
around after touchdown but could not guarantee it was a safe
thing to do. In other words, once a BAe 146, the main user of this
airport, is down it must stay down. Once down all its systems
must work correctly or it could be in serious trouble.

It is clear from the AAIB report that an overrun, with potentially
disastrous consequences, had been narrowly averted but that a
repetition was not as unlikely as it should be. The AAIB's dry
warning stated: "The situation of London City Airport is such that
there is a limited amount of land in the overrun area of either
runway and the consequences of a high-speed overrun are
potentially very serious."[17] The "basic defence" against this, the
report added, was simply to make sure that the aircraft land in the
correct touchdown area while correctly configured. There is no
failsafe here whatever, and no room for errors.

In its report into the incident, the AAIB considered the by no
means improbable scenario of a similarly loaded BAe 146 landing
on a dry runway with brakes operational but with spoilers
inoperative. In that case it would have stopped with just 55 metres
to spare; if the runway had been wet the stopping point would
have been 105 metres beyond the end of the runway. In other
words, penetrate the diplomatic and dry language at work in the
report and it becomes clear that the aircraft in this incident could
have crashed if it had been raining. In south-eastern England in
mid-November rain is not considered particularly unusual.

This plane was not even loaded to its maximum extent. If it had
been, and if the spoilers had failed to deploy or another adverse
combination of events affected braking (like touching down too

far down the runway and in wet weather) the outcome would also have been a crash.

The report remarked that the airport was looking into the possibility of installing a pit filled with ash or sand to retard an aircraft overrunning the runway. Left beyond the scope of the investigation was the question of why nobody had thought of this before, especially as the airport was built in the mid-1980s. Not considering the possibility of runway overruns at an airport with one of the shortest runways in the country is a clear compromise of safety.

The US FAA, which often takes the lead in introducing safety measures which are frequently adopted wholesale by other countries, legislated for all US airports to have a 1000-foot over-run area. But it made exceptions, including Love Field, in Dallas, and LaGuardia, as well as others.[18] At Washington National Airport (now known as Ronald Reagan National Airport), which has other safety concerns – being huddled in the middle of a major city, with high-rise blocks frighteningly near the airways – the operators decided to extend their runways. Subsequently, several aircraft have aborted take-offs and fetched up in overruns. Without the new tarmac areas, they would probably have ended up in the Potomac river.[19]

One aircraft that did get its feet wet was a World Airways DC-10 arriving at night at Boston-Logan International Airport in January 1982 after flying from Newark, and before that Oakland, California. The plane landed 2500 feet from the beginning of the 9200-foot runway but the surface was a dangerous mixture of hard-packed snow, rain and ice, the temperature on the ground being only just above freezing. The pilot had not been informed about the condition of the runway by the tower.

When the plane landed, braking and reverse thrust did barely anything to slow the heavily laden jet, and as it slewed towards the end of the runway the pilot swerved to avoid a lighting installation. The plane slipped off the end of the runway, which juts into the sea, and the nose broke off, coming to rest half in the water. Two of those on board were swept away by the currents and their bodies were never recovered.

The NTSB decided that the pilot was not to blame in this situation. Instead it took the FAA to task for not giving airport managements any yardstick for measuring the slipperiness of runways in bad weather conditions, or how these would translate into ways of calculating stopping distances. In this case the NTSB did address the point about runway length, observing that when the FAA drew up rules on minimum runway lengths it took no account of the reduced braking effectiveness of aircraft on icy runways.

Overrunning the runway on take-off or landing can result in impacts, but these are by no means the only types of landing accident that occur. In the United States in particular, runway collisions happen because an aircraft has landed on the wrong runway, or landed on a taxiway instead of the runway. Normally such crashes are judged to have been the responsibility of air traffic controllers, like the crash of a USAir 737 into a small airliner, a Skywest Fairchild Metroliner, a turbo-prop with just twelve people on board on 1 February, 1991, at Los Angeles International airport.[20]

There are heavy operational pressures on airports and air traffic control in the United States to improve the throughput of aircraft. Airlines gain because they can increase their services and airports earn more with more landings. The FAA, which runs US air traffic control, is very sensitive to such pressures from the airlines who, after all, are only trying to expand their businesses. However, when new procedures are introduced, proof that they are safer than the pre-existing situation is not required. Instead, educated guesses are made about safe operation, and figures are then produced to show how improbable it is an accident will occur. Translated into commonsense language, the new measures come in and are judged worthwhile if they "only" cause new crashes at such and such a remote rate.

A good example concerns parallel runways. There is absolutely no safety argument in favour of parallel runways and simultaneous landings, which are now established at a number of US airports, with still more airports anxious to win official approval. Certainly, the standards under which parallel runways are operated are extremely strict, and well policed. Pilots are extensively trained to guard against anything untoward in such operations. Nonetheless, the pressures continue. While San Francisco International airport's parallel runways are 750 feet apart, there is pressure to lower the permissible distance down to 150 feet.

It is no good saying, after a major crash involving parallel runways, that it may have been the pilot's fault. The possibility of an operating error needs to be built into such systems so that the same level of safety that existed before is maintained. So far, there have been no fatal accidents involving parallel runways. If (more probably *when*) one does occur, the airline, the airport and the FAA are likely to refer to the millions of landings that were made without incident and how unlikely, improbable and out of the ordinary this crash was. The fact that it would not have happened if parallel runways had not been introduced will not be considered relevant.

One recent example of the pressures that airlines put on the traffic system came in the summer of 1997, when the FAA brought in new rules for taxiing aircraft at airports. Under one of the FAA's air traffic orders aircraft would then be permitted to land, take off and taxi on intersecting runways and taxiways. Typically, a landing aircraft would be told to land and then hold short of an intersecting runway or taxiway. The ALPA complained that the procedures were so tightly timed that sooner or later a mistake was bound to be made and that would result in a collision. They instructed their members not to obey some of these instructions.[21]

A runway incursion is when an aircraft or other vehicle, for whatever reason, strays on to a taxiway or runway assigned to someone else. In the United States, runway incursions have been increasing at a high rate, owing to the FAA's failure to implement various systems it has promised to the airports. In 1991 John Lauber, a prominent figure in US air safety who was then with the NTSB, said, "The Safety Board views runway incursions as one of the most significant hazards to aviation today, and we expect that the potential for a ground collision involving an arriving or departing airplane will increase." This was shortly after the Metroliner/737 collision at Los Angeles.

Collisions are not all that frequent but are potentially the most serious crashes, since they usually involve two aircraft, although airport surface vehicles frequently feature in such incidents. Tenerife, after all, was a runway incursion accident. In the main, the runway crashes have been happening because the FAA and the airport authorities have failed to deal with the increase in overall traffic. Signs and procedures are not standardised, and pilots are frequently confused.

What seems particularly dangerous to the non-US observer is the fact that most of the runway violations are made by general aviation planes: small private aircraft. The owners of such planes are highly influential in the US Congress, and resist efforts to impose more safety features on them and to exclude them from major airports. The United States' most serious mid-air collisions to date have involved passenger aircraft striking private planes.

The main failing of the FAA here is that it has set itself a target it has no hope of reaching. In 1994 it decided to try to reduce runway incursions by 80 per cent by 2001. Between 1993 and 1996 runway incursions rose by 54 per cent.[22]

Similar to the desires of airlines and airports to land more planes is the desire to lower what are called "separation standards". Separation is the technical term for keeping aircraft apart. This is done not merely in the sense of preventing mid-air collisions, but also to keep planes from following too close to each other. Behind every aircraft trails an invisible trap called a wake vortex. One crash in May 1972 illustrated the problem well. An American Airlines DC-10 was practising landings and take-offs, known as touch-and-gos, at Greater Southwest International Airport, Texas, while a Delta DC-9 was also on a training exercise at the same airport. The DC-9, which is about half the size of a DC-10, came in to land behind the DC-10 and was too close, although nobody realised it at the time.

From each wing tip of a jet trails the vortex, a wide corkscrew of air currents swirling backwards. Imagine the aerial equivalent of the whirlpool you see in the plughole of an emptying bathtub.

In certain atmospheric conditions the vortex can persist for two minutes or more behind the plane that created it. With its undercarriage down and configured for landing, the DC-9 entered the invisible spiralling maelstrom behind the DC-10's left wing, which could have had a wind-strength of over 200 mph.

The DC-9's left wing was suddenly forced down as the current hit it, and as the pilot attempted to correct in the other direction, the other part of the spiral hit the right wing, dipping it sharply. The left wing dipped once more and then the right wing span violently round, hit the ground and the aircraft crashed on its back in a massive explosion which killed all four men on board. That crash, in full tribute to the Tombstone Imperative, put wake vortices on the map.[23]

Wake vortices had been known since the early days of manned flight, but while aircraft were small the vortices were small and the planes could cope. Then came the jets, and the main threat of wake turbulence, as the vortex effect is also known, was to light aircraft following jets. In the early 1970s the full implications of small jets following in the wake of the relatively new wide-bodied jets were not fully understood until the investigators of the DC-9 crash started to gather data from other pilots who had already experienced similar upsets but had had enough altitude to recover. The consequence was new rules to provide for five nautical miles of separation behind "heavy" jets, i.e. 300,000 pounds and above.

Unfortunately, the lessons learned from the 1972 tragedy were not applied correctly. When it was certified, the Boeing 757 just missed classification as a "heavy" and so separation standards were not as generous as they were for the larger jets. It was not fully realised at the time that the intensity of wake vortex is not simply a function of the mass and speed of the aircraft. According to a US study, the 757's especially aerodynamically efficient wing allowed it to produce "vortex tangential velocities greater than any ever recorded, including those of the Boeing 747 and Lockheed C-5A". A large military transport, the C-5A is similar in size to the 747 and both are far larger than the 757.[24]

One 757 vortex claimed the lives of everyone on board a Cessna Citation private jet at Billings, Montana, in 1994 even though it was over two miles behind the Boeing. Several more fatal crashes involving the wakes of 757s had to follow before the FAA mandated greater separation behind them, its reluctance to take prompt action being motivated, many observers believed, because such action meant fewer landings at airports, with unwanted consequences for the profits of airlines and airports alike.

Despite recommendations in the investigators' report on the DC-9 upset, studies on wake vortices did not follow except by serendipity. The largest amount of research ever undertaken into the mysterious physics of the wake vortex followed the disaster that befell the twenty-five occupants of a Boeing 737 which plunged earthwards very suddenly from a height of 6000 feet as it approached Colorado Springs airport in April 1991. This accident – along with a similar 737 crash at Pittsburgh in 1994 – has so far been given no official cause.

These days, it is believed that a failing in the hydraulic piston that controls the 737's rudder may have been at fault in those two disasters, but as part of the investigation the NTSB fully considered the possibility of a wake vortex upset. The political pressure on the NTSB to come up with an answer to the Colorado Springs conundrum was so great that the government authorised the spending of millions of dollars on a research programme to establish the effects of this phenomenon.

When it was complete the research enabled Greg Phillips, the senior NTSB investigator for Colorado Springs, to discount a wake vortex as the cause of the crash, but in the course of the vortex tests the researchers had accumulated a large amount of new data, which eventually led to new NTSB recommendations on the distances that ought to separate aircraft. Despite the NTSB calling for such research over twenty years beforehand, it was only done in the context of a non-wake vortex-related crash.

Retired NTSB air crash investigator Rudy Kapustin has publicly decried the industry and the FAA's failure to act on wake vortices or to act on the investigators' 1972 recommendations in increasing separation standards. He said: "recent NTSB correspondence to FAA shows that there were at least 51 wake vortex-related accidents and incidents between 1983 and 1993 in the United States alone. These 51 occurrences resulted in 27 fatalities, eight serious injuries and substantial damage or destruction of 40 airplanes. Two of the most recent cases involved a McDonnell Douglas MD-88 and a Boeing 737 conducting visual approaches behind B-757 airplanes."

Mr Kapustin pointed out, furthermore, that in March 1994 the NTSB wrote to the FAA making nineteen recommendations on this topic. He adds: "one must wonder why in-depth investigations inquiring into the vortex-generating characteristics of large and heavy wide-bodied airplanes were not conducted sooner". Why indeed? Such hints are common fare in the debates between investigators and regulators, and what he is implying is that the FAA is too beholden to the industry to consider such changes.

The NTSB continued to hammer away at separation standards, in particular those affecting the 757, and finally succeeded in 1994 when compulsory separation behind the plane was increased from three to four miles. Crashes still happened, so the distance smaller aircraft had to observe behind 757s was increased by the FAA to five miles in August 1996, twenty-four years after the Delta DC-9 had crashed in Texas.

Avoiding wake vortices is difficult to regulate for, because their precise mode of operation and how long they persist in the air is little understood. To err on the side of safety, however, would lead to loss of revenue for airports and airlines. The FAA, therefore, needed harder evidence and more corpses before acting.

Anecdotes of pilot encounters with wake vortices are legion. NASA operates an anonymous reporting system whereby pilots can allow others to learn from their mistakes or experiences. In one sample of wake vortex reports to NASA, half the dangerous experiences reported were when the aircraft concerned were at or above the FAA's recommended minimum separation standards.[25]

In Britain, however, separations standards are more conservative. The CAA has come under less pressure than the FAA to lower separation distances, which is why it has not blindly followed suit when the FAA has relaxed standards. One would no doubt be accused of cynicism if one were to suggest that separation standards are lower in the United States because the pressure to land more aircraft is greater.

Crashworthiness

Just as important as how aircraft crash is the question of how the aircraft structure itself behaves in a crash. The cabins of passenger-carrying aircraft are not designed to be crashworthy in any important respects, unlike the average motor car. Certainly, the fuel tanks must maintain their integrity as far as possible, the regulations state, and seats have to withstand a shock of 16 g, but is this enough?

The aviation industry's unwillingness to tackle this issue is aided by a popular misconception. Most people believe that an airliner accident crash is an all-or-nothing proposition and that everyone dies when they crash. In fact, some 60 per cent of fatal air crashes have survivors, and the numbers of those killed can amount to any percentage of the number of people on board, from one dead to one survivor.

Although we now take much of the crashworthiness of cars for granted, this was not always so. When the advocates of greater car safety proposed removing the sharp edges from inside the compartment, having the steering column collapse, and using safety glass they were ridiculed. The important point, they were told, was to prevent the car crashing in the first place and only the driver could do that. Therefore, all that should be done was to educate the driver.

Now, however, not only the above points have been covered, but we have safety-belts, air-bags, roll-bars, child-seats, head-rests, crumple zones, safety cages, side-impact protection beams, detachable rear-view mirrors, and so on. The list is by no means complete.

The aircraft industry, however, remains in the state of denial that the automobile industry was in before the drive towards greater crashworthiness and occupant protection got going in the mid-1960s. It is true that the chances of a car having a crash during twenty or so years of life on the road is greater than that of an aircraft, but so many people are carried on jets that it may be worth considering carefully what could be done to protect passengers better. And although fewer planes crash, in relation to the number flying, than in the days of piston-engined passenger aircraft, just as many people are being killed in each individual crash as were then. This implies that the crashworthiness of aircraft has not improved.

This is somewhat ironic, seeing as the first steps in making cars more crashworthy were adopted in the United States from the experience of designing small aircraft during the Second World War – chiefly by removing sharp edges from cockpit panels, introducing crush zones in the nose and using four-point harnesses.[26] A measure of how low down crashworthiness is on the agendas of regulatory authorities is the fact that the FAA only made belt and shoulder harness restraints compulsory on small, private aircraft in 1978. Pilots had been wearing restraints in American military aircraft since the First World War, and shoulder harnesses since the mid-1930s.

UK accident investigators had an unusual opportunity to study survival aspects of an aircraft crash in some detail as they looked into the destruction of a nearly new British Midland Boeing 737-400 just outside East Midlands Airport, in January 1989, by the village of Kegworth.[27] Of particular interest was the fact that this was the first survivable crash of an aircraft fitted with the new, 16 g seats, well above the standard required for most aircraft.[28]

The aircraft was flying its scheduled service from London to Belfast when smoke began to enter the cockpit and a series of loud bangs was heard. This famous exchange followed.

> Co-pilot: "Got a fire . . . It's a fire coming through."
> Captain: "Which one [engine] is it?"
> Co-pilot: "It's the le . . . the right one."
> Captain: "OK, throttle it back."

They mistakenly shut down the healthy right engine while the left engine struggled on. They were close to East Midlands Airport and requested and received permission to make an emergency landing there. The situation was unusual, but it was a "normal" emergency so far and no problems were anticipated in making a one-engine landing, something all pilots of such aircraft practise assiduously. The crisis that had afflicted the left engine appeared to go away after the autothrottle, a sort of cruise control, was disconnected. But the mechanical failure within it was still consuming the engine.

The captain lined up the aircraft for landing at the airport, which sits atop a broad plateau of ground. The airport is convenient for Birmingham and the dense industrial belt of the East Midlands, with the M1 motorway running perpendicular to the eastern end of the single runway. The motorway – the busiest trunk road in the UK – lies in a deep cutting and then has two moderate slopes down to the six lanes of heavy traffic.

When the plane was 900 feet over the village of Kegworth and less than three miles from the runway, the left engine suddenly gave up the ghost, without giving the crew time to attempt to relight the right engine.[29] As the co-pilot shouted, "Jesus, there's a motorway," the 737's tail hit the ground at the top of the eastern embankment of the motorway at roughly 125 mph. It then sailed over the eastern slope of the embankment and through its trees, and impacted with the embankment on the other side at over 100 mph, slewing to a halt in three pieces, with the tail assembly upside-down.[30]

Of those on board, 47 had been killed (including some who died later in hospital), and of the 79 survivors, all but 5 suffered serious injuries, many breaking both arms and legs and fracturing hips and pelvises. Fire-tenders from the nearby airport were almost immediately on the scene and they quickly extinguished the small fire burning in the remnants of the engine which had started the emergency. It took eight hours for the last injured occupant to be removed, the fire and ambulance crews enlisting the help of motorists in rescuing the injured from the aircraft.[31]

What made this crash of special interest to the investigators was that it involved a new, extremely common type of aircraft suffering an impact but without fire. The final maximum deceleration in the crunch into the western embankment of the motorway was 26.5 times the force of gravity, a very high loading but one which it is well known that humans can survive. The AAIB had extensively investigated survivability factors in the last major survivable air disaster, the British Airtours 737 which caught fire in August 1985 at Manchester airport and killed fifty-five (*see* Chapter 3). While they had concentrated on aspects of surviving fires then, on this occasion they had an opportunity to research impact survival thoroughly.

In addition, the casualty doctors at the four local hospitals to which all the injured were taken received funding to enable them to make an extensive study of all the injuries and how they related to seat position. The report shows that most of the dead were sitting in the seat-rows immediately forward and aft of the wing. The wing-box is a structure that holds both wings together and passes through the fuselage and is extremely strong. The seats that were bolted to the wing-box were less disrupted than the rest.

The other seats simply flew forward during the crash because on impact the floor structure disintegrated, freeing the seats. On entering the cabin in this area rescuers noticed that the head level of those inside was where the floor level would normally have been. Many of the dead had, simply, been crushed by the weight of other passengers sliding into them, concertina-style, from behind. Many were injured by being struck in the back of the head by heavy objects flying out of the overhead bins, all but one of which detached on impact and spewed themselves and their contents all over the passengers. One doctor involved in the investigation said three passengers sitting in aisle seats were struck violently in the back of the head by objects shooting out of the bins. Two of them were killed, but this could not be included in the official report because it was impossible to prove beyond doubt exactly which objects had been in which bins and done the damage.[32] The mess created by the overhead bins and the general pile of people at the front of the cabin were what made the rescue work so difficult and prolonged.

In studies of emergency evacuations, it has been found that the bins and other debris often seriously hampered evacuation.[33] That overhead bins should present such risks is ironic, because they are relatively recent innovations. Earlier aircraft had open shelves above the passenger seats, and because of the risk of injury from flying objects in a crash only coats and hats were allowed to be stored there. The installation of the overhead bins thus appears to be a direct exchange of passenger safety for convenience, since enclosing the bins clearly does not prevent their contents from spilling out.

A much more important observation, however, was made from the Kegworth experience. To great astonishment, it emerged that this aircraft had two contradictory standards for seat and floor strength. According to rules introduced by the FAA and adopted by the CAA, new aircraft had to have seats designed to withstand a 16 g deceleration. However, the specification for the floor was still only 9 g. This was an absurd situation. There is no point in having a 16 g seat attached to a 9 g floor. It's like wearing a seat-belt in a car and then unbolting the seat from the floor. At Kegworth the seats flew forward still attached to the seat-track.

The question of how passengers should be seated and the specifications for the crashworthiness of the seats and floor have changed very little since 1952, when the FAA set standards for static and dynamic loading of the seats that were only marginally changed by the new rules affecting this plane.[34] Oddly, the general attitude of the airlines and the aircraft manufacturers appeared to be similar: don't fix the plane, just prevent it from crashing.[35]

However, not only do most air crashes have survivors, but many individuals have survived crashes which were, technically speaking, not survivable. In December 1972 an Eastern Airlines Lockheed L-1011, or Tristar, crashed in the Florida Everglades after descending at a rate of 3000 feet per minute (that's about 35 mph in the vertical axis alone) and moving at a forward velocity of 190 knots (or nearly 210 mph). Nonetheless, 67 of the 161 passengers lived. The reason so many survived what the NTSB officially termed an unsurvivable crash was that, owing to special circumstances, the seats were attached in a secure fashion to the floor and they maintained their integrity much longer than did the seats at Kegworth. Unfortunately, this lesson did not translate itself into recommendations for stronger seats, or better attachment of them to the floor.

The AAIB studied some thirteen crashes and noted:

> *On comparing these accidents with ME [the Kegworth plane], it was apparent that the structural disruption to ME was characteristic of other off-airfield accidents which had involved landing undershoots, failed go-arounds and power-off forced landings. Accidents involving rejected take-offs and landing over-runs were generally less severe. Two recurrent features of these accidents were the major disruption which had been caused by an impact after the initial ground impact, and the occurrence of two major fuselage failures, one forward and one aft of the wing.*

The implication seems reasonably clear. If the same level of strength had been available to the floor fore and aft of the wing as over the wing then a lot more people would have survived. The AAIB added that another "recurrent feature" of the crashes they studied was that many of those who survived the impact but were incapacitated by their injuries died in a post-crash fire because they were unable to escape the plane.

It was the earlier crash of another British Midland aircraft that provided one of the grimmest illustrations of this theme. On 4 June 1967 a British Midlands Argonaut, an aircraft with four piston engines carrying eighty-four people in total, crashed in the middle of Stockport, near Manchester.[36] The crash site was 100 yards from Stockport police station so help was immediately at hand. Nevertheless, only twelve people could be rescued before a fierce fire broke out killing all who remained on board. Crucially, just like at Kegworth twenty-one years later, many passengers who survived the crash were immobilised by broken legs. They were the ones killed by fire.

The cause of injury in the Kegworth crash raises important questions about seat design. The AAIB report says that the first injury a typical passenger on this plane suffered was hitting the back of the seat in front. (If the seat parted from the floor the passenger suffered other injuries from being crushed.) And then, as the pelvis was heavily loaded by the body being thrown on to the lap-belt, there were fractures of the pelvis and the iliac spines, dislocation and or fracture of the hip joint. What then tended to happen was that legs and arms flailed forward, lower legs, arms and feet often being broken in the process. Most seriously, thighs were broken by the crossbar running under the cushion at the front of the seat. In other words, most of those who were not killed in the impact were comprehensively smashed up.

Much as the AAIB research and investigation served to draw attention to these failings, it is not as if they were unknown. Indeed, many investigators privately say that situations like this have to be approached as if they are new, because that makes it easier for effective remedial action to be taken. A study by the NTSB published in 1981 found that in crashes they had investigated at least part of the seat and its restraint systems had failed in 84.4 per cent of cases. They found that 77.7 per cent of overhead panels, rack and bins had failed and caused injuries, and that galley equipment or parts of it had failed in 62 per cent of cases and had sometimes blocked the emergency exits.[37]

This raises the spectre of rear-facing seats, one of the great controversies of the airline industry, and one of the clearest illustrations of the industry's reluctance to embrace new measures to improve safety. In 1945 the Royal Air Force adopted a regulation that from then on all its transport aircraft would have 25 g-resistant rear-facing passenger seats.[38] In a UK government study in 1954 it was found that in crashes involving RAF transports with a mix of forward- and rear-facing seats, the occupants in the rear-facing seats fared better. In 1951 it had been proposed that rear-facing seats be mandated in all civil passenger aircraft and incorporated into the British Civil Aviation Regulations, but this proposal died on the vine.

Since then there have been no further RAF air transport crashes from which to gather more data. Some Comet, Trident and Boeing 737 passenger aircraft were fitted with rear-facing seats, but these were not installed for safety reasons, only to provide a lounge-style arrangement of passenger seats facing each other as on trains. All air crash investigators seem to be in agreement that survivability would be enormously improved if all transports had rear-facing seats. Equally, however, they are convinced that the airlines "would not allow it" because it is too expensive.

The heat of the industry and regulator response to arguments in favour of rear-facing seats is out of proportion to its content. One safety expert who wanted to remain anonymous stated: "The trouble with rear-facing seats is that anybody with common sense can understand that they would be much safer in an impact. And aviation industry people do not like the fact that they cannot retreat into engineering jargon to discuss it."

An official at the CAA argued that a survey had been done showing passengers wouldn't like rear-facing seats. On being asked for details, it turned out no such survey had been carried out.

From the evidence found by the AAIB and old research done by the FAA, it seems that only a small weight penalty, if any, would result from all passenger seats facing the rear, but both the CAA and the FAA have shown extreme reluctance to countenance the suggestion. One objection is that people in rear-facing seats would be struck in the face by loose materials being ejected from overhead bins. The AAIB answered that one by saying that the bins need to be made more secure anyway, so that heavy objects do not fly about the cabin during a crash.

The AAIB recommended research into new ways of restraining passengers, including rear-facing seats, and revising the brace position (see Chapter 4). No action followed on passenger restraint, but a new brace position was adopted. One does not have to plumb the depths of cynicism to suggest that it was easier to adopt a measure that cost nothing than one that did not.

As far as the overhead bins are concerned, little has improved here either. They are still designed, as they were then, to pass a static loading test. That means, essentially, you fill it up until it breaks. By this test the bins are very strong. They can take about three pounds of weight for every inch of bin. Since the bins, at least in the Kegworth 737-400, were sixty inches long, that means each one was capable of taking 180 pounds without collapsing, thus providing a clear safety margin. However, they have never been tested with dynamic loading: that is, subjecting them to a deceleration.

Ask an aircraft manufacturer about crashworthiness and you will get the response, "we build 'em to fly not to crash". Presumably, the Swedish car-makers Volvo might take offence if one implied that their cars were good for crashing but not for driving. Both functions are now regarded as indispensable for cars, and regulations provide tests that cars must undergo to prove their crashworthiness. The airline industry, however, has been protected from this.

The industry is doing the absolute minimum it can in order to improve safety. Instead of concentrating on a wide variety of measures, each of which contributes in a small way towards improving the overall picture, they concentrate on CFIT in the hope that one big push will lower the incidence of that kind of crash and thus let the industry off the hook on other matters.

The NTSB put it well, if a little ponderously, in its 1981 report.

The Safety Board believes that there is sufficient data currently available to support the upgrading of the occupant crash protection standards in the regulations; and further, that the substantial body of knowledge and practical experience in design, construction, testing and use of crashworthy structures and cabin furnishings can be applied successfully to large transport aircraft, in many cases without substantial penalties in cost and weight and without major modifications to existing structures.[39]

That was 1981, and still nothing has been done to raise crash standards beyond the woeful 9 g standards that currently exist. The aviation industry is working with outmoded designs where crashworthiness is not a serious consideration. Airbus-340s or Boeing 777s may be twenty-first-century technological marvels when it comes to navigational aids, flight computers, aerodynamics and operating efficiency, but both are stuck in the 1950s in terms of crash performance.

We should leave the last word with Donat Desmond, who was travelling with his wife to Belfast on the British Midland 737 and wrote this moving account of his experience for the benefit of a British parliamentary committee looking at improving cabin safety.

Eight seconds before the impact we were informed that we were going to crash land by the Captain's terse announcement: "Passengers. Do not prepare for emergency landing. Prepare for crash landing. Prepare for crash landing!"

Everyone in the plane was buckled into their seats but we did not have time to push down the seat immediately in front (which in many cases had a passenger seated who prevented the collapsing) and little time to get into the crash landing position. Eight seconds later the Boeing 737-400 impacted very solidly with a "forward" velocity of an estimated 120 mph, and a "downward" velocity of something like 30 mph. Most of the 47 who lost their lives were killed instantly on impact. The front section of the plane was hit especially badly (my wife and I were seated in seats 5D and 5E respectively) and a block of passengers were killed in rows 6 to 10 which included the section of the fuselage where the plane snapped.

The actual impact was incredible, with an initial grazing of the opposite bank of the M1 followed by the crash where I felt my back literally explode. The next thing I knew I was gazing unbelievably at a scene of terrible devastation illuminated strangely by the light from the left-hand engine which was still on fire and the lights from the motorway streaming through the fractured fuselage immediately behind me.

My seat had apparently broken through the floor and partly descended into the luggage hold. The row of seats in front of me, however, had concertinaed on impact and were pinning my legs down. I was totally unable to move except shuffle in my uphill-facing seat. I had nearly severed my left arm off the seat in front of me and my right upper arm had somehow exploded through my skin and dislocated my shoulder; both ankles and my back were also broken (although I am now able to walk as the shaft of my spine physically compacted and did not snap my spinal cord).

On boarding the plane I was 5 ft 11½ inches tall, I am now 5 ft 10 inches, having lost height in my compacted spine and broken ankles.

My greatest fear on becoming conscious after impact was the very real risk of fire. Incredibly, the plane did not ignite; I have been told . . . we hit a hill, with the consequence that the fuel ran downhill soaking into the soil and did not fan out to ignite with the burning engine. The prompt response of the East Midlands Airport firemen was also a major contributory factor in eliminating this risk.

The actual impact . . . could have been made potentially more "survivable" by the provision of restraining harness-type or seat-belt-type restraining straps. The present buckle seat-belts are seriously deficient in that even when in the emergency landing position the main body and head flail outwards in a significant impact, and are broken by the seat in front.

I remember a man in front of me dying as his lungs filled with blood caused I imagine by his smashed ribs piercing his chest cavity. Marja, my wife, died when she broke her neck off the seat in front of her, thankfully she died instantly.

I would like to express my admiration and gratitude to the firemen and emergency services who got me out of the plane alive at 11.05 pm on that Sunday night and to a young man I know only as "Graham" who saw the plane coming down as he and his wife drove home to Hull. He tried to keep five of us conscious and alive during the following hours as we drifted in and out of consciousness. I felt so sorry for him, as I watched him give his everything to keep us alive. Sadly two of us five died. But I admired him as I watched him trying to bale out that vast pool of human suffering with his small thimble.[40]

CHAPTER 3

Fire and survival

THE UNFORTUNATE FACT about most crashes is that there is a disturbingly high probability of fire breaking out when the aircraft has come to rest. Next to deaths resulting from crash impacts, fire and toxic smoke are the leading causes of fatalities.

In the United States it has been estimated that 22 per cent of all deaths in civil transport aircraft are due to fire, an extremely high proportion given that the total includes death by blunt trauma in non-survivable crashes. One study said that over a twenty-six-year period 2400 people had been killed in aircraft fires.[1]

The irony of surviving a crash only to face the threat of death by fire was not lost on Jerry Schemmel, a survivor of the Sioux City DC-10 crash in July 1989, as he hung upside-down in the wreckage. He had already spent forty-five minutes in the air knowing a crash was going to happen. "What an irony. Here I survive the crash of a jumbo jet, but now will die in the aftermath, either by the suffocating smoke or the fire or both."[2]

Realists might say, however, that fire cannot be an unexpected outcome in a crash when the fuel on board can amount to one-third of the aircraft's total weight.

The story of how fires on planes are fought, and the regulations to control their severity, is a fascinating one. Unfortunately, it is characterised by delay and foot-dragging by the certification and regulatory authorities, whose inherent bias towards inaction is most obvious in this aspect of air safety.

On the face of it, avoiding post-crash fires in aircraft might seem to be a fanciful notion. Fuel is stored in the wings and often in a central tank between the wings, in the middle of the fuselage, and some aircraft even carry fuel in the tailplane. A Boeing 737 can carry more than 16 tons of kerosene, and some Boeing 747s as much as 145 tons. If a plane is to crash and break, keeping the fuel from spilling would seem to be a fruitless task. If it atomises as it is spilled it will burn extremely fiercely.

Many precautions are taken to prevent fires. Aircraft that are returning to the airport after an emergency have to dump fuel in the air, both to reduce their weight and to lower the risk of fire in the event of a crash. If a lowered undercarriage is ripped off in a crash landing it must not open holes in the fuel tanks. The same goes for engines and engine pylons that may fall or be torn off the wings.

More could be done, perhaps, to prevent the fuel tanks from rupturing in a crash, but the debate between the regulators and their critics on fire is hottest in the area of what could be done to protect aircraft occupants from the effects of fire once it has started. On the whole, the regulators are much more concerned with preventing fires than trying to protect passengers once they have broken out. The difference between these approaches is a crucial one.

In the early morning of 22 August 1985, one group of would-be holiday-makers was sitting on a British Airtours Boeing 737-200 doing whatever people do to reassure themselves on take-off and looking forward, presumably, to exchanging the climate of Manchester for the heat of Corfu. The first officer, who was the pilot flying this leg, applied full power for take-off. The aircraft was approaching take-off speed when the two pilots heard a thud and, fearing a birdstrike or a burst tyre, immediately abandoned take-off. Nine seconds later they got an indication of fire in the left engine, which they confirmed with the tower.

The thud they had heard had been part of the left engine

disintegrating. Debris flew out of the engine nacelle and punched a hole in the equivalent of the filler cap for the wing fuel tank, which is on the underside of the wing. Aviation fuel gushed from a dinner-plate-sized hole and was ignited by the engine exhaust. As the aircraft turned off the runway to the right, a light wind blew the stream of flames on to the fuselage, and within one minute of the plane stopping fire had burned through the fuselage and entered the cabin.

This early in the sequence of events a conflict is obvious between operational and safety issues. The pilot was correct in observing the British Airtours operator's manual on procedure, i.e. leaving the runway. Yet why did the rules state they should clear the runway for other aircraft when the first priority would seem to be to stop and assess the emergency? In fact, that is precisely what the manufacturers, Boeing, recommend in their own 737 manual.

Although aircraft manufacturers always supply their own recommended instructions for operating their products, airlines are permitted to adapt the manuals, with the approval of the regulators, to fit in with their historic operating procedures and their own "culture" of safe piloting. This outdated practice is confusing and dangerous. It is easy to imagine how an airline's experience might be valuable in adapting the manufacturer's manual, but common sense suggests there should be just one manual, with contributions from the airlines, rather than as many different manuals as there are airlines.

British Airtours' change regarding leaving the runway was unnecessary and contributed to the severity of the disaster. Had they not turned the aircraft off the runway, the wind would not have blown the fire on to the fuselage. In deference to the Tombstone Imperative, the manual has since been changed to order halting the aircraft where it is.[3]

Confusion and panic reigned in the 737, escape being hindered by people blocking exits and contradictory instructions from cabin crew. Many failed to get out in time. Despite an extremely rapid response by the airport fire brigade, considerable courage from some cabin crew and fire-fighters, and the severity of the fire being less than that planned for in an emergency, 55 of the 137 people on board died, most of them from toxic-fume inhalation. In common with most fires, those in homes included, the cocktail of poisonous gases claimed about 80 per cent of the dead, with the heat of the fire taking the rest.

The AAIB's determination of the causes was fairly simple:

Major contributory factors were the vulnerability of the wing tank access panels [the "filler cap"] to impact, a lack of any effective provision for fighting major fires inside the aircraft cabin, the vulnerability of the aircraft hull to external fire and the extremely toxic nature of the emissions from the burning interior materials.

The major cause of the fatalities was rapid incapacitation due to the inhalation of the dense toxic/irritant smoke atmosphere within the cabin, aggravated by evacuation delays caused by a door malfunction and restricted access to the exits.[4]

The pilots could not see the relevant part of the left wing or engine – no passenger jets give the pilots a complete view of the wings and engines. The commander therefore asked the tower whether they thought they should evacuate the plane, to which the tower replied in the affirmative. Some forty-five seconds after the thud which caused the captain to abort take-off, the aircraft had come to a halt, and the captain had asked over the PA system for everyone to evacuate via the right-hand side of the plane.

Confusion followed. Passengers at the back and on the left saw intense fire, but those on the right saw nothing at first. So when those who had seen the fire moved into the aisle they were shouted at to sit down and stay calm by cabin crew and other passengers. Soon after stopping, the pilots saw flames creeping up the left-hand side of the plane and they left via their emergency rope through the cockpit side-window. The cabin crew got people going through the front-left door before the flames cut off that route.

The front-right door was useless until the purser had cleared an obstacle on its slide, and the rear-left door was opened, but nothing came out of it except thick black smoke. The investigators found that when such doors were opened "aggressively", as would be the case in an emergency, they frequently jammed. They repeated these tests and confirmed their results.

Boeing, however, told them that they had never encountered this phenomenon in twenty years of 737 operation. Little, even in the accident report, was made of this strange discrepancy. If these doors were prone to jamming when treated roughly, surely there was an important problem to be addressed. It was not, however, covered in the AAIB's recommendations.

The official report into the crash by the AAIB says what happened next.

As the aircraft came to a halt and at the instigation of other passengers, a young woman sitting in row 10 seat F (10F), beside the right overwing exit, attempted to open it by pulling on her right hand arm-rest which was mounted on the exit hatch. Her companion in seat 10E, the centre seat of a row of three, stood up and reached across to pull the handle located at the top of the hatch marked "Emergency Pull". The hatch, weighing 48 lbs, fell into the aircraft, pivoting about its lower edge to lay across the passenger in 10F, trapping her in her seat. With the assistance of a man in row 11 behind the women, the hatch was removed and placed on vacant seat 11D. The passengers in 10F and 10E then left the aircraft cabin through the overwing exit on to the wing followed by other survivors. This exit was open about 45 seconds after the aircraft stopped.

Twenty-seven people escaped through this door, access to which was just 10.5 inches between the seats, before it became clogged with struggling passengers, and those waiting to get through it were overcome by the smoke. The majority of the dead were found slumped around this exit. One of them died slumped across the threshold of the exit. The last person to be rescued from the plane was a boy, whose hand a foam-vehicle driver had seen moving above the body of the man in the exit. The rescuer climbed up on the wing and pulled the boy out.

The largest number of survivors had got out through the front-right door. Nobody escaped through the two rear doors. After seven minutes all who were going to escape had done so.

Nobody will know whether it would have made any difference, but the airport fire service was delayed for ten crucial minutes by a shortage of water. One fire officer had gone into the plane but had been blasted back out again by an explosion, possibly an exploding aerosol can. The officer in charge wanted no one else to go back in until he had a secure water supply. Tragically, the nearby hydrants were all dry.[5] When fire tenders from outside the airport joined them on the tarmac, fire-fighters went back into the plane and found one man still alive.[6] He was extricated but died six days later in hospital.

The sight of the charred tail section of the Boeing 737 lying collapsed on the runway was possibly Britain's most enduring news image of that disastrous year for aircraft accidents.

Unusually, the dry language of the official report manages to convey the desperation inside the aircraft as the emergency developed, and dispassionately describes the immediately handicapping effects of the hot, thick, black smoke generated by the materials used in the cabin trim and the seats.

As the aircraft stopped, the aft cabin was suddenly filled with thick black smoke which induced panic amongst passengers in that area, with a consequent rapid forward movement down the aisle. Many passengers stumbled and collapsed in the aisle, forcing others to go over the seat-backs towards the centre cabin area, which was clear up until the time the right overwing exit was opened. A passenger from the front row of seats looked back as he waited to exit the aircraft, and was aware of a mass of people tangled together and struggling in the centre section, apparently incapable of moving forward, he stated "people were howling and screaming".

Many survivors from the front six rows of seats described a roll of thick black smoke clinging to the ceiling and moving rapidly forwards along the cabin. On reaching the forward bulkheads it curled down, began moving aft, lowering and filling the cabin. Some of these passengers became engulfed in the smoke despite their close proximity to the forward exits. All described a single breath as burning and painful, immediately causing choking. Some used clothing or hands over their mouths in an attempt to filter the smoke; others attempted to hold their breath. They experienced drowsiness and disorientation, and were forced to feel their way along the seat rows towards the exits, whilst being jostled and pushed. Many, even in the forward cabin, resorted to going over the seat backs in order to avoid the congested aisle. This was reported by passengers in seats 7A, 6B, 5D, 3E, 3F and 2F, in addition to statements from passengers who confirmed that they had gone forwards over the seats. Some stated that "the smoke generated an immediate sense of panic".

Forty-eight of the fifty-five who died had been rendered unconscious or killed by toxic fumes, and the remainder had been killed directly by fire.

It can take up to forty hours for the damage of smoke inhalation to show itself, even among those who appear to recover quickly afterwards, and many survivors suffered terrible after-effects of the toxic fumes. One survivor found just outside the aircraft had thick mucus issuing from his mouth and nose and was covered in soot. Many had a white film, like cataracts, over their eyes, and suffered dizziness and weakness in the knees from the first whiff of the smoke.

A wide variety of synthetic chemicals is used in aircraft trim and fittings, including polyurethane foam for the seat cushions, and PVC for the wall panels – both can produce hydrogen chloride, carbon monoxide and hydrogen cyanide. The acrylic materials for the curtains were found to be extremely toxic when alight. Less than six pounds of modacrylic curtain material can produce a lethal concentration of hydrogen cyanide in the aircraft cabin. These and other materials produced an extraordinarily dangerous mixture of toxic gases, with effects ranging from narcosis (unconsciousness) to irritation in varying degrees of the nose, mouth, throat and lungs, aside from the fatal effects.[7]

The investigators noted also that the fire was worsened, although by how much was difficult to tell, by the presence of duty-free alcohol and aerosol cans. There was evidence on the roof of the cabin of fires from broken and exploding bottles of spirits. They contributed to the fire because they were in the overhead lockers, which was the part of the cabin that became the hottest quickest. They also found twenty-seven aerosol cans in the wreckage, fifteen of which had exploded.[8] The AAIB has recommended that all duty-free purchases be made at the destination airport rather than before boarding, but this has been ignored.

Camping-gas cylinders are not allowed on with hand baggage, but the highly inflammable butane that they contain is the same ingredient found in many aerosol products, like dry air fresheners. Since ozone-friendly aerosols appeared, butane has been the main propellant. The investigators recommended that spirits be kept at floor level or below, and that the same restrictions be put on aerosols as on camping-gas bottles.

The explosion of an aerosol can can be dramatic.

During a test detonation of an aerosol can located in an aircraft forward toilet, the overpressure was sufficient to blow out the toilet door, allowing the compartment pressure to vent into the cabin. Despite the cabin itself being vented by open rear doors and overwing exits, the resulting overpressure in the main cabin blew the flight-deck door out of its aperture and forward several feet into the flight-deck, where it jammed between floor and ceiling.[9]

They also suggested that medical oxygen cylinders should be stored below the floor. Currently they are in the upper part of the cabin, where fires would be hottest, and once they have ignited the pure oxygen would strongly intensify the fire in the area of the cylinder.

None of these recommendations has been acted upon.

The investigators reviewed the literature on fires in cabins and researched the history of the regulations on fire standards in aircraft. Toxic compounds, after all, were a relatively new phenomenon, products of the jet age. Before the 1960s, cabin materials did not include high proportions of plastics and other petrochemical-based compounds that give off such deadly fumes.

Research on this had previously been carried out in the United States. A United Boeing 727 had crashed at Salt Lake City in November 1965 and most of the forty-three passengers who died in the fire had extremely high levels of toxic compounds in their bloodstreams. The FAA then commissioned research into smoke-hoods. The toxicity of the smoke became an even bigger issue after the death of 46 of the 219 passengers and one of the crew aboard the Capitol International Airways McDonnell Douglas DC-8 which crashed on take-off at Anchorage, Alaska, on 27 November 1970. The passengers were US servicemen being flown to join the war in Vietnam.

Owing to a mysterious malfunction, the plane's brakes were still on when the pilots applied normal take-off power. But because the runway was icy, the aircraft still moved and picked up speed. The pilots only noticed something was wrong when it was too late. As they accelerated the tyres progressively blew, slowing the plane so it could not reach take-off speed. It ran off the end of the runway, struck several obstacles and then caught fire disastrously.

In this case there had been no flashover, and the fuselage had broken into two pieces. Post-mortems showed cyanide in the blood of the victims. The FAA then began to seek the source of the cyanide and looked at the cabin trim and furnishings.

The main standard on fire protection was issued in May 1972 by the FAA, setting flammability standards, under which cabin materials had to be exposed to a Bunsen-burner flame for a specified time before ignition. While this standard would be effective in terms of preventing passengers from starting fires, either accidentally or deliberately, in the cabin, it took no account of fires already in progress, or those fed by aircraft fuel, and the resulting toxic gases.

The FAA announced in 1974 that it was considering setting a standard for how much toxic gas could legally be allowed to be generated from cabin materials. The US aviation industry, however, responded to the proposals by questioning the FAA's testing methods and casting doubt on the overall safety benefit of any such changes. Accordingly, the FAA dropped the proposed rules.

However, it did not give up entirely. In 1978 it set up a committee to "Examine the factors affecting the ability of the aircraft cabin occupant to survive in the post-crash environment and the range of solutions available." A series of fire tests were carried out using the hull of an old Lockheed C-133. When the investigators from the AAIB went back to previous research on cabin fires to compare notes they reviewed all the FAA-produced material. They found that despite the new FAA tests on the C-133 the American agency was still reluctant to take preventive measures against toxic emissions, and was still wedded to the idea of preventing fires in the first place.

Strangely, in the AAIB's view, the FAA tests in the old Lockheed fuselage detected only small concentrations of highly toxic gases. The chief threat to life the FAA identified was flash-over. This extremely dangerous phenomenon occurs when hot smoke and gases which have been confined and have gathered, typically, close to the ceiling suddenly ignite to create a raging ball of flame which charges through the compartment. The tests in the Lockheed fuselage caused the FAA to establish as conventional wisdom that flashovers inevitably occur in aircraft fires when the fuselage is intact. However, there was no flashover in the Manchester disaster, and the AAIB's research showed that flash-overs are by no means inevitable.

Flashovers tend to be associated with fires in spaces which are poorly ventilated, like the King's Cross underground station fire in 1986. The AAIB hypothesised that the FAA had failed to take sufficient account of open exits and breaches in the hull caused by crash damage and their effect on ventilation.

When flashovers *do* occur, however, they are devastating. In August 1980 the worst aircraft fire occurred when a Saudi Arabian Airlines L-1011 Tristar returned to Riyadh airport after a fire was detected in the cargo hold shortly after take-off. After the plane landed rescuers had to cut their way into the aircraft because all 301 souls on board had been killed by smoke or flame.

The flight-deck crew was heavily criticised for being indecisive and for taxiing much longer than was necessary after returning to the airport.

It is believed that the already serious fire became catastrophic when the flight-crew shut down the engines, and thus the air-conditioning system, as they came to a halt on the runway. The ventilation provided by the air-conditioning had probably been preventing the flashover from occurring. When it did occur, however, it almost certainly killed everyone who had not already been claimed by the toxic fumes.

The FAA's belief in flashovers as the chief danger led to flammability tests as their principal safeguard against fire. However, these were little different from the Bunsen-burner tests of yore, and ignored fuel-fed fires altogether. In other words, the FAA stayed concerned only with preventing fires from breaking out in the cabin, and not with the levels of toxic gases or fires from outside the cabin.

Reading between the lines, the AAIB report betrays a whiff of scepticism about the FAA's priorities. Indeed, the authors chose to pinpoint what looks very much like an abdication of responsibility by the FAA in regard to setting standards on smoke and toxic-gas emission from cabin materials. The report said:

A discussion document issued by the FAA in July 1986 requesting further comments on their "Improved Flammability Standards for Materials Used in Interiors of Transport Category Airplane Cabins" is of interest. In response to requests from two commenters from the materials industry for assurance that no rule-making with respect to smoke and toxicity was anticipated in the foreseeable future, the FAA replied: "Based on the information currently available, the FAA has no plans to establish standards for either smoke or toxicity; however, this does not preclude taking such action in the future . . .".

In other words, the industry was anxious to know that toxic-gas standards would not be applied and the FAA, despite earlier declaring that such standards were important, meekly complied.

It would have been rude and undiplomatic for the AAIB to criticise the FAA's efforts in this field, which were, undoubtedly, scientifically correct. But the FAA had certainly taken its time. The Civil Aeromedical Institute in Oklahoma City, which is part of the FAA and is the body conducting the research, has been working on toxic emissions and aircraft fires ever since the DC-8 disaster in Anchorage.

CAMI published a report on smoke toxicity in 1995. After twenty-five years of research, what was their recommendation? More research. Despite all the evidence of death by fire in air crashes, they said, "Continuing fundamental research in smoke toxicity, fire safety and fire hazard assessment in aircraft accidents is clearly warranted."[10]

The reason for this bizarre state of affairs is the FAA's relaxed, academic and slow approach to the problem. Instead of trying to prevent smoke killing people by whatever means are most appropriate, or investigating fire-suppression systems fully, they have insisted on attempting to come up with a definitive toxicity test for cabin materials. It is this which has caused the delay.

Different types of fire, different types of cabin furnishings, and varying rates at which fires develop mean that each fire is unique. And since the cabin trim and furnishings give off different proportions of toxic chemicals according to the type of fire, devising a standard test for toxicity is extremely difficult. Mandating smoke-hoods, of course, would mean that much of this research would be unnecessary.

The FAA's point of view seems to be that if it cannot come up with a standard test for the toxicity, then it will take no action. That does not mean they are not trying. But, they say, it will take several years. This approach does the air traveller no favours whatsoever. An analogy might be that of the authorities refusing to set a speed limit for cars in residential districts because they cannot predict exactly how many of a pedestrian's bones would be broken by a car going at 100 mph as opposed to one going at 90 mph.

An example of where the FAA's priorities lie, and of its thinking, was given in its response to observations from the CAMI researchers that cabin water-spray systems would clean the air of toxic chemicals as well as suppress the fire. Rather than look on the positive side and investigate the system's potential for saving lives, the FAA first decided to commission research into whether passengers could be harmed by breathing hot steam generated by the cabin water-spray hitting the flames!

Because the FAA has failed to act on toxic emissions, no other aviation authority has taken any initiative, least of all the UK's CAA, despite the immense amount of research done both by the CAA and the AAIB in the aftermath of the Manchester disaster. In that period of research they developed immense expertise, and there is no excuse, in this field anyway, for waiting for initiatives from the USA.

In the absence of any action on toxic emissions, the FAA relies on flammability tests, i.e. preventing fires starting. A new standard for flammability tests came into force in the United States in August 1986. The CAA adopted it wholesale for application to UK-registered aircraft in March 1987, despite the fact that the AAIB was still conducting its massive investigation into the Manchester fire, and was developing an expertise in the issue under consideration that few could rival.

Even though there was incontrovertible evidence from Manchester – as well as fire-related accidents dating back to the mid-1960s – that people can be incapacitated by just one or two breaths of the thick black smoke of a cabin fire, there are still no regulations to control the toxic-gas output of cabin materials.

What was particularly ironic about the adoption of the new flammability standards was the fact that in certain circumstances they could make the fire worse. Making cabin materials less flammable means using more flame-retardants. However, in cases where fire has taken hold already and overcome the flame-retardants, these chemicals only add to the toxic cocktail swirling around the cabin interior. Typically, they produce hydrogen chloride when burned, and when that combines with water in eyes, noses, lungs and throats it makes hydrochloric acid.[11]

Next to CFIT, fire is the biggest hazard to aircraft passengers, so it seems strange that it is not policed as strongly. Despite its lethality there is no "task force" as there has been for CFIT, and no new initiatives to reduce the toxicity of the smoke products of cabin materials. The case history of flammability and toxic gases shows that the FAA and the airlines are locked into a particular view of the problems, namely to strive to prevent fires from breaking out or crashes from happening. It concentrates on the high or low probability of the first event in the sequence leading to disaster and little else.

The mechanism of a disaster sequence tends not to be analysed. If fire leads to clouds of toxic gases incapacitating and then killing the occupants, the FAA tends to address what started the fire, not its consequences. This antediluvian thinking is hardly fitting for an industry that prides itself on its modernity and use of high technology. It is as if the FAA were telling people not to run away from the falling tree until they have identified its species.

And then there is the problem that the FAA mandated the flammability standards only for new aircraft and for parts being replaced. A US government agency reported that the whole US airline fleet would only be in compliance with the 1988 standards in 2018. Smoke-hoods, on the other hand, would be introduced universally and immediately if mandated.

Observers and safety experts have commented that natural materials like cotton, wood and wool are more expensive than their artificial cousins, and weigh a good deal more. It may well be that there is no realistic alternative to the highly toxic materials in use in aircraft, but if that is so there could still be a shift towards better protection of passengers.

Over the years following the 1965 air crashes involving fire, the FAA tested and improved the smoke-hood, evaluating a variety of important factors, such as the effect of finding it and donning it on evacuation time, possible disorientation, claustrophobia, amount of air, visibility, effects on hearing, and so on. They concluded that smoke was the most important inhibitor of evacuation, not the hood.

In much the same way that it went about setting standards for toxic gases, in 1969 the FAA notified the industry, as it must do by law, about its proposed mandatory introduction of smoke-hoods to passenger aircraft. (In 1967 the FAA had made it compulsory for smoke-hoods to be provided for all its own aircraft.) Once again the dead hand of the industry fell on this proposal and over a year later it was quietly dropped.[12]

Despite the fact that its own research said the extra delay caused by passengers having to don smoke-hoods was minimal, the FAA cited this as the reason for withdrawing the proposed rule. This was also to be the CAA's line, despite all the AAIB's research. The CAA published its supposedly definitive study, "Smoke-hoods: net safety benefit analysis" in 1987.[13] It examined a large number of past accidents involving fire and studied them in the light of the various systems on offer.

Many scientists and outside observers criticised the report for being biased against smoke-hoods. At a conference in 1988 the former top toxicologist at the FAA's CAMI, C.R. Crane, said the CAA report contained "systematic bias" because "the contribution from FBL [fire-blocking materials] is consistently over-estimated while that from PPBE [passenger protective breathing equipment] is underestimated". He added, "I would characterise the general model [in the CAA report] as one that would inadequately, if not incorrectly, represent the real world of aircraft fires."[14] Statisticians also attacked the report for its partial consideration of the issues (see Chapter 8 for a critique of the cost–benefit analysis contained in the CAA report).

The non-scientists were less polite and formal. They said that industry lobbying and its worries about cost and convenience were what were really driving the regulatory agencies' refusal to adopt the smoke-hoods.

Research nonetheless continued, and as more passengers died from smoke-inhalation around the world the topic came up again. In 1980 the FAA once more tried to start the ball rolling on smoke-hoods. More research followed, but the issue was little advanced beyond the work done in the 1960s. However, they also produced cost-benefit analyses that showed that smoke-hoods were the most cost-effective way of saving lives in cabin fires.

Minds should have been concentrated by another disaster. In June 1983 twenty-four occupants of an Air Canada DC-9 died in

Cincinnatti from poisonous smoke. The accident report noted that this fire, which had started in the air, had been almost a real-life experiment for smoke-hoods. Most of the survivors, it emerged, had been breathing through wet hand-towels which had been distributed by a resourceful flight attendant. The NTSB recommended protective measures be implemented, but nothing was done.[15]

Investigators, however, had been having these experiences for some time. Captain Bill Tench, who was the head of the AAIB until 1981, had personal experience of the dangers of the new materials being used in aircraft when a Boeing 707 doing training exercises at Prestwick airport in Scotland crashed and caught fire in 1977. Ironically, the plane belonged to British Airtours, the subsidiary of British Airways which was operating the Boeing 737 that caught fire at Manchester. Although the crew escaped safely, he says, "It caught fire and burned like hell, and the fumes were all highly poisonous, mainly cyanide. I made recommendations about the fire aspects in aircraft. We wrote a long screed saying, 'If you don't do something about prohibiting these plastics which create cyanide then somebody is going to get killed.' And then years later we had Manchester. All it did was verify everything I had said in the other accident report."[16]

Action on this issue has still not been taken. In the United States most corporate jets have smoke-hoods and the US Defense Department's Air Mobility Command, which is charged with moving large numbers of troops by air, ordered 50,000 of them in 1996.[17] The commercial passenger has no such luck unless he or she wishes to find out who makes the devices and then buys one (they are not on sale in most airports) at upwards of fifty dollars.

Normally, the British CAA trails behind the better-funded US FAA and there is a more or less unspoken assumption that whatever is good for US airlines is good for those of the rest of the world. But the CAA paid scant attention to the AAIB's research.

Having visited the Civil Aeromedical Institute in Oklahoma and finding that the FAA had not advanced the issue, the AAIB commissioned its own research into smoke-hoods. It conducted extensive trials and tests of smoke-hoods with and without filters, and published the results. The AAIB invited the CAA to set the standards that the products would have to meet.

The hurdles the smoke-hoods had to clear were set so high it almost looked as if they were designed to invite failure. Smoke-hoods for crew members, which are already mandatory, must permit fifteen minutes' breathing and weigh three to four pounds. For the passenger hoods under test the CAA demanded they had to give twenty minutes' breathing and weigh only one pound. Nevertheless, some products met the standard. The AAIB's test results had a simple message: inexpensive, low-tech, lightweight smoke-hoods could easily be made and could protect passengers long enough for them to get out of the plane while outside assistance arrived.

The CAA, however, was not going to let independent research get in the way of the time-honoured tradition of simply doing everything the Americans do, and it came up with various objections to the smoke-hoods. Said Geoff Ratcliffe, chairman of the Royal Aeronautical Society's airworthiness maintenance safety groups, "I can't imagine 400 passengers evacuating an aircraft in 90 seconds having all initially obtained and donned smoke-hoods."[18] This obsession with the ninety-second limit is misplaced, particularly as the FAA already addressed the question in its original late 1960s research. Then they concluded that smoke-hoods would add 8 per cent to evacuation time.

Frank Taylor, director of Cranfield Aviation Safety Centre at Cranfield University and an authority on accident investigation, said, "The possibility that it may take ten seconds longer to evacuate with a smoke-hood is of little consequence if passengers live to tell the tale."[19]

One important point the regulators seem to have forgotten completely is that the presence of smoke greatly delays evacuation. If it is delayed beyond the magic ninety seconds, then it would seem sensible to protect passengers against that smoke. Furthermore (at Manchester, for example), fire and smoke may appear without the aircraft commander knowing about it, and smoke-hoods would allow passengers to take measures to protect themselves on their own initiative.

A more plausible but unproven explanation for the CAA's attitude is that it will not order airlines to do anything which could cost them significant sums. Although smoke-hoods would cost little, they would still cost more than nothing, and that is evidently too much.[20]

If that was to be the legislative fate of smoke-hoods, then what chance would other systems have? The AAIB and the CAA both considered the viability of having a water-sprinkler system in cabins. The idea is simple. An overhead pipe or array of pipes uses a small reservoir of water to produce a fine spray-mist which would suppress flames while also "scrubbing" the atmosphere of many of the harmful gases and smoke particles. Having first ruled out smoke-hoods on the grounds that cabin-water-spray systems were more promising, the CAA abandoned research into the latter in 1993, saying they would cost too much for the expected savings in lives. Many of the relatives of the dead in the Manchester fire were furious with the CAA when the research ceased. It appeared that the CAA's apparent commitment to sprinkler systems had been merely a means to avoid answering tough questions on smoke-hoods.

Water is heavy and many were worried by the significant weight penalties in such a system. However, one system could provide a protective three-minute spray with just thirty to forty gallons of water. Even more effective was a system, complementary to the above, whereby fire crews could "plug in" their water supply and thus supply effectively unlimited quantities of water to the cabin sprinkler.

There are other issues to be considered in conjunction with the water systems, such as the potential threat the stored water for the cabin-spray system might pose to other parts of the aircraft. However, none of these was considered before the idea was abandoned.

The advantages of the sprinkler systems and smoke-hoods would be particularly strong if the aircraft were in the air when the fire broke out. Although this scenario makes up a very small proportion of the fires that do occur, it can have horrific consequences when it does happen.

On 11 July 1973 a Boeing 707 of the Brazilian airline Varig carrying 17 crew and 117 passengers was approaching Orly Airport near Paris after the long flight from Rio de Janeiro when the cabin crew reported a fire in one of the rear toilets. The situation rapidly deteriorated and the pilot told air traffic control that thick black smoke was asphyxiating his passengers. The crisis escalated when the smoke entered the cockpit and the pilots put on their oxygen masks. They could not see their instruments for the smoke and, desperate to escape the toxic cloud, the pilot put the aircraft down in a field after scraping some trees, five kilometres short of the runway.

The undercarriage collapsed and the engines were torn off but the fuselage remained intact. Despite the unusual fact that the fuel spilled in the crash break-up did not ignite, the situation could hardly have been worse. Only ten members of the crew escaped the aircraft under their own steam. One passenger was rescued alive by fire-fighters, who arrived only seven minutes after the crash, but by then the fire had already burned through the roof of the cabin. All 123 others were killed by the toxic smoke.[21] It is worth remembering that at the time of the crash the conflagration was only in the rear toilet area. The reports said nobody was killed by heat.

The CAA's attitude towards smoke-hoods has been so controversial that Malcolm Keogh, a partner in a leading British legal firm specialising in seeking compensation for air-crash victims, has said he would argue that "if there should be another accident involving a British-registered aircraft where people die through asphyxiation in circumstances which could have been prevented by the use of smoke-hoods, the CAA will bear full legal liability by reason of its breach of a clearly defined statutory duty".[22]

The Manchester report concentrated on survival issues in general, an approach the AAIB successfully carried forward with its report on survivability in the January 1989 Kegworth crash, which occurred two months before the official publication of the Manchester report. It was scathing about the overwing exit and how it was depicted. "The passenger flight safety card exercised a large amount of artistic licence in representing the area local to the overwing exit." It showed more room to manoeuvre than there was in reality, and depicted the person using it in uniform, thus leading people to believe the crew would do it if necessary. Most contentious of all, however, was the question of how wide the access to the emergency exits should be. What seemed questionable to the investigators and the survivors who are still campaigning for improved cabin survivability was the fact that, with the way this aircraft was configured, there was only a 22.5-inch gap between the two forward bulkheads close to the forward galley. In other words, to escape through the two front doors all the passengers coming forward could only pass between the bulkheads in single file, greatly reducing the speed at which they could evacuate. In addition, passengers became jammed between the two sides of the forward galley, and a stewardess had to pull a passenger out to free the flow. There may as well have been only one door to the outside situated at the front.

The certification standards applicable in Britain and the United States state that all persons on board must be able to be evacuated within ninety seconds of the order to do so being given, and when using only half the exits. Just such a test of a similar Boeing 737 with the same number of passengers and crew was performed for the CAA's benefit in 1970. Everyone was evacuated in seventy-five seconds.

William and Linda Beckett, whose daughter died in the Manchester fire, have been campaigning for the AAIB's recommendations to be adopted by the CAA ever since the official report came out. They have concentrated on lambasting the CAA over what they see as its failure to address the AAIB's points on access to the exits, protection against toxic fumes and water-spray systems.

The Becketts produced a chronology of what they call deliberate delay. The CAA announced in January 1986 that it was enforcing, as a temporary measure, the removal of the seat nearest the overwing exit. The Becketts and others, however, objected that this did not widen access to the exit from the aisle. Indeed, since the CAA rule was introduced before the publication of the

AAIB report, the investigators were able to respond to this measure. They said: "Removal of the outboard single seat adjacent to each exit, in the light of the evacuation difficulties encountered at Manchester, does not address the total problem of identification of and access to the exit in dense smoke."

Next, in 1987 the CAA commissioned research into the ideal width of access to the overwing exit. Two years after that, in December 1989, it released a paper suggesting that eighteen inches was the optimum width for access to the exit. In September 1990 the CAA notified Parliament that it would be putting forward eighteen inches as a requirement for all such exits, to be included in the Europe-wide aviation regulations.

Time passed but failed to dull the Becketts' interest in these regulations. In November 1993, they recorded, the CAA said that a new European body, the Joint Aviation Authorities, was now in charge of the exit-access question. In August 1995 the JAA announced that it was proposing ten inches as the standard width to access the exit. Since then, no new standard has been set in Europe or the United States. Despite it being a live issue and the subject of much research, fourteen years have passed since the disaster with no action. "Is the CAA dishonest," asked the Becketts, "or just ineffectual? What happened to the eighteen inches that they claimed for all those years that they would 'require' and 'pursue'?"

Whatever the CAA's reasons and motivations, the above process is typical of the length of time it takes. One British investigator, who wishes to remain anonymous, told me, "The whole point of the CAA commissioning research is to kick the issue into touch for a couple of years. Then the research comes back and they say the costs outweigh the benefits. By then, everybody has moved on and forgotten about the horrors of the original crash in the first place. It is a deliberate tactic. And it works." The Becketts believe the function of CAA research is primarily to wear down the proponents of change, and help it to stall these awkward customers until they lose interest and go away.

A very similar story was recorded regarding access through the forward bulkheads to the forward doors. The gap in the stricken

Boeing 737 had been 22.5 inches, although the statutory minimum was 20 inches. Although this standard was also adopted by the JAA, no initiative has come forward. Thus, despite all the research effort of the CAA, the AAIB, the FAA and academics and researchers worldwide, nobody has a full answer to the question of whether access to the doors and emergency exits should be improved fourteen years after the Manchester disaster.

It is clear that if access to exits is widened seats will have to be removed. Taking out seats means losing revenue, and airlines never want to lose revenue. If one were to say that this is the real reason why no regulator has addressed the issue, one would be accused of cynicism.

Another aspect of the AAIB's recommendations has also been ignored, namely, the idea of fire-hardening the hull so that it takes longer for fire to penetrate the fuselage. The report says, "In the long term, a more fundamental review of attitudes to fire is required. Historically, the aircraft industry has adopted a somewhat fatalistic attitude to the problems of aircraft fires and it is quite apparent that the hull has received scant attention when it comes to the consideration of fire at the design stage."

The investigators were not proposing massively thick aircraft walls, just some redistribution of insulation that could slow fire penetration. They noted that beneath the cabin floor there were ventilation routes that help spread fire which could easily be blocked by rearranging some internal walls without adding to the plane's weight. In the main, though, they were asking manufacturers simply to consider a question they had not considered. None has yet risen to the challenge. When asked about such questions the manufacturers tend to repeat the same line, "We are in compliance." True, but not relevant.

In general, the regulators often feel that they are having to hold a sober, responsible line against hysterics who want to see adopted standards that would prevent a recurrence of the tragedy they are particularly concerned with, but would have little useful application to most accidents. And yet the Manchester disaster occurred in spite of considerably better conditions than those that the regulations are designed to deal with.

The fire crews arrived in twenty-five seconds, not three minutes, as accounted for in the regulations; the fire cover was in excess of what the regulations specify; and the pilots acted entirely correctly. The wind force was minimal and the 700 gallons of fuel that was involved in the fire was well below what could be expected and is planned for in thinking about fire emergencies. The cabin crew showed courage and initiative, receiving bravery awards later, and fire-fighters also went beyond the call of duty. And yet, fifty-five people still died.

The AAIB expended all that research effort because it wished to prevent a recurrence. The CAA, however, seems to have taken the view, a common one among regulators, that this event was so rare that it is not worthwhile attempting to prevent a recurrence.

Reminders of the terrible consequences of fires were soon in coming. Less than two years after the Manchester report was published, on 1 February 1991, a USAir Boeing 737 was cleared to land on runway 24L at Los Angeles airport. Under a heavy workload, the tower controller had forgotten that she had cleared a Metroliner, a small aircraft with ten passengers and two crew, to wait for take-off permission on the same runway. The 737 landed on top of the Metroliner, its main gear straddling the smaller plane and crushing it, killing all on board instantly.

The grisly union of 737 and Metroliner slithered on and came to a halt against a building, a fierce fire breaking out which killed twenty-one people on board the 737, all but one by smoke inhalation. Eleven of the dead were found, as at Manchester, within eight feet of the overwing exit. They had almost certainly got to their feet to escape after surviving the crash and had been felled, as if by a blow, by the deadly fumes. The NTSB again called for stricter flammability standards and smoke-hoods.[23]

What follows is the testimony of David H. Koch, a survivor of the crash.

The impact of the 737 against the stone building caused an enormous fireball to shoot up past the windows on the left. The cabin lights immediately went out and people began to scream hysterically and rush down the aisle towards the rear of the plane. A few seconds later the interior of the plane began to fill with intense, heavy black smoke, which was extraordinarily painful to breathe and very toxic.

I reached for my suit jacket, which had been on the chair to my right, but could not find it. My thought was to use it as a face mask to protect my lungs from the smoke. I was on my hands and knees attempting to crawl down the aisle toward the rear of the plane. Several people stampeded over me. It quickly became pitch black in the cabin from the heavy smoke, in spite of the bright light from the fire on the left side of the plane. I could only make out the vague outlines of people directly in front of me. As I moved down the aisle I encountered a mob of fighting, frenzied people jamming the aisle.

At that point I stood up on my feet, choking heavily from the smoke, and walked back toward the first-class section. My state of mind was objective about the condition I was in. I had a real sense of curiosity about what it would be like to die.

Suddenly, an inspiration came over me as I realised that the heavy smoke must have come from an opening in the fuselage somewhere. I walked forward in calm desperation to the front of the plane behind the cockpit. I looked to my left at the entrance door through which passengers enter the plane, and saw a terrible inferno through the porthole of the door. The doorway to the cockpit was closed and I sensed heavy smoke coming from the cracks around the door. I next turned to the right and felt my way to the service door in the galley. To my astonishment, I detected an opening between the door and its frame on the right side of about several inches width. It was possible to see light on the other side.

By this time, I was feeling very faint and I later guessed I only had about fifteen to thirty seconds of consciousness left. Every breath caused me to convulse and was extremely painful. I put my fingers in the opening and pulled. The door moved somewhat, which enabled me to put my head out and take a deep breath of fresh air. A tremendous feeling of strength came over me and I felt like Superman. I revived somewhat. With this added energy, I pulled the door more and it moved to the left a couple of feet. This permitted me to step into the doorway and jump to the ground below.

I crawled and stumbled away from the plane and ran about thirty yards before stopping. My lungs hurt terribly and I coughed and choked badly for about five minutes before I could breathe normally again.[24]

Mr Koch, not surprisingly, is now a strong advocate of compulsory smoke protection for passengers.

Initially, Mr Koch had done the right thing by crawling. A fire in a stationary cabin, with holes in the fuselage and at rest will concentrate heat in the roof of the cabin, meaning it is coolest by the floor. Those remaining standing are not only exposed to the worst of the smoke, but visibility in such situations is so limited that they may not even be aware that by sticking close to the floor they would be able to breathe more easily. At Manchester, several passengers survived because they lost consciousness relatively quickly in the thick smoke, and came to after they had hit the floor, which the smoke had not yet reached.

Irrespective of cabin survivability, there is another area where regulators could easily make a difference: the flammability of fuel itself. When aircraft were powered by piston engines fires took a terrible toll of aircraft, in flight and on the ground, because the fuel was gasoline, which is extremely flammable, especially as a vapour. Fires began to fall in number when jet engines were introduced because they do not need fuel that is as flammable. The fuel that mainly succeeded petrol on airliners, JP 4, was still quite flammable and extremely dangerous in a crash. A safer alternative, available even in the 1960s but barely used then, was paraffin, or kerosene, which is less flammable but more expensive than JP 4. Kerosene vapour, for example, does not become flammable until it has warmed up to a relatively high temperature, while petrol vapour is inflammable at normal temperatures. It is only when it is atomised into a mist that kerosene becomes flammable and explosive.

Japan Airlines and KLM both lost aircraft in terrible fires during the 1960s and that persuaded them to move to Jet A 1, one of the types of kerosene which is less explosive and has a lower flashpoint than JP 4. PanAm and TWA had already moved to Jet A 1 from JP 4 after suffering their own bad aircraft fires. In fact, airlines generally moved over to Jet A 1 in piecemeal fashion, and usually only after their passengers had been killed. Regulators had nothing to do with it.

Let us not be misled into thinking safety was the main reason for the switch from JP 4 to Jet A 1. The US military had a great deal to do with it. One lesson from the Vietnam War was that reducing the flashpoint of the aircraft's fuel meant that it was less vulnerable to small-arms fire. Once the US military noticed the benefits, it started to order Jet A 1 in large quantities. Thus, the economics of kerosene use improved for the civil aviation industry too, and prices came down. Only in Australia, a country which stands out in aviation history for having taken many safety initiatives long before others, was the move to Jet A 1 enforced. JP 4 was banned there in 1962.[25]

JP 4 and Jet A 1 have something in common, however. Although the latter is far safer in terms of creating explosive mixtures in fuel tanks, there is not much to separate them in crash conditions, i.e. when the aircraft strikes obstacles and the fuel bursts out of the tanks, forming a highly explosive mist which then ignites and kills those who survived the impact.

In the early 1970s the British chemicals multinational ICI designed an "anti-misting kerosene", or AMK, in conjunction with the Royal Aircraft Establishment at Farnborough. It looked very promising because, by adding an ingredient to the kerosene, the fuel was prevented from forming an aerosol, and thus a highly explosive mixture, should it burst from its fuel tanks.

AMK did present a few technical difficulties, such as the fact that the effects of the additive had to be removed before it was burned in the engines, because atomisation is essential to the process. So research carried on for answers to the problems. That research received an enormous fillip when the FAA decided to become involved, prompted by the Tenerife disaster of 1977, where 70 per cent of the 576 who died were killed by fire. Frank Taylor, air accident investigator, director of the Cranfield

Aviation Safety Centre and fuels specialist, says that the FAA did not go into the subject very scientifically: "Most effort seems to have been put into proving yet again, but on a larger scale, what was already known, that AMK helped during a survivable crash; comparatively little was spent on getting around the problem of using AMK safely day in, day out, throughout the world."

The FAA duly steamed on, ignored the difficulties of using AMK operationally, and put all its eggs in one basket with the setting up, on 1 December 1985, of one spectacular test. It summoned mass media from near and far to witness an organised crash. A radio-controlled and unmanned Boeing 720 (a smaller version of a Boeing 707) would be flown into a set of blocks and barriers that would cause the wings to smash up, and the fuel to be thrown forward into flame-pots. The anti-misting properties would be well demonstrated. Unfortunately, the stunt was a disaster. The media were incorrectly briefed and failed to understand that fire was expected, but it would hopefully be much less severe than it would have been otherwise.

The aircraft became misaligned on its obstacles and the crash was much more fierce than predicted. The fuel flew out of the plane and detonated in a stunningly spectacular orange fireball. The world gasped at the amazing footage they saw on TV and read the stunt as a failure. Surely, this new type of fuel did not work. That was the message that the world received, but the scientists and engineers present knew that the conflagration had not, in fact, been as serious as it would have been with ordinary fuel. The fireball did not penetrate the fuselage, as it certainly would have done otherwise, and the dummy passengers were unscorched. But the public relations damage had been done and funding for AMK research was withdrawn.

AMK was not a panacea, however. Using it posed operational and safety problems, too. Frank Taylor commented that "had the test been perceived by public and Congress as being successful it might have proved to be too difficult to prevent AMK being introduced prematurely, before all the operational problems had been solved, with potentially disastrous consequences".

However, despite the regular recurrence of disastrous aircraft fires, AMK has remained stuck where it was when the FAA crash test took place. Research on solving AMK's operational problems has not been carried out, and there has been no new research and no new quest for better standards of fuel. Despite Manchester, TWA 800 and the runway collision at LAX, no more is being done.

As matters stand, civil and military jet aircraft use Jet A 1, but most navies use JP 5, or AVCAT, a fuel that is safer than Jet A 1. The consequences of fires breaking out on an aircraft carrier are much more serious than on land, hence the need for the added safety margin. The problem is that it is more expensive.[26] The flashpoint of JP 5, or the temperature at which it can explode, is much higher than Jet A 1. The higher the flashpoint, the safer the fuel. JP 5 is now under active consideration by the FAA. It is considering mandating its use by the commercial airliner fleet, although its cost is a significant obstacle.[27]

In Chapter 8 we consider the methodologies of the regulators and why it is that topics like CFIT can attract the attentions of a task force grouping regulatory organisations with industry bodies, while fire, which kills almost as many people, is brushed under the carpet. One problem might be solved by forcing better performance out of the pilots, and the other needs money to be spent on expensive new systems and materials. You can guess why the industry concentrates on the former rather than the latter.

CHAPTER 4

Survivors

WHEN WE READ accounts of catastrophes or warfare which killed thousands we always identify with the survivors. It is only natural. For one, it is hard to imagine being dead, and, of course, the accounts we are reading were written by the survivors. We cannot delve into a book called *How I Nearly Made it out of the Titanic* or read an autobiography entitled *One of the Fallen*, so we tend to condition ourselves to thinking that even when only 5 per cent survived, we would be in that number.

This may be illogical, but thinking otherwise is simply not useful. If we read a survivor's account of a great disaster, what we are looking for are clues as to how we could maximise our chances of surviving. Was there anything in this person's behaviour or personality that singled him or her out as a survivor?

In most matters we take precautions if there is some risk, whether it is fastening a seat-belt in a car or washing our hands before eating. All too often, we take a fatalistic attitude towards air travel, saying that crashes are just one of those things, and there is nothing one can do about it. In this respect commercial aviation forces recall, once again, of how attitudes towards car safety have changed in the last twenty to thirty years.

Once upon a time car crashes were also regarded as "just one of those things" and effectively beyond anyone's control. Hard as it is to remember such a time, survival on the road was simply regarded as being in the lap of the gods. As drivers, we are in a good position to improve our chances on the road, much less so as air travellers. Nevertheless, we can still take precautions that could make a difference in a crash.

The average traveller thinks of the enormous speeds and heights at which planes fly and then assumes that a crash is not survivable. Since, as we have already seen, most crashes occur at landing or take-off, the speeds and heights have moderated considerably, offering more opportunities for survival. Indeed, far from being the all-or-nothing proposition it is normally considered, an air crash does not inevitably result in 100 per cent fatalities. Some 60 per cent of all air crashes fall into the "survivable" category, meaning that the deceleration forces on impact were well within tolerance for the human frame.

Before we read accounts of crash survivors it is worth going through some of the precautions that all air travellers ought to take.[1]

Precautions

Generally speaking, the people who do best in aircraft emergencies do not panic, even though they may well be afraid. One of the best ways of avoiding panic is to have devised a plan of action in the event of an emergency. The difference between death and survival in an aircraft emergency could be a matter of seconds. Making a plan saves on thinking time when you can least afford it.

Before boarding

It is well worth arriving early, at the two hours before departure that is usually specified. It may well be boring to hang around an airport, but there are two main advantages. The first is that you may be able to get your choice of seat position at check-in (*see* "Where to sit?" below). The second is that if there are any security scares, or special measures being taken, you can get clear of them quickly. Incidentally, never accept a package or bag from anyone, either as carry-on or as luggage. It could be a bomb, or it could be drugs: you don't know. Beware, though, because the people asking this favour know that most passengers are well aware of the warnings against doing it. As a result they have pretty convincing stories prepared, which may include offering you a look inside the bag to "make sure" there is nothing untoward. Don't be tempted; there could be something in the lining.

Before boarding you should ensure that you have a life assurance policy. On domestic flights the liability of the airline is unlimited, meaning that there are no limits on the compensation payable for death or injuries, depending on the laws of the country concerned. That might seem favourable, but the courts and legal systems in different countries vary enormously. The courts in the United States, for example, rate the monetary value of a human life in a court judgement much higher than courts in the UK, even though the two legal systems greatly resemble each other. In France the compensation available may be good, but it could be several years before the judgement is handed down. Court procedures in France and Italy, in particular, are incredibly slow.

International tickets, which can include purely domestic legs, are governed by a complex and outdated treaty called the Warsaw Convention. Under Warsaw the liability of an airline is automatically limited, in most cases to $75,000 for death, but in some countries the figure is much lower than that. The treaty came into force in 1929 and was designed as a measure to protect the then infant airlines from being sued into bankruptcy in the event of a crash, thus smothering civil air transport at birth.

However, if "wilful misconduct" can be proved on the part of any party responsible for the accident, usually the airline or the aircraft's manufacturer, the Warsaw limitations do not apply. This can necessitate immensely long litigation between the lawyers for the victims' families and for the insurers of the airline and other possible defendants. The relatives of the passenger-victims of the Lockerbie air disaster had to wait eight years before their favourable judgement came through.

There have been many examples of tragic cases where the family of one person who died in a crash was fully and satisfactorily compensated while the family of the person sitting next to them got $75,000 or less because they were flying a domestic flight on a multi-destination international ticket. Irishman Michael Kavanagh was just such a person. He was killed along with 130 others when the USAir 737 he was travelling on crashed mysteriously on the approach to Pittsburgh airport. The compensation being paid out to the families of the American business executives and others who had been sitting next to him was running, observers said, at between $2 million and $3 million. Because he was on a domestic portion of an international ticket bought in Ireland, his compensation was going to be just $75,000.[2]

Warsaw also covers injuries and baggage loss, so you may want insurance to cover that eventuality too.

Some credit card services automatically give you life assurance when you use their card to buy your ticket. Business travellers, in particular, should make sure that their company is providing them with cover.

What to wear

Most experts advise air travellers to wear cotton, wool and leather in preference to synthetic garments. The latter have a very low melting point — that's why you don't iron them — and can melt on to the skin in a fire and make burns worse than they might otherwise have been. You can also receive minor burns from such material overheating as a result of friction with the inflatable emergency slides. This is worth remembering. It can be easy, for example, for women to forget not to wear synthetic tights on a plane journey.

Similarly, ordinary flat shoes are best. High platforms or – even if fashion did permit such a throwback – stiletto heels are definite no-nos. The latter could puncture the inflatable slide that is used to evacuate the passengers.

If you wear glasses, attach a lanyard to them, so that in case of an emergency you won't lose them or waste time looking for them.

What to take

Another pre-flight tip is to try to keep your carry-on baggage to a minimum. One of the nuisances to all passengers, as well as the airlines, is the amount of time it takes to board the plane. An aisle does not have room for two abreast, so the line can only move as fast as the slowest person in it. Grandma and Grandpa with five pieces of carry-on luggage can take quite a while to be seated.

The US trade union representing flight attendants estimates that 4500 passengers are injured every year by carry-on baggage, and that is in the United States alone. They also reported just under 4000 baggage-related injuries to their members in 1996, the hurt usually being incurred while carrying, lifting or stowing passengers' baggage.[3]

All this could be minimised, and safety helped, though, if we took less on. Many airlines permit only two carry-on items, and some of them one, but these rules are hardly ever enforced. Since most current aircraft were designed the amount of material that people are unwilling to trust either to the honesty or sensitive manipulation of baggage-handlers has greatly increased. Laptop computers, mobile phones and delicate purchases made on holiday have to go into the overhead bins.

Many people do not look at what they are carrying on, or ask themselves whether they really need it on the voyage, let alone think of minimising it. Even worse is when people who are anxious not to wait at the luggage carousel cram everything they can into a bag which only just fits into the overhead locker.

Overhead bins can open quite easily during in-flight turbulence or on an emergency landing. Should this happen, a heavy object could fall out and injure somebody. In the event of a crash the bin doors fly open or collapse altogether and heavy objects within fly forward, striking passengers in the back of the head, as we saw with the Kegworth crash. The bins have a load they are not supposed to exceed, but this is a static, not a dynamic, load.

The difference between static and dynamic loading is a useful concept to know about when considering the mechanics of a crash. Depending on the speed with which the aircraft stops – the deceleration – any object becomes heavier. One car manufacturer promoting the use of seat-belts in the rear seat pointed out that an unsecured child in a 30 mph crash will hit the front seat and its occupant with the weight of a baby elephant. In other words, while the overhead bin seems perfectly capable of taking all that luggage, in a crash it could disintegrate and spew its contents all over the cabin.

It would be better then to take as little as possible on to the plane, and would help further if you placed the heaviest objects you were carrying under the seat. No matter if others are putting bowling balls and collapsible bicycles in the lockers. It is best to use them only for things that you would not object to hitting you on the head. Some airlines are beginning to enforce stricter rules for carry-on items, which would make it sensible to prepare for observing them.[4]

As recommended in the AAIB report on the Manchester fire, bottles of spirits are best kept on the floor. Once a fire has taken hold they would make it worse if they caught fire, and in the overhead bins they would be in the hottest spot.

Electronic devices

Most airlines tell you not to use mobile phones, laptop computers, computer games or other electronic equipment – including ordinary radios, CD players and computer games – during take-off or landing. Dangerous emissions can even come from mobile phones that are switched on although not in use, or from computers that are switched on but dormant.

Some people may remember the days where not all the electrical systems of cars and trucks were shielded, and your radio would emit ugly noises as an unshielded vehicle went past. Imagine your radio as the direction-finding needle tuned to a navigational radio beacon in an aircraft cockpit and your mobile as the unshielded vehicle and you can see the threat.

These restrictions are not precautionary. These devices have been proved to interfere harmfully with the aircraft's navigation equipment, and the more electronic devices are used to control the aircraft, the more important it is to ensure that passengers' electronic devices are not being used. One reason this is especially important is that the kind of fault that such an electronic device can cause may often not be detectable as such by the flight-crew.

Some forms of interference are not fully understood. Devices which ought not to interfere with aircraft systems have been known to do so. Most aircraft systems have been designed to be as immune as possible to such interference, but they cannot be completely protected. And the radio-receivers that take a bearing on a radio-transmitting beacon cannot, for obvious reasons, be shielded from radio waves.

For reasons of air travel, among others, most electronic devices have to be tested for conformity to standards that limit the amount of radiation they can emit. However, the shielding can be removed, during a repair perhaps, or in the course of some modification. As a result, a strong signal would probably play havoc with certain cockpit instruments. Weak interference, however, is more hazardous since the disruption to the cockpit instruments would be less obvious to the pilots.

On smaller aircraft the dangers are greater because the aerials are much closer to the potentially interfering equipment.

Very few passengers are aware of the dangers these devices can pose, and some may be scornful enough of the warnings to use them when they have been told not to. A child might carelessly switch on a Game Boy without being aware of the prohibitions on its use. So many and varied are the kinds of electronic device that can be used, it would be too much to expect the cabin staff to notice every one. If you see someone using such a device before take-off or when electronic devices have not been cleared for use, tell a flight attendant.[5]

Where to sit?

Are there more or less safe places to sit on a plane? It is an old question, and there are no easy answers. There are pros and cons. In several cases passengers sitting at the rear of the aircraft survived when all others died. These were crashes when the impact forces, rather than any subsequent fire, were the mechanism that killed. No part of the aircraft, other than immediately next to an emergency exit, is safer than any other when it comes to fire, but an impact usually precedes a fire.

In August 1985 one of the most extraordinary brushes with death was experienced by three women and an eight-year-old girl. They were passengers on a Japan Airlines 747 making the thirty-minute hop between Tokyo and Osaka. Because Japan is such a mountainous country, air travel saves a lot of time, even on relatively short journeys.

What then followed was the worst single-aircraft crash ever, with 520 dead. While the aircraft was still climbing the rear pressure bulkhead blew out. Passenger jets only need to pressurise the part of the plane that the people are occupying. So, the pressure is held between the cockpit and the tail, where the bulkhead, an umbrella-shaped dome, seals off the rearmost part of the cabin. The tail itself is not pressurised. When the rear bulkhead blew out, which was caused by a faulty repair carried out years earlier, the surge of pressure in the tail blew off most of the vertical fin, as well as disabling all of the four independent hydraulic systems.

Although the plane continued to fly for another thirty minutes, a crash was inevitable because without hydraulics the crew had no effective means of controlling the plane. When it crashed into a mountain ridge the 747 was going at some 260 knots. Nevertheless, the women and the girl, all of them seated in the rear four rows of seats, survived, although their neighbours did not. All had several broken bones but were able to make full physical recoveries. One of them had been thrown clear during the crash and was found in a tree.

It is believed that several more passengers may have survived the crash but died before rescuers arrived.[6] The crash happened almost at dusk in a mountainous and inaccessible area miles from the nearest road and no rescuers arrived until morning.

Basically, the survivors made it because they were at the rear of a large plane. The official report said that those at the front of the aircraft died from multiple injuries caused by deceleration of "hundreds of g" while those who died at the rear were killed by "tens of g". In essence, the crushing and destruction of the forward fuselage acted as a kind of shock absorber for those in the rear.

Although her story sheds little light on the physics of crash impacts, the account of Yumi Ochiai, an off-duty flight-attendant who survived that crash, speaks volumes on other matters.[7]

Just about when we should have been levelling off there was a big noise . . . It was like a ricochet gunshot you hear on TV films . . . a high-pitched "ping". Nothing else happened to warn us of what was in store . . .

There was a "Waah" from the passengers. The women made a sort of strangled cry, but there was no general screaming. My ears did not hurt but they felt blocked. Just like the feeling you get before they pop. Soon they were back to normal.

When the loud noise happened a white mist suddenly appeared. It was quite thick, and you could barely see in front you . . . The mist went away in a few seconds and after I had put on my oxygen mask it had cleared completely . . . There was no smell. Of course, we were taught in training that the white fog would appear if there was a decompression . . .

From where I was sitting, I couldn't see the outside of the plane or the sky . . .

There was no talk, all this time, because the passengers had their oxygen masks on. With the mask on, desperately trying to breathe, maybe there was no time for conversation. But they looked worried, looking around and out of the window. I don't remember if there were any babies crying . . .

There was no feeling of the aircraft descending. While we were putting on the oxygen masks and afterwards there was a movement like a big gradual turn to the left and then to the right. This was about ten minutes after the loud noise. Breathing was not hard at this time, even without the oxygen mask . . .

I didn't then know the phrase "Dutch roll".[8] The plane continued tilting to the right and left as though it were circling. There were no vibrations at all. It was just a continuous movement banking left and then right. There were no sudden movements or harsh vibration, just a slow move.

All I could see from the window nearest me was white clouds. It was thick cloud and you couldn't see the ground. The passengers were looking out of the windows and some of them were asking the flight attendants if everything was OK. The atmosphere was not flustered or panicky. I think, at this stage, people still thought that everything would be all right. But there was no word from the cockpit so everybody was worried.

Even towards the front I could see that people were putting on their life-vests . . . I took out my life-vest and pulled it over my head.

I kept hoping we would go back to Haneda. But we were still in the clouds at high altitude, so we couldn't be doing that. I started to get worried.

But there were some passengers who didn't know that the life-vest is under their seats, or some who knew, but couldn't put them on. Near me some of the young girls couldn't find theirs and they started to panic. That's when I got out of my seat and started to help the passengers, at about the time the passengers started to take out the safety card from the pocket in front of their seats.

As I got out of my seat, a man sitting next to me by the window asked if I was a stewardess. I said yes and helped him put on his life-vest. He was a very calm man. After he got his life-vest on he stretched over to help others put theirs on.

Once I was in the aisle I helped the passengers whom the . . .

stewardess was responsible for with the life-vests. She went to those behind me, while I went to those in front of me, about two rows.

But just then the aircraft started shaking from side to side so much we could not stand straight. It wasn't a violent shaking but the angle became so steep that you had to take two or three steps while holding on to the seats, get the vest out from under the seats, sit down, and then take two or three steps again. We could not walk straight.

Life-vests are supposed to be inflated when you leave the plane, after it has hit the water. If you inflate it inside it becomes difficult to adopt the crash position, bending the body forward and putting your head between your knees. But near me there were about four or five passengers, all men, who had inflated their vests. In this sort of situation women seem to be calmer. The people who looked like they wanted to cry were all men. I remember this very clearly.

One of the young men who had inflated his vest asked anxiously what he should do. There was nothing to do, so I told him to adopt the brace position as he was.

If one passenger inflates a vest then others copy them. Another stewardess, myself and the calm man who was sitting beside me all shouted out for people not to inflate their vests.

There were some empty seats. The passengers who were sitting alone probably got worried. They left their seats while putting on their life-vests and then sat down next to someone.

I wasn't asked anything but the stewardesses in uniform were getting all sorts of questions, "What's going to happen?", "Will we be all right?", "Will we be saved?" It was only the men who were asking. Even where there were women with families – perhaps because they were also with a man – the men did the asking . . .

I heard a child calling, "Mother," not a shout but a sharp cry. The adults didn't shout or scream. It was like nothing would come out. It was very tense and anxious . . .

The pitching of the plane got worse. It wasn't possible to stand up any more. As soon as the life-vests were on almost everyone took up the brace position. Usually, you tell everyone to take off their glasses, put sharp objects in the pocket in front of them or if you have a jacket, to wear it, in order to protect you from shock. But there was no time for this.

I went back to seat 56C . . . Just before adopting the safety posture I told the man sitting next to me, "If we make an emergency landing and I cannot move, please open the rear door and let the passengers out." He replied in a very calm voice, "Leave it to me." These were my last words with him.

About this time I could see Mount Fuji out of the window. It was quite near. It was how you normally see it on this route. There was a white cloud on the black surface of the mountain. I could see it in the top part of the left window, then moving to the bottom of it. When Mount Fuji came into sight I adopted the safety posture and lowered my head.

As I did so I looked round the cabin and saw a lot of the oxygen tubes pulled straight down. Probably, most of the passengers took the safety position with their masks still on. I could feel my body jolt uncontrollably in the safety posture. Not like the roll of a boat, an enormous shaking from side to side, not vertically. From the front I heard a girl scream . . .

Then there was a steep descent straight down, completely upside-down just as if your hair was being pushed back by the wind in a fast descent. It probably wasn't like that, but it felt like it. It was frightening. I was frightened. Please don't make me remember any more. It is a fear you do not want to relive. The passengers could not say anything. I also thought I was going to die. We went straight down. There was no vibration, no time even to look out of the window. You don't know when you will crash. You just have to keep the safety position.

I can't even remember if I was sweating . . . My whole body was tensed and I probably had my eyes shut. They say that it was thirty-two minutes from the loud noise to the crash. It was a long time; it felt like a couple of hours. I waited for an announcement saying we were returning to Haneda. If that announcement came it meant that we could fly and if we were communicating with the airport we would be all right. But the announcement never came. There was an impact.

I felt only one impact. It all happened at once, that's all I can remember. I didn't feel that we turned over, just that I was thrown. You have to keep the safety position even after the impact but I was so scared I looked up. At that moment lots of things were flying around and they hit my head. I don't remember any sound. The sound, impact, it all happened at the same time.

After the impact there was a cloud of dust and everything appeared blurred. I thought, we've had a crash. I realised then what a terrible accident it was.

It smelled very bad, the smell of machinery. Not oily, but the smell you get when you go into a machine room. I was stuck in a seated position. My left hand and both my legs were stuck against something solid and I couldn't move them at all. The back of my foot was touching something. I didn't feel much pain, but was limp.

It was painful and difficult to breathe. I was panting rather than breathing. I thought vaguely, "So this is what it is like just before you die." I was so limp and exhausted that I thought then that I wanted to end it. I thought it would be better to die, so I tried to bite my tongue off. I didn't want to suffer, that was my only thought. But it hurt, so I stopped biting.[9]

Just after the crash I heard harsh panting, and gasping noises from many people. I heard it coming from everywhere, all around me. There was a boy crying, "Mother."

The next time I remember it was dark. I don't know how much time had passed. I could vaguely see in front the shadow of the back of a seat or something like a table. I seemed to be still in my seat but wedged underneath everything. On my left cheek I could feel someone, I think it was the calm man who had been sitting next to me, touching as though he was leaning on me. He wasn't breathing. He was cold.

My seat-belt was still on and it was biting into me and getting painful. I used my right hand to unfasten the belt. My right arm was all I could move. There was a gap above my head where I

could move my arm freely. I moved my hand in front of me to
push at something solid that was in front of me. It would not
budge, so I reached around it and felt about three heads as if
sitting in a row together. One had longish hair in a perm, so it
was probably a woman. The head was cold, but I was not
afraid.

From somewhere around me I could clearly hear a young
woman saying, "Come quickly." I could still hear the harsh
panting of a couple of people.

From then on I lost all sense of time. Sometimes I passed out.
I wasn't cold; in fact my body felt hot and I sometimes raised
my right hand into the gap above my head to feel the cool air.

Suddenly I heard a boy's voice, "OK, I'll hang on," he said.
It sounded like the voice of a boy of just about school age.
Although I could hear it clearly I couldn't tell if it was the same
boy who had been calling, "Mother," earlier.

I was so weak that I could only listen to the panting and
gasping or the voices that I could hear coming from somewhere. I couldn't smell the machinery smell any more. I
couldn't feel whether I was bleeding, but there was no smell of
blood. I didn't throw up.

In the darkness I could hear the sound of a helicopter. I
couldn't see any light but I could clearly hear the sound, and it
was quite near too. We'll be saved, I thought, and I raised my
right hand and frantically waved. But the helicopter went
further away. "Don't go." I waved desperately. "Help. Someone come," I think I shouted too.[10] But it faded . . . Even then
I could hear the heavy breathing of a couple of people, but I
could no longer hear the voices of the boy or the young woman.

My body was hot. While raising my right hand into the cold
breeze I was thinking in the pitch darkness; things like "My
poor husband, what if I die like this?" I thought about my
father as well. My mother had died three years previously so if
I died he'd be so unhappy. When I first became a stewardess my
mother said, in a slightly surprised way, "If something happens,
aren't the stewardesses supposed to be the last ones to get out?
Do you think you can do that?" I wondered why we had

*crashed. I wanted us to go back and do it again, and this time
we wouldn't fail, we would do it better. Many things welled up
in my mind.*

*I never cried. Not at all. The tremendous sensation of the
crash, I don't want anyone ever to have to go through that. I
thought things like that too. And I passed out again. When I
came to it was light. There was no sound. It was absolutely
quiet. I thought, "Am I the only one still alive?" But I called out,
"Let's all hang on," which came quite naturally. There was no
reply and I couldn't hear the heavy breathing any more either.*

*I felt a strong wind. I felt bits of wood or something like
straw fly and hit my face. When I came to I heard the sound of
a helicopter close by. I couldn't see anything, but there was
bright light in front of me. It wasn't sunlight, it was much
brighter.*

*Near by I heard a voice saying something like, "Wave your
hand" or "Raise your hand." I couldn't tell if it was someone
else being rescued or whether they were calling to someone. I
raised my right hand and waved. They said, "That's enough,
that's enough, we'll come immediately." Soon after, I lost consciousness. I thought vaguely, "I've been rescued, I'm saved." I
don't remember how I was dug out of the wreckage or how
I was transported.*

In any impact, the longer the time between starting to come to a
halt and coming to rest, the less severe the forces on the people. In
other words, much of the energy of this impact was absorbed by
the forward part of the aircraft before it reached those in the rear.
That is why the front of a car is called a "crumple zone". If it
collapses gradually, the deceleration is slow. If it is very rigid, the
impact forces are transferred much more quickly to the occupant,
who suffers greater injury.

In the Kegworth crash the least injured of the passengers were
those in the last three seat rows, despite the fact that their section
of the fuselage snapped and came to rest upside-down. Their
deceleration had also been slowed by the crushing of the fuselage
in front of them.

The survival of the four passengers on the JAL flight was little short of miraculous and in itself cannot prove that choosing seats in the rear is a safe option. And there are some disadvantages to sitting right at the back. First, whatever motion the aircraft is experiencing will be strongest there, especially in turbulence, and it will also be noisier than forward of the wings. On those aircraft where smoking is still permitted it is likely to be in the last few rows.

However, another crash illustrated the value of sitting in the rear as well as one other part of the plane, over the wing. Wings are not, from the structural point of view, simply attached to the side of the fuselage, as we might imagine. Between the two wings is the "wing-box", which usually contains some of the plane's fuel load as well as linking the wings for strength. During the Kegworth crash, the key problem was the disruption of the floor, and the consequent piling together of the seats. But the seats over the wing-box held.

In January 1992 an Airbus A-320 of the French internal airline Air Inter crashed on a mountain just short of Strasbourg airport in foul weather at night. It was a classic CFIT, with the plane hitting the rounded top of a hill at a fairly shallow angle. It was only fifty or so feet from clearing it altogether. There was virtually no fire in this crash, mainly because the wings were sheared off by trees early in the crash sequence and the ground was deep in snow.

There were eight survivors in all out of the ninety-six people on board. All but one of the survivors had been seated at the rear of the plane, and the man who was not had a seat over the wing.

Similarly, an unusually high proportion of the passengers in the Eastern Airlines Tristar that crashed into the Everglades in 1972 survived because their seats were firmly attached.

The Korean Airlines Boeing 747 that crashed on the island of Guam on approach to the airport in August 1997 killed 230 with twenty surviving. Roughly one-third of the survivors were in overwing seats, one-third at the rear and one-third in the upper deck seats in the "hump" behind the cockpit.

For crash survivability then, choose seats closest to an exit, and over the wing, or in the rear.[11] Even the same type of aircraft can have different seating configurations, so it may be no use asking for a specific seat-row expecting to get, say, the seat next to the overwing exit. On the other hand, check-in may be able to help if you specify that you want the overwing-exit seat. (These also have more leg-room.) In general, the overwing position is best for seat-strength, but the rear is best for having a crumple zone in front of you.

Having boarded

Unless you were the last to board, you are likely to have some time to kill before take-off. The best advice, in general, is to spend the time waiting for the cabin staff's safety briefing to look at the safety card and get the measure of the layout of the aircraft and your position in relation to the emergency exits. If you are next to an exit, look at it carefully and work out exactly how it is opened and where the emergency slide is located, and how it is operated. Main-door exits have slides, and overwing exits usually do not, but bear in mind that every aircraft is different. Some accidents have happened while the aircraft has been taxiing, some even while still at the gate, so the sooner you get to grips with your plan the better.

Following the Kegworth crash a new brace position for impact was adopted by the CAA. Noel Crymble, a survivor of that crash who was highly critical of the CAA's failure to follow through on the AAIB's safety recommendations, told me the CAA adopted the new brace position because it was the only recommendation that would not have cost the airline any money. The new position has been adopted by the FAA, too (*see* diagram on p. 123).

This is a sensible position for the passenger to take and shows what a regulator can do when someone has bothered to give a little thought to the question, even if it does beg the question as to why, before 1990, nobody else had. It is a position that you ought to adopt in preference to others, since many airlines have not updated their safety cards and may not be aware of its advantages.

This new brace position has two advantages over previous, or

**FORWARD-FACING PASSENGER
BRACE POSITION**

alternative, brace positions. The first is that the arms are already up against a surface. Kegworth showed that a lot of damage was caused by arms flailing forward. They might still suffer injury, but if they are already forward, there will be less flailing. The second change is placing the feet just behind your knees, another lesson learned from study of the injuries at Kegworth. If the feet are forward of the knees, then there is nothing to slow down their flailing forward, increasing the possibility of them being broken. If they are behind the knees they cannot swing forward so easily.

Some estimates put the average number of passengers who observe the safety briefing as low as 5 per cent, and one study showed that less than a third had read the safety card.[12] Even if it is drearily familiar to you, it is useful and important to watch the safety briefing by the cabin crew. It is not commonly known, but flight attendants are not mere aerial waiters and waitresses: they are trained in safety drills and evacuation procedures and their presence on the aircraft is mandated by the safety regulations.

(They do not help the cause of getting an audience for their safety show, however, by handing out newspapers as people board.)

Even if it is not telling you anything new, the briefing helps put you in mind of the remote possibility of a crash. Cabin staff and pilots often despair of getting passengers to pay attention. Many of them, especially the business travellers, seem to think it "cool" to be seen ignoring the briefing. Yet their short-sightedness does not only affect them alone, for people who do not know what they are doing during an emergency or evacuation usually hinder the escape of others.

Choose the nearest exit and count the number of seat-rows until you reach it. If a crash occurred in total darkness or smoke impaired visibility you would need to find the exit in darkness. Although the emergency lighting on the cabin floor should guide you to an exit, there have been occasions when it did not illuminate. It can be useful to close your eyes and imagine making the journey to your exit; this also helps you to memorise the route. If there is fire, or an exit is otherwise blocked, remember there is always another exit on the opposite side of the fuselage.

Look also at the seat-belt. Although many passengers scoff when the flight attendants are showing you how to do it up, there is a good reason for the demonstration. In panic or fear some people intuitively reach for the buckle where they would find it in a car, at the side. But the aircraft buckle is in the middle of the belt. The lever also has to be pulled all the way out for the webbing to be released.[13]

Like all safety-belts it should fit snugly, but not too tight, over your pelvis. Over the legs or the stomach is wrong. However tempting it may be, one should never – nor in a car – strap a small child into your own belt. At first glance it might seem safer than the child being loose, but this is wrong. In a severe impact all your weight will be thrown on to the child and then the belt, which could kill the child. If there is no seat for the child, placing it on the floor in front of you is best. Some airlines have a belt which loops around your own belt. It is not ideal, but if it is provided it is worth using.

The issue of providing safety-seats for children under two is a controversial one. There are safety-seats intended primarily for use in cars but which are also approved for use on aircraft. The airline ought to know those which are approved and you should be able to check with them. It ought to be possible, but only by checking with the airline, to bring an approved safety-seat with you and use it, if there are spare seats on the plane, without any extra charge. (In most countries, under-twos are not charged for tickets.)

In the United States the FAA has approved certain child's safety-seats but refuses to mandate them for passenger air travel. This makes the small child the only unsecured object in the whole cabin. It is impossible for an adult to hang on to a child in his or her arms in a severe impact. As mentioned above, the best place for such a child, in the event of a crash, is on the floor in front of your seat.

The NTSB has clamoured since 1979 for mandatory child restraint on aircraft, but the FAA's main reason for refusing to do this is that it claims that the extra cost would discourage families from travelling and that means they would go by road – which, they argue, is more dangerous. However, if the seat were compulsory, airlines would probably come up with a way of carrying the baby at minimal extra cost. The incentive for the airlines would be strong, because if they did not do so they could be losing the ticket of at least one adult, possibly two or more, and the baby's siblings, if any.[14]

The FAA put some of its topsy-turvy logic on full view when a document it produced on improving child safety in aircraft considered a number of scenarios. "Scenario No. 4" was the best, they said. In this, the family pays for and reserves a seat, if it is available, for their own child's safety-seat, and duly puts junior in it for the journey. The FAA calculated that this would save the most lives at the least cost to all concerned. Of course, that is the present situation. In other words, in order to improve safety, the FAA recommended one "scenario" as the best solution which just happened to be the status quo. Thus, to improve safety, it recommended doing nothing!

What not to do

It can be useful to remember what not to do. Your actions during an emergency when you are terrified can be semi-automatic. People often function in such situations in an almost dream-like state, so it can be worthwhile remembering that when you have to escape, you must do nothing else. Absurd as it may sound, on many occasions people who should have been rushing out of the plane to save their lives paused to try to take their carry-on luggage or coats with them as they left the burning and broken plane. It is second nature, but giving in to this instinct could be fatal. Take only your self and get out.

A Canadian study found that in nearly half of all the emergency evacuations under consideration passengers had attempted to take their carry-on baggage with them. Better to lose it than your life.

Evacuation

Most emergency evacuations are precautionary, and most airline captains will try to avoid them if possible. Getting hundreds of people out of a plane in ninety seconds, as required by the regulations, demands a lot of the cabin staff, and somebody almost always experiences injury from going down the slides. But if they are going to be used, do what you are told and jump. Some slides can be blown about by the wind, for example back under the aircraft. If you have escaped it would be helpful to reposition the slide and hold it down against the effects of the wind. However, if the slides are working correctly, once you are out it is essential to get far away from the aircraft. Fuel could be spilling out without yet having caught fire, or an explosion could be in the offing.

Sometimes, especially if, say, the nose-gear of the aircraft has collapsed, the rear end of the fuselage can be high in the air and the slide will be near the vertical. Whether to go or not depends, clearly, on balancing factors. If the cabin is full of smoke and fire, get out anyway. If there is no sign of fire or smoke it might be possible to use another exit.

Many passengers, especially those who have not been paying attention to the cards or the briefings, will attempt to leave by the exit they entered the plane by, no matter how many other exits are available or visible. In fact, as the passenger who knows what he or she is doing, you could see a lot of ignorant or sheep-like behaviour. Best to follow your own counsel, unless you are being directed in an orderly fashion by cabin staff.

Panic is probably the most serious hindrance to emergency evacuation. Aircraft evacuation experts have classified panic into two types: overt panic, i.e. screaming and shouting, and negative panic, in which a person freezes and cannot move. The latter syndrome is especially dangerous if the affected person is sitting next to an overwing exit, the kind that passengers are expected to operate. Cabin staff are supposed to make sure that the people sitting next to the overwing exits know how to operate them and are strong enough to do so. Disabled people, the very overweight, the elderly and people with young children are not normally seated there.

But there is no way of telling how someone is going to react in an emergency. There have been plenty of occasions when the person next to the exit either froze or fumbled getting the door open.

Types of emergency

The cruise portion of flight is the safest, statistically, and the flight-crew have least to do. But crashes aside, there are two important types of in-flight emergency to be aware of.

The first is a sudden decompression. The cabin is pressurised to about 8.5 psi (pounds per square inch), or roughly the atmospheric pressure at about 3000-feet elevation. So when the aircraft is at great heights, it is more heavily pressurised that the outside atmosphere. That means that if a hole should appear in the cabin, the air will rush to escape through it.

No aircraft can be hermetically sealed, so the air-conditioning units are working permanently, boosting the air pressure on a continual basis. This compensates for small leaks, which present no problem. Bigger holes that appear suddenly do.

Holes can appear in aircraft for various reasons, but they are never in themselves enough to cause a plane to crash. Under special circumstances, a sudden decompression can be the first domino to topple in a catastrophic sequence of events, but it ought not to, and normally it does not. In the notorious DC-10 disaster near Paris in 1974 (see Chapter 9) the decompression caused by a cargo door blowing off pushed down the cabin floor and severed critical flight controls. It was the linking of the floor failure to the decompression that caused disaster, not the decompression alone.

Pressure bulkheads have failed, and while this resulted in the loss of the JAL 747 in August 1985, on other occasions the same bulkheads on a Lockheed Tristar and a DC-9, for example, have failed without any lives being lost.

Other holes have appeared thanks to fan blades from exploding jet engines penetrating the fuselage, or the cockpit windscreen being blown out, or bombs. Of the exterior doors, only some types of cargo door can open during flight, even if they are not supposed to. The doors in the passenger cabin proper are plug-doors, meaning that irrespective of latches and locks the cabin pressure keeps them shut.

A sudden decompression is nothing if not alarming. There will be a loud bang, followed by a rushing of air towards the hole, wherever it might be. Like a colossal vacuum cleaner, it will lift all the dust and dirt in the stream of rushing air, frequently temporarily blinding people. The rushing of air will quickly subside and at that time one will notice a thick white mist in the air. This is the water vapour condensing out of the warm cabin air as it meets the cold outside air. The cabin will also appear colder and soon the mist will clear.

Emergency oxygen masks drop automatically from the overhead compartments when there is a sudden pressure loss on most planes. In order to operate them it is necessary to pull sharply. Contrary to popular belief, the oxygen cylinders do not contain pressurised oxygen. They hold two chemicals which, when mixed, produce oxygen. Pulling on the lanyard attached to the oxygen mask sets off a small explosive charge in the cylinder which allows the two oxygen-generating chemicals to mix and provide oxygen for about ten minutes.

In some emergencies passengers have stood up or moved near the mask, but because they have not pulled on it, it has not operated. Only moderate force should be used. Some passengers who have pulled too hard on the lanyard have found the cylinder dropping into their laps, which is to be avoided since the chemical reaction heats it to about 260 degrees Celsius. Oxygen is odourless and colourless, so one should not make the other potential mistake, that of discarding the mask because you imagine it is not working.

When wearing the mask, remember that a perfect seal around the cup is not necessary. The oxygen supply is being mixed with the normal air, which is why, incidentally, the mask will not protect against smoke.

As if to add to the alarm that will inevitably be occurring, while you and the cabin crew are putting on oxygen masks the flight-crew, after donning their own, will put the plane into an emergency descent to an altitude where you no longer need the oxygen mask, about 10,000 feet. The only purpose of the oxygen supply to the passengers is to bridge the gap until the plane gets to a safe altitude. Getting there is an easy matter, but from up to 40,000 feet it could be a steep descent and it can be easy for people already alarmed by the decompression to imagine that the plane is diving to its doom. It will level off, however, at the new altitude and the pilots will land at the nearest airport.

It is likely one would experience some pain in the ears during the decompression but no permanent damage should result. On a couple of extremely rare occasions, no doubt closely studied by the screenplay writer of the James Bond film *Goldfinger*, a passenger has been sucked out of a window during a decompression. Many airlines ask you to keep your safety-belt "loosely fastened" at all times, presumably because it would be harder to make people comply if they were asked to keep it securely fastened, but that is better.

On a single occasion this was not enough. In November 1973 a National Airlines DC-10 was in cruise on its way from Miami to San Francisco. Owing to a mechanical condition influenced by the pilot and the flight engineer conducting what they thought would be a harmless experiment, the engine on the right wing blew up. The plane buffeted, there was a series of loud bangs and a piece of the engine damaged a window. Mr F.H. Gardner was in the window seat with his seat-belt loosely fastened.

The outside part of the three-layered window gave way, followed by the rest of it. Mr Gardner was sucked halfway out of the window, his seat-belt now catching on his legs and his neighbour trying to hold on to him. The decompression was still in full flow and a few seconds later the other passenger could not resist the force and Mr Gardner was sucked out of the window completely. Although many parts of the engine were found on a wreckage trail all over New Mexico, Mr Gardner's body was never located. Fortunately, the plane landed safely twenty minutes later and there were no other serious injuries.[15]

Clear-air turbulence

The remote possibility of clear-air turbulence, or CAT, is the clinching reason for keeping the seat-belt fastened at all times. It is a more serious version of ordinary turbulence, which is greatly under-reported as a cause of injury on aircraft. One report said that 7611 people were injured by turbulence in US aircraft in 1996 alone.[16]

When an aircraft runs into CAT it is like falling into a hole. Planes are held up by the wings moving fast enough through the air for there to be less air pressure above them than below, so that the pressure differential lifts the wings. A stall is the technical term for when this effect no longer applies. In CAT an aircraft can suddenly run into following winds of 200 knots or more. This causes the plane to lose lift and drop like a stone, albeit only for a few hundred feet.

Alternatively, the plane can be pushed up or down by powerful draughts of air. The movement can be so sudden, though, that unbelted passengers, flight-attendants with their meal-carts and anything else that is unsecured will slam violently against the cabin ceiling. Many of the overhead lockers will also probably open and heavy objects could fall out. It is, in other words, about the most shocking and scariest experience it is possible to undergo in-flight, short of an actual catastrophe.

A severe example of this untypical event occurred on a United Airlines 747 flying at 33,000 feet en route from Tokyo to Honolulu on 29 December 1997. The aircraft shook violently and plunged 1000 feet when it hit the CAT, and one female passenger was killed while 110 others were injured, some of them seriously. A newspaper report said:

> *The mêlée was videoed by a passenger: it showed the aircraft shaking, and screaming passengers bouncing against the ceiling, with oxygen masks released above the seats. One passenger said later: "The plane suddenly sank and, bang!, people were thrown out of their seats."*[17]

The natural reaction of the pilots, whether the aircraft is pushed up or down, is to lower the nose in order to gain speed and thus stability. If they do it too violently, though, it will merely exacerbate the turbulence the plane is passing through, especially at the back. In the same way that the end of a see-saw moves faster than the part close to the fulcrum, the rear of the fuselage will be subjected to more violent movements than the front or middle. In fact it is now recognised that the severity of many CAT incidents is increased by the pilots' instinctive pushing forward on the control column, although most airlines do not train their pilots to cope with these incidents.[18] The United 747 was so badly damaged during the incident that it was written off as being beyond economical repair.

Barely any crashes have been caused by CAT or other forms of turbulence. The most famous example of a fatal turbulence event was that of the BOAC Boeing 707 whose captain, on leaving Tokyo on 5 March 1966, obtained permission to fly close to

Mount Fuji so as to give his passengers a spectacular view of Japan's most famous natural feature. Unknowingly, the captain flew the plane into a "mountain rotor", a swirling vortex of winds associated with the disrupted air-flows over mountains. Normally, it is visible as a cloud, but there was little moisture in the air that day, and so nothing for the meteorologists to warn the flight-crew against. A gust of turbulence slammed into the side of the plane like a giant's hand swatting a fly. The shock broke off the vertical fin, smashing it against the left elevator and breaking that off before part of one wing snapped and the rest of the aircraft disintegrated, crashing to the ground 16,000 feet below.

Just five months later, on 6 August, a Braniff Airways BAC 1-11 had its tail smashed off by an extremely violent upward gust. On this occasion the aircraft had been trying to thread a path through a line of thunderstorms. Unfortunately, by going between two thunderstorms the pilot had inadvertently flown into an area of extremely powerful upward and downward currents, known at lower altitudes as "windshear".[19]

Before aircraft carried radar that could warn them of severe weather conditions ahead, especially thunderstorms, pilots gave storms and the like a wide berth. Flights would have been cancelled. Having the radar has been useful to keep aircraft out of trouble, but it could equally be argued that because of it aircraft fly closer to danger because they can see it. The same is true of new windshear-warning radar, which we will deal with later.

Despite the extreme rarity of such turbulence, it should be remembered that an aircraft is similar to a ship. There is only so much it can take from the elements it is navigating. No aircraft can be made completely proof against structural failures caused by extreme turbulence, but it can be kept out of harm's way relatively easily.

Fire

Surviving a crash itself is often not enough. It may turn out only to be the prelude to a fire, in which more lives will be lost. A cabin fire is possibly the best example of the kind of situation which becomes more survivable the more you keep your head.

In discussing what occurred at Manchester (*see* Chapter 3) the basic outline of what to do was covered. When trying to evacuate stay close to the floor if possible. If you don't have a smoke-hood, a pillow or seat cushion could be useful to hold over one's mouth and nose to filter out some of the harmful particles in the smoke, and if a drink is to hand, wet material is better than dry. Smoke-hoods are commercially available, especially in the United States, and would be a wise buy, especially for the frequent flyer, although the type that uses a bottle of compressed air is illegal in most countries.

The fact that the aviation regulators are opposed to the installation of smoke-hoods in aircraft for use by all passengers does not mean they are opposed to the individual carrying one on. Indeed, as we have seen, the FAA has them on all its own aircraft, and most air-safety professionals carry their own when flying commercially.[20]

The aircraft does carry fire-extinguishers, near the cabin-crew seating stations, often in the overhead lockers, but passengers should not attempt to use them. Time spent looking for a fire-extinguisher would be much better spent trying to get out. If a fire broke out in flight the cabin staff would attempt to use the extinguishers.

Ditching

This needs to be mentioned, despite its rarity. The runway over-runs we have described at LaGuardia that put the aircraft in the water were not ditchings as such. It is ironic, however, that nobody evacuating those planes was told to take their buoyant seat-cushions with them.

In the United States, under pressure from the industry, the FAA permitted the substitution of inflatable life-jackets with seat-cushions that float, although all British-registered aircraft continue with the life-jackets. The floating seat-cushions are not nearly as good as a life-jacket, which comes equipped with a light, a whistle and a nozzle for inflating it, should it lose pressure. But the supposition in the United States was that the ditching of a jet airliner is an emergency of such major proportions that help would very soon be at hand.

An Ethiopian Airlines Boeing 767 ditched just offshore one of the Comoro Islands in the Indian Ocean, an event spectacularly captured on a home video by a holidaymaker on the beach in November 1996. Those who survived the crash easily made it to shore themselves or were helped by the tourists on the beach and in boats. These were bizarre circumstances which it would be virtually impossible to legislate for. Hijackers had taken over the plane and ordered the flight-crew to fly to Australia. They refused to believe the plane did not have enough fuel for the journey, and when it ran out ditching was the only option.

A more unusual ditching occurred in October 1963 when an Aeroflot Tupolev 124 ditched in the River Neva, Leningrad. While holding for landing the aircraft ran out of fuel. The crew landed the plane on the river, where it remained, floating, and after the passengers and crew were all evacuated safely it was even towed ashore.[20]

During the piston-engine age ditching was, if not common, an eventuality to be guarded against strictly. The provision of life-jackets is a hangover from that era, but they did come in useful during the ditching of a DC-9 of ALM Dutch Antillean Airlines in May 1970.[21] Owing to bad weather at his destination on St Maarten, in the Caribbean, the pilot approached but decided not to land. While he diverted to other airports the plane ran out of fuel and had to ditch.

The worst problem was that there was not enough warning of the impending ditching, meaning that some flight attendants and passengers were not belted in and received serious injuries when the plane hit the water, although it was landed as well as any pilot could have managed. Despite there being five lifeboats on board, only the inflatable escape slide was usable as a raft and 22 of the 57 people on board drowned, either inside the plane or while awaiting rescue by helicopter.

As the safety cards state, the life-jacket must not be inflated before leaving the aircraft. If the fuselage is intact, the overwing exit is the best place from where to leave the aircraft, since it may be possible to walk along the wing, and inflate the life-jacket before having to get into the water.

It is a mistake to shed clothing and shoes before getting into the sea. Provided the life-jacket is working, having more clothes on helps provide an insulating layer. All life-rafts and individuals floating in the water should stay as close to each other as possible. It is good for morale as well as making a bigger target for rescuers to spot from above.

Is something going wrong?

Pilots and flight attendants do not have much respect for a passenger's view of the safety of the aircraft. If a passenger says something dangerous is going on, the flight attendant is liable to give them the kind of treatment a doctor gives a patient with a runny nose who thinks he has green monkey disease. And, of course, the vast majority of us are totally unqualified to pass any kind of comment on the operation of a modern jet. Consider, however, the 1989 crash at Kegworth of the British Midland 737.

When the left engine started to bang and shudder, smoke, sparks and flames issued from it, all of which was visible to the passengers on the same side of the cabin and behind the wing. After the pilots had shut down the right engine, the chief flight attendant entered the cockpit and said, "Sorry to trouble you, but the passengers are very, very panicky."

The captain then told the passengers over the public address system that there had been trouble with the *right* engine, that it had been shut down and that they would be landing in about ten minutes.

The official report states: "The flight attendants who saw signs of fire on the left engine later stated that they had not heard the commander's reference to the right engine. However, many of the passengers who saw fire from the No. 1 [left] engine heard and were puzzled by the commander's reference to the right engine, but none brought the discrepancy to the attention of the cabin crew, even though several were aware of continuing vibration."

The captain, they knew, was wrong, but nobody had the nerve to say so. In this case the disastrous results are well known, although it must be added that it would take a brave non-pilot to contradict the professional pilot of a big jet with over 120 people on board. There is no guarantee, furthermore, that a flight attendant would necessarily have brought any such passenger's comment to the captain's attention. This captain had a reputation as something of a martinet, and cabin staff might well have feared getting short shrift from him with any comment that could be interpreted as calling his judgement into question. As it was, they knew he had an emergency on his hands and would have been extremely reluctant to interrupt him. The average flight attendant, after all, knows little more than the average passenger about flying planes.

Here was, however, an opportunity, and it was not taken. Perhaps, had the passengers on the left been aware that the engines cannot be seen from the cockpit of any commercial jet transport, somebody might have ventured a remark.

Another example of deference and the "they must know what they are doing" syndrome concerned one of Aloha Airlines' elderly Boeing 737s before a short flight on 28 April 1988. This was the famous flight when the entire upper half of the fuselage between the cockpit and the leading edge of the wings was ripped off, creating what some people called the Boeing "convertible".

With substantial helpings in equal measure of luck and skilful flying the aircraft flew on and landed safely. One flight attendant had been killed as she was sucked through the developing hole in the roof, and several passengers were seriously injured by exposure to the cold and the powerful air currents.

But a passenger on the fateful flight told the accident investigators that as she boarded she noticed a crack in the side of the fuselage just to the right of the front door she was entering by. This turned out to be part of the crack that eventually opened up and unzipped the roof later on the flight. She decided, however, that: a) they must know what they are doing, b) that she would be treated with scorn if she mentioned it and c) there was no point in making a fuss.[22]

One rare case is recorded where a passenger did make an intervention which made a difference. He wrote a letter to the *New York Times*, published on 10 April 1992, saying what had happened to him.

> *The plane was fully loaded and we sat locked inside for two hours while the plane was de-iced, taxied out, came back for a second de-icing and got in the take-off line again. After we had waited for about a half-hour, the wind shifted, and we had to go to the other end of the runway, with ice all the while building up on the wing, next to my window . . . When the pilot announced that we were next in line for take-off, I rang and requested that a stewardess ask the cockpit if they were aware that what seemed an inch of ice had built up on the wings. The flight engineer came back into the cabin and observed the wings. The pilot announced that we had to return for de-icing again.*[23]

This occurred at LaGuardia Airport in circumstances similar to those which resulted in the crash of the USAir F-28 in March 1992 (*see* Chapter 2). Passengers on that flight had also noticed ice on the wings, one of them being quoted as saying, "We take off like this, we're all dead." They kept quiet, however, and a fatal crash followed.[24] Again, it is easy to forget that the flight-deck has no view of the engines or most of the wings.

Excessive creaks, groans and cracks should be reported to the cabin staff, especially cracks. Unless the crack is in your plastic cup, it has no place on an airliner and you should tell a flight attendant about it. Another kind of useful intervention a passenger can make would be to remark on any unpleasant or burning smells. Fires can start anywhere in a cabin, from the cargo holds to the toilets, or amid wiring between the cabin walls and the outer skin of the fuselage. The first signs of any such fire may well not turn up on cockpit instruments. Obviously, if you tell a flight attendant, they can smell it too, if it is there. You are very unlikely to be upbraided by cabin staff, who are supposed to be polite anyway, for bringing up something like this, even if it turns out to be a false alarm.

A passenger was first to notice the beginning of a disastrous fire in the Air Canada DC-9 in 1983. The passenger told the flight attendant that there was a burning smell coming from one of the rear toilets, and she noticed smoke seeping under the closed door when she went to investigate. That was the beginning of a crisis which resulted in the plane diverting to the nearest airport and twenty-four people dying of smoke inhalation. After the evacuation fire consumed the rest of the aircraft. Although there is no way to be sure of it, the passenger's warning may have saved time that prevented all on board from dying.[25]

It is worth pointing out, for instance, that a kerosene smell can be present at the beginning of a flight, usually before it has taken off, although it is likely to clear quickly. Since the air for the cabin comes from the engines, it is possible, initially, for the kerosene-heavy air outside the plane to be momentarily transferred to the cabin. This is a good example of a concern that could be brought to a flight attendant's attention, who can then put your mind at ease about what it signifies.

A few alarming incidents have resulted from the design of the auxiliary power unit (APU) on the Boeing 727. The APU is a separate jet engine used for generating electrical power which is usually at the extreme end of the tail. On older 727s it is on the bottom of the fuselage. When the APU starts up it can sometimes belch smoke and a large jet of flame before it kicks in. Unfortunately, this vent is in full view of some of the passengers, and the event has resulted in unnecessary panic.

In addition to the engines, the wings are very visible parts of the plane, and those who stare out of the windows will see a lot of them. A certain amount of flexing, especially on landing and take-off, is normal, and you should not be concerned with vapour or streams of vapour coming off or out of the wing. The former is simply condensation and the latter could well be fuel being vented out of the wing-tanks.

In October 1996 passengers on a British Airways Boeing 777, however, did get worried about what seemed excessive flexing of the wings during a flight from Heathrow to Saudi Arabia. It seemed the wing flaps were moving apparently randomly and the aircraft rolled while at 37,000 feet. They told the cabin staff, some of whom reportedly became extremely distressed themselves, and they informed the pilot. Although it is not certain that the action of the passengers caused the decision to return to Heathrow, the captain did turn around shortly afterwards. The incident apparently involved uncommanded movements of the rudder and rudder pedals, and glitches in some of the computers were suspected.[26]

It should be clear by now that if you have been on commercial jets once or twice and are wondering about reporting something that may be worrying you, it is better to speak up than not. Provided you are not alarming other passengers as you do so, cabin staff ought to thank you for raising your concern.

CHAPTER 5

Don't shoot the pilot: The human factor in flight

PILOT ERROR IS the primary factor in over 70 per cent of all crashes. This is what the industry tells us, but, as the old saying goes, "Some humans are caused by accidents, but all accidents are caused by humans." In all accidents human error, if not the primary factor, was involved in 85 per cent of crashes.[1]

Some of those mistakes cast the pilots concerned in the worst possible light, but many others were errors that anyone could have made, and some of them, under the circumstances, were almost inevitable. It is these last which are most worrying, since many investigations stop analysing crashes once pilot error has been identified. And yet, manufacturers often build machines which are inviting operator errors. Legislation lets the manufacturer off the hook, however, and so not enough is being done to correct the situation.

Piloting is a profession which has some of the highest personal-satisfaction ratings of any job. In the United States, rates of pay for low- and middle-ranking commercial pilots are, by other professional standards and by those of pilots in other countries, extremely low. This is because the competition to enter the profession and the urge to fly are so strong that employers can offer less pay.

One US commuter airline pilot I met told me that it actually cost him money to fly as a first officer on an ATR-72 twin-engined turboprop. The pay was low but he had a business of his own which paid him enough and did not need all his time. The joy of flight for him was so intense, it was worth every penny. He says he knew others who felt the same way, giving up higher pay or a quieter life for the joy and prestige of being a professional pilot.

Pilots not only enjoy having the best views in and of the world on a daily basis, they also take pride in their ability to operate the aircraft as efficiently and comfortably as possible. Professionals they may also be, but one rarely meets a coach, truck or train driver who gets the same amount of satisfaction and pride out of what they do for a living.

Add to their personal commitment a high level of continual and refresher training and medical examinations and it may be hard to see how pilots ever make mistakes.

In Chapter 1 we discussed two bad crashes, Tenerife in 1977 and Cali in 1995, caused by flight-crew probably trained to the peaks of what was humanly possible who nevertheless made serious errors which cost the lives of all or most of their passengers. In both cases, however, other factors were pulling them in opposite directions to their training. At Tenerife, the captain was anxious to return to Amsterdam and avoid an unnecessary overnight stay for himself and his passengers, and seems to have cut a corner. At Cali the captain wanted to make up time near the destination for the delay suffered at departure, and he and his co-pilot allowed themselves to lose track of where they were.

Anyone can see the pressures these pilots were under, but how to deal with them is more problematic. Much research has focused on why pilots err, but, sadly, the answers usually tend to demand more training. If the pilots were in situations where they forgot their training, then the answer comes back, "Train them not to forget their training." Clearly, this is not good enough.

One famous example of this kind of circularity is often cited by pilots. A DC-8 was approaching a US airport in July 1970 when one of the pilots mistakenly deployed the air brakes. The plane was so low that the deployment of the brakes caused the plane to

crash and all 109 people on board died. The US FAA suggested
that a notice be placed by the air brakes lever reading, "Do not
deploy in-flight." The acid comment came back that a notice may
as well be placed in the middle of the instrument panel reading, "It
is forbidden to crash this aeroplane." After a couple more similar
incidents, the FAA required the installation of a device preventing
the use of the air brakes while airborne.

If insufficient or inappropriate training is a problem, it is not
being addressed now. Most of the "big" aviation countries
operate anonymous reporting systems whereby pilots, air traffic
controllers and other professionals can tell their anecdotes of
near-disaster so that others can learn from them. In the UK it is
called the Confidential Human-factors Incident Reporting Programme (CHIRP). In October 1997 one pilot for a low-cost airline
reported: "Further pressure has been brought to bear in the
training regime, with a reduction in the simulator sessions per
year, on a fleet where most co-pilots have less than 1000 hours'
total time, and 50 per cent of captains have less than two years'
command experience. Again, 'ticks in boxes' are adhered to but
very little real training/development can be achieved in the limited
time that is now available."

The same person added something that is a commonplace
nowadays in airline operations. "These actions lead me to the
assumption that flight safety is being de-prioritised by my company, with regulatory limits now being regarded as targets to
achieve month in, month out. It is my hope that this situation can
be reversed before a major incident takes place that forces a
rethink on the question of what constitutes 'business efficiency'."[2]

One suspects, however, that a "major incident" will be necessary before the issue is properly addressed, but because the pilot is
still responsible, even when under heavy commercial pressure, it
may not be. At a time when the left hand of industry is proposing
more pilot training to help deal with CFIT, automation problems,
upsets, icing and so on, the right hand is removing training
opportunities in the name of cost reduction and profit maxi-
misation. What we are left with, in an accident, is "pilot error".

It is worth considering a case study of an apparently appalling error, however, if only to illustrate how no "pilot error" is quite as simple as it might sound. It surprises many to discover that in the Kegworth crash, on the M1 motorway in January 1989, there was more to the shutting down of the wrong engine than meets the eye.

In Britain the incredulity which met the information that the wrong engine had been shut down was so great that there was considerable speculation as to whether the aircraft's instruments had been mistakenly cross-wired. When the public found out that this was not the case the incredulity was replaced with scorn for the pilots. The truth turned out to be more complicated. When the left engine began to play up, the pilots felt a rattling, a shuddering, smelled burning and saw smoke. Most of the captain's previous experience had been on aircraft, including other 737s, where the air-conditioning system was operated by the right engine, so that if an engine were to catch fire or issue smoke into the cabin or cockpit, then the right engine would have to have been responsible. On this aircraft the air-conditioning air was supplied by both engines. The first officer did not notice anything untoward on the instruments for either engine when he responded to the captain's query with "It's the le . . . the right one."

When the captain ordered the right engine throttled back, the first officer disconnected the autothrottle and then throttled the engine back. The shuddering stopped and the smoke cleared. They believed they had corrected the problem, when in fact it was the disconnection of the autothrottle which had given them some temporary relief, not the shutdown of the engine. The autothrottle is a system, like cruise-control on a car, which automatically keeps the engines at power or speed settings selected by the crew.

To cut a long, fairly technical story short, the autothrottle's attempt to maintain thrust on the left engine after it had lost a fan-blade was what was causing the shuddering and smoke. When the autothrottle was disconnected and the engine run at a lower power setting, the vibrations diminished strongly. The problem seemed to go away. But the vibration and fuel-flow gauges were still registering abnormal readings and had either pilot paid close attention they would have noticed something untoward. They had many other fish to fry, though, and there was a long list of jobs to do in declaring an emergency, going through checklists and preparing the plane for landing at a new destination.

After having the engine on low power during the descent, they increased it as they neared the airport. Increasing power on the engine precipitated the catastrophic failure that had never been far away, but at that stage in the descent there was not enough time to restart the right engine. Had the left engine's failure come a couple of minutes earlier they would probably have had time to restart the other engine and make a safe landing.

At this point two other factors came into play. The first was that indications of engine vibration on earlier versions of the 737 were notoriously unreliable and, for better or worse, pilots frequently ignored them. In this 737-400, however, they were much more effective. In their conversion training from the 737-300 to the 737-400 the pilots' attention had not been specifically drawn to this feature of the aircraft, although there was a reference to it in the aircraft manual. The captain had only flown fifty-three hours on the 737-400 and his co-pilot even less. British Midland did not even have a 737-400 simulator for the men to train on. This was much less training than was ideal.

The second problem was that the crew became engaged in what the investigators later concluded was an unnecessarily lengthy exchange of reports and instructions over the radio which distracted them from cockpit tasks. They were even asked to make a test transmission to the airport fire station. The frequency was also being shared with several other planes when, the investigators later reported, the British Midland aircraft should have been given a frequency for its exclusive use.

Despite all this, the captain attempted at one point to review their actions, saying, "Now what indications did we actually get – just rapid vibrations in the aeroplane, smoke . . ." Whether that review would have detected their false diagnosis we will never know because at that point he was interrupted by air traffic control with a new heading and an instruction to change radio frequency. He did not resume the review afterwards.

Distinguished pilots, among them personnel from Boeing, later said that they could see exactly how these pilots could have mis-interpreted the available cues to diagnose a fault in the wrong engine. Mistakes certainly, but understandable ones any honest, professional pilot would be loath to say he or she would never make.

One other feature of the sequence of events almost slips past without notice. The engine failed. The CFM-56 3C engines were uprated versions of a type of CFM engine that had already given long and reliable service. When it was uprated the manufacturers argued for and received permission to enter it into service with only ground tests having been performed, instead of flight tests, as would have been usual. Had it been flight-tested then the entire accident might have been avoided because the engine problem might have been identified then. Two similar engines failed in flight within the next few months, one of them a sister aircraft to the Kegworth plane. On those occasions safe landings followed, and it was found that there was metal fatigue in the fan-blades. Under flight testing, the fault might have emerged before the engines entered revenue service, and if that precaution had revealed the problem, nobody would have been fiercely blaming two men, both of whom were seriously injured.

An understandable mistake it may have been, but the aircraft was the pilots' responsibility and an error it remained, for all that. The AAIB noted the actions of the pilots but without criticising them unduly. However, the CAA, when it was shown a draft of the report, insisted that the phrase be inserted "contrary to their training" after the remark which said they had shut down the engine prematurely.[3]

The justification for this is simple. By accentuating the pilots' responsibility, the CAA seemed to be saying that, whatever the mitigating factors, the plane and passengers are the pilots' responsibility and that there are no "understandable" mistakes. Former chief safety pilot for Lufthansa Captain Heino Caesar told me once, "We emphasise the mistakes of pilots too much perhaps. But that is because all humans have the potential to improve their performance, and we cannot tell machines to improve." In other words, it is not necessarily a bad thing to keep pilots on their toes.

That is to look at the situation generously. More cynical types would say the CAA wanted to emphasise the alleged culpability of the pilots to detract from the engine's deficiencies and the paucity of conversion training, which were also major factors.

Many pilots have been wrongly blamed. In October 1952 Captain Foote's fully loaded BOAC Comet was taking off from Rome's Ciampino Airport. Just as the plane's nose rose there was a shuddering and the aircraft ceased to accelerate or to lift off. He abandoned the take-off but could not stop in time and the aircraft was destroyed as it ran into obstructions off the end of the runway. Nobody died, but Captain Foote was roundly blamed for the crash, and attracted considerable odium from having been the first person ever to crash a jet airliner.

The Comet had been flying for less than six months and Foote had encountered a problem unknown to piston-engined airliners. If the nose was raised too high and too soon during the take-off run the drag resulting from the angle of the wings to the air would prevent it reaching take-off speed. Test flights confirmed the problem and a new procedure was adopted. When the Boeing 707 was being tested for its airworthiness certificate, test-pilots tried to reproduce the problem, albeit on a runway with plenty of space. They found the same phenomenon that Captain Foote had encountered.

As a result of the tests on the 707 a fin was attached to the bottom of the rear fuselage so that the pilot would be physically unable to raise the nose so high that the aircraft would encounter the phenomenon that undid Captain Foote. Later, all jet transports were designed so that it was not possible to encounter the same problem by changing the shape of the fuselage at the rear.[4] It took some considerable time, but Captain Foote's name and reputation were cleared in the end.

If Foote was affected by the opprobrium of being the first man to crash a passenger jet, Captain James Thain attracted even more hatred by being blamed for killing seven members of the Manchester United football team in February 1958. In what was known in Britain as the Munich Air Disaster, Captain Thain's twin-engined Elizabethan aircraft failed to make it into the air during a foul night on his third attempt to take off from Munich airport. The plane ran off the runway, hit a house, which was too close to the runway, and twenty-one people in total died in the crash, for which the German authorities held Captain Thain entirely responsible. They said he had failed to check the wings were clear of snow and ice.

He protested and was backed by his trade union, the British Airline Pilots' Association, but owing to diplomatic peculiarities in Britain's relations with Germany at the time, he was vindicated at home while remaining responsible for the crash on the official record. British research backed by work from NASA showed that even a small amount of slush on the runway could slow an aircraft's speed to the point where take-off was impossible. Captain Thain never managed to regain his pilot's licence before he died, unvindicated, at an early age of a heart attack.[5]

Pilots tend to be blamed less squarely nowadays, but there are exceptions, one of the cruellest of which involved Captain Glen Stewart of British Airways. Captain Stewart had the unedifying distinction of being the first British commercial transport pilot to be criminally prosecuted for endangering his aircraft by the Civil Aviation Authority. He was flying his Boeing 747-100 on an instrument landing system approach to Heathrow on a foggy night on 21 November 1989. On this kind of approach the pilot has to engage two radio signals, the glideslope and the localiser. The glideslope tells the pilot where he should be on the horizontal axis, and the localiser on the vertical. Stewart evidently had trouble getting the aircraft correctly aligned, but instead of executing a missed approach, that is going around and trying again, he persisted, taking the aircraft to just seventy-five feet above the ground and just a few feet from the roof of the airport's Penta Hotel. At that point he did go around and landed safely on the second attempt. Some 255 people were on board the flight from Australia.[6]

Another pilot, who wishes to remain anonymous but is familiar with the case and with Captain Stewart, did not pretend that Stewart had not made a mistake, but added that there were mitigating circumstances. He said, "People think that ILS landings are easy, but they are not. It can be very tricky to get everything correctly aligned. There is a special checklist to follow for it, that varies slightly according to the different version of 747 that you are flying. It is possible, especially when you are tired, to get confused about which checklist you're working from, and the different sequence in which things have to be done."

This, he believes, is what happened to Captain Stewart. He had been flying for over seven hours and made a mistake due to fatigue. But there was also another factor present, my source told me. The rules state that both pilots must be qualified for ILS landings. In this case, however, the co-pilot was not so qualified, but he had been given a special dispensation by BA to operate the flight with Captain Stewart.

Unusually for the UK, the matter was investigated by the CAA itself, since the AAIB was wholly taken up with the investigation into the Lockerbie disaster. Captain Stewart, who had, undoubtedly, committed a serious error, had already resigned from BA, but the CAA decided to prosecute him and in May 1991 he was convicted of "negligently endangering" his aircraft and the passengers. He lost his captain's qualification on the 747 and was fined £2000.

The pilot familiar with Captain Stewart adds, "Being prosecuted by the CAA really pushed him over the edge." Rumour has it that Captain Stewart had other personal problems as well, and he slipped into a serious depression. In November 1992 he committed suicide. Pilots had no doubt that, however much he may have erred, Captain Stewart had been victimised and while he ended up facing criminal prosecution, the airline was not criticised for permitting the flight to proceed on such a long sector with a co-pilot unqualified for ILS landings. For a period after Captain Stewart's prosecution, many pilots acted with hostility towards CAA personnel and flight inspectors, frequently refusing them the right to inspect their flights, or not allowing them passage on the jumpseat, the extra seat in the cockpit reserved for inspectors and other non-flying personnel.

Given the fact that a pilot error is usually only one part of a confluence of events in an accident, many experts prefer to use the term "pilot action". If the error is the kind that 90 per cent of all pilots would make in similar circumstances then it is surely misleading to call it an error. At this juncture, opinion tends to diverge into two schools of thought: one says blame or negligence is an important concept legally and helps prevent people ducking their responsibilities. The other school says that assigning blame gets in the way of identifying the true sequence of accident causation and thus preventing repetitions.

Some pilots nevertheless believe that blaming the pilot is the default option in an air-crash investigation. I have heard that allegation made against the NTSB in the United States as well as, separately, the opposite charge that the NTSB is so beholden to the US airline pilots' trade union that it does not dare blame pilots. Both charges are wrong, but where there is uncertainty the pilots may attract blame on the simple basis that, whether or not they erred, they were responsible for the aircraft. One study said that pilots who died in their aircraft were statistically more likely to be blamed than those who survived.

The attaching of blame to pilots can be the result of pressures brought about by the legal system, the American one in particular. A fascinating account of how strict legal responsibility and fault-finding can obscure the reasons for a crash rather than bring them to light was given by pilot and author Laurie Taylor. He quoted the misgivings of airline pilot Captain Dale Leppard, an accident investigator with the US pilots' trade union, the ALPA.

A few years ago, an aircraft crashed in the fog during a non-instrument approach. The co-pilot survived. He testified under oath that he misread the altimeter by 1000 feet. Why? Nobody asked. Why didn't the captain catch the fatal error? His life literally depended on it. Nobody asked why. Why weren't these vital questions asked and answered? Because the Cockpit Voice Recorder revealed some extemporaneous conversation by the flight-crew several minutes before the accident. From the moment the CVR was read out, the probable cause became crew inattention, and we lost an opportunity to correct an altimeter known to be subject to 1000-feet misreads, and which the [US] Air Force rejected as inadequate over twenty years ago.

He went on to point out that if the twenty minutes of tape previous to the ten minutes that were published had also been revealed, it would have shown the captain's extreme fatigue, including the comment, "I'm so tired. I can't wait to get to the hotel so I can rest." Captain Leppard went on:

> *So, we also lost an opportunity to study fatigue and scheduling rules. Here the CVR performed a function opposite to its intended purpose in that it caused the investigation to be suppressed. Of course the crew made mistakes – fatal ones – but we never really explored why, and thus our primary mission of accident prevention was denied.*[7]

Captain Leppard had clearly identified the disturbing influence of the perceived legalities on the investigators. Equally insidious was the presence of evidence from one quarter – the CVR – apparently precluding investigation in other areas. However, none of this excuses investigators from not taking a multiplicity of factors into account when determining what happened.

The cockpit voice recorder has always been at least slightly suspected by pilots, especially Australians who, until a strike in 1989, had an extremely powerful trade union. They were very upset when Mr Justice Spicer decreed the CVR into existence in the course of his inquiry into Australia's worst air crash, the destruction of a Fokker-F27 in June 1960, in which twenty-five people died. A highly experienced crew had been in a "hold" in fog while waiting to land when the plane crashed into the water. Little added up in the investigation, and no satisfactory reasons for the crash were established. The judge had thought that having CVRs would reduce the possibility of any crashes this mysterious happening again.

He ordered the CVRs to be operational on Australian-registered large passenger aircraft by the beginning of 1963, making Australia the first country in the world to do so. It was a widely admired initiative from a nation generally regarded as having one of the strongest safety cultures in the world. Australia was the first country to make seat-belt use compulsory in cars and to permit the random breath-testing of motorists.[8] In most of the rest of the world, pilot opposition to CVRs was not that great, because the main battle had already been fought over the introduction of flight data recorders.

But in Australia the pilots fought the CVR tooth and nail, holding it to be a spy in the cockpit and a slur on the airmen's professionalism. In the end, the union was able to negotiate an agreement with the authorities that CVRs would only be used when investigating fatal accidents.[9] For a country whose safety culture is so admired, this was a retrograde step. Events which had come within a whisker of claiming dozens or hundreds of lives could not be properly investigated, at least from the point of view of the actions of the crew.

This was illustrated on the night of 29 January 1971 at Sydney airport. A Canadian Pacific DC-8 had just landed and been ordered by the tower to take a certain taxiway off the runway. Instead of doing so, however, the pilots turned the aircraft around and started to taxi. Meanwhile, an Ansett Boeing 727 had been cleared for take-off on an intersecting runway. The 727 saw the DC-8 ahead at the intersection while on its take-off roll, continued to gather speed and took off. The belly of the 727 was slit by the fin of the DC-8, damaging part of the hydraulic system. Fortunately, no other critical controls were affected and after dumping fuel the 727 landed without further incident.

It was an extremely near thing, but the Australian pilots' union was absolutely unbending and would not permit the CVR on the Ansett plane to be examined because nobody had been killed. The investigators nevertheless obtained a copy of the CVR and listened to it on the quiet, although they could not base any formal conclusions on it. The investigators knew that the pilot of the 727 had had enough time to abort the take-off but could not say so.

The investigators' luck changed when they heard the audio-tape of air traffic control. The 727 pilot had been using an intercom to talk to his co-pilot, a common practice, especially in noisy aircraft.

Instead of pushing the intercom button he had pushed the "transmit" button on the air traffic control frequency. He was heard to say, "How far ahead is he?" When correlated against the time, this showed that he had had enough time to abort the take-off.[10] Since his statement had been recorded on the audio-tape of the tower it was admissible in the investigators' report and could be used for disciplinary action.

Despite the Australian practice in this department being uncharacteristically "unsafe" it remains in full force. If Captain Leppard was justly concerned at investigators stopping at "pilot error" and going no further, this incident illustrated the problem of going too far in the other direction. Pilots and their representatives are continually on the alert for efforts to heap unjustified blame on them, especially when they are not there to answer back.

When a Lauda Air 767 crashed in Thailand in 1991, it soon became clear that a thrust-reverser had deployed in mid-air, causing the disaster. From Boeing, however, came hints that it must have been the pilots who had inadvertently done it. And if not, then they had failed in their duty by not recovering a rectifiable problem (see Chapter 9 for a full account of the crash).

It emerged only much later after detailed analysis that the thrust-reverse had not been commanded by the pilots and that it would have been virtually impossible for them to recover once it had. Since that information came out many months later, the blame had already stuck.

Similarly, Boeing was saying, albeit not in public, that pilot input was responsible for the crash of a USAir Boeing 737 near Pittsburgh on 8 September 1994. This was to prove an extremely controversial crash since, up to now, it remains one of an extremely small number of unsolved crashes. The investigation into it threw up all sorts of potential scenarios for what had happened.

The bare facts were that the aircraft was at about 6000 feet on its approach into Pittsburgh airport when, without warning, it suddenly rolled to the left on to its back and then nose-dived into the ground, the pilots' attempts to recover notwithstanding. The aircraft and its 132 occupants were smashed into tiny pieces in a

The Tombstone Imperative at work. Although it had failed disastrously before, urgent action to fix the DC-10's rear cargo door (in normal operation below) did not come until it was implicated in one of the world's worst air crashes. Above: Gendarmes picking through the wreckage of the Turkish DC-10, which crashed north of Paris in March 1974, killing all on board.

The industry has done a lot to prevent fires breaking out, but virtually nothing to cope with their effects, especially toxic fumes. The 1980 fire on a Saudi Tristar (above) was one of the worst, claiming 301 lives. Note how in all these fires heat is concentrated at the top, burning through the roof. In the Air Canada DC-9 (below) which caught fire in the air in 1983 and landed at Cincinnati, survivors lay on the floor clutching wet cloth to their faces before landing. However, this lesson did not translate into practical measures to protect passengers from the poisons generated by typical aircraft cabin fires.

After the 1985 Manchester Airport disaster (above), the CAA's own research showed wider access to the exits was necessary. The regulations remain unchanged. Toxic smoke also claimed many of the lives lost during the collision (below) of a USAir 737 with a Skywest commuter aircraft (invisible beneath the much larger 737) at Los Angeles Airport in 1991. Mandatory smoke-hoods are still a distant prospect.

Explosive decompressions inside aircraft ought not to be catastrophic but often are. In the world worst ever single air crash, of a JAL 747 in Japan in August 1985, killing 520 (above), such a decompression blew out the hydraulic lines and much of the tailfin. The Boeing 747's cargo do have been prone to similar problems to those of the DC-10's. In 1989 a United 747's front cargo blew open, expelling nine passengers and stopping the two engines on the right wing. Skilful pilo and a lot of luck brought the aircraft back without further deaths.

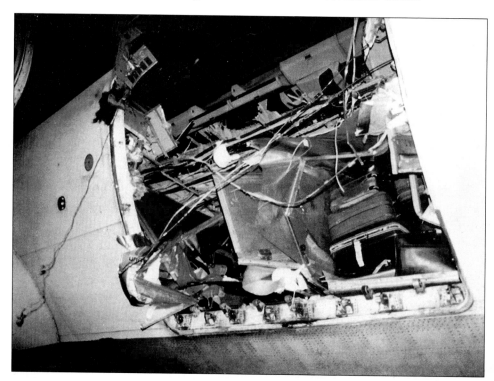

ety margins are narrower than they should be, and many aircraft and systems are highly intolerant error. In freezing rain the ATR-72 (above) has to be handled very precisely. Failure to do so can, has, caused fatal crashes. A series of errors resulted in this 737 ploughing off the end of the La rdia runway in New York in 1989 (below). If it had been one of the much longer runways typical of most airports the disaster probably wouldn't have occurred.

Highly computerised aircraft can crash in ways unknown to their more primitive forebears. Thi Airbus A330 (above), painted in the client's livery but still under test, claimed the lives of seve company officials, including the chief test-pilot, when he failed to account for a subtle feature of flight control software. The pilots claimed not even to be aware of computerised engine control which were a factor in this non-fatal crash of an SAS MD-80 near Stockholm (below) in 1991.

The crash of a Korean Airlines' 747 at Guam in August 1997 (above) seemed to confirm that airline's poor safety record, as well as underlining the ubiquity of Controlled Flight Into Terrain, i.e. flying into ground you didn't know was there. Guam threw up questions of crashworthiness, too, which was the major safety issue to arise out of the January 1989 Kegworth crash (below).

Rescuers removing one of the survivors from the wreckage of the Korean 747 at Guam. Many of survivors had been travelling in the "hump" behind the 747 cockpit, meaning that much of the aircraft in front and below them acted as a kind of crumple zone. Jean-Noel Chatre, seen below be carried off the French mountain which the Airbus A320 he was flying on hit in January 1992, survived, burned and terribly injured, despite having to wait four-and-a-half hours to be rescued

small wooded valley. Barely a single recognisable piece of aircraft or occupants remained.

The woefully inadequate flight data recorder gave no clues to what had happened. One theory that had to be tested at great expense before it was discarded was that the wake vortex of a preceding Boeing 727 might have caused the upset. The 727 was too far away, the weather conditions were not right, and 727s are simply not heavy enough to cause problems for a 737.

After various other scenarios were considered the investigators' best guess remained that for some unknown reason the rudder had swung suddenly to the left as far as it could go. Changes to the hydraulic servo units that power the 737's rudder have now been instituted, as well as limiters preventing it from swinging too far in either direction.

Misbehaviour by the rudder, however, has not been determined as the definite cause. Quite apart from some uncertainty about the precise mechanism of the crash, the evidence – from eye-witnesses, an aircraft following behind and from the CVR and FDR – does not support that conclusion to a legal standard of proof.

However, the implication that Boeing's engineering could have been at fault, inherent in the idea of the "rudder hardover" theory, was a ghastly prospect for the company. At that time about 2700 737s had entered service, it was the most numerous jet airliner in the world, and it had an above-average safety record. If Boeing's design or manufacturing methods were found to be at fault the financial implications of bearing all the cost of compensation and of modifications to the fleet would have been horrendous, not to mention the effect on the company's prestige.

It was in such an atmosphere that Boeing floated the idea that the pilots might have been at fault; that, somehow, they had crashed the plane, if not deliberately, then as a result of some kind of momentary aberration. A *Seattle Times* reporter, Byron Acohido, uncovered the allegations that Boeing was making against the pilots. In the course of a meeting with the NTSB in Washington in March 1995, Boeing presented a thick file of papers on pilot error, including psychological studies on why pilots make mistakes.

At Boeing's request the NTSB investigators formed a committee on "human performance" and during the meetings that followed a Boeing psychologist and a Boeing test-pilot put forward the idea that one of the pilots must have not only depressed the rudder pedal all the way to the floor, thus causing the rudder to swing over to the left, but must have kept his foot there. Perhaps, the Boeing psychologist ventured, the pilot was reverting to an early childhood memory involving use of the left foot. Or maybe he had suffered a seizure.

The meetings continued and in January 1996 the two Boeing representatives on the committee presented a twenty-five-page paper outlining an argument that the aircraft could not have been responsible for what happened, and it must have been the pilots. The other members of the human performance committee and the rest of the investigating team were so horrified that the paper was rejected out of hand for inclusion in the final "human factors" report.[11]

Some of the most illuminating efforts to try to find out why pilots err have, simply, analysed what kind of mistakes are made and when. One of the most important of these was a special study by the US NTSB of crashes in which flight-crew errors were cited as primary or contributive causes. They selected thirty-seven accidents of US jet transports between 1978 and 1990 and classified various features of the accidents. The sample was not very large, but there were various important findings, some of which surprised the investigators.[12]

The most intriguing discovery in the NTSB study was that in 80 per cent of the accidents the captain had been flying the aircraft. Captains and first officers usually share flying duties, with the non-flying pilot managing radio communications as well as monitoring the instruments and the actions of the pilot flying.

The NTSB was unable to correlate this finding with any other data or to draw any conclusions from it. There was nothing in the crews' general experience, level of fatigue, familiarity with each other, or other reasons why the captains should have taken the lion's share of the prangs.

The NTSB found that the commonest kind of error a captain

made was one of omission, and the commonest of those was the failure to declare a missed approach, or to "go-around", where the pilot abandons the landing in progress and goes around to try again. Correspondingly, the commonest error of the first officers noted by the NTSB was failure to monitor the pilot's flying, and pick up on the error of his colleague.

It is tempting to venture, however unscientific it may be to do so, that it is easier for a captain to contradict a co-pilot than the other way around. In the KLM cockpit at Tenerife a co-pilot contradicted his captain and was rewarded with a testy answer. He and the flight engineer failed to overrule the captain again and disaster followed. The way seniority can get in the way of open communications is sometimes called the "flight-deck gradient".

Other NTSB findings included the fact that 55 per cent of the accident aircraft were running late, compared with between 17 and 35 per cent of non-accident aircraft. This seemed to confirm the dangers of the "hurry-up syndrome" and put a hard figure to the anecdotal evidence of pilots worrying about safety being compromised by operational pressures. Cali, Tenerife, the Airbus crash at Strasbourg in 1992 (discussed Chapter 6), and dozens of other crashes have seen these kinds of pressures affecting the judgement of pilots. Indeed, some pilots consider their ability to balance the demands of the company with the safety, of operation as their biggest professional challenge. Despite the evidence that such pressures compromise safety, there are still airlines which punish pilots who divert to other airports, refuse to take off or otherwise cite safety reasons for deviating from the schedule.

Many pressures on safety, for example, flow from operations that are being ruthless on costs, like ValuJet, the "no-frills" airline which lost a DC-9 in May 1996 in the Florida Everglades, with 110 dead, owing to dangerous cargo being mistakenly loaded. ValuJet has since acquired another airline, AirTran, and now operates all its aircraft in Air Tran's less controversial livery.

In the study the NTSB also found a correlation between the likelihood of an accident and the degree of familiarity that existed between the pilots, since a significant proportion of accidents happened during the pilots' first day of duty together, several happening on their first flight. In other words, the better the pilots knew each other, the safer the flight. The investigators also found that a significant number of the accident flights were flown by pilots who had been awake longer than twelve hours. Another factor was the time of day. Flights after midnight were prone to danger, but the two "low spots" of human alertness, the late afternoon and between three and four in the morning, were also shown to be significant.

The NTSB's findings highlighted the importance of two aspects of preventing pilot error. One has been the relatively recent inclusion of "management factors" in accident investigation. Now a firm part of every NTSB investigation, this aspect of the inquiry into a crash examines operational pressures on the pilots in question, and probes pilot morale, management relations with aircrew and, above all, the "safety culture" of the airline.

More critical was the emphasis on cockpit resource management (CRM), which came to prominence in the wake of the Tenerife disaster and was in the early stages of development into a full-blown aviation discipline at the time (see Chapter 1). It may sound like a work-creation project for people with fashionable theories, but there is more to it than that. For one thing, the NTSB study indicated that, much as making sure pilots are not too tired was very important, a good working relationship between the two pilots was even more crucial.

CRM has been defined by the veteran air-safety analyst John Lauber as "the effective utilisation and management of all resources – information, equipment and people – to achieve safe and efficient flight operations". This definition is broader than pilot and co-pilot relations because more than two people are involved in "keeping the pointy end forward and the shiny side up". At Kegworth, the cabin staff were clearly wanting in CRM training, since they failed to draw attention to the fact that the engine the captain was shutting down was not the one on fire. Cabin staff are vital in the preparation of the cabin for a crash, and communications between them and the flight-deck are essential. CRM also involves air traffic control. Nonetheless, the normal definition of CRM is "make the captain listen and the co-pilot speak up".

The best example of CRM saving lives was the United Airlines DC-10 flight in July 1989, which ended at Sioux City airport with only 112 of the 296 on board perishing, despite there being an extremely violent crash. Captain Al Haynes co-operated closely with the cabin staff in preparing them for the crash landing, and supervised a more or less collective endeavour in the cockpit. He even accepted an offer of help from Denny Fitch, a United DC-10 instructor who had been travelling as a passenger. Fitch worked the stricken aircraft's throttles.[13] There can be no member of the piloting community who has not heard of the UA-232 crash at Sioux City, and the forty-one minutes of improvisation and ingenuity that preceded it. Captain Haynes has been lecturing on it ever since and the near miraculous survival of so many people is generally attributed to the collaborative skills of him and his crew.

They faced an unprecedented situation and coped with it. There was no known procedure for dealing with their emergency – total loss of all hydraulics – because such a situation was assumed to be too improbable to be worth guarding against. The pilots on the flight-deck eventually worked out that the plane could be controlled to some extent by differential thrust, i.e. altering the thrust on the right and left engines to make the plane move left and right, and reducing and increasing thrust to iron out oscillations and to lose height.

A flavour of the extraordinary combination of skill and luck that the United flight-deck crew had that day is given in Captain Al Haynes's own account.

> We had no ailerons to bank the airplane, we had no rudder to turn it in, no elevators to control the pitch, we had no leading-edge flaps or slats to slow the airplane down, no trailing-edge flaps for landing, we had no spoilers on the wing, to help us get down, or help us slow down, once we were on the ground. And on the ground, we had no steering, nose wheel or tail, and no brakes.
>
> So what we had . . . was the throttles on Number 1 [left] and

Number 3 [right] engine to control us. And by manipulating those throttles, we were able somewhat to control the heading, by skidding the airplane into a turn. And controlling the pitch was just about out of the question. We kept saying we think we have the elevators under control. We never had the elevators under control. We thought we did, but we didn't . . .

So you see, with those two things to work with – two engines – just getting the airplane on the ground was a tremendous piece of luck. Amazing. Because it has been tried again, and it didn't work. Everything had to work in the right sequence, and it happened to work, so we got the airplane, at least, to an airport . . .

The preparation: how do you prepare for something like this? I gave a talk at Anchorage to the Alaska Air Safety Foundation and they subtitled my talk: "Disaster in the air, are you ready?" No, you're never ready. But you might be prepared . . .

As for the crew, there was no training procedure for hydraulic failure. Complete hydraulic failure. We've all been through one failure or double failures, but never a complete hydraulic failure.

. . . Not having any experience at all in flying an airplane under those conditions, our basic problem was keeping the airplane in the sky and trying to find an airport. Besides losing all of our hydraulics, which gave us no control, we had . . . a problem that I was not really familiar with . . . a term called "phugoid" . . . [A]s soon as you cut power on one engine, you lose speed, the nose drops, airspeed starts to build, you'll go through that speed, the nose will come back up, you'll go through the speed again on the slow side, and you'll just oscillate like this. Maybe you can stop it, maybe you can't.

We found out the way you have to stop it. Not as much as we know now, a lot of this is after-the-fact knowledge, we weren't this smart in the air. But we found that in order to stop a phugoid, you had to do the opposite of what you would normally do. When the aircraft reached its apex and started down, you had to add power . . . to create lift in the wings to get the nose to pitch up. The hardest thing to do though was, as the nose started up and started to slow down, and you're approaching a stall, you'd have to close the throttles. And that's very difficult to do. We found out, though, that's what we had to do.

. . . Another thing that added to our problem, though, was that the damage to the tail was such that the aircraft constantly wanted to roll to the right. If we left the power alone, the aircraft would roll over.

. . . We immediately determined that we could not control the airplane: it wouldn't respond to the inputs of the crew. At this time, we were in a right bank, the bank was increasing, we were up to 38 degrees of bank, we closed the Number 1 throttle completely, and firewalled the Number 3 throttle, and very slowly the wing came back up. And three times on our attempt to get to the ground, we got to 38 degrees of bank, and we were . . . overpowering the airplane, over-controlling because panic was one thing, although we didn't appear to be panicked; not having any idea what we were doing was another, and an airplane about to roll on to its back at 35,000 feet is pretty scary, so you just do anything you can to make it stop. But by manipulating the throttles this way we kept the wings fairly level – for a while. Then we had to start down.

. . . Well, we felt – like everyone else – that this cannot happen – you cannot lose all the hydraulics in a [DC-]10. That's been told us . . . "It can't happen, – you just can't lose your hydraulics". And we believed it like everybody else. And now while we were reasonably sure we weren't accomplishing anything with the yoke, we kept flying the yoke . . .

To let go of the yoke completely is extremely difficult to do. After almost forty years of flying airplanes and holding on to something, not having something to hold on to – I don't know if we could do that. But what we found out is that it was very difficult to move the throttles. We were told there was a DC-10 captain in the back, who was an instructor, and we like to think instructors know more than we do – so I figured maybe Denny knew something that we didn't, so we asked Captain Fitch to come up. Well, he took one look at the cockpit, and that's his knowledge. It was sort of reading the transcript [of the CVR], because he's about fifteen minutes behind us now, and he's trying to catch up, and everything he says to do we've already done. And after about five minutes – that's twenty minutes into this operation – he says, "We're in trouble!" We thought: "That's an amazing observation, Denny."

. . . He says, "Now, what can I do?" I said, you can take these throttles, and try to help us with the throttles. So what he did, he stood between us – not kneeling on the floor, as the news media said – and he took one throttle in each hand, and now he could manipulate the throttles together. With the Number 2 [the tail engine] throttle frozen, we couldn't get hold of the throttles together. Now he could. As we said, "Give us a right bank, bring the wing up, that's too much bank, try to stop the altitude," he'd try to respond. And after a few minutes of doing this, everything we'd do with the yoke, he could correspond with the throttles. So it was a synchronised thing between the three of us . . . So that's how we operated the airplane, and that's how we got it on the ground. . . .

. . . [The tower] did tell us how long it [the runway] was, 6600 feet, and then he said at the end was a wide-open field. So our scenario was: probably what we do is land, and hopefully stay on our [landing] gear, go off the end of the runway, shear our gear, and go on our belly. If we did go sideways, since we couldn't steer it, and we did have a quartering tail-wind that was turning us left to right across the runway, we might go off into the field and shear it en route. We kind of hoped we would do that.

We came pretty close to the runway. We got the right wing tip in the centre of the runway, the right main gear off to the side. We touched down on the right wing tip, the wing flap fairing, the Number 3 engine, the one on the right side, the right wing gear, and the nose wheel, all pretty much simultaneously. The right wing broke off – that's the reason for the fire here, spilling all the fuel. The right main gear separated from the airplane. The left gear stayed on. And the airplane slammed on the ground, and we did not hit and cartwheel, like all the news says. We hit and slid on the ground, on the left main gear and the right wing stub. Slid along sideways, for about 2000 feet or so, when the left wing came up.

Also, on impact, the tail broke off, the entire tail section of the aircraft broke off, so there's no weight in the tail at all. So when the left wing came up – probably because of our speed – the tail came up. The aircraft went up on its nose, bounced on the runway three times, on the nose, leaving . . . marks on the runway. We went upside-down and airborne . . . There was so much fire and smoke . . . We hit . . . upside-down. And, fortunately for us, the cockpit broke off, and unfortunately for the first-class cabin. And then the aircraft went over on its back and skidded to a halt . . .

You normally land the DC-10 at approximately 140 knots. We were doing 215 knots and accelerating. You normally touch down at about 200–300 feet per minute at the most, as a rate of descent. We were doing 1850 feet per minute. And increasing. And you normally like to go straight down the runway, and we were drifting left and right because of the quartering tail-wind of ten knots, which gave us ten knots more of speed, as we hit the ground.

But that picture [of us] in the air is very deceiving. It looks like we have everything pretty much in control. We were starting a down phugoid, and starting a right bank, 300 feet in the air. And . . . that's where our luck ran out. We just ran out of altitude, trying to correct it. We had the time in the air, trying to correct it. But that close to the ground, we didn't have time. In an attempt to stop the phugoid and the turn, Dennis added power, and unfortunately the left engine spooled up faster than the right, the first time in the day we noticed that it happened, and the bank increased. And in four seconds we went from 4 degrees of right bank, to 20 degrees of right bank, and hit the ground.

However, safety experts say the tumbling of the aircraft probably saved a lot of lives. It took up most of the inertia, most of the shock, and allowed the people to get out of the airplane. As soon as we hit the ground, I went out. I have

absolutely no recollection of anything from the time we hit the
ground until I came to in the cockpit. Trying to figure out
where I was. And then we had some conversation, and then the
operation started, and I was in and out throughout the whole
thing. I remember parts of the rescue, I remember parts of the
ambulance ride. I don't remember the ride into town at all.[15]

Many pilots have commented on the difference here between the
team-based, problem-solving approach of this United crew and
the JAL crew that was flying the 747 that lost all its hydraulic
power over the Japanese mountains in August 1985. In the
newsletters and Internet forums to which many pilots contribute,
the Japanese crew has been criticised for not using differential
thrust on its four engines – as opposed to the two the United crew
had available – to gain greater control of the aircraft and steer it
to an airport. They were in the air for approximately the same
length of time.

This is probably unfair criticism. The unfortunate Japanese 747
crew had no inkling of how to control the jet with differential
thrust, and such techniques were not even attempted until after
the crash which claimed their lives.[16]

Nevertheless, especially given the international nature of civil
aviation, cultural differences between pilots of different national-
ities have been closely analysed. The airlines for the Far East, in
particular, employ many expatriates from Britain, the United
States, Australia and Canada, and they will often be flying with
Koreans, Japanese, Malaysians, Chinese and others. The cultures
are very different and express themselves in the cockpit. Put
broadly and crudely, Japanese people, for example, tend to think
of themselves as part of a collective and also as occupying a very
specific place within a defined hierarchy of power. Westerners,
Americans and Australians in particular, have a more individual-
istic image of themselves and a more egalitarian outlook. Put the
two cultures together in a cockpit and you could well experience
significant problems. Certainly, teachers of CRM to Asian airlines
found that their idea of CRM was highly culture-specific, and that
many of the peoples of the Far East were uncomfortable with the

idea of interfering with a superior's prerogative.[17]

Several observers who know both piloting cultures criticise the Far Eastern-origin pilots as being unwilling to disagree with the captain when in a subordinate role, for being too rigid in their attitudes when in command. The kind of skill in improvisation that a pilot may need to employ in a crisis comes much more easily to an American or Australian, they say, than to a Korean or Japanese pilot. Too much, however, can be made of this. While the improvisational skills of Americans and Australians may well be superior, it could be countered that the conformity of the Far Eastern individual means that he is possibly less likely to be in need of improvisational skills. Piloting modern passenger jets involves barely, if ever, seat-of-the-pants extemporising. "Going strictly by the book" could well be a more useful quality to have in a pilot.

As if to support this, the NTSB study of cockpit errors found a large number of faults were made in the reading of checklists. This kind of error, it would seem, is less likely among highly conformist individuals. The legendary meticulousness of Japanese quality control in manufacturing, so well known from the car industry, for example, is evident in that country's aircraft-maintenance skills too. It could well be that the relative cultural weaknesses of each society are cancelled out by their different strengths. While there are statistical differences between the relative safety of Asian as opposed to US carriers, none of these can reliably be narrowed down to differences in cockpit styles.

Equally important to safety have been airline "cultures". The Dryden Commission was a ground-breaking Canadian inquiry into the crash of a Fokker F-28 in Dryden, Ontario, in March 1989. Twenty-four were killed, including both pilots, and forty-four survived when the ice-contaminated plane crashed on take-off. The commission took in an unusually wide number of factors into account, not least of which was the fact that there were no hard and fast national rules, or aircraft operators' rules, for when the F-28 should be de-iced.

Something judged extremely important in this crash was that the pilots had come from very different airlines, one a major scheduled carrier, the other flying smaller planes on short routes.

After the merger of the two airlines, there was much resentment among the "airline-type" group of pilots at the domination of flight operations by the "bush-pilot" types. This also translated itself into the cockpit, where each set of pilots had a different way of doing things. Such difficulties, the commission said, could well have influenced the crew's decision to take off regardless of the snow and ice on the plane.[18]

It also pointed out that poor morale after industrial disputes can affect safety considerably. This was thought to be an important factor in the crash of a BEA Trident at Staines, just after take-off from Heathrow on 18 June 1972. The captain of that flight was heard having what a witness described as the most violent argument he had ever heard in the airline offices just before taking command of his aircraft. The subject was industrial action then in progress which had pitted senior pilots like him against junior officers of the sort that accompanied him that day.[19]

There are still many pilots, though, who think of CRM as Californian psycho-babble – those who say, only half-jokingly, that CRM really means "cockpit run by me". Another version is: "This is the Cockpit, you are the Resource, I am the Manager." It is not just a question of training pilots to love and understand each other, with hugs all round. Quite apart from the fact that most pilots are not the hugging type, it misses the point. Being too relaxed and casual can be just as dangerous as being at daggers drawn.

John Lauber drew attention to the fact that leadership skills are vital in the cockpit, and that CRM ought not simply to be a matter of getting people to like each other.

I do not care whether people like each other or not. They can fly together very safely even without liking each other. It is possible to develop effective leadership skills on the part of individuals. Leaders can be effective in terms of setting the tone, of inviting assertiveness on the part of the subordinate crew members and yet retaining command and the responsibility that goes along with command in the cockpit.[20]

Bad air days

Crashes always involve a seeming conspiracy of disparate
elements that may be innocent enough when present alone but
make a fatal cocktail when mixed. If one puts together the NTSB
research on pilot errors and combines it with the cross-cultural
information one can construct a set of circumstances most
conducive to having a crash. Take two pilots who don't know
each other and have been awake for more than twelve hours.
Have an Australian captain with a Korean first officer, who
crossed a picket line in a recent strike which was honoured by the
captain. Have them trained by different airlines on the same
aircraft type. Make sure the captain is flying, and that the flight is
late. Add a departure time in the late afternoon, stir in bad
weather and a full load, and *voilà*.

Fatigue

On 18 August 1993 the three-man crew of a Douglas DC-8 cargo
plane flying into the US naval base of Guantánamo Bay, Cuba,
met several of these criteria.[21] Cargo aircraft are not normally any
more dangerous than passenger aircraft, although they are almost
invariably much older, and are usually flown during the night.
Unfortunately, they do not normally attract the same publicity as
passenger aircraft when they crash, even though they are of
similar designs and could well have lessons to offer operators of
the same planes.

They also occupy air space, are equally capable of having a
collision with another aircraft, and can kill people on the ground
as easily as any airliner. The El Al Boeing 747 that killed so many
people in the Amsterdam tower blocks in 1992 was a cargo plane,
after all, as was the Russian aircraft that collided with the Saudi
747 over India in 1996, not to mention the other Russian aircraft
that crashed into an apartment block in Irkutsk in December
1997. The operational pressures, too, are not very different from
those affecting the pilots of commercial air carriers.

The old DC-8 at Guantánamo Bay had, like most air freighters, been retired from revenue passenger service and been converted into a cargo-carrier.[22] Flying it were two pilots and a flight engineer, all known to be highly competent professionals. However, it was the co-pilot's first time working with the captain. It was his first flight into this airport since his service with the US Navy in small jets many years beforehand, and the captain had never landed there before.[23]

Neither pilot had received special training or information on the Cuban airfield, which poses exceptional difficulties. With hindsight, it was obviously a bad choice, but the captain decided not to land on the runway they planned to use, but the more challenging alternative runway. Only three-quarters of a mile from the threshold of this runway lies the fence separating the US base from Cuban territory which no aircraft may stray over. To get an aircraft, especially a fully loaded large one like a DC-8, on to that runway necessitates an extremely sharp turn to the right, with the wings coming level again only when the plane is right over the end of the runway.

The NTSB did not consider it probable that any pilot landing there for the first time could have completed the landing successfully. Compounding the difficulty the captain of the DC-8 had set himself was the fact that he had been on duty for eighteen hours, nine of which he had been flying, and awake for nearly twenty-four. The co-pilot and flight engineer were only slightly better rested. Also, the arrival, at nearly five in the afternoon, fell in one of the two periods in the day in which alertness is at its minimum and which was identified by the NTSB study as particularly error-rich.

The captain turned the plane into the bank to line up with the runway, lost sight of it, allowed his speed to slow and, despite warnings from the other members of the crew, persisted with the approach. The plane banked too far, stalled and smashed into the ground, hitting it with wing and nose first before spreading itself and a fire over a wide area.[24] The crew were extremely lucky because the nose section sheared off the fuselage on impact and was not affected by the post-crash fire. They suffered serious injuries but were able to assist in the investigation of the crash, making the event unique in several ways. Because they were alive to give testimony, they could speak of their fatigue, rather than have others speculate about it. Tiredness cannot be identified during autopsies.

The captain said, "I remember looking over at him [the co-pilot], and there again, I remember being very lethargic about it or indifferent. I don't recall asking him or questioning anybody. I don't recall the engineer talking about the air speeds at all. So it's very frustrating and disconcerting at night to try to lay there and think of how this – you know – how you could be so lethargic when so many things were going on, but that's just the way it was."

Statements like that helped the NTSB conclude that it was fatigue that had affected his judgement in making several bad decisions, like opting for the more difficult runway, ignoring the warnings of the crew, failing to increase power when a stall was imminent, failing to go-around, and so on.

There was one other item from the NTSB checklist of factors most conducive to pilot error: bad industrial relations. The flight-crews at American International Airways had just voted to join a trade union, having previously had no representation.

The operational pressures also became fully evident in the accident report. American International Airways was found to be an airline which did as much as it needed to "stay legal" but no more, and where a "lean management" philosophy prevailed. Individual managers had vast ranges of responsibility, all of which they had little hope of covering adequately. The FAA found it difficult to police the airline because it was short of staff and funds, and AIA's base was very remote. Where it was able to carry out inspections it found several violations of the rules, and a general reluctance on the part of management to correct them.

The NTSB interviewed the chief executive of AIA. "He said", the NTSB report recounted, "that in order to remain competitive, the company must often assign long duty times and `work every-thing right to the edge of what was allowed by federal regulations. He indicated that this practice was 'common' in the air freight industry." Furthermore, the AIA contract with the US Navy specified financial penalties if too many cargo flights were late departing the base at Norfolk, Virginia.

The pilots themselves had said that in discussing the assignment they got that day they thought it was "pushing the edge" in terms of duty and flight time, but they knew it was legal and so did not complain. The co-pilot told the NTSB that "you better really be tired" to refuse to fly.

After the crash ex-AIA pilots contacted the NTSB complaining of long duty time, flight hours and safety violations. One pilot said he had been intimidated by company managers for cancelling a flight for reasons of fatigue. And yet, incredibly, if the crew of that DC-8 had overcome their fatigue and landed successfully at Guantánamo Bay, they would have been expected to fly the empty aircraft back to Atlanta straight after unloading. There was a loophole in the US aviation regulations permitting "ferry flights", whereby the aircraft is just being flown to be positioned at the right airport, not to be counted when calculating maximum crew duty hours.

The NTSB report noted that only the United States and France, for different reasons, calculate flight time and duty time for aircrew as separate. Other countries have the more sensible approach of considering time on duty as just that. Common sense would seem to indicate that when assessing how tired you are, it is how long you have been awake and working that counts, not whether the work has been on the ground or in the air.

Lest anyone should believe that these problems are confined to cargo operators, increasing complaints are being received from pilots on passenger operations who are being pressured to train less and fly more. One pilot who reported his woes to the UK's CHIRP said: "I am becoming increasingly concerned that pressure to improve business efficiency is seriously eroding the long-term safety of the operation." The airline was short of crews and as a result: "Whilst remaining (just) within the letter of the law, the company is operating well beyond the spirit of it by exposing its crews to a risk of long-term fatigue."

Another pilot reported to CHIRP where this could lead: "The

flight departed at around 2200. During cruise, four hours into flight, first officer asked captain if he could take a nap. This he did. Whilst this was happening the captain fell asleep. This lasted on and off during the flight for approximately half an hour, [the aircraft] passing and turning over various waypoints during this time." Cruise is the safest part of a flight and the flight management system was evidently handling the plane fine, but it must have been alarming to both crew members to wake up and realise that the other was asleep at the same time. It is not the kind of thing to raise the morale of passengers very much either, should they get to hear about it.[25]

This kind of incident is fairly common, especially during the cruise part of flights. In 1996 the US pilots' union, the ALPA, compiled a selection of war stories of fatigue from American and Japanese pilots to submit to the FAA when it was considering issuing a new rule permitting longer duty times. Here are a few.[26]

> . . . *25 minutes after departure both first officer and captain sound asleep. The autopilot levelled at 16,000 feet. Woke up when aircraft entered convective activity (towering cumulus) and hit moderate to severe turbulence with airspeed at redline, since climb power still set! No exaggeration whatsoever!!*

> *After seven days in the Pacific, we fly all-night from Bangkok to Narita [Tokyo], have a short day layover, then fly all night to Honolulu. Some or all of the crew passes out on that leg from fatigue. We are [so] tired by the [time of] approach and landing that our thinking and reaction time is similar to being drunk. If the weather wasn't consistently good in Honolulu, I'm sure we would have lost an airplane a long time ago.*

> *Last leg to base after long day, little sleep time, night before leg – Pittsburgh to Akron. Both crew members tired and forgot to do approach course, almost landed with gear up. Caught it on final and got it put down in time.*

> *On duty all-night trip . . . First officer flying, both very tired, on*

final to Pittsburgh first officer called for flaps 40. I reached over
and shut down number two engine. On the F-100 with flaps at
25, the fuel lever is at the same relative position as the flaps
lever. Single-engine landing accomplished OK. Fatigue
definitely a factor.

Another kind of pilot error derives from simply having had a bad
day, and emphasises the importance of keeping him sweet. Having
a Captain Ahab at the controls might be imagined to be fairly
good for flight safety, for at least there would be no questions over
leadership. Yet as the experience of the martinets in charges of the
KLM 747 at Tenerife and the British Midland 737 at Kegworth
demonstrate, bad tempers are bad news.

This was particularly true for the New Yorker who captained a
Northwest Airlink British Aerospace Jetstream 31 leaving
Minneapolis/St Paul international airport on 1 December 1993.[27]
The captain's day started badly, with the company notifying him
that he would be required for duty the next day as well. This made
him angry because he had expected to have the day off, and he
filled out a form to start a grievance procedure with the airline
over it.

His day meant travelling as a passenger out of Minneapolis/St
Paul to International Falls, Minnesota, flying the plane back to
Minneapolis/St Paul and then flying another one on to Hibbing,
and then to International Falls, where he would stay the night
before returning to Minneapolis/St Paul as a passenger in the
morning. But the paperwork had not come through for his first
flight as a passenger. He insisted that the airline official dealing
with passengers drop everything and get his authorisation for him
immediately. He was so rude that the official's supervisor
suggested she make a formal complaint. This captain had already
shouted at this official in another confrontation a month earlier,
although he had later apologised.

Then the plane had to be stopped to let the captain on board.
After he and his co-pilot that day arrived at International Falls
they flew the plane they had been passengers on back to
Minneapolis/St Paul and switched planes for the next flight. The

captain said the first officer had failed to carry out the visual check of the aircraft's exterior properly and, indeed, when he did it himself, he found that the landing lights were not working, something which should have been reported by the previous crew. He dealt with that problem and had the lights replaced and finally allowed the ramp agents, whom he had already refused twice, permission to board passengers.

His day was not getting any better. The weather report for his destination was not up to date, and when the passengers were on board he discovered that the ramp agent had miscalculated and the aircraft was 130 pounds too heavy. The luckiest air traveller in the US that day volunteered to leave the aircraft.

The flight was fifty minutes late leaving because of these complications, but once it was in the air, being flown by the first officer, the flight was uneventful until they neared the airport of Hibbing. Although they do not put it in quite such bald terms, the NTSB report indicates, presumably based on listening to the tone of voice used on the CVR, that the captain was being at best offhand with his colleague, if not downright condescending.

A witness before the departure of the flight had noted the first officer's embarrassment at having been caught out on the landing lights question and the captain's temper seems to have persisted well into the flight. The report said that he had frequently humiliated or berated his subordinates on other flights. He disliked the airline, apparently, and it was even alleged that he used to throw the aircraft around deliberately so as to cause passengers to complain and thus give the airline a headache.[28]

If the captain was being domineering and distracting the first officer from vital monitoring tasks, the first officer, as is the conventional view in these days of CRM, was equally at fault for allowing himself to being intimidated or overawed.

The aircraft is not a type that behaves particularly well in icing conditions, and it was a cold day on which other pilots had reported icing. In an unauthorised manoeuvre, but one which the NTSB believed was pretty common practice, the captain initiated a very rapid descent so as to expose the plane to as little ice as possible. However, he clearly lost awareness of how rapidly they were descending. Neither man even had time for an expletive before the plane smashed into trees, killing both of them and their sixteen passengers. In all, there are mistakes, understandable mistakes, and days better spent in bed.

CHAPTER 6

Who needs pilots?

WITH HUMAN BEINGS so intractably fallible, and most training concepts having been tried repeatedly, aircraft designers have looked for a technical fix for human errors, most enthusiastic among them a number of bold French thinkers at the heart of the Airbus Industrie consortium. About fifteen years ago they began to look to autopilot computerisation and the application of fly-by-wire technology for a new dawn in thinking about passenger aircraft.

The result has been a fascinating mix of success and disaster. On the one hand, computerisation has enormously eased a vast number of pilot tasks, making normal flight operations a much less stressful and complicated business. Also, the software involved has helped to prevent a wide variety of errors common on earlier-generation aircraft. On the other hand, however, this same new technology has introduced terrifying new ways of crashing a plane that never existed before.

We are now faced with one of the most vital problems of aviation safety, the human-computer interface. Humans are pretty good at what they do, but computers can be even better. Binary logic, however, has little in common with human reasoning and if you put the two together in a safety-critical situation you soon realise that the different methods of problem-solving do not always match perfectly. Losing a file or mistakenly deleting a paragraph is the kind of thing we can live with if we are doing word-processing in an office or at home. The same type of error translated into the management of an aircraft with hundreds of people aboard involves losses on a somewhat greater scale.

Computerised autopilots, flight management computers, are quite distinct from flight control systems, which use fly-by-wire (FBW). It is important to know the difference between the two when discussing the computerised operation of aircraft.

From the Wright brothers' plane to the Boeing 707 the pilots' controls were always linked directly to the control surfaces by cables and pulleys. Turning the wheel to the left, for example, pulled cables attached to the ailerons to make them change the shape of the wing, which in turn made the plane roll to the left. When the jets got so big that it was beyond human strength to move those control surfaces, first electric and then hydraulic power were added. The first wide-bodied jets, the Boeing 747, the DC-10 and the Lockheed L-1011 Tristar, could not be controlled without hydraulic power. Certain earlier jets, like the Boeing 737, also use hydraulics but have retained the option of controlling the aircraft manually if they fail or are not desired.

Then came FBW. Instead of the hydraulic valves being operated by cables attached to the control column, on an FBW aircraft the control column sends an electrical signal to the hydraulic units telling them what to do. Despite one terrible crash involving FBW it is not as susceptible to problems as flight management systems. FBW is only the hand, while FMS is the brain. FBW and the associated flight control system governing it work in a very simple fashion, while the ways in which FMSs can be mishandled or misprogrammed are legion. (*See* Chapter 9 for a discussion of FBW and its role in the crash of a Lauda Air Boeing 767 in 1992.)

Almost all civilian aircraft manufacturers also make military jets and they had been using FBW on those for many years before deciding to install it on civilian jets. In combat, pilots could improve their control of the plane by using fly-by-wire technology. Thus those military jets terrorising livestock and walkers over remote countryside are not being "flown" in the normal sense, certainly not at a consistent 200 feet over hilly ground. No human could possibly maintain that altitude at 600 knots and avoid all the obstacles at the same time. The computer is reading the ground and adjusting the control surfaces while the pilot watches on a monitor. At higher altitudes the pilot takes over if necessary. Without FBW such manoeuvres would be impossible.

Airbus Industrie, whose first commercial aircraft flew in 1970, was a relative newcomer to the aviation game and in order to be competitive with its much larger American rivals it had to steal a march on them. It was decided that fly-by-wire and cockpit computerisation were the answers.[1]

The computerisation takes place within what is known as the flight management computer, which is the main hardware behind the flight management system (FMS).[2]

Conceptually, FMS has been around for a lot longer than FBW, since it is simply a 1980s term for what used to be called the autopilot, although FMSs are capable of much more. Autopilots, at first purely mechanical in nature, existed conceptually even before manned flight, and practical versions based on mechanical principles were first installed in the early 1930s. Then, in the late 1950s British engineers developed an "autoland" system, whereby passenger aircraft could be brought into the airport whatever the visibility, so long as both airport and aircraft were properly equipped, and the pilots correctly trained. Fog had been seriously curtailing flights to Heathrow and a technical solution had long been desired.

Since then, computers have transformed the capabilities of the mechanically based autopilots. Sitting as a guest in the cockpit of an Airbus A-321 in 1996, I watched in some amazement as the plane flew between two airports in France. The pilots entered the waypoints (radio beacons along the route), and the altitudes which air traffic control had told them to use en route, and various other data into the computer. When they had taxied to the end of the runway and obtained clearance to take off, the order to the FMS to "go" was given. The correct thrust for take-off was selected and the FMS controlled the plane completely from take-

off to landing. The pilots watched out of the cockpit window –
still a vital function – exchanged important messages on the radio,
and monitored all the instruments. Since no deviation to the route
or timing of the flight was needed, they did not fly, in the classical
sense, from take-off to touchdown.

A pilot for a major US airline told me a similar story. Provided
no route changes or deviations were necessary, and there were no
technical problems, all he had to do to get from Los Angeles to
Auckland, New Zealand, was to punch a four-digit number into
the FMS of his Boeing 747-400. The number referred to a pre-
programmed flight plan for the journey.

The advantages of computerisation in the cockpit are threefold.
First, it lowers operating costs because so many functions are now
performed automatically and thus at their optimum. When Airbus
were designing the A-320 they also believed that the computerisation would make the pilot's job less skilful, and thus less prone to
error. Training, they believed, would take less time and thus cost
less money.

Another innovation was to plan the cockpit from the outset so
that other aircraft in the same family would have the same layout
and controls. This "commonality", as it is known, permits
upgrading of pilots to a different type of Airbus with a minimum
of new training. The A-320, A-330 and A-340 share virtually
identical controls. This, incidentally, has proved an immense commercial advantage to Airbus when competing against Boeing.

Airbus also wanted to abolish the flight engineer's post on the
plane. His job had traditionally been to calculate fuel loads,
monitor the engines and take care of all technical aspects of the
aircraft not involved in actually flying it. When the A-320 came
along, the flight engineer went the way of the steam locomotive's
stoker when diesel engines were introduced.

The second advantage of computerisation was that the FMS
and the FCS were not simply taking the burden of flying from the
pilots. They were also monitoring all aspects of the flight from the
point of view of economy. They calculated optimum speeds and
trim of the machine so that fuel use was kept to a minimum. On
longer-range aircraft the on-board computers can also auto-

matically shift fuel between the different tanks so as to maintain an optimum centre of gravity, and thus the most aerodynamic presentation of the plane to the airflow. The computers can even automatically change the trim of the aircraft to compensate for the slight change in centre of gravity when passengers leave their seats to go to the toilet, or when the heavy service trolleys are moving in the cabin.

Third, and most controversially, the potential was created for the computer to prevent unauthorised manoeuvres. If the pilot, by some mischance, tries to make the plane climb so steeply that it stalls, or attempts some other manoeuvre that could endanger the aircraft or cause serious discomfort to passengers, the system will simply not respond to the commands. Although this feature has been severely criticised, it is mostly pilots' pride that has been compromised, not safety.

Indeed, the capability of the plane to overrule a pilot is not entirely new. Eric Newton, now long retired from his job as one of Britain's most experienced air-accident investigators, remembers how during the Second World War pilots were capable of ripping the wings off their fighters when executing desperate manoeuvres to escape enemy aircraft. The designers, he told me, then came up with a counterweight attached to the joystick. The effect was that as the pilot pulled back on the stick, the increase in g forces made it progressively harder to pull back the stick. This made it virtually impossible to pull it so far back that the plane would start to break up.

Some of the new automatic functions are important advances. "Alpha floor" protection, for example, is an aspect of the computer programming in Airbus planes that recognises when the aircraft is about to stall and automatically applies the correct amount of power and control surface position to get the plane out of this dangerous condition.

The "go-around" programme is also superior to any American passenger jet's system when it comes to emergencies. Without having to push the limits of the aircraft manually, as the Boeing 757 pilots tried to do just before they crashed on the approach to Cali, the computer uses maximum thrust and maximum climb angle to get out of trouble automatically. It has even been claimed that if the pilots had been flying an A-320 at Cali they might not have crashed.[3]

Airbus believed that by removing some of the responsibility for flying the plane from the pilot they could remove some of the causes of accidents. In normal operation, the crew would be prevented from stalling the plane, banking it at more than 30 degrees, and various other "protections", as Airbus termed them, were programmed in.

A jokey description of the A-320 started to circulate among pilots. The new cockpit would have a pilot, a computer and a dog. The computer was there to fly the plane, the pilot was there to reassure the passengers, and the dog was there to bite the pilot in case he tried to touch the controls.

Airbus's most controversial idea was that the capabilities of the FMS were so great that pilots would henceforward need less training. Pilots would, effectively, be given information on a "need to know" basis by the system which was flying the plane for them. The "glass cockpit", as seen on advanced Airbuses and their American equivalents, has few traditional dials. Three video screens give the pilots most of the information they need.

Early on, Airbus was making a virtue of this and informally describing the plane as both idiot-proof and uncrashable. Captain Heino Caesar, formerly Lufthansa's chief safety pilot, illustrates the point from the experience of one of his Boeing 727 pilots who went to Toulouse to do conversion training on to the A-320. After being introduced to the plane the young man was subjected to one of the silly aphorisms that gave Airbus such a poor reputation in the earliest years of the A-320. "It is so easy to fly," he was told, "a fifteen-year-old child could do it." The Lufthansa man was not impressed. "Get yourself a fifteen-year-old, then. I am an airline pilot." And with that he stormed off.

Captain Hubert de Gaullier was, until he retired in late 1996, an A-320 pilot for the domestic French airline Air Inter (now known as Air Inter Europe). He was not encouraged when, just before his training began, he heard Bernard Ziegler, the A-320's chief engineer and a highly experienced pilot, deliver the homily,

"My maid could fly it," during a radio interview.

When he arrived for training the instructors did little to disabuse de Gaullier of the impression that pilots could be next in line for the flight engineer's fate. "They told me, 'The computer flies the plane, so you only need to know how to programme the computer,'" he recalls. "When I said I wanted to fly it in the simulator as well as programme it, they said you don't need to." Having first flown jets for the French Navy in the early 1960s before moving on to the Caravelle with Air Inter, and then other conventionally controlled jets, this was not what he was accustomed to. He insisted on being allowed to fly the aircraft and eventually, as a concession to his seniority and persistence, they allowed him a few hours' "hand-flying" of the A-320 simulator, as opposed to merely programming it.

Two expert authorities on the problems of automated aircraft, Nadine Sarter and David Woods, have said, "The role of pilots in the modern glass cockpit aircraft has shifted from direct control of the aircraft to supervisory control of automated machine agents." In other words, the pilot flies the computer and the computer flies the plane. Moving the pilot from an active to a supervisory role is one of the chief problems of cockpit auto-mation. Having a pilot as supervisor carries the inherent risk that he or she could easily end up "behind" the aircraft, following the actions of the automated systems rather than leading them.[4] This was part of what went wrong before the Cali crash.

Some might call the attitude that led to this change French arrogance, but whatever their *amour propre* over their new machine, it was undoubtedly revolutionary. It was easier to operate and offered huge savings in costs over the US-made planes, especially the ageing Boeing 737 and McDonnell Douglas DC-9 descendants. It gave Boeing its biggest commercial scare since the British-made De Havilland Comet became the world's first jet-powered airliner in 1952.[5] It also nearly followed the Comet's example in a more grisly respect. A series of A-320 crashes occurred that left observers speculating whether, as with the Comet, Boeing would reap the benefits of learning from the mistakes of the Europeans.

When the A-320 was first flown at air shows in 1987 and 1988 Airbus showed off its capabilities. Air France's chief training pilot for the A-320, Michel Asseline, used to amaze the crowds by displaying manoeuvres that only the A-320's FBW technology combined with the FMS could offer. The plane is capable of flying in the manner of jet fighters at air shows, flying extremely slowly but with the nose pitched up in the air at a high angle. No civilian Boeing could do that. This was possible because the system of "flight envelope protection" would automatically prevent the high angle developing into a stall.

However, the shine came off, and some of the French hubris began to show, when, at an air show at Habscheim, Alsace, on 26 June 1988, in full view of several TV cameras, Asseline misjudged his height and flew the plane, together with 130 passengers along for the ride, straight into trees at the end of the runway. The plane's fuel load exploded as it crashed. Three passengers died and several were seriously injured.

Later the same day the French authorities said Asseline was to blame. Judicial investigations vindicated that finding, albeit only eight years later, and Asseline received a conviction for "negligent homicide", which he then appealed. But the A-320's problems were only beginning. To come was a series of air disasters which seemed to derive not from failings in the plane, but from over-confidence in its capacity to take responsibility or skills away from the pilot. A new type of aviation accident was about to enter the lexicon – "mode-confusion". Again, innovation and cost-reduction were in the driving seat, not safety. For this experimentation passengers and aircrew alike were to pay with their lives.

On a fiercely hot 4 June 1990 at midday an Indian Airlines A-320 was approaching Bangalore airport. A relatively in-experienced co-pilot was flying the plane under the command of a check captain, whose role in these flights, as on airlines all over the world, is partly to be in command of the flight and partly to instruct the co-pilot. Without knowing it, the co-pilot had selected the wrong computer mode on his FMS as they began the approach. The aircraft gradually lost speed and fell below the glide-path for the airport while they believed it to be managing their approach. Too late they realised the plane was descending too fast and tried to extricate themselves. They were, investigations later revealed, less than ten seconds too slow off the mark. The engines were in the process of spooling up to full power to get them out of trouble when the plane bounced heavily on the baked earth, shearing off the undercarriage, landed again and burst into flames. Fifty-six of the 146 on board survived, not including the pilots.

Fully understanding what went wrong in this crash demands too much familiarity with the way in which the A-320's FMS works, but in essence the FMS was operating in one mode, with one set of rules applying, when the pilots believed it to be operating in another, where different rules held. Put crudely, the pilots were not flying the aircraft.

This disaster was thus, strictly speaking, the fault of the pilots, because they had not been paying strict attention to all the instruments, something Airbus was quick to point out. However, critics said that one apparently minor error could put the plane into the wrong mode, and because the pilots were unaware of the mode-change, their subsequent actions were not merely inappropriate, but disastrous. Never before in living memory had anyone known of a correctly configured aircraft without any systems failures crashing so close to an airport in such perfect weather. Airbus brushed off the criticisms, blamed the pilots, and moved on.

However, the next two Airbus crashes were harder for the company to ignore. No longer would anybody be speculating about the pilot one day becoming redundant, and no more Airbus officials would be heard talking about "the uncrashable plane".

On the night of 21 January 1992, in appalling weather, an Air Inter A-320 crashed into La Bloss mountain, a few miles short of Strasbourg airport and only a minute or so's flying time from the airport where Michel Asseline's A-320 had crashed. Eight of the 96 people on board survived, but only because the plane had hit the mountain at a shallow angle. Captain Hubert de Gaullier's son, a steward on the flight, died in the crash. As so often in

CFITs, if they had been fifty feet higher everybody would have made it.

What eventually emerged was a different kind of mode-confusion, but too similar to Bangalore for comfort. The investigators' best information was that, as they neared Strasbourg airport, one of the pilots had selected an angle of 3.3 degrees for the final approach to the runway. But he should first have switched a simple knob, like an on–off switch on an old-fashioned radio. Apparently, he did not. When he entered what he thought was a 3.3 degrees of flight-path angle, he was in fact entering a rate of descent of 3300 feet per minute, a very fast rate considering their altitude. It was this that caused them to hit the mountain.[6]

Again, pilot error, according to Airbus. And again, Airbus was technically correct. The pilots had made a mistake, but it was beginning to look as though such mistakes were shockingly easy to make. Indeed, in one of the starkest and most shocking examples of the industry's failure to learn from previous mistakes, this very error had occurred twice before non-fatally, near Gatwick in 1988, and over San Diego in 1990. In both the non-fatal dress rehearsals for the Air Inter crash it was daylight and the pilots simply noticed from visual clues that they were descending abnormally fast.[7]

Such is the sophistication of the automation that when a descent rate is selected, the computers automatically make sure that it is done without jerks or sudden sinking so as to maximise passenger comfort. The Air Inter plane was flying in the dark and entirely on instruments and so no visual clues were available to alert the pilots to their high rate of descent.

Just after the Strasbourg crash the secretary-general of one of France's pilots' unions, Romain Kroes, spoke up: "Each time [an A-320 crashes] the crew is blamed, whereas the responsibility is really shared in the hiatus between man and machine," he said on French radio. He added, "There are numerous faults in the way man–machine communication and the cockpit have been designed on the A-320 . . . Since the Habsheim and Bangalore crashes, it has been clear to us that the crews were caught out by cockpit layout."[8]

Air Inter crews were, traditionally, always under intense

pressure to meet deadlines, because the success of the airline in large part depended on competing on punctuality with the TGV, the high-speed train. Generally, the airline operated 85 per cent of its flights with less than a fifteen-minute delay, and won an award for such efficient operation of the A-320 from Airbus in 1988 and 1991. Air traffic controllers were always aware that Air Inter planes were in a hurry and often helped them along by suggesting quicker ways of getting down.

On this occasion the tower controller had suggested that instead of the approach they had planned, the crew of the Airbus could use a different runway, thereby saving time. This meant doing a non-precision approach, however. Had they stayed with their original runway choice, they would have performed an ILS approach and would almost certainly not have crashed.

One safety device which observers were amazed to find absent on the Air Inter A-320 was the ground proximity warning system, which gives warnings if the plane is sinking too fast or if terrain is approaching. On such short journeys – no Air Inter flight ever lasted more than forty minutes – GPWS was regarded as a threat to the timetable, and so the airline management, incredibly, did not install it. At the time, Air Inter was the only major airline in the world not to have GPWS, a fact that was kept quiet. On one occasion, government inspectors arrived to go over the A-320 fleet and were astonished to find a hole in the equipment bays in the cockpit where GPWS was normally installed. Had GPWS been present on the aircraft it might have given the crew sufficient warning of the approaching mountain to avoid it.

If Strasbourg dented Airbus's apparent complacency, it was punctured altogether in June 1994, when another fatal Airbus crash occurred, albeit one of a crucially different character. This time the plane involved was the bigger brother of the A-320, an A-330, Airbus's answer to the Boeing 767, which has capacity for fifty more passengers than the A-320 and a greater range.

Destined for Thai Airways and already painted in its livery, the twin-engined A-330 was still being put through a series of flight tests for the plane's airworthiness certificate at Airbus's base in Toulouse by the chief test pilot, Englishman Nick Warner.

Warner and his six companions on board were flying an exercise in which they would mimic the effect of an engine failing shortly after take-off. The idea was to engage the autopilot at this point and observe its employment of "pitch protection" to get the aircraft out of trouble. Just after they took off, they idled the left engine to simulate the failure, and the nose pitched up as the plane lost speed. The aircraft was then operating in a mode called "speed reference". But the altitude elsewhere in the system had been set to 2000 feet. What then happened was that the FMS switched from "speed reference" to "altitude acquire". For special reasons, the "pitch protection" does not function when the aircraft is governed in "altitude acquire" mode.

The flight-crew watched, expecting the aircraft systems to rectify the extreme angle. Too late, Warner realised that the aircraft was not going to recover, and he took control manually. He was pulling the plane out of its crisis, but was already too close to the ground. It crashed, burned and all seven on board perished.[9]

This was a different story from Bangalore and Strasbourg. Here was Airbus's chief test pilot crashing a plane, and it had not even got off company property. Pilot error was, yet again, the cause but if Airbus's chief test pilot was going to fall victim to such an error, what chance for the lesser mortals flying their Airbuses daily in line operation? Although no public evidence of a major rethink emerged, it is generally believed that Airbus reviewed its earlier, overambitious idea of how the pilot–computer relationship would develop.

It was soon realised that the logic of the computerised system was not something pilots did not need to know about. Maids and fifteen-year-olds would have to go elsewhere for their first flight. Far from making the pilots' job less skilful, all Airbus pilots would have to undergo more training, not less. They would have to become intimately familiar with the system logic so they were aware at all times of "where" the computer was and what it was going to do, as well as the interaction of all the modes.

The captain on the A-320 which crashed short of Strasbourg airport had spent only 162 hours flying the plane, and his co-pilot less than half that. By the standards of other aircraft that was an extremely low level of experience for a captain, but it was fully in accordance with the Airbus training philosophy of the time. Weren't the computers supposed to be doing the flying for the crew? One of the first changes Air Inter brought in following the crash was that the captain of an A-320 always had to have a minimum of 300 hours' experience of flying the plane behind him. They also installed GPWS, stable-door fashion, at last.[10]

All this is not to say that American-made aircraft do not suffer similar problems. The "pioneering" crashes have been of Airbuses possibly because Airbus was the innovator. But many American-made planes have had mode-confusion accidents and others related to the FMS. Indeed, the FMS for both Boeings and Airbuses are manufactured by the same company, Honeywell. The only substantial differences in the "architecture" of the Honeywell FMSs for both planes have been put there at the insistence of the plane-makers. Such bitter rivals in the market-place do not want it thought they even share the same brand of seat-covering, let alone FMS. The need for greater training and familiarity with the logic behind the operation of the FMS is just as great with US-made aircraft as with the Airbuses.

Airbus's initial problems have now been corrected and the Airbus family of planes has now reached an average level of safety. But for a revolutionary new aircraft to succeed only in achieving an average rate of fatal accidents is surely not good enough for cutting-edge technology in the late twentieth century. It may have eliminated, through its FMS, human errors that claimed lives beforehand, but in safety terms has only robbed Peter to pay Paul. The cost savings, however, are anything but average. There has been a revolution in technology and airline economics, but safety has stood still.

The Airbus experience indicates a process of learning by your mistakes and experimenting until you get it right. Many might question whether that should be done with aircraft in revenue operation. That said, all new aircraft begin their service lives with up to three times the level of accidents that they experience five years after entering service.[11]

The manufacturers are left, however, with a problem that will go on claiming lives and probably only be corrected by the Tombstone Imperative. It lies in the nebulous area beyond mere electronics, mechanics and automation. How much should the pilots do, and how do they interact with the computers? The human–computer interface is a baffling area. If the computer tells the pilots too much, they are overloaded with information they cannot absorb. Tell them too little, or in too obscure a way, and the aircraft can be heading for destruction without the pilots being aware of it.

Before we pass on to the generic problems of cockpit automation and the challenges they present, here is another reminder that these fascinating technical questions always have a human component. What follows is the testimony of Jean-Noel Châtre, one of the eight survivors of the A-320 crash near Strasbourg in January 1992.[12]

The accident itself I remember absolutely nothing about. I have no memory, none at all of the crash. The only thing I remember is waking up. The doctors told me that I had probably been unconscious for between thirty and forty-five minutes after the accident, and I was lying in the snow with bare feet, in my socks, to be precise. I was lying between two tree trunks and I regained consciousness and looked around me . . . It was quite strange because I remember asking myself: "But where am I? What am I doing here? What's happened to me? Has there been an accident? OK, it's not a car accident; it couldn't have been in a forest." And it maybe took me one or two minutes to realise that I had been in an airliner and that the plane had crashed.

After that I tried to stand up. I had two broken ankles, so I fell down again right away, but I felt nothing at all. I had been lying in the snow . . . and I think that my hands and feet must have become frozen, I had no feeling in my hands or feet.[13] And then I succeeded in hauling myself up and sitting on the tree trunk behind me. I looked for my glasses, which I didn't have any longer and without them I can't see much, and then I started to look around, to worry about whether there were people near me, so I called out and when I called, and even when I didn't, I could hear other voices. I heard other cries, not exactly cries for help, I heard people calling, murmuring and groans.

. . . The fuselage of the plane was in front of me, about five or six metres away. There were two or three fires. There was one not very far from me, about three or four metres to my left, and then another fire a bit further away on the left. I knew I was not alone. I knew that there were other people, but I guessed that those people were more or less injured and they probably could not do much . . . I think that went on for about fifteen to twenty minutes roughly. And in that time I called out every thirty seconds or so, hoping that someone would say something to me.

At the end of this period of time, about an hour, maybe seventy minutes after the crash, I noticed someone who was not very far from me, who was between me and the fuselage of the plane and whose legs were crushed underneath a tree trunk . . . And this person, who must have been unconscious at first like me, must have woken up, regained consciousness and he lifted himself up, but he had the tree trunk on his calves.

. . . I approached him on all fours, since I couldn't walk, and I said I was going to try to help him. I wanted – my intention was to find a branch to try to lever, to lift the tree trunk. I think he woke up after a little while, he must have realised the state he was in and he started to panic, to flail around in all directions. In fact I had to get away from him to avoid getting hit by an elbow after a few minutes. So I left him, and wandered off in a circle on all fours, . . . and while crawling around like this I went around two tree trunks, the ends of which were in the biggest fire nearest me, and as I came around again in the circle I wanted to climb over these tree trunks. OK, the first I had no trouble with, but the second, when I put my hands on it, the bark crumbled. It had been eaten away from the inside by the fire and I fell into the burning wood on the inside and it was then I burned my hands and torso. So I obviously got out very quickly and went back to where I had been to begin with.

I went back to the guy who was stuck under the tree, who was calling for help.

It's one of the surprising things, I think, about these situations, that there is no communication. You are so panicked, you are so outside your normal experience, there is no logic any more to your behaviour, or what you say . . . I just said to him I was going to try to help him, but, look, I couldn't. This tree trunk had to be seventy centimetres thick – and it would have taken four or five men to lift it.

So, after an hour and a half to two hours after the accident, it was so cold that, although I was afraid of getting close to the fire because of the kerosene, all the same I came close to it because it was very cold . . . I sat astride this tree trunk, leaning against the standing tree, and I warmed myself up as best I could. I was so numb that I even put my feet in the fire without feeling anything. Since my feet were frozen I felt nothing at all; my feet weren't actually in the fire, but were resting on some branches that were.

I was still hearing talking going on from time to time, so I knew there were other survivors, but I didn't know where and in fact I found out later that they were only about ten metres away from me. I believe I shouted out every now and then, maybe every five to ten minutes. I never got an answer. The only response I got was hearing these voices, talking from time to time . . . Time went by and it was getting colder and colder, I was more and more numb and I was hoping that help would come.

During the last hour – I wasn't really afraid during the first four hours because I didn't think there was much wrong with me, apart from the broken ankles – but during the last hour, I believe I really started to be afraid . . .

I have talked about it once with Pierre Lota [one of the other survivors], who told me that he went back into the wreckage of the plane to find some blankets and he saw me. He saw me but he didn't try, at least I think not, to attract my attention. But you know when you are in a situation like that which is so bizarre nothing makes sense. I think there is the survival instinct and nothing else.

As for the man under the trunk, I think he was simply trying to get himself free, he realised he was alive and he must have known what had happened and he realised that he was trapped because his legs were crushed by a tree and he tried everything to get out, exhausting himself . . . unfortunately, he didn't make it. It's difficult to put it over, I think it was two to two and a half hours after the accident, there was a branch of a pine tree near where I was which caught fire and fell down on him. Well, I didn't think I could do anything and I just turned my head away. And maybe ten or fifteen minutes later, I thought he must have fallen, that he had collapsed. I couldn't see him any more.

. . . It was an odd situation because without my glasses I can't see so well – the fires gave some light, but only lit up the upper parts of the trees. Along the ground after a metre, a metre and a half, it was pitch dark. The wreckage and the tree trunks stopped the ground from being lit up and you couldn't see anything on the ground.

I asked the judge eighteen months after the accident. They tried to locate the man whose description I gave them but they found no trace of anyone who had been trapped under a tree trunk.

I believe I had a good sense of the time that was passing because two days after the accident my father asked me in hospital: "Do you know how long you were waiting for help?" I told him it was between four and five hours. And in fact it was four and a half hours, I had a good consciousness of the time.

It was long, you know . . . The accident must have happened at about 7.30 I think. The rescuers got to me at half past midnight, a quarter to one, and I arrived in hospital at 4 a.m.! It's a long time![14]

. . . It disrupts your existence. I got the feeling that day that I won a kind of sordid lottery. Why am I here alive in the middle of all these corpses? Happy to be alive, but not proud.

. . . I lived through one crisis but my family lived through a different crisis and when you get back together again it's not easy. It was difficult for us to understand each other. I came back, psychologically shocked and damaged physically, and

that changed a lot of things in our relationship. It changes your way of looking at things. Am I wiser? I don't know. I see things differently. Very difficult for me for years, living a parallel life to what I had before. I think that in the space of one or two years I lived what someone would normally live over ten or twenty years.

I am not bothered by flying now. I have flown seven or eight times since. I don't sleep well the night before but I don't have a problem boarding. I was initially afraid of contacting the relatives' group, but then I went to a meeting and I realised they needed everybody's help, especially that of the survivors, to find out the truth of what happened.

Automation-related problems have been present on modern passenger aircraft as long as there has been automation, and the earliest automation-related crash is generally reckoned to have been the destruction of an Eastern Airlines L-1011 Tristar in the Florida Everglades on 29 December 1972.

The aircraft was in a mode called "altitude hold", which does what it says, keeps the aircraft at a selected altitude. Everyone on the flight-deck gradually became obsessed by a malfunctioning indicator light on the control panel. During their investigations of this problem the captain inadvertently nudged the control column. Unbeknown to him, a push or pull on the control column disengaged the autopilot. With the altitude-hold function now disengaged, the aircraft began imperceptibly to descend. The crew were so preoccupied with the rogue indicator light, which was totally unrelated to the automation, that they failed to notice the drop in altitude until the aircraft crashed, killing about a hundred people, including the flight-crew (*see* Chapter 2).

Another automation-related point in this crash is that if the aircraft had not had an automatic function for maintaining altitude the pilots would have been constantly monitoring their altitude.

Since then it has became well established that touching the control column is the main way of disengaging automated functions in the cockpit, but this is no longer always the case, because there is simply too much automation to be turned off.

A similar incident once befell a DC-10 in the middle of cruise flight at high altitude, although the consequences were not as serious and have a lighter side. The captain had left the flight-deck and a flight attendant had brought refreshments to the co-pilot and flight engineer, who were still there. The flight engineer helped the flight attendant place the tray on a flat area between the two pilots' seats by moving forward the co-pilot's seat. The crew seats in a typical passenger jet cockpit are moved by pressing buttons activating electric motors. What he did not know was that the co-pilot was sitting with his legs crossed below the knees, so his left foot was where his right foot would normally be, and vice versa.

When the seat moved forward the co-pilot found his legs trapped between the control column and the seat. By the time he was able to tell his colleague to stop, it was too late. The forward motion of the seat had pushed the co-pilot's legs against the control column, the column had moved and thus disengaged the autopilot and with its continued forward motion put the plane into a steep dive. Fortunately for all concerned, they regained level flight, although some injuries had been caused during their recovery.

More typical of an automation-related fatal mishap was the crash of an ATR-72 turbo-prop aircraft with sixty-eight people on board at Roselawn, Indiana, on Halloween 1994. In this type of automation-related problem we can see the conceptual difficulties very clearly. Basically, the automation can be managing a "problem" which may be growing in intensity. Yet, because the computers are coping, the pilots are unaware that a crisis is developing. The crisis, however, can become so severe that the automation is no longer capable of handling it. At that point, it switches itself off and hands control back to the pilots, who then have a very short space of time in which to deal with a large number of problems of an immediate nature. Since they were "out of the loop" while the situation was developing they did not have a chance to observe the problem as it grew, and use the time that would have afforded them to come up with an answer. Automation is meant to relieve the pilots of unnecessary work. It simply does its job, being unable to distinguish between coping with a crisis and operating normally. An analogy might be that of water dripping into a vase. If it is made of glass you can see when the water is about to overflow, but if it is made of china, you won't know about the spillage until it happens.

In the case of the American Eagle ATR-72 the problem was ice. This plane had made a brief flight to Chicago's O'Hare Airport and was in a "hold" awaiting landing clearance in cloud and freezing rain. The pilots had switched on all the aircraft's icing protection systems and they were functioning normally. The pilots knew ice was present but there were no indications of any abnormalities, so they were not concerned. However, this aircraft has proved to be particularly susceptible to control problems in freezing rain, which is just one of a range of icing conditions that aircraft can encounter. Although it is relatively rare, freezing rain is particularly threatening to the aerodynamic properties of the ATR's super-efficient wing.

What was happening to this plane, as occurred to others of the type on previous occasions, was that the freezing rain was flowing back from the leading edge of the wing and then solidifying to form a ridge of ice parallel to the leading edge. The leading edge is protected by an inflatable "boot" which inflates and deflates periodically, thus breaking off any ice that forms there, but the ridge of ice parallel to the leading edge was forming *behind* the boot and thus was unaffected by the ice protection systems. Because the wing is on top of the fuselage, it was also invisible to the pilots. As the ice started to accrete in a ridge on top of the wing, the autopilot compensated for the increased drag. When the wing wanted to drop it provided the appropriate input to keep it level. It continued in this fashion until the tendency was too strong for the autopilot to handle. Then, suddenly, the autopilot disengaged, saying, as it were, "Over to you, boys, I can't handle it any more."

The ridge of ice had become so large that it caused a vacuum above the aileron, forcing it up and rolling the aircraft suddenly to the right. The co-pilot, who was flying the plane that day, righted it again, but almost instantaneously the aircraft rolled to the right once more. This time, no matter how hard the two pilots pulled, the wing would not come back up again. They went into a dive and the plane smashed into a soya-bean field nose-first at about 500 mph. Instead of the pilots coping gradually with a deteriorating situation, and thus having time to develop a solution to the problem, a full-fledged crisis was dumped on their laps without warning and without time to do anything about it.

Something similar happened to a China Airlines Boeing 747SP in a famous incident on 19 February 1985 near San Francisco. In this case, the aircraft had left Taiwan and was only 300 nautical miles from San Francisco. As is typical of this type of aircraft at this phase of a long flight, it was flying at a relatively high altitude, 41,000 feet. At very high altitudes the aircraft travels faster and uses less fuel. The downside, however, is that the higher it goes the closer it is to stalling, because of the lower density of the atmosphere. Although it can be perfectly safe to fly at 45,000 feet, in this case the difference between the aircraft's top speed and its stalling speed was only three or four knots.

Like the ATR-72 the autopilot here was masking the onset of a problem, although it should be pointed out that the crew was at fault for flying at an altitude where their safety margin had become virtually non-existent. One of the engines was suffering a loss in power. Accordingly, the autopilot attempted to compensate by increasing power on the other engines, and applying rudder to correct the imbalance caused by the difference in power between the engines on each wing. As a result the plane started to tip over, but the pilots did not believe their instruments when they showed this. Still they did not disconnect the autopilot to regain positive control. They only did so after the tipping of the aircraft had suddenly magnified itself into a roll on to the aircraft's back.

Having turned upside-down, the 747 started to do something it was never designed for, spinning earthwards and upside-down. The spinning aircraft moved incredibly violently, it and the passengers experiencing a terrifying roller-coaster ride ranging from one-quarter of the force of gravity to six times the force of gravity. Hardly anybody on board can have believed they would survive. Some of the aircraft's movements were so violent that the landing gear was thrown, by centrifugal force, through the gear doors. These doors sheared off because they were never designed to be opened at such high speeds and struck the tailplane and the rudder, breaking off large sections of both. Despite all this the flight-crew managed to regain control of the plane at only 9500 feet, before landing safely at San Francisco airport with only two serious – physical – injuries being recorded.

Despite the failings of the crew in allowing themselves to be placed in such a dangerous situation in the first place, the automation masked the growing problems until it was no longer able to cope, thus handing the pilots a crisis instead of a developing problem.[15]

Automation that is present without the pilots, or even the airline, being aware of it is even more alarming. This strange condition had a role in the crash of a Scandinavian Airline Systems McDonnell Douglas MD-81 shortly after it left Stockholm airport for Copenhagen on 27 December 1991.[16] This aircraft, part of the DC-9 family, has two engines mounted at the rear of the fuselage. Despite sub-zero temperatures being a common feature of Scandinavian flight operations, it turned out that SAS had inadequate icing procedures. Clear ice was on the wings as the aircraft took off. Shaken by vibration, the ice broke off the surface as the plane rose and was sucked into both engines.

What the pilots did not know was that the plane was equipped with automatic thrust restoration, a system that automatically restores engine thrust at low altitudes, which is helpful if an engine fails after a take-off limited by noise-abatement regulations. Whatever the reasons for the system, when one of the engines started to surge, and the pilots throttled it back, the system automatically restored the thrust. The first affected engine thus started to burn up and the pilots shut it down. Ideally, a lower power setting would have allowed flight to continue. But then the other engine, its power being raised by the system constantly, also burned itself out, leaving the aircraft completely unpowered.

Fortunately, however, they were not at a great height, never getting above 3200 feet. Assisted by an SAS captain travelling as a passenger, the crew managed to extend the flaps and lower the gear before clipping some trees, losing most of the right wing, and coming to rest in a field after slithering along for 110 metres. Although the plane broke into three pieces, it did not catch fire, and only one person suffered a serious injury.

McDonnell Douglas claimed that SAS had been fully informed about the thrust-restoration program, but SAS denied this. Quite possibly, information on the automation had been deemed "something you don't need to know about", whether it was the manufacturer failing to tell the airline, or whether it was the airline failing to tell the pilots. Either way, it was hardly possible for the pilots to be more out of the loop than here.

In 1996 the FAA published a report by its Human Factors Team on precisely these problems, and although there was no ballyhoo about it, it had some alarming points to make both about the nature of the problem and what was being done about it.[17] Worst of all was the conclusion that computers were throwing up systemic problems, ones that could not be addressed by better software or computer design.

Rather than specific items cropping up and causing problems, although there were a few of those, it was the generic nature of the problem of marrying the pilot to the computerised systems that worried them most. The human–computer interface was growing into a situation where human and computer were attempting to have a conversation, as it were, while speaking different languages. This "larger pattern", they said, "serves as a barrier to needed improvements to the current level of safety, or could threaten the current safety record in the future aviation environment".[18]

The team found that designers of software and trainers of pilots, for example, do not know enough about human performance under conditions that can easily arise. In other words, both parties are leaving too many opportunities for pilots to be taken by surprise by, for example, counter-intuitive actions of the flight control systems, expressed in the all-too-familiar modern pilot's cry of "What's it doing now?" Woods and Sarter entitled one of their papers "Strong, Silent, and out of the Loop".[19]

The software designers, however, respond that "human-centred" automation is what they are designing, making it as user-friendly as possible. The FAA report retorted: "It is relatively easy to get agreement that automation should be human-centred, or that potentially hazardous situations should be avoided; it is much more difficult to get agreement on how to achieve these objectives."[20]

One famous example concerns the yoke, or control column, the tall pillar with a horseshoe-shaped handle on top that sits between both pilots' legs. On an FBW aircraft it is no longer necessary because the cables that were once attached to the column have been replaced by electrical linkages. Airbus has installed side-sticks, which look almost exactly like a home computer's games joystick, one for the left hand of the left-hand pilot, and one for the right hand of the right-hand pilot.

Boeing, on the other hand, has retained the yoke in the 777, its latest and only civil FBW aircraft. The company believes that it is better to retain this symbol, even though all the "feel" in it is artificially produced, to reassure the pilots. They think it is better ergonomically too. Once the pilots are familiar with their aircraft they operate them professionally, and thus do not quibble about whether the sidestick is better than the yoke. In forums on the Internet pilots are continually debating the relative strengths of Airbus versus Boeing in cockpit design as well as many other aspects. But the harshest criticisms of either design come from the pilots flying the other aircraft.

In ergonomics, it seems that Boeing may have a slight advantage over Airbus in its retention of the yoke. This is not because the Airbus system is inferior but because it takes a nibble at one of the problems of the glass cockpit, that of all information to the pilots having to be interpreted visually. Both manufacturers and their computer designers have to face the fact that almost all the information the pilots need is displayed on computer monitors or visual display units. In earlier types of aircraft visual information was often presented in different ways. The needles of an altimeter, for example, can convey a rough idea of the altitude to the pilot from a quick scan, while the modern system gives him or her a precise reading in numbers. Instead of scanning the information, the pilot has to read it.

A glance at the position of the throttle handles, for example, will tell the pilots roughly what power setting the engines are at. With non-moving throttle handles, as is standard on the current Airbus family of aircraft, that information can only be gained by further perusal of the computer screen. The visual channel is having so much demand put on it that the opportunities for mis-interpreting it would seem to be increasing, as well as increasing the stress of instrument monitoring on the pilots. It ought to be possible for computer designers to use other means of providing the pilots with basic information than simply putting everything on a screen.

This is not merely a luxury. One of the particular problems about monitoring computerised instruments is that the monitoring has to be done continually, but the systems hardly, if ever, go wrong. It is easy for boredom and thus inattentiveness to set in and monitoring is well known to be a task that humans tend to perform erratically. It is not unheard of, particularly in the cruise portion of a long flight, for both pilots to drift off to sleep.

Citing the rise of "problems of inattentiveness, boredom and complacency on the flight-deck" one of the foremost experts on the human–computer relationship on the flight-deck, Dr Charles Billings, has thus characterised the attitudes of pilots towards the FMS, which they tend to view almost as a third pilot: "it is far easier now for a tired or distracted human operator to simply 'let George do it', for 'George' is now far more able to do most of it without much help".[21]

The industry, however, has learned how much time and effort automation can save. Airlines want more of it and don't question its effect on pilot attentiveness, let alone train pilots for the eventuality of the automation failing and hand-flying being necessary.

This is a key dilemma. On the one hand, it might be argued that if automation does the job so well you should use it all the time. Against that it could be said that should any of the automation go wrong, you would want to know that a competent pilot knew what to do. If, however, the pilot is to keep his or her skills at the highest peak, then the automation will not be used to its fullest extent. It is only a slight exaggeration to suggest that, in an ideal world perhaps, pilots should do their hand-flying in the simulator, honing their skills, while in real operations they should use the automation to its fullest extent.

Simulators, however, are expensive, and many airlines use them as little as they can. It remains the job of the airline to find the right balance between making pilots maintain their flying skills and taking full advantage of the extraordinary powers of auto-mation. Since it is always cheaper to rely solely on automation, and keeping up skills that are used less and less is expensive, airlines will therefore be tempted, even if not all will succumb, to skimp on training.

The FAA Human Factors report lit upon this as the most alarming trend they noticed during their research. Airlines are spending less on training because of economic pressures. "It is of great concern to this team", they remarked, "that investments in necessary levels of human expertise are being reduced in response to economic pressures when two-thirds to three-quarters of all accidents have flight-crew error cited as a major factor."[22] The modern, competitive airline environment means that cockpit automation is being used as a reason not to train pilots to the extent that they used to be. The report is saying that the com-puterised systems have to be understood by the flight-crews if they are to be safe.

One might have imagined that after the Strasbourg, Toulouse and Bangalore crashes the awesome potential for disaster inherent in very slight pilot errors would reinforce the need for greater training. However, airlines are concerned with normal operation of aircraft, not emergencies, and so the trend towards less training has been reconfirmed.

One of the special dangers lies in the fact that the logic of the FMSs is not always properly understood by the flight-crew, particularly as computers often have several different ways of achieving the same objective. One pilot, for example, or one particular airline, may use the FMS's ability to capture a certain altitude level in order to climb away from the airport. Another may use, for example, the computer's ability to set and maintain a rate of climb to do the same job. These are not dangerous methods but each "mode" of the computer's operation allows and forbids certain other ways of operating the plane. Ideally, a pilot should be aware of both these and all of the other methods of doing the same job and what can and cannot be done within each "mode".

Prior to cockpit automation there was very little variety in how a pilot could do his job. By and large there was only a right way and a wrong way. Unless the pilot of the computerised aircraft knows all the peculiarities of all the different modes, he or she could be in trouble, particularly if operating in an unfamiliar mode and then trying to do something that may be permissible in the usual mode but not in this one, possibly without even being aware that the mode has changed. That was the type of error that killed Nick Warner and his colleagues.

Reading between the lines of the reports, it seems that computer and software designers have failed to account for the special problems posed by having this new technology controlling aircraft. They have continued on the traditional path of solving problems and automating actions in the most economical fashion, as elsewhere in the computer industry. What gets left out in this approach is ergonomics, and there is often failure to consider the effects on people of having to monitor these machines for long periods of time, failure to quantify all the idiosyncrasies of the system ("you don't need to know that") and an inadequate appreciation of the way in which humans respond to their wonderful machines. Many flight-deck systems, for example, do not provide much feedback. One may have programmed a certain action into the FMS, but it could help if more of these actions are then fed back to the pilots, confirming to them that they have correctly entered the command.

Too often, computers are designed by people who live, work and breathe computers themselves. They thus assume familiarity with a culture of computing that pilots, for example, may not share.

In reply, it might be said that they do not need to know, so long as they stick to their training and to the company's rules. Unfortunately, unexpected situations sometimes arise, the machines sometimes misbehave, and then the pilots need to know more about the logic that drives their computers so that they have an idea of what is happening when something starts to go wrong. And many pilots of such aircraft, while admitting or even being proud that this new type of plane is much easier to operate, confess that when reprogramming is required, and the flight deviates from the norm, they face considerable difficulty and a massively increased workload that can sometimes leave them "behind" the aircraft, as at Cali.

If manufacturers, regulators and airlines do not consider the issues more carefully, the current problems could well turn the clock back on air safety. As each automation-related accident is so dissimilar from the last, the industry's already strong tendency to ignore preventive action on the basis that a repetition will be very unlikely would be accentuated.

Although the figures suggest that third-generation aircraft, which include the Boeing 757, 767 and 777 as well as the A-320, 330 and 340, among others, are statistically safer than the second-generation planes that preceded them (like the 737 and 747), this may have something to do with the first models being owned by large airlines with good safety records. They may well continue to be safer, in the longer term, but when something does go wrong with a flight computer, be it as a result of poor inputs or faults internal to the software code, the errors are usually impossible to reproduce.

So mysterious are the ways of the software that the aircraft designers have acknowledged, to some extent, that mystery bugs could appear. Airbus, but not Boeing, ordered their software from two separate teams working completely independently. They have also duplicated the computers on board, so that no one safety-critical system is dependent on a solitary computer. That is not to say they can't go wrong.

Computers and software constitute one of the great problems of modern living. Much is controlled by computers, but when software goes wrong there is often absolutely no way of correcting the problem. Peter Mellor, an academic expert on software reliability with particular knowledge of the Airbus A-320, has written, "Software is the most complex thing ever made. It is difficult to visualise. Various diagrammatic conventions can be used to represent its structure . . . and though each elucidates one aspect of its structure or behaviour, none captures the whole of the interrelationships between the different parts of a program."[23]

The more the lines of code, the written instructions from which software is constructed, the greater the complexity and thus the difficulty of tracing a fault. Furthermore, the type of error that occurs, when it does, tends to be dramatic. "When digital systems go wrong, they tend to go very wrong, very quickly, and in unpredictable ways," writes Mellor.[24]

The incident that took place on the BA 777 en route to Jeddah in October 1996 (see Chapter 4) worried all on board and the captain decided to return to Heathrow, but the technicians could not reproduce the fault once at base.

Another fault befell the computers on a Martinair Boeing 767 flying from Amsterdam to Orlando on 28 May 1996. The electronic flight instrumentation system (EFIS) failed completely, meaning that all the computer displays, which have all but replaced the clocks and dials in the cockpit, went blank, after a series of minor but worrying failures in instruments and their displays throughout the flight. Fortunately, mostly due to pressure in the past from pilots, the EFIS is backed up by more old-fashioned instruments and the pilots used these to ensure a safe but hairy landing. They had to land fast and without flaps or many of the usual braking aids, like ABS and reverse thrust. Nobody could subsequently work out what kind of failure had been involved and why it had blanked out the screens. The aircraft went to Seattle for Boeing to have a good look but the results of the investigation were not published.

The early days of the A-320 saw several tragic accidents, although none was thought to be related to the operation of the software. One Air France A-320, however, did suffer what were believed to be important software faults during a flight from Paris to Amsterdam in August 1988. As the plane took off, a message came up on the display telling the pilots that they could only control the pitch of the aircraft manually, implying that the computer dedicated to that purpose had broken down. Everything seemed normal, however, so the pilots ignored it. The problems, however, were just about to begin. As they climbed, more and more display messages started to appear. The right main landing gear had a fault, so did one of the computers, the ground spoilers were wrong, one of the hydraulic systems was inoperative and so on. The last warning declared that smoke had been detected in the lavatory. The pilots decided to return to Charles de Gaulle Airport, but more was in store. They had to use the emergency system to lower the landing gear, and the displays would not confirm the gear was down. They had to fly past the control tower to get visual confirmation that the landing gear was in the correct position.

The cabin was prepared for a crash landing, but they landed safely and normally. Afterwards three of the computers were replaced, but later still it was thought that the flight warning computer, which has a role in showing the fault messages on the displays, was responsible. It was not until over a year later that the problem, which had only recurred once afterwards, was definitively overcome. Precisely why things had been going wrong was never solved.[25] It looked like the gremlins were back, this time in electronic form.

The crew of an Airbus A-340 had an equally alarming experience on 19 September 1991 on their way back from Tokyo to London. Something was wrong with one of the fuel computers, but they were allowed to leave without it functioning, relying instead on the one that remained. After they had reached cruising height the captain's map display on the EFIS disappeared, as did the electronically displayed flight plan. The displays of the first officer, who was flying the plane, were working all right, so the captain used his. Later he tried his own instruments again and this time they were working.

Everything went normally until they neared Heathrow. When they were close to a VOR beacon, giving the aircraft guidance to the airport, the captain's map computer suddenly lost its display and its data. Up came that distressing command familiar to all computer users, "PLEASE WAIT". Shortly afterwards, the first officer's instruments did the same thing. They were on the approach now, with no time for tinkering with the computers. They were just manually adjusting the instrument landing system – an entirely visual approach was not possible due to worsening weather – when a message came up on the display warning them they were short on fuel.

The captain accordingly asked for his approach to the airport to be expedited and permission was granted as he declared an emergency, which is mandatory when there is a concern you may run out of fuel. Then, however, when they were at less than 5000 feet, the ILS started playing up and they could not rely on the glideslope indicator. This meant they had to be guided in by the controller on radar headings until they could see the runway. Official and commercial secrecy mean that we are obliged to imagine the tension in the cockpit as the pilots, ably and resource-fully, coped with one problem being heaped on top of another without the luxury of time to take a longer view of what was on their plate.

The instrumentation went through one more mad moment as the co-pilot ordered a left turn, and the plane went right. After pulling the plane desperately back on to the centreline of the runway they were talked down by the tower, and at 500 feet they saw the runway and landed safely. After landing, the fuel computer perked up again and informed them there was plenty of fuel still on board.[26]

The post-mortem by the AAIB revealed human, technical and, alarmingly, software errors. The error that caused the right turn when left was ordered was due to a strange condition. If the pilot commanded a change in heading, the aircraft would turn in the diametrically opposite direction to the heading desired, but only if the original heading was 180 degrees. The official report said, "this software error was known to Airbus Industrie", but did not reveal why they kept it to themselves.[27]

At the time this aircraft was relatively new in operation, and the fuel computer's odd behaviour was due less to software than to other technical factors. Nevertheless, the combination of errors was extremely alarming and had extremely serious potential safety concerns. The AAIB report gingerly requested the certification authorities to make sure they knew about all these problems, pointing out that the reliability of these crucial systems was less than was desired.[28]

It is best, perhaps, to leave the subject with quotes from US pilots who have contributed anonymously to the Aviation Safety Reporting System run by NASA. These were quoted in an appendix to the FAA Human Factors Team report and illustrate in plain language the worries that many professional pilots feel about the unprecedented challenges that automation is presenting to them. Each quote is from a different pilot's report.[29]

The climb rate the autopilot had . . . nearly resulted in a stall as the aircraft bled its speed to maintain the climb [rate]. I relied too much on the autopilot and allowed myself to become distracted with my chart review. I'll never underestimate the potential for disaster that over-reliance on an autopilot holds again.

The FMC is something that takes a lot of hands-on experience before a pilot gets much proficiency and speed on it and six months' practice over the last two years is not very much.

Too much emphasis was placed on programming the FMS.

FMC can give you a false sense of security because it's always accurate. This time it was off three to five miles . . .

Needless to say, confusion was in abundance. There are just too many different functions that can control airspeed and descent rates, all of which can control the altitude capture.

My first priority was data entry rather than situational awareness.

The first officer was too concerned about the FMS entry instead of starting the descent properly.

My inexperience led me to attempt to generate a computer solution for a simple manual VOR problem. Attempting to reduce the workload though automation created a more demanding situation, distracting us from the basics of flying.

Being new in an automated cockpit, I find that pilots are spending too much time playing with the computer in critical times rather than flying the aircraft.

As routine as this flying becomes, it is easy to get in a trap of trusting the "magic" of the glass cockpits instead of the old reliable raw data.

This is not an isolated case. I have experienced similar scenarios before. We spend hours doing nothing at cruise while the electronic wonderware does all. Near the airport, the wonderware fails, the airport equipment and personnel put unnecessary burdens on us . . . which can lead to very serious consequences.

The automation is great under normal conditions and works well when you have the time to monitor. When there isn't time to monitor you need to fly the airplane without deliberately trying to override systems that were never designed to perform these non-standard take-off profiles.

I was led down the primrose path relying too heavily on the normally reliable programmed FMC computer, great as long as correct.

Rather than ignore the map and concentrate on raw data, the captain was playing catch-up with the computer.

With over 4000 hours in advanced cockpits, I have found that these supposedly "failsafe" systems can occasionally set us up and then let us down in a big way.

Heading select knob doubles as heading hold button and an imperceptible extra push in on it activates heading hold. Multifunction knobs should not be accepted on aircraft. It is simply too easy at night when you are tired or distracted to activate the wrong function.

Both of us were engrossed in trying to figure out why this computerised marvel was doing what it was, rather than turning everything off and manually flying (which we finally did) until we could sort things out.

Chapter 7

Other humans' errors

OF ALL THE factors that get aircraft into dangerous situations, and that are not the fault of the pilots, maintenance provides the largest category. There are special types of mistake that can be made by maintenance engineers for which no amount of skilful piloting can compensate. The hazards of normal operation are bad enough without having to worry about improperly maintained aircraft.

The kind of crash that results from such failings is getting more common because airlines are increasingly subcontracting the care of their aircraft to outside companies in an effort to reduce costs. The maintenance contractors, in turn, are obliged to cut costs more and more aggressively in order to bid for and win the maintenance contracts. It is a worrying situation and is not going to improve.

This very factor was cited in the NTSB's report on the crash of the ValuJet DC-9 in May 1996. Untrained engineers in the employ of a contracted-out maintenance company had mistakenly stored live oxygen generators in the cargo hold of the aircraft. When they were sparked off, probably by shifting around in the cargo compartment, they generated enough heat and oxygen to cause a furious fire which claimed the aircraft.

In Chapter 1 we saw a horrifying example of bad maintenance practice by American Airlines, which resulted in the United States' worst crash when a DC-10 lost an engine on take-off and stalled without the pilots being aware that a stall was in progress. Responsibility for the bad practice of the maintenance people should probably be shared with McDonnell Douglas for making an engine so hard to service. And then there was the poor repair of the rear pressure bulkhead which claimed the lives of 520 people on Japan Airlines Flight 123 in August 1985, seven years after the repair had been made.

Recognition that maintenance problems are a growing area of safety concern was shown in the UK CHIRP system, the UK's confidential anonymous reporting system. The editors of CHIRP's publication said, "in recognition of the fact that incidents/ accidents with maintenance-related causal factors have shown an increasing trend in recent times, there has been more widespread support to bring engineers into the system as one of the measures to combat this unwelcome characteristic".[1]

Engineers had just been invited to join the category of aviation worker, then including air traffic controllers, aircrew and cabin crew, who could put reports into the system. Curiously, the UK Civil Aviation Authority vigorously resisted the inclusion of engineers in CHIRP. Why this was so was unclear, but it may have had something to do with the fact that the managers of engineering departments of airlines and maintenance companies were also strongly opposed to the move.

Accidents and incidents involving maintenance have been increasing steadily. Between 1986 and 1996 in the UK flights increased by 55 per cent, but incidents where investigators listed "maintenance concern" as a factor increased by 100 per cent. One of the accident investigators who has drawn attention to the phenomenon is David King, of the AAIB. His basic message is simple: "Human-factor-related causes to accident are not restricted to the flight-deck," he says.[2] It may seem a self-evident point, but it rarely receives enough attention.

One of the most famous maintenance-related cases happened to a BAC 1-11 over Oxfordshire on 10 June 1990. As this aircraft was climbing through 17,000 feet the left windscreen blew out under the increasing cabin pressure. The captain was nearly sucked out of the cockpit, but survived because two of the cabin crew clung to his legs while the co-pilot executed an emergency landing.

What had happened was that a maintenance manager had fitted the wrong bolts when replacing the windscreen, but behind that apparently simple mistake lay a series of worrying factors. First, the safety-critical task was undertaken by one person and was not checked by anyone else. Second, the engineer was no neophyte, but a man with thirty-three years' experience behind him, twenty-three of them with British Airways, who were responsible for maintaining this plane.

Although he carried out a variety of tasks in an incorrect manner, it was mainly his enthusiasm that had let him down. He had arrived at work early in order to clear a backlog of tasks. He was under time pressure to get the work done so the plane could be washed. He was also working at a time, between 3 a.m. and 5 a.m., when alertness can be compromised, and he had not been on the night shift for five weeks. In addition, he ought to have been working in a supervisory role but was not because there was a shortage of staff on the shift. Despite the safety-critical nature of aircraft engineers' work, their working hours are not governed, as aircrews' hours are, to prevent fatigue from causing mistakes.

However, when the incident was investigated, he alone was made to carry the can. He was sacked ignominiously, and British Airways escaped any criticism for allowing staff shortages and for not having proper quality assurance, supervision of engineering jobs, or adequate monitoring of this man's work.

Far more serious was the problem that arose during a flight by a British Midland 737-400 on 23 February 1995, a sister aircraft, incidentally, to the British Midland 737-400 that crashed at Kegworth in January 1989. The plane had left East Midlands Airport for Lanzarote, in the Canary Islands, and was climbing to cruise altitude when the crew noticed that the oil quantity in the engines was falling. Soon the oil pressure was falling too, on both engines, and they quickly decided to declare an emergency and asked to divert back to East Midlands.

However, the oil was continuing to disappear and the crew realised they would not make it all the way back. The oil-pressure warning lights came on, they declared a Mayday and air traffic control sent them to Luton airport where they landed safely with barely any time to spare.

It was subsequently discovered that both engines had been inspected the previous night, and during the maintenance two items called high-pressure (HP) rotor drive covers, one for each engine, were removed and then not replaced. The result was that the oil started to drain away once the engines were started. As the plane landed at Luton it was seconds away from both engines seizing. Had the engines failed in flight it was possible, indeed probable, that all 189 people on board could have been killed.[3]

The engineer responsible and the fitter helping him were both sacked and the airline was fined £150,000 plus £25,000 in costs. However, there were disturbing similarities with the BAC 1-11 incident. The main person responsible was a highly experienced engineer who was doing an engineering job instead of acting as supervisor because the engineering department was short-staffed on the shift. The work was also being done in the low-alert time of circadian rhythms, and even though the airline had a quality assurance department, it had not noticed the poor working practices. Nor was the work double-checked.

Even though it is mandated after any engine work or inspection, no "ground run" of the engines was performed, nor was it common practice for this to happen. Had the engines been run on the ground, the leaking oil would have been noticed immediately. Surprisingly, the CAA had, just before this incident, noticed shortcomings in the airline's quality assurance department, but gave its approval anyway because it believed the issues were being addressed. This casual attitude was not criticised.

The judge imposing the fine called it "exemplary", although opinion might be divided on that. A fine of £150,000 might seem something of a let-off for a company that had, through carelessness and flouting maintenance procedures, nearly succeeded in killing 189 people. By contrast, the American airline America West was fined over £3 million ($5 million) for failing to carry out structural inspections per schedule on its fleet of Airbus A-320s.[4] Bad though America West's breach of good practice and the law was, it was not even a specific event with catastrophic potential.

All had not been well at British Midland in this case, or at British Airways in the case of the BAC 1-11. Not only had the working practices, and the workloads on the engineers, been previously identified as serious problems, but quality assurance, which is meant to be a guarantee against poor working practices, had failed in both cases. Nothing that had happened in the first incident was used as a lesson to prevent the second.

Some might say that such slippage is inevitable. Quality assurance is a method that has replaced quality control. Under the latter, work is inspected by a different person and authorised as having been completed correctly. Under quality assurance, the working methods in general are inspected and approved, not the work itself. This must, axiomatically, be less safe than quality control, especially when applied to safety-critical tasks like aircraft maintenance. Of course, it is not hard to guess which is cheaper. Quality control involves using more personnel since they have to be on hand to inspect the completion of tasks.

David King of the AAIB is a civil servant, and so has to mind his words, but the implication in the question he put could scarcely have been clearer. "Have commercial pressures", he asked, "resulted in minimal staff allocations to the task, allocations which rarely materialise due to absences for leave, sickness, or training?"[5] Much as the individuals concerned may have merited criticism, the faults were deeper. King added, "the real causal factors are systemic and do not stop at the individuals, but reside within the culture of the organisation – an organisation approved by the Regulator". Here was an implicit slap on the wrist for the CAA.

The near-disaster of the British Midland 737 exposed another failing that had long been known and also had not been rectified. Best engineering practice says that all the engines of an aircraft should not be serviced by the same person or team at the same time. If they make the same mistake on all the engines the aircraft could find itself trying to stay airborne without the means to do so.

The most famous such incident occurred to an Eastern Airlines Lockheed Tristar on 5 May 1983.[6] It left Miami on its way to Nassau and was twenty minutes into the flight when the low oil-pressure light for the tail engine came on. The captain decided to return to Miami, and shut down the engine. With two of the three engines still functioning the aircraft still had more than enough power to continue, so it was ordered to climb to a new altitude on its way back.

Shortly after the crew shut down the tail engine the low oil-pressure lights came on for the remaining two engines. They could not shut down both of those and so they continued. However, ten minutes after the first engine was shut down, the left engine flamed out, and five minutes later the right engine died too. Once they noticed problems developing in the wing engines, the crew had tried to get the tail engine to start again, but could not do so at first. The plane descended from 13,000 feet to 4000 feet under no power whatsoever before the crew got the tail engine started again, and they made a safe, if white-knuckled, one-engined landing back at Miami.

Engineers had failed to replaced O-ring seals on what are called master-chip detector assemblies. The effect was similar to that on the British Midland 737. Without these items, the engine oil just started to drain away once the engines were started.

When the NTSB enquired later of the FAA what had been done in response to this incident, it replied that it had informed all the engineering vice-presidents of suitable airlines. The NTSB pointedly remarked that they were not the people who do the work on the engines. One European airline adopted a different approach. It modified the O-ring seals so that it was not possible to reassemble the engine and forget to put them back in.[7]

That should perhaps have served as warning – a "precursor" incident – to British Midland, but it obviously did not. Not working on all the engines at the same time may seem to be common sense, but British Midland only adopted this practice after its own incident. More surprisingly, perhaps, Boeing itself only altered its manuals to reflect this suggestion after the British Midland incident. Yet again, the lesson learned from the experience of one manufacturer was not carried over to the other, even though it was a problem common to any multi-engined aircraft.

It seems, however, that many such lessons are hard to learn. On 6 November 1997, a BAe 146 of the Royal Air Force's Queen's Flight, i.e. one of the aircraft specifically designated for carrying the British royal family, experienced just such an incident. Working on critical parts of all the engines at the same time turned out to have been only one of the mistakes made during maintenance.

The aircraft in question was leaving its base on a training flight. After fifteen minutes in the air the pilots noticed low oil quantities on all four engines, and shortly after that the number 3 engine's low oil-pressure warning light came on. The pilots shut that engine down and immediately requested clearance for an emergency landing at the nearest airfield, which happened to be Stansted Airport. The oil-pressure warnings came on intermittently on number 2 and number 4, so they idled those engines and pushed number 1 engine to maximum power. Fortunately for the crew, they managed to land only seven minutes after declaring the emergency, but even so they had to shut down numbers 2 and 4 while still on the landing roll.

The detail on this incident comes from an interesting source, CHIRP, which gave a full account of the incident in a newsletter; but all identifying features of the company, plane type and even engine type were removed. (The details made it obvious that it was indeed the BAe 146 of the Queen's Flight.) In a further clue, CHIRP acknowledged the permission of the Inspector of Flight Safety, Royal Air Force, for publishing the report.[8]

This was a very narrow squeak for the pilots, and only slightly less of one for the royal family. The engines hold 24.2 pints of oil, and each one needed twenty pints to refill them, apart from number 1, which needed twelve. As the CHIRP commentary stated, "only prompt action by the flight-crew and some good fortune averted an accident".

In this case, the aircraft had just been through major maintenance work during which all the engines were serviced, but O-ring seals in the chip detectors (the same items that were left out of the Eastern Airlines Tristar in 1983) were not replaced, allowing the oil to drain away. Yet again, the engineers had failed to run the engines on the ground. If they had, the fault would have been noticed immediately. The company concerned, FRA Serco, was put under a "full safety audit", the UK Ministry of Defence announced shortly after the incident. The maintenance contract for these aircraft had gone to tender under privatisation schemes run by the British government.

The incident showed all the evidence of poorly qualified, under-resourced and understaffed maintenance work, combined with dangerous practices becoming established as standard. The maintenance shift was three senior engineers short out of a complement of twelve. A "leading hand" who was not specifically qualified to work on engines was asked to change the chip detectors, but when he went to get the appropriate spares there was no one present in the engine bay. Recent manpower cuts meant the engine bay was unstaffed outside normal working hours. The engineer consulted his boss and then proceeded to take the wrong chip detector parts from the engine bay. The ones he had did not have the all-important seals attached.

This man was meant to pass the actual fitting job on to someone else, but no one was available, so he did it himself. As the report stated, "The Leading Hand then persuaded an airframe/engine fitter, who had been working elsewhere, to sign for the task and the Leading Hand then signed as supervisor." In yet another breach of best practice that is all too common, people who had not been involved in the work were signing off on it. Other editions of the CHIRP journals are filled with examples of aircraft engineers coming under pressure to cut corners like this.

It also turned out that the leading hand never consulted the aircraft's maintenance manual, where the correct procedure is spelled out, and he and his colleagues apparently told the RAF inspector that it was common practice, which they had inherited from RAF maintenance, not to carry out ground runs of the engines after chip detectors had been replaced.

This was not the only fault in the saga. Oil from the engines has to be drawn and analysed regularly for signs of excessive wear.

The samples were being taken at the wrong time and from the wrong place, meaning that the opportunity to catch problems with engines early on was being lost.

The inspector used phrases like: "inadequate number of supervisors . . . Inadequate planning . . . No advance notice . . . Not following procedures . . . Inadequate training and authorisation procedures . . . Poor communication . . . Consultation . . . was inadequate . . . equipment was inadequately marked."

Had any members of the British royal family died in a crash resulting from such maintenance procedures, no full complement of engines on an aircraft would ever have been serviced at the same time again.

Mistakes that are made in maintenance are often less obvious than this one. However, there are still mistakes that recur time and again, and which, like this one, are not addressed. In the cockpit, attention has been drawn to how pilot errors can be induced by confusing ergonomics. The pilot may well retain responsibility for error, but some systems are easier to get wrong than others.

Similarly, some maintenance errors are accidents waiting to happen, and better design could prevent them. An obvious one was pointed out by Eric Newton in a paper he wrote over twenty years ago. He investigated an accident in which a one-way fuel valve had been screwed in the wrong way around. The part had two threads on either side of the valve. Fuel was meant to go through the valve, but when the time came for it to do so it could not. The result was that the engine was starved of fuel, stopped and there was a crash. If the valve had been designed with a different thread on one of the sides, it would not have been possible to install it the wrong way around.[9]

There are many examples of poor design contributing to maintenance errors in this way. One study showed that 20 per cent of in-flight shutdowns of aircraft engines involved maintenance, and another that about 15 per cent of all accidents involved maintenance factors. Wayne Glover, a former maintenance human factors engineer for Boeing, says, "the [aircraft] design process currently does not include human error, especially maintenance error, in a systematic method".[10] The trouble with checking a normal maintenance procedure is that you assume the engineer has the right tools, is in the right place at the right time and doing the right things.

What Glover suggests is that the design of parts should be looked at from the point of view of seeing what can go wrong, as in failure mode effects analysis. This is the engineering method used in aircraft design where all possible failures of a part or system are analysed to see whether they would result in further failures. "Aggressively seeking human error may produce failure paths not anticipated by the designers, allowing the design to be improved." Obvious candidates for this approach, given the above incidents involving various oil seals, would be engine assembly. Like the airline that adapted the O-ring seals on the L-1011 to make them impossible to leave out, perhaps all engine manufacturers should look at ways of making it impossible for engineers to forget to replace particularly important parts. Obvious it may be, but common practice it is not.

The chief determinant, however, of what kind of maintenance error is made is usually financial. One report said:

> There could be a strong temptation, in the short term at least, to cut back expenditure on crew training and engineering maintenance because immediate savings can be made in these areas without affecting revenue. Staff at all levels will sense the economic situation and some . . . may feel the need to adopt procedures which benefit the company's financial position in the short term but which also jeopardise the safety position.

Those profound remarks did not follow any of these recent incidents. They were made in the context of a committee of inquiry into British air transport which reported in May 1969.[11] Thirty years on we are still failing to learn that lesson.

CHAPTER 8

Investigators and regulators

OF ALL THE insiders in the aviation business, the air-crash investigators are the airline passenger's best allies. Their job is to attempt to prevent the thing we fear most. They do this chiefly by carrying out exhaustive examinations of crashes and almost always come up with convincing explanations of what occurred, even events that can appear unfathomable. They tend to be qualified pilots or engineers – or both – and often have to use great ingenuity and patience in finding out what went wrong.

Their basic task is to investigate the causes of a crash and report on it, making recommendations to enhance the safety of future air travel if necessary, with a view to preventing repetitions. Every country's rules and laws are different but most investigators take as their brief attempting to prevent recurrences of the crashes they investigate.[1] It is then up to the national regulatory body, which is responsible for ensuring the observance of the law and of safety standards among airlines and airports, to act on those recommendations or not.

Investigators have something in common with passengers: they are the orphans of the aviation business. Unlike pilots, airlines, government aviation departments and the manufacturers, they do not pretend to the public that crashes hardly ever happen, and that when they do they are random and unavoidable. Investigators have no interest in declaring that everything in the garden is rosy. The investigator must, as a matter of course, witness the grisly consequences of a mistake in aviation that can rival any battlefield for gruesomeness. Having experienced such scenes, many of them develop a strong passion to see the errors and oversights they have come across corrected, and sometimes are criticised for an excess of zeal.[2]

There are advantages and drawbacks to being seen in this way, a point made by Thomas Farrier, a top US Air Force safety official.

> *Air safety investigators, like safety professionals in other disciplines, suffer an undeserved (or at least somewhat undeserved) reputation for zealotry. We often stand accused of a lack of vision, of too narrow a perspective. However, some safety professionals wear such labels as badges of honor, defending extreme nay-saying as "the conscience of the organization", and arraying themselves in the armor of righteousness.[3]*

In 1997 some of this came into the open. Since the early 1980s the NTSB had been recommending that all large passenger jets, as opposed to merely the wide-bodied jets, have smoke detectors and fire-suppressing systems in their cargo holds. The FAA persistently opposed such measures, declaring them not worthwhile, but appeared to have egg on its face when it turned out that warning of a fire in the cargo hold could possibly have saved the unfortunate occupants of ValuJet Flight 592. This DC-9 crashed in the Florida Everglades due to a fire in its cargo hold, just a few minutes after take-off on 11 May 1996, killing all 110 on board. It was speculated that if a warning system had been present to alert the crew to the fire before it burst through the cabin floor they might have been able to make it back to the airport.

The sensitivity of the issue must have become apparent to the airlines as well as the FAA. In December 1996 top executives from sixteen US airlines pledged directly to President Clinton and Vice-President Gore that they would install fire-detection and suppression equipment in cargo holds, as requested by the NTSB, even before the FAA required it.

Five months later, nothing had happened, leading the chairman of the NTSB, Jim Hall, to remark that the delay "makes the public announcement meaningless, and that is regrettable".[4] Carol Hallett, president of the Air Transport Association, the US body representing the airlines, responded angrily, saying, "suggesting to the press that airlines are not acting responsibly in this matter may advance various causes, but safety is not one of them".[5]

It was not clear what she was objecting to, nor how the cause of safety was being compromised by calls on the airlines and the regulators to be safer. She was clearly putting the NTSB firmly in the "zealot" compartment. Afterwards, however, it emerged that the stately pace of the regulatory system was not, in fact, going to be leap-frogged by the airlines' promise to the President and Vice-President. The airlines were going to wait for the FAA to produce a standard for the equipment in question, and estimates made at the time suggested that it would be another two to three years before the changes were implemented. A classic case of making a pledge when media interest is high and failing to make good on it when the media's short attention span moves them on to another story.

Accusing crash investigators of an excess of zeal is almost required behaviour by regulatory agencies when defending themselves against accusations of inaction on safety. The investigators' safety recommendations go to the UK Civil Aviation Authority, the US Federal Aviation Authority or their counterparts elsewhere, and these organisations are heavily influenced by both the airlines and manufacturers, who are little interested in guarding against what they see as a very remote event with the expenditure of large sums of money. Much as they will deny it, no airline happily spends money on safety measures.

The scope of the responsibilities of the regulators and the investigators vary from country to country. In the United States the 350 staff of the NTSB have other departments responsible for investigating marine and road safety matters, while the 40,000-strong FAA runs the air traffic control system among many other

responsibilities. In the UK the AAIB is divorced from its marine
and road equivalents, while the running of air traffic control is
separate from the CAA, the main regulatory body. Each has been
in the field for a long time and exhibits different strengths and
weaknesses.

Both countries, though, are lucky enough to have separate and
relatively independent bodies for the two tasks of air accident
investigation and regulation. The investigators propose, and the
regulators dispose.[6] There is no obligation on the regulatory body
to follow any safety recommendation made by the investigators,
but it is customary for the regulators to respond publicly to safety
recommendations by saying whether they believe them appropriate or not, or what further action they intend to take.

Between the two types of body there is what could be described
as creative tension at the minimum, or an adversarial relationship
at its worst, which is not surprising given that in the United States,
20 per cent of investigators' safety recommendations are rejected,
and many more are listed as accepted but in fact do not accept the
spirit of the recommendation. Frequently what the regulator is
doing is saying, effectively, "Yes, we accept your recommendation, but that does not mean we are going to do anything about
it." This helps lift the percentage of recommendations that are
listed as having been accepted but results in no change.[7] Much as
they decry failure to observe their safety recommendations the
investigators do not desire the regulatory role for themselves. It is
outside their expertise. What is most valuable about the US and
the UK is that there is a relative degree of openness in the process
whereby recommendations are made and then debated, rejected,
or implemented.

In most countries the investigators and regulators are part of
the civil aviation ministry, and while tension between the two no
doubt also exists, it does not take place in open view.

The UK has seen many battles between the investigators of the
AAIB and the CAA, several of which we have touched on already.
The most heated confrontation came over the issue of smoke-
hoods, in the aftermath of the Manchester air disaster (*see*
Chapter 4), and cabin water-spray systems. Less well known,

perhaps, although typical of many disputes that occur even now, was the background confrontation between the investigators and the regulators over the issue of cockpit voice recorders in the early 1970s.[8]

Bill Tench, who was with the British AAIB for twenty-six years until his retirement as its chief in 1981, remembers the industry's resistance to the installation of this device that we now take for granted as an essential safety feature of all larger aircraft. "This was my pigeon in the AAIB," he says. "Ever since the early sixties we had been recommending the installation of CVRs, but the airlines would not countenance the expense involved in retrofitting all their aircraft."[9] Pilots were comfortable with them, the main battles over privacy and "spies in the cockpit" having already been fought over the installation of FDRs, flight data recorders.[10]

"I was battling all the time with the big noises of BOAC and BEA," Tench says. "They had the clout, and they adopted the attitude, 'Oh, we've put in these damned FDRs that you've insisted on, and we're not going to change our equipment now for you.' And the resistance that they could put up was very considerable." He remembers prominent airline officials successfully lobbying the government to help prevent CVRs being made compulsory: "We made recommendations until we were blue in the face." As so often it was the Tombstone Imperative that brought in the change and, ironically, it involved a BEA aircraft.

On 18 June 1972 a BEA Hawker-Siddeley Trident 1C, under the command of Captain Stanley Key, was climbing normally after take-off from Heathrow on its way to Brussels. At 1700 feet someone in the cockpit then withdrew the "droops". These devices extend from the leading edge of the wing, just as the "flaps" extend from its rear. Both devices increase the surface area of the wing, giving it more lift at low speeds, and are retracted at higher speeds for more efficient flight. However, the plane was only flying at 162 knots and the droops were not meant to be retracted until 225 knots.

All was not yet lost, though. This plane was equipped with an automatic system designed to help recovery from a stall, which is what happens when a plane flies too slowly. When the airspeed fell, first the "stick-shaker", which alerts the pilots to the stall, and then the system's "stick-push" triggered.[11] Somebody, however, cancelled the stick-push, thereby sealing the plane's fate. The nose went up 30 degrees, the plane stalled, and then dropped to the ground like a stone. It crashed, wings level, into a field, killing all 119 on board.

It was discovered that the captain had advanced heart disease and had probably suffered a heart attack, but there were several other pilots on the flight-deck and the reasons for their subsequent incorrect, even bizarre, actions remained totally mysterious.

Unusually, the crash was investigated by a judge at a public inquiry, a very different process from that normally used in British air-accident investigations. It was chaired by Geoffrey Lane, who went on to become the Lord Chief Justice, Britain's most senior judge. Unencumbered by the baggage of membership of the aviation community, his report was highly critical of the absence of CVRs on British aircraft. He also revealed – and roundly criticised – the apparently deliberate delays that had so frustrated Bill Tench, a series of textbook civil service obstructions.

In 1969 the AAIB had revised various regulations on flight recorders in conjunction with the Department of Trade and Industry, including provisions for the fitting of CVRs in all aircraft of the relevant type after mid-1972. This may have seemed far enough in the future, but the airlines were not happy. Their lobbying got the ball kicked into touch in 1970, through the setting up a "Working Party" to "reconsider the whole matter of FDRs and CVRs and to make recommendations".

The Working Party reported in May 1971 that they believed, as far as CVRs were concerned, that they should only be introduced on new aircraft. (Given the very long service life of commercial aircraft, this meant that the majority of British-registered aircraft would not have had CVRs for decades to come.) The recommendations went to the Department of Trade and Industry, which waited for nineteen months before responding in December 1972. It announced it was implementing the suggestions, but only bringing them into force in a further two years, January 1975.

This long and winding road, so typical of aviation regulation in general, was still being travelled in this leisurely fashion despite the fact that the Trident crash at Staines had already occurred and that a CVR could well have solved the mystery.

"This, at least as far as CVRs is concerned," inquiry commissioner Lane commented drily, "we do not regard as satisfactory. CVRs were first introduced in Australia in January 1965 and soon afterwards by the United States. They are fitted as standard equipment to all BOAC's 747s and most large United States transport aircraft. It is nearly four years since the first proposal for their adoption in this country was made . . . The time has come for expedition." Belatedly perhaps, but it was then expedited, owing more to a judge showing his displeasure than to air-accident investigators making recommendations.[12]

There have been many more recent examples of the CAA being all too ready to accede to airline pressure not to implement new safety measures. Part of that industry bias is also shown in the fact that engine and aircraft manufacturers are always represented on official crash investigations. Although they undoubtedly participate honestly and professionally, by being first on the scene they are given an important edge in preparing for possible product-liability litigation. No representative of victims or survivors is permitted to join the investigation. In the UK accident investigation reports are circulated in draft form to any party whose reputation may be affected by the contents, so that they can argue for a change, if they wish. Relatives of victims or survivors receive no such privilege because, absurdly, their reputations are not in question.[13]

In Chapter 3 we documented the delays in consideration of the question of the width of access to overwing emergency exits, and the minimum allowable gaps between bulkheads. If one plots a chronology of the submission of reports, commissioning of research and deliberations of working parties, the conclusion that the delay is deliberate is inescapable.

Occasionally, after some deft footwork, the CAA can even avoid responding to AAIB safety recommendations altogether. In the wake of the Kegworth crash the AAIB report recommended to the CAA that it "initiate and expedite a structured programme of research, in conjunction with the European airworthiness authorities, into passenger seat design, with particular emphasis on: (i) effective upper torso restraint, (ii) aft-facing passenger seats".

The CAA is not obliged, as we have seen, to follow such recommendations, but in this case it never said whether it was accepting the recommendation or not. What it did was propose a "general review of cabin safety/occupant survivability research" through the Joint Aviation Authorities Research Committee. This involved no "particular emphasis" on what the AAIB recommended, and no specific answer on "effective upper torso restraint", let alone "aft-facing passenger seats". Despite the AAIB recommendation having been made in 1990, nothing further had yet been done by the time this book went to press. The CAA's apparent decision to ignore this AAIB recommendation has gone unnoticed by the government and is generally unremarked upon.[14]

The CAA is bound by clear duty, if not by law, to respond to AAIB recommendations, and its failure to do so here is remarkable in itself as much as for the fact that it has attracted no comment. All CAA responses have been folded into research in a European context, and that has dragged on for years without the results, if any, being reported.

In several cases the CAA has dealt with recommendations it is uncomfortable with in the manner of a politician who, when asked a straight question, gives an answer to the question he wants to answer, not the one that was put.

There have also been reports of draft AAIB reports being changed by the CAA after lobbying by manufacturers of aircraft or engines, and in one maintenance-related accident reference to poor maintenance procedures was dropped altogether. In another maintenance-related incident what appeared to be an attempt at news management was recorded. An extremely serious violation of safety procedures during maintenance nearly resulted in the loss of an aircraft (*see* Chapter 7) and when the airline, British Midland, was prosecuted, the date of the court judgement was exactly the same as the date of publication of the AAIB report.

Much of this may be a thing of the past, however, since European aviation authorities are increasingly handing over responsibilities to the JAA, the Joint Aviation Authorities, a secretariat grouping some twenty-six member-nations centred on Europe. Although it lacks formal status and is not an organ of the European Union, it is progressively taking over the functions of the national aviation authorities, especially in regard to certification.

This may seem a move in the right direction, but there are serious dangers, chief among which is the fear that in the drive to get common standards the regulations that result will be compromises. In other words, while the standards of some of the less stringent authorities in the alliance would be raised, those of the most stringent will be lowered.

FAA

The US FAA has been, until the JAA started to rival it for size, the lead agency in international aviation safety standards worldwide, often to the point that if the FAA has not legislated on something other aviation authorities, on principle, will not act. We have seen, for example, how the CAA bowed to FAA precedence on fire regulations despite the fact that, owing to the intensive research following the Manchester air disaster in 1985, it possessed better and more up-to-date information.

However, until very recently, the FAA was saddled with dual and conflicting responsibilities: maintaining aviation safety standards on the one hand, and "promoting" civil aviation on the other. As one of its critics, Mary Schiavo, a former inspector-general at the US Department of Transportation with responsibility for assessing the performance and effectiveness of the FAA, put it, "the FAA couldn't reconcile its conflicting duties, and . . . often it supported the business of aviation at the expense of safety".[15]

The FAA's mandate has now been changed to emphasise the safety side more strongly, but a remit to "encourage" civil aviation remains, and thus so does the double standard. Schiavo

left her job and immediately went public with her savage
criticisms of the FAA after the ValuJet crash in the Everglades in
May 1996. Her chief concern was that in its desire to help Valujet,
a new, low-cost airline, the FAA had not applied the strictest
safety standards in case they were too onerous on the fledgling
business. She also found that, despite an enormous inspection
staff, the FAA did not focus its inspection efforts carefully enough.
In 1990, while still in her government job, she had said, "We
audited FAA's inspections of commercial airlines. Our audit
disclosed that 84 aircraft operators were inspected between 200
and 18,000 times each. In fact, one plane, operated by a major
commercial air carrier, was inspected 200 times in one year,
although no significant violations had been identified. Conversely,
1100 aircraft operators for whom inspections were required were
not inspected."[16] It was speculated that the much-inspected
aircraft plied a route popular with FAA inspectors. For obvious
reasons, inspectors get free travel on planes they are inspecting.

Schiavo's office also uncovered a wide variety of failed inspection procedures in other departments and the fact that many
regional FAA officials become too friendly with their local
operators, leading to laxity in enforcement.[17]

Many of these failings appear to be faults in a system which has
grown complacent, and where there is a greater sense of identity
and comradeship between the inspectors and the inspectees than
between the inspectors and the public. This can happen to any
organisation, especially a highly politicised government body.

To blame or not to blame

An important question for the investigators, if a slightly more
philosophical one, concerns how much finger-pointing there
should be when reporting on the causes of a crash. Blame is one
of the biggest issues in accident investigation. For behind that
simple word lie immense differences over the approaches to be
taken towards the safety of commercial aviation. They concern
the pragmatic question of how investigators get their recom-

mendations accepted, and how they may tailor their advice to what they believe is doable, rather than what needs to be done.

In an increasingly litigious world apportioning blame for a crash is thought by some to be counter-productive. "All we are trying to do is to work together to make things safer and pointing fingers won't help that process," it could be said. The reply often comes, "If responsibility for a crash is clear cut, not blaming anyone lets them off the hook, and relieves them of pressure to resolve the problem. The accident will, therefore, happen again."

However, blaming those responsible for a crash is not really important to the cause of safety. Nor even, necessarily, is finding the definitive, or probable, cause of a crash. Much more important is to find out how the crash can be prevented in the future. Veteran air-crash investigator Chuck Miller says, "I couldn't care less about the cause of the crash. Preventing it from happening again is why I went into this business." This is no mere semantic distinction but a key point in terms of how safety is regarded by the professionals, and is the key to reforming the way safety is thought about by airlines and regulators.

Indeed, Miller and other investigators have called for the elimination of finding "causes" from the investigation process. They feel that fixing causes is similar to fixing blame and that is a legal process, not properly belonging to the cause of accident prevention.[18] Miller quotes the first chairman of the NTSB, Joseph J. O'Connell, on this theme from a speech he made in July 1968.

> *Is it always vital that we identify beyond peradventure which one [cause] was the culprit? I think not. If the alternatives are all possible causes, shouldn't we seek remedies for all? I think so.*[19]

Identifying causes is not the same as finding ways to prevent other crashes in the future. As Miller says, "Any trained safety professional will tell you that classifications of accident causes or factors are merely convenient cubby holes in which to place investigative findings. Further analysis is needed to identify the most practical remedial actions."[20]

Some, like the air-safety investigator Ira Rimson, go further, saying the NTSB, for example, is compromising the goal of preventing recurrence by overemphasis on causes. "The two objectives which the NTSB attempts to achieve – determining cause[s] and prevent[ing] recurrence – are countervalent; that is, they are so fundamentally inconsistent that increasing concentration on one diminishes the worth of the other. Assigning causes is passive. It is little more than assigning responsibility and accountability, or 'blame'. Preventing recurrence requires action."[21]

The arguments for and against finding causes as the primary purpose of accident investigation have gone on for decades in the context of ICAO, within national aviation communities and in domestic law. Unfortunately, this complex consideration of cause, which involves the philosophy of science, moral philosophy and several more obscure branches of human disputation, has prevented the primary emphasis of accident prevention being the goal of every investigation from coming fully to the fore.

Prevention versus cure is a good way of characterising the main differences between investigators and regulators. The FAA's position tends to be the latter, with its critics, among them the investigators, in the former camp. An analogy might be the quest to eliminate lung cancer. One effort is directed at seeking surgical and chemical answers to the disease, while others simply try to prohibit or discourage the smoking of tobacco.

The two approaches clashed most obviously recently in the US National Transportation Safety Board's tussles with the Federal Aviation Administration over the probable cause of the explosion of TWA 800, an elderly Boeing 747 with 230 people on board, over Long Island, New York, on 17 July 1996.

The NTSB acknowledged after a lengthy and exhaustive investigation, which was sidetracked for many months by the assumption by many experts that sabotage must have been responsible, that it could not pin down exactly what had caused the explosion. It was positive that the central fuel tank was the seat of the explosion. These tanks, positioned within the wing-box which connects the two wings, are rarely used on 747s, even on transatlantic crossings, but they are never completely empty.

There is always a certain amount of fuel sloshing around in the bottom of the tank.

The aircraft in question had been sitting on the ground at New York's Kennedy Airport on a hot July day for several hours with its air-conditioning units running at full blast. These units are located adjacent to the central wing tank and can generate considerable heat. The NTSB's best theory was that this heat, combined with the high general air temperature, made the fuel vapours in the tank hot enough to become explosive. With jet aviation fuel, this is quite a feat, it being inherently much less volatile than, say, petrol. However, eleven minutes after take-off, with the air-conditioning units still generating heat, something ignited the explosive vapours, causing an explosion which ripped the aircraft apart. All on board were killed.

Conspiracy theorists aside, nobody has seriously challenged this conclusion.[22] There was much more mystery about the potential ignition source. One speculation by the NTSB was that the fuel itself had accumulated a charge of static electricity, and that a spark caused by its grounding on to some part of the tank set the explosion off. A process similar to this had caused explosions in the storage tanks of marine oil-tankers.

There was also the possibility that an electrical short in the scavenge pump, a pump designed to transfer fuel in the tank to other tanks, had initiated the explosion. But the scavenge pump was not among the 95 per cent of the wreckage brought to the surface. Much later on, the possibility that there may have been arcing across frayed wires whose insulation was much easier to damage than had previously been thought emerged as a strong contender. Although the insulation issue has lately moved to the forefront of probable causes, nothing has yet been definitively shown as the ignition source. Nevertheless, wiring changes have been ordered by the FAA on many 747s and 737s.

The failure to find the culprit in the initiation of the explosion sequence on board TWA 800 is what divided the NTSB and the FAA. The NTSB, with its stated objective of preventing the repetition of disasters, wanted airlines to be forced to do what the military have done with the fuel tanks of their combat aircraft since the middle of the Second World War – to inject an inert gas, usually nitrogen, into empty tanks in order to expel the oxygen and make any explosion impossible. They were still ignorant of the cause of the ignition, but they proposed a way to prevent any ignition occurring.

In the past, FAA concerns over fuel tanks had always been directed towards preventing the possibility of any sources of ignition inside them, reflecting its point of view over fires in aircraft cabins (*see* Chapter 3). It continued with this attitude in response to the NTSB recommendations about inerting fuel tanks. It felt it could not legislate in this way unless it knew the source of the ignition. It said: "The FAA has considered that design features which are intended to preclude the presence of an ignition source within the fuel tanks would provide an acceptable level of safety."[23]

This bizarre statement was a mixture of engineering and bureaucratic code. What it meant was that since the FAA had already done all it could to preclude sources of ignition in fuel tanks, TWA 800's fate must be within the realm of "acceptable levels of safety". In effect, they were saying that such an event is so rare that it is not worthwhile attempting to prevent a repetition. For obvious reasons, nobody put it quite this baldly.

The NTSB's Dr Bernard Loeb said, "It is not a safe thing to have an explosive vapour and there needs to be a way to preclude that."[24] The difference between the two bodies was simple: the NTSB wanted to preclude the possibility of explosive vapours, the FAA to preclude sources of ignition. And since the FAA did not know what had caused the ignition it had, effectively, no proposal to make.

It is clear that methodologically the NTSB attitude here is inherently safer. There have been disastrous fuel-tank explosions before, some on the ground and some in the air. In no case was the cause ever definitively determined. All the more reason, one might imagine, to preclude the possibility of explosive vapours. The FAA, however, wanted to work on precluding sources of ignition, despite not knowing what they were in the case of TWA 800 or the other two cases.[25] It issued six "airworthiness directives", changes to aircraft that manufacturers and airlines must make if the planes are to be allowed to fly, designed to reduce the risk of ignition taking place in Boeing fuel tanks.[26]

Under public pressure and with the high profile of the TWA crash refusing to disappear, the FAA did bend somewhat on its insistence on discovering the ignition source in the tank before legislating. It is now actively considering mandating the use of JP 5, a fuel with a higher flashpoint, and thus less likely to explode, throughout the US commercial jet fleet as a result of the debates about fuel that have arisen during the investigation (*see* Chapter 3 on types of aviation fuel).

In a statement from the FAA, one of its chief technical officers, Tom McSweeny, wrote, "The big issue is infrastructure costs to produce it [JP 5], which is why we asked the American Petroleum Institute to study the infrastructure issues and possible costs. A rough calculation is that the US transport fleet uses 17 billion gallons of aviation fuel each year. Looking at the number of passengers that represents, a 2 per cent increase in fuel, for instance, would be less than a penny per passenger."[27]

This illustrates one of the oddities of air-safety regulation: the balance of costs. The aviation industry is a mature and well-capitalised industry. It is absurd that in this day and age a government agency, paid for by the taxpayer, should be making a large and lucrative industry's cost–benefit analysis on its behalf.

Mr McSweeny went on: "If JP 5 were doable, with a little insulation between the air-conditioning packs and the center fuel tank, on those airplanes that have them, you would be able to say 'no explosive fuel mixture would ever occur in airline operation', even assuming 120 degree F fuel. That is certainly worth going after." So worth going after that it is extremely difficult to understand why it has not been gone after before, especially given the low cost.

This brings us to cost–benefit analysis, one of the most controversial aspects of legislating for air safety. The FAA is bound by law to consider the cost of improvements to safety. US Presidential Executive Order No. 12,291 section 2b says: "Regulatory action shall not be undertaken unless the potential benefits to society for the regulation outweigh the potential costs to society." To work this out a number of variables have to be quantified. First, the FAA look at an estimate of the number of lives that would have been saved in past air crashes had the proposed safety improvement been installed.[28] Then they estimate the cost of implementing the said improvement. And finally, they multiply the number of lives saved by value of a life (about $2.7 million currently in the United States, although the figure changes frequently) to get benefit to society. This is compared with cost and if the value of the lives saved exceeds the cost then the safety measure can be implemented.

In making the argument against fire protection in narrow-body jets' cargo holds, for example, the FAA claimed that the cost would be $350 million, and the value of lives saved $159 million. No change was therefore warranted.

The disadvantages of this system are many. In the United States such means of calculating costs gained considerable notoriety in the 1970s. One *cause célèbre* concerned the Ford Motor Company. Ford had worked out it would cost less to pay compensation to people who would be injured when a poorly designed fuel tank in its Pinto model exploded after being rear-ended than it would to install a five-dollar piece of metal that would greatly reduce the number of probable tank explosions. Such calculations have given cost–benefit analysis a bad name. Indeed, there would not be much popular support for the little-known presidential executive order if it read, "Regulatory action shall not be undertaken unless the potential benefits to society for the regulation outweigh the potential costs to *airlines*."

That, however, is what it amounts to, and this is the method used, albeit with less transparency, in the UK and by most regulatory agencies. In its defence, there needs to be some way in which to calculate how much safety society wants from its machines, and cost–benefit analysis is a reasonably good method. The problem arises from what inputs are used. Currently, all the calculations of the cost of the safety improvements come from the airlines and the manufacturers themselves, and few others have the knowledge to generate alternative numbers.

The calculations of how many lives would be saved by the new safety measure is also controversial, mostly because it is secret and we often do not know what type of crash is being included and which excluded. If costs that are set artificially high are set against figures of lives saved that are unnecessarily conservative, then the proposed measure will fail the cost–benefit test.

No one would seriously suggest not putting a price on life, unacceptable though it may sound on a personal level, for the purposes of making global calculations like this. However, few would agree with the currently semi-secret way of making the cost–benefit calculations. Widespread disappointment, for example, greeted the UK CAA's decision on cost–benefit grounds not to mandate the installation of cabin water-spray systems on commercial aircraft. The CAA had already cut off debate about the introduction of smoke-hoods by saying that they would be superseded by the water-spray system, which showed much greater promise. When the water-spray system was ruled out on cost–benefit grounds, they returned to smoke-hoods, dismissing them as unsafe.

Many were suspicious of the CAA's reasoning in ruling against cabin water-spray systems because fire and smoke inhalation are such important causes of death in air crashes. Unfortunately, what was included and excluded as data was not revealed.

Some of the dubious science at work in these cost–benefit analyses was exposed at a seminar on aviation safety organised by a British transport safety organisation in 1988. Many experts present at the seminar heavily criticised the UK CAA's "Net Safety Benefit Analysis" study which pronounced on the unviability of smoke-hoods in 1987. This was the research that countered the demands of air-safety investigators, survivors and victims' relatives which had risen so vociferously in the wake of the 1985 Manchester air disaster (*see* Chapter 3).[29]

Attracting the strongest criticism was the fact that the CAA excluded from its cost–benefit analysis the Saudi Tristar fire, which claimed 300 lives in 1980. The report supposed that the toxic fumes only came from burning seats, not carpets, curtains, PVC cabin trim or anything else, and that adequate fire-blocking of the seats would have saved those lives. If this disaster had been considered from the point of view of the beneficial effects of wearing smoke-hoods, their economic viability under the cost–benefit method would have been much greater. Many experts suspected, therefore, that the Saudi disaster was excluded for precisely this reason.

The FAA's arguments against using inert gases to prevent the possibility of explosive vapours arising in aircraft fuel tanks are similarly biased. Early in 1998 the US FAA commissioned the Aviation Rulemaking Advisory Committee, a industry-wide think-tank, to consider ways of preventing fuel-tank explosions in the light of TWA 800. In July 1998 ARAC reported it was recommending that the FAA continue to look into cost-effective ways of doing the job.[30]

More important than this statement of "carry on as usual, guys", however, was that the industry body considered various methods of preventing the problem, and dismissed them on cost grounds. It struck down the NTSB's favoured method, making the fuel-tank vapours inert by adding nitrogen. ARAC claimed it would cost $3 billion over ten years if the nitrogen were added on the ground, and $30 billion if the nitrogen system were carried on the aircraft.

The only non-industry person on the ARAC body, however, Paul Hudson of the Aviation Consumer Action Project, said that recommendations of the report were inadequate and that the cost estimates were inaccurate. Asking a commercial organisation to produce a cost-figure for a measure it does not want to implement is unlikely to produce any other outcome.

If virtually unending research does not put off those pressing for change, cost–benefit analysis usually provides the *coup de grâce*. Eddie Trimble, one of the British AAIB's most senior and experienced investigators, put it like this, "We do research to say we are doing research. The idea is not to do anything, say you are doing research and wait until the fuss has died down. Also, they say, 'we can't do anything'. If they are told they must, they do research, and hope the research doesn't turn up anything. If, however, it does result in something they should do something about, they then apply cost–benefit analysis and say it is too expensive."[31]

Systems safety

Prevention versus cure, and cost versus benefit demonstrate different philosophical approaches towards aircraft safety, but probably the most important concerns systems safety. This term signifies a way of looking at a system as a whole to consider the consequences of a fault arising. The Cold War's "domino theory" may have been full of holes when it came to imagining what would happen to neighbouring countries if a country fell to communism, but it is a good analogy when looking at the way failures can come about in complex engineering systems.

Chuck Miller, who was boss of the NTSB's predecessor organisation at the time of the 1974 DC-10 crash near Paris says he has come to be regarded as something of a maverick in the aviation safety business by fighting his corner. "If you use the concept of safety systems analysis," he explains, "you look at the whole system and structure and you say, 'Suppose such and such happens, what would then follow?' You are not concerned about how likely the failure is, you look at the system holistically and look for ways in which one minor fault can trigger another, triggering another and so on to disaster. Under this way of looking at things, you try to break up those chains of errors."

The worst case of this was the Turkish DC-10's cargo door (see Chapter 9). If the cargo door failed when the aircraft was pressurised, the floor blew out, so that the controls through the floor were severed and the pilots thus lost all control.

The FAA, however, and other regulatory authorities look at the probability of the event in question taking place, not the consequences if it does. Miller says, "The FAA and many others in the industry are fixated by probabilities of failure and use that calculation to work out safety. But this is not the same as a system safety analysis, where the interdependence of critical systems is looked at. For example, instead of looking at the effect a door coming off could have on other parts of the system they only look at the probability of the door coming off."

The cargo door's propensity to have knock-on effects in cases of failure was known, but the remoteness of the event was thought by the FAA to be so great that it was not worth preventing.[32]

The difference between the two positions is sometimes called safety engineering versus reliability engineering, the latter being the normal way in which engineers calculate risk. The systems safety approach can be vindicated by looking at the remoteness of the probability of many of the fatal crashes that have had design or engineering factors near the top of the list of accident causes. If such an approach can break the sequence of dominoes falling, safety is enhanced. In order to work well this approach needs to be adopted at the design stage and onwards. Indeed, the fixation on mathematical probability at the heart of the reliability engineering approach can become an alibi.

It also has cynical implications. By saying such and such an event is too remote a possibility to be worth preventing, if the event *does* occur it can be argued that it is not worth attempting to prevent a recurrence. In reality, this does not usually happen. Boeing took action to prevent the possibility of a recurrence of the JAL 123 disaster in August 1985 even though, from the probability point of view, the mathematics had not changed. Had systems safety approaches been adopted from the beginning it is probable the solution they adopted after August 1985 could well have been adopted before the aircraft ever flew, especially given the inexpensive nature of the fix for the problem.

Nor were the mathematics or the systems safety implications any different before and after the ValuJet crash in May 1996. If a fire in a cargo hold is so serious that immediate action is necessary in a wide-bodied jet, it is just the same in a narrow-bodied jet.

Close relations

The UK and the USA are not the only countries where over-familiarity and cross-fertilisation in the jobs market lead to cosy symbiosis between the regulators and the operators.

France is a country where the state still dominates many business operations, and in the field of civil aviation it is supreme. Until recently its predominance was so total, and its confidence in itself so complete, that no effective supervision was taking place. The French civil aviation world is a hermetic society, a masonry of like-minded pilots, engineers and officials who all know each other, and take turns in the merry-go-round of state bureaucracies and state-owned companies. In this cosy, closed world, so similar in its clubbishness to the US and UK aviation communities, a mentality of surveillance and checking did not exist, at least until the Air Inter A-320 crash near Strasbourg in January 1992 (see Chapter 6). This tragedy proved to be a wake-up call for the entire French aviation scene.

Until very recently, both the national airline (Air France) and the domestic airline (Air Inter Europe), one of the main jet-engine manufacturers and the lion's share of the Airbus consortium were totally owned by the government. Its investigative body and its regulators are civil servants too, and the personnel share a common education at the prestigious École Polytechnique, the training ground of top French engineers. This has combined to create a conspiracy of like-mindedness.

When the news from Strasbourg came through everything changed. The new wonder-plane had just had its third fatal crash in as many years of operation, a disastrous situation. The Bureau Enquêtes Accidents (BEA, the French investigators' body) dropped everything and mounted its most exhaustive investigation ever. From its report comes some startling and disturbing information about the absence of oversight.

Worst was the absence of GPWS from the cockpit. One might have expected this to raise eyebrows in the French civil aviation authority, the Direction Générale de l'Aviation Civile, but it did not. In fact, the investigating judge formally charged the DGAC with negligence, for failing to require GPWS installation.[33]

DGAC personnel had carried out no general inspection of Air Inter in the seven years prior to the crash. Furthermore, the airline had no safety department, and none of its A-320 instructors had undergone any competency checks between 1988 and 1992. The DGAC's flight inspectorate had carried out no flight inspections on Air Inter A-320s since 1988. Nor had the DGAC's technical and training inspectorate been able to conduct any inspections, although sometimes this was due to resistance from Air Inter flight-crews working to rule. Indeed, industrial relations at the airline were particularly bad as it had enforced the two-man cockpit on a reluctant workforce.

On hearing that the captain of the plane that crashed only had 162 hours on the A-320 and the co-pilot 61 hours, pilots in other countries gagged in disbelief.

Commandant de Gaullier says that the fact that the state owned Air Inter was the reason why Airbus paid no attention to the pilots' criticism of the cockpit ergonomics, which were believed to have played a crucial role in the crash. Airbus knew that Air Inter was a captive market, and as another state company it was not about to be permitted to buy anything but Airbuses. There was thus no fear that the pilots' complaints could lead to the airline shopping elsewhere.

The Strasbourg crash exposed something rotten in the state of French civil aviation in a very dramatic fashion.

Certification

Once an aircraft has been granted an airworthiness certificate it is generally assumed that the regulators have guaranteed that the aircraft is perfectly safe. This, however, is not necessarily true. What the certificate states is that the aircraft has satisfied the regulatory authority on the minima specified in law on how the aircraft must perform. It sets maximum stalling speeds, criteria for the amount of time all passengers can evacuate the plane in an emergency and various other standards. Manufacturers are expected to exceed the minima because the regulations cannot keep pace with the constantly evolving and changing technology involved in the manufacturing of the aircraft.

Aviation technology is changing so fast and becoming so

advanced that frequently the best expertise on technical questions resides with the manufacturers. Thus, the certificating authorities are having to take the manufacturers' word on certain safety matters, because they do not have the expertise to cross-check it themselves.

This occurred, controversially, in 1995 with the certification of the Boeing 777. The aircraft's fly-by-wire technology and computerised systems were too complex for the FAA to certify;[34] as a result, 95 per cent of the work in certifying the plane was outsourced to Boeing itself. In effect, major manufacturers like Boeing supply their own airworthiness certificates. Not only was the company being asked to certify its own products, it was actually being asked by the FAA to design the tests that the new aircraft would have to pass.[35]

Although such delegation is usually performed honestly, it has serious drawbacks if the supervision process is to have credibility.[36] More worrying, in the 777's case, was the fact that Boeing had been permitted to "put a stake in the ground". It had set a certification date of April 1995 and was working flat out to achieve it. When certification or other tests looked like interfering with the deadline, they were adapted, changed or deemed inapplicable so that it could be met. In the case of the 777 an enormous amount was riding on it because of its commercial importance. It was easy to persuade the US government that the country's largest corporation was facing a deadly contest with the government-subsidised European company Airbus Industrie – and nothing could be allowed to stand in its way.[37]

Mary Schiavo, while still Department of Transport inspector-general, heavily criticised the FAA's failure to supervise the regulatory process over the 777, saying that the Transportation Secretary, Federico Peña, and the two top men at the FAA, David Hinson and Tony Broderick, "interfered with the certification process to keep Boeing's schedule".[38]

To do this, it was necessary to make certification exemptions and exceptions for the aircraft on a frequent basis. The plane was first certified, for example, before it had been shown it was safe to fly passengers on it, which has been the customary definition of airworthiness, so as to keep to the schedule. It also was permitted to fly ETOPS without any testing period.[39] Boeing also had to show that the engines were capable of long periods of continuous operation without breakdown, but during the test schedule a breakdown *did* occur. Boeing nonetheless obtained permission from the FAA to continue with the test schedule as if the breakdown had not occurred.

The FAA is not the only authority that can be pressured by a major domestic manufacturer, especially one with the clout of Boeing. France's DGAC, which also, according to legend, used to hand out blank airworthiness certificates for Airbus Industrie to fill out at its leisure, was accused of not operating sufficient surveillance when it certified the ATR-42/72, a twin-engined turboprop aircraft whose number designated roughly the amount of passengers it could take. The ATR-72 is a stretched version of the smaller ATR-42, which was launched first. Subsequent events vividly demonstrated the difference between being safe and having an airworthiness certificate.

In the ATR-72 crash at Roselawn, Indiana, which killed all sixty-eight on board on 31 October 1994, we saw that growing dangers to a flight can be concealed from the pilots by the autopilot. That was just one of the issues. Controversy also arose because the NTSB believed that one of the factors involved in the crash was an alleged failure of the DGAC to monitor the performance of the aircraft, particularly in ice.

The DGAC responded furiously to the accusations of the NTSB, accusing it in return of not sufficiently criticising the behaviour of the flight-crew and of thus compromising safety. It was a dispute of unprecedented bitterness and the publication of the NTSB report was delayed for many months while the DGAC and the Bureau Enquêtes Accidents tried to get the report toned down and offered alternative explanations. There were reports of diplomatic *démarches* by both sides and rumours, which proved unfounded, that the French certification of the Boeing 777 might have been held up.

Because they were unable to resolve their differences, the NTSB published a second volume of its investigation report consisting solely of the BEA's responses to the criticisms made in the first volume.[40]

The ATR-42/72 came into its own in the mid-1980s because the deregulation of the US airline market meant an explosion in the number of short-range routes flown.[41] The chief technical innovation in this plane, and similar designs from Saab and Embraer, as well as others, was a new composite-material wing so smooth and efficient that large fuel savings became possible.

The issue here is a combination of manufacturers' and the regulators' failings. Icing regulations had been devised in the United States in the late 1940s and, generally speaking, are perfectly adequate. Large jets fly higher and faster than commuter planes, but the latter's lower operating altitudes expose them to significantly more icing than the larger planes. The new, super-efficient wings could not tolerate the quantities of ice older models could, which was a strange compromise to make, since ice has been known to be extremely dangerous to aircraft and has been much feared by pilots since the earliest days of aviation.

The type of icing that caused the worst problems for the ATR-42/72 is freezing rain, a fairly unusual phenomenon involving rain that is liquid but solidifies as it hits the aircraft. This condition was considered so rare by the FAA that it was not thought worth including in the certification requirements when they were drawn up shortly after the Second World War. It turned out, however, to be commoner than supposed, especially in the altitude range that commuter planes usually operate in, between 10,000 and 25,000 feet. The problem would also have seemed less significant when the planes that did encounter these conditions had wings that were more tolerant of ice than the ATRs.

The first serious accident involving an ATR happened in October 1987 to an Italian ATR-42 overflying the Alps. It suddenly rolled to the right and went into a dive it could not exit. Thirty-five died. Exactly the same disaster happened at Roselawn, although then it was an ATR-72.[42]

When rain hit the leading edge of the wing, it ran back over the top of the wing before freezing. The main ice-protection system on this plane was de-icing boots. These are like an inflatable salami arranged on a part of the wing's leading edge. When they are inflated the ice that has formed over them breaks up and is swept off in the air-flow. Pumping them up and down – an automatic process controlled by the de-icing system – prevents a layer of ice forming on the leading edge.

However, because the freezing rain was running back before solidifying, the de-icing boot could not affect it, and a ridge of ice parallel to the leading edge would develop. This would normally cause so much vibration, loss of airspeed and sluggish controls that the pilots would notice and quickly leave the icing environment. When the autopilot was on, however, the effects of the ice would be masked until instability became so great that the autopilot snapped off.

By then, as at Roselawn, it could be too late. On that occasion, the passage of air over the ridge of ice created a temporary vacuum over the wing. This caused the aileron to snap up, sending the plane into a roll. Pilots had managed to recover from this situation in five "precursor" incidents, but, owing to special circumstances at Roselawn, they were unable to do so. The aileron stayed up no matter what they did, the plane rolled on to its back and although the pilots were beginning to regain control, the plane was going too fast and they were too low. The extreme speed tore the wings and tailplane off before they crashed.

The special tragedy here was that it was known that the ATR could be hard to handle in ice, and some preventive measures had already been taken. After a couple of scary incidents following the aircraft's entry into service in the United States the FAA required modifications.[43] These were implemented but did not prevent the problem from happening, and still nobody was alerted to the possibility of this sudden upward movement of the aileron, which caused the Roselawn crash, sometimes called "aileron snap".

The NTSB, however, was in no doubt about what had gone wrong when it published its report into the disaster. It said, "ATR failed to completely disclose to operators, and incorporate in the ATR-72 airplane flight manual . . . adequate information concerning previously known effects of freezing precipitation on the stability and control characteristics . . . when the ATR-72 was operated in such conditions." A further "probable cause" of the crash was given as "The French DGAC's inadequate oversight of the ATR-42 and 72, and its failure to take the necessary corrective action to ensure continued airworthiness in icing conditions." It further criticised the DGAC for failing to keep the FAA up to date with information on the plane, and lambasted the FAA for having poor icing certification standards.

In plain language, the NTSB was alerting everyone to the fact that a plane that had extremely dangerous flying characteristics in certain weather conditions was allowed to fly because there was a loophole in the regulations, meaning those weather conditions were not covered. Manufacturers and regulators were aware of the tricky handling required, but in setting the new piloting rules little attention was drawn to the potentially appalling consequences of even a minor deviation from them.

Had the dangers of freezing rain been included in the certification requirements of the regulators this aircraft and others like it would have had to demonstrate much better ways of dealing with the problem. They were not, and so the plane was dangerous – but legally so.

In its report on Roselawn, the NTSB was implying that ATR had been morally deficient in allowing the aircraft to fly normally when they knew there were conditions in which it could, despite meeting certification requirements, turn into a death-trap. Various alerts and brochures were published by ATR pointing out that there were hazards associated with flying in icing conditions but they did not, the NTSB affirmed, emphasise how dangerous these could be.

ATR, backed by its test pilots, as well as the DGAC and the BEA, has always maintained that the Italian crash and Roselawn were avoidable by better pilot actions.[44] The BEA reply to the NTSB report said that the crew had been inattentive, distracted, and not operating sufficient vigilance. It even questioned their qualifications and skills. It further said that the aileron snap had not been previously known (which the NTSB denied), although it admitted that better icing regulations should be specified.

One French official, who wished to remain anonymous, told

me, "Yes we know there is a problem with this plane. But we set rules for the pilots to follow, and they go and break them. Then we set new rules, and they break those too. There is a limit to how much we can do."

Against this it might well be protested that if something can be done wrong, it will, and that modern aircraft ought to be more error-tolerant. My unnamed informant was guilty of one of modern aviation's greatest sins: using the pilots as Band-Aid's to cover inadequate design. The small-capacity aircraft that preceded the ATR type of plane, like the Shorts 360, were much more tolerant of ice, but they were less cost-effective. It seems unwise for the fate of an aircraft to depend so critically on special subtleties of how it should be flown, with particular operating speeds, propeller speeds and so on. That, it would seem, is a price to be paid for operating more cost-effective planes. The public, however, remains unaware that these planes have a smaller than desirable safety margin, because they require much more precise piloting, and are less forgiving of error.[45] The new technology has been applied here, as ever, to costs, not to safety.

Another reason why large jets do not suffer such problems is that they operate what is called a "hot wing". Spare power from the plane's engines is used to heat the wing and thus prevent ice building up. There have been many crashes of large jets involving ice, but all involved failure to de-ice before take-off. No large jets have crashed owing to in-flight ice accumulation. The ATR and its sister types do not have enough spare power to operate the hot wing. In other words, in the interests of operating economics these aircraft have less safe de-icing systems. To operate a hot wing would require a higher proportion of the engine's power than de-icing boots, and that translates into higher costs.

The FAA had known of the dangerous characteristics of the ATR before Roselawn, even before the crash of the ATR-42 in Italy in 1987. After incidents involving two ATR-42s at the end of 1986 the FAA forbade flights by these planes into icing conditions. Rules on how the planes must be flown and changes to the de-icing equipment were made, after which the prohibitions were lifted. The FAA was keeping the ATR legal, but it was not keeping it safe. It was, however, going as far as it could, given the fact that the icing conditions which put the aircraft in danger had not been legislated for.

It was especially tragic, therefore, to see that similar circumstances to the Roselawn crash were involved in the crash of a similar aircraft in frighteningly similar weather conditions just over two years later.

On 9 January 1997, an Embraer EMB-120, a Brazilian-made twin-engined turboprop commuter aircraft operated by the US airline Comair and similar in design and function to the ATR-72, was approaching Detroit Metro airport. It was in a holding pattern, again like the Roselawn aircraft, with the autopilot on, when it entered icing conditions. A thin layer of ice built up over the wings and tail, which might not have been too serious if the aircraft had been going at the right speed, over 160 knots. Unfortunately, air traffic control had asked the pilot to fly at 150 knots and he complied.

As at Roselawn, the autopilot was masking the growing problems caused by the ice until the aileron snapped up, the autopilot switched off and the plane rolled. The pilots had no control and the plane plunged 4000 feet, crashing and killing all twenty-nine occupants.

In the discussions of what went wrong it was found there was considerable confusion about what pilots were meant to do in icing conditions, despite the Roselawn experience and the furious controversy over the flying qualities of the ATR. Embraer had stated that the EMB-120 should not be flown below 160 knots in icing conditions, after it had performed some tests, and that crews should activate the de-icing boots as soon as ice was encountered.

Embraer informed the US airlines operating the plane of all this in April 1996, but only one of them implemented the changes. The other airlines were not remiss; it was simply that they believed that if de-icing boots were activated too soon, a bridge of ice could form over the boots, thus rendering them useless. The NTSB later called this a "pilot myth" that might have been true in the 1930s or 1940s. The Comair plane was travelling at 150 knots when the upset occurred, but it was not established that the crew knew ice was present or whether the de-icing boots had been active.

The US airline pilots' union, however, squarely blamed the FAA. "The handwriting was on the wall," said Captain Mitchell Serber, of the Airline Pilots' Association. He added, "The opportunity was there for the FAA to take action to prevent the accident." There had been at least six previous upsets of EMB-120s in non-fatal incidents arising in icing conditions. And yet, ALPA said, the FAA had not done anything about it. Comair itself sued Embraer for failing to disclose information about the aircraft's vulnerability to ice.[46]

In May 1997 the FAA had proposed new regulations for the EMB-120 and how it should be flown in ice, as well as a new way of detecting ice. However, a catalogue of warnings and alarms had been ignored. The inadequacy of the icing regulations was already known, the Roselawn crash had already drawn attention to the problem of freezing rain, the icing certification regulations had not been revised, and the susceptibility of the super-efficient wings on these aircraft was already known. And still another crash occurred.

In its examination of the Comair crash the NTSB did not mince its words. The *Washington Post* called it "as brusque an indictment as the safety board has ever issued about the FAA".[47] The report asserted:

> [T]he probable cause of this accident was the FAA's failure to establish adequate aircraft certification standards for flight in icing conditions, the FAA's failure to ensure that an FAA/CTA-approved procedure for the accident airplane's deice system operation was implemented by US-based air carriers, and the FAA's failure to require the establishment of adequate minimum airspeeds for icing conditions, which led to the loss of control when the airplane accumulated a thin, rough accretion of ice on its lifting surfaces.[48]

The FAA failed here, and it failed to listen to its own people. One FAA certification engineer wrote a report saying that the EMB-120 had special problems in ice, and called for warnings to be issued to pilots about what to do, and for minimum speeds in icing conditions to be set, along with other precautions. The report was never formally drawn up, although some of the advice was incorporated in the plane's flight manual. Absent, however, was any sense of urgency.

Certification is a minimum, not a guarantee. Both Embraer and ATR knew they had aircraft that had dangerous tendencies in certain icing conditions, and regulators allowed them to adopt flying solutions rather than fix the design and err on the side of safety.

Enough safety

Many of the problems that regulators face, or create, and the reasons for their reluctance to take action, have much to do with the continuing perception that air travel is "safe enough". This tendency is still there, despite the fact that all the regulators and the international bodies have set themselves the task of significantly increasing the safety of air travel, so that the number of accidents does not increase in line with the increase in air traffic.

One of the saddest examples of the "safe enough" philosophy is the alleged degradation of safety margins in Australia, which has historically had one of the strongest, if not the strongest, aviation safety cultures in the world. Australia's official air accident investigators have been at loggerheads with the Civil Aviation Safety Authority over a demonstration of a new kind of air traffic control in late 1998. The trials involved much less surveillance than had been customary and after a couple of near-misses, the air accident investigators used their legal powers to stop the trial over safety fears and got into a fierce row with CASA.

Air safety investigator Graham Braithwaite has offered an explanation of how it is possible to turn the clock back. After a series of crashes in Australia he commented, "How could an apparently good safety culture start to go into decline? Surely no one lets the safety margin start to erode? One word haunts anything that is apparently safe – complacency."[49]

CHAPTER 9

The Tombstone Imperative

MOST AIR-SAFETY specialists subscribe to the old maxim, "Those who cannot learn from history are condemned to repeat it." The saying is particularly apt for the aviation industry because many of the same mistakes keep coming up again and again in accidents. They do so because the cause of accident prevention is not what drives the process of regulating air safety. Certainly, bad accidents are investigated very thoroughly indeed. Sometimes, however, lessons are not learned, even in the course of major investigations. In addition, the analysis of minor or non-fatal accidents may yield crucial lessons for air safety, but these are not picked apart in the manner of, say, the TWA crash in July 1996, because they do not reach the front pages.

Dr Ted Ferry, Professor of Safety Management at the University of Southern California, says, "When deciding what to investigate there is little question about matters that may be of public concern or that involve serious injuries or fatalities. That is spelled out by law. Where we fail is in making an investigation detailed enough to confirm our seriousness about preventing similar accidents."

Determining the cause of an accident is, of course, vital. However, most people would have thought that ensuring the prevention of others is even more so. And the two approaches are not identical. Whichever point of view you take, we are still not learning enough about preventing accidents from the experience of both fatal crashes and those that nearly became fatal. For every fatal accident, from which most safety improvements come, there are thousands of non-fatal accidents, the study of which can be equally valuable in preventing fatal events.

Rudy Kapustin, now a safety consultant and freelance air-accident investigator who had a twenty-five-year career with the US NTSB, shares Dr Ferry's concerns about where aviation's priorities lie. Both agree that publicity is the key factor. Resources are drawn to particular problems by the amount of media and political attention they attract. As the regulatory and investigatory organisations are controlled by politicians, it is they who will respond to the sight of weeping relatives by demanding answers.

"Unfortunately," Kapustin says, "the dollar value and the level of injuries are still essentially the determining factor as to the extent of the reporting and the investigation requirements in the United States and probably many other countries." In the United States, no accident or near-accident needs to be reported unless someone has been injured, or $25,000 worth of damage has been caused. There need not necessarily be an investigation if a flight-crew avoided hitting a mountain with seconds to spare, so long as no one was injured. In contrast, if someone slips on a bar of soap in the toilet and bangs their head badly on the toilet-bowl rim, dozens of officials would become involved.

Kapustin illustrates this in simple terms:

If a fully loaded Boeing 747 or an Airbus A-340 overruns the runway during a landing for any reason such as runway surface condition, excessive touchdown speed, malfunctioning aircraft flight instruments, air traffic control errors or mistakes by the flight-crew, and there are no injuries, no damage to the aircraft or ground equipment, the occurrence may well not be reported or investigated. However, if the airplane continued down the overrun an additional fifty feet, struck an obstruction, ruptured the fuel tank and half the passengers and crew died in the ensuing fire, a major investigation team would be launched and

*eventually involve in excess of one hundred or more highly
skilled participants in the investigation. A public hearing would
probably be convened and every possible factor which could
have caused or contributed to the accident would be explored
in great depth, many safety recommendations would be made
and an impressive final report would be issued and distributed
worldwide.*[1]

When the rules were first laid out decades ago, damage to
property or injury to persons probably seemed a sensible way of
determining what should be investigated. Now, however, much
more is known about how analysing non-fatal accidents can
prevent disasters, and yet the rules under which investigations are
mounted have barely changed.

One of the scariest examples Kapustin cites of this crazy logic
was also one of the more recent. In April 1991 a German-operated
Airbus A-310 was approaching Moscow airport for landing
when, at about 2000 feet, the captain was ordered by the tower to
"go around" because there was an obstruction on the runway. On
"go around" an aircraft must abandon its approach, immediately
climb to a pre-assigned altitude and circle the airport until cleared
to land again. On this highly computerised plane all the commands to the ailerons, flaps and engines to perform the "go
around" are pre-programmed. The pilot simply selects "go-
around" on his instruments and the computer does the rest. However, neither the airline nor Airbus Industrie had thought it
necessary to school pilots in precisely how this programme would
play itself out.

As the plane began to climb, using full power, the captain
thought that the angle of ascent was too steep. Pilots are cautious,
so when they are climbing they do it gently, well within the
capabilities of the plane. On this aircraft, quite correctly, the way
the computer is programmed means that the "go around" command is exactly the same as that used when a pilot has to take
emergency action to avoid hitting something. The computer
accordingly uses maximum power and the maximum climb angle.

Not having selected "go around" before, the pilot thought the angle of ascent was too alarming for the passengers, so he adjusted the elevator (the horizontal surfaces on the tail) to make the angle shallower. The elevator controls are operated independently of the computer, but the computer sensed the change in angle, and sought to re-establish its original, programmed angle of ascent.

The pilot did not know that the computer was compensating for his actions, so when the angle of ascent failed to ease, he applied more down-elevator. The result was that the computer and the captain were fighting each other without him being aware of it. The upshot of this struggle was the plane pitching up to the vertical, as it slowed to just 30 knots, then pitching suddenly down in a terrifying, almost vertical dive, and then gaining altitude once more. The aircraft suffered four further terrifying roller-coaster-type stalls, convincing all on board that their last moment had come, before the captain regained control and landed the plane without injury to the passengers or damage to the aircraft.

Technically, the pilot might not have had to report the incident, but his unintentional aerobatic display had taken place in full view of the airport, and the many passengers whose lunch now decorated the interior were not about to smile and chalk it up to experience. As a result the German air-accident investigation department fully investigated the incident.

The report of the German investigation described exactly what had happened and criticised the crew – but under the section of the report headed "safety recommendations" was written "none".[2] In April 1994 the pilots of a China Airlines Airbus A-310 fell into an identical misunderstanding over the "go around" mode of their computer as they came in to land at Nagoya airport in Japan. This time, they did not have the height to recover, and the plane crashed, killing 267 people.

After the Nagoya crash, all pilots on this plane were briefed on the characteristics of its "go around" and it became part of basic training. This was by no means the first time stable doors were being slammed shut after the horse had bolted. Adding insult to injury, however, China Airlines crashed another Airbus in similar circumstances at Taipei airport, killing 202, in February 1998 (*see* Chapter 10).

The aviation industry recognises that not reporting and sharing all non-fatal accident information is a brake on safety, but there are many problems associated with it. Full reporting of every little incident can reveal a great deal about how an airline operates its aircraft, and in such a cost-sensitive industry airlines could be giving away secrets to the opposition. Furthermore, by telling the government what they have been doing wrong, the airlines could be inviting enforcement action, particularly in the litigation-rich environment of the United States. As if that were not enough, the United States faces a particular problem in that federally collected information can be forced into the open by the use of the Freedom of Information Act. Airlines would not be happy about anything they gave the government becoming public property.

As a result, in the United States the FAA has proposed a voluntary system of reporting and is "urging" the industry to implement it. Rather than overcome the legal and commercial obstacles in a manner which places the safety of the travelling public at the top of the agenda, they have opted for yet another voluntary code of practice. Requests for the industry to improve its act voluntarily have rarely worked in the past, so there is little reason to suppose this will do any better.

At the same time, the International Civil Aviation Organisation, the UN body setting the rules for international aviation, is implementing other incident-reporting rules, but this body moves in an extremely sluggish fashion, since it needs the consent of many different members with very disparate interests in order to proceed.

The regulating agencies are not entirely ignorant of the problems. In late 1997 the ICAO's members voted to expand its Safety Oversight Programme and give it enforcement powers for the first time.[3] Owing to domestic political pressure, the US FAA had already started a programme under which it has been inspecting the facilities of countries whose planes are flying into the United States, banning some, and restricting the activities of others. With this already in place, ICAO had to follow suit in some fashion, and now it has. What sanctions will be taken against non-compliant members, and what bodies would be formed to carry out the inspection duties, was not clear as this book went to press. By the standards of past performances, the nations that are derelict in their duties need not hold their breath before the ICAO takes steps. As matters stand countries only get safety audits from the ICAO when they request them. It is those that do not request them that we should be worried about.

Under the treaty, for example, member-organisations are supposed to provide copies of their investigations to the ICAO. Many member-countries provide them five years or more late, and many others do not bother. They are not punished. The fault tends to lie with Third World countries which are operating broken-down aviation systems, bad airports and air traffic control, and shoddy airlines. They are the ones that have most to lose, but their votes count as much as those of the industrialised countries.

It is worth looking at the operation of the Tombstone Imperative in detail, to see how it is possible not to learn what seem to be obvious lessons. Possibly the most notorious example concerned the McDonnell Douglas DC-10. This aircraft came to have such a dreadful reputation with the flying public that McDonnell Douglas even abandoned the "DC" label it had given all the civilian aircraft it had been putting in the air since the 1930s. Later versions of the DC-10 were called the MD-11, and updated models of the DC-9, a much smaller jet, are now known as MD-80.[4]

On 3 March 1974 a Turkish Airlines DC-10 took off for London from Orly Airport, near Paris, loaded not only with Japanese bankers, Turkish immigrant workers and returning holidaymakers, but 185 Britons who had transferred to that flight because industrial action at Heathrow meant their own flight had been cancelled. The plane was at 12,000 feet, eight minutes into the flight, and banking over the beautiful woods where Jean-Jacques Rousseau contemplated man's relationship with nature, when the rear cargo door blew off. The door had not been closed correctly and when the difference between the pressurised air in the cabin and the outside of the plane peaked, the latches could not take any more and it flew off the rear of the fuselage.

The technical term for what followed is an explosive decompression. All the air in the wide-bodied jet surged towards the hole in the fuselage like air from an inflated balloon which has been let go. So powerful was this rush that the floor nearest the rear cargo door instantly collapsed, and an entire row of seats, together with its eight occupants, shot out of the plane. All the hydraulic lines, and the control cables for the tail and the rear engine, which ran through the cabin floor, were severed, leading to an almost total loss of control. Some seventy-seven seconds later the aircraft smashed into the forest of Senlis at over 500 miles an hour, killing all 346 on board. At the time it was the world's worst airline disaster.

And yet, a rear cargo door had already blown off a DC-10 nearly two years beforehand. Miraculously, that plane landed safely, but because nobody had died, next to nothing was done to prevent a recurrence.

The sorry tale shows both the kind of influence a major manufacturer can bring to bear on regulatory authorities as well as the kind of thinking about the probability of accidents that still dominates the aviation scene. It shows that compromises on safety for the sake of increased revenue are made all the time, and are, in fact, in the nature of the business.

It is worth looking in some detail at the history of the DC-10's disastrous door.

The Convair division of the General Dynamics Corporation was McDonnell Douglas's subcontractor for door design. As part of the whole manufacturing process, Convair had to supply McDonnell Douglas with what is called a "Failure Mode and Effects Analysis" for every part it was making. This exercise involves predicting every conceivable way the system can fail and what the consequences might be. Among other things, the analysis said that if the cargo door was closed but was not properly locked *and* the "door open" indicator light in the cockpit failed, then it could blow open. This could possibly lead to collapse of the floor and/or damage to the tailplane from cargo or seats being expelled.

In May 1970 Convair conducted a pressurisation test on Ship 1, the first DC-10 off the production line, in connection with a test of the air-conditioning system. Suddenly, the forward cargo door

blew open and a large area of the cabin floor collapsed. The
companys' response was to blame the person who failed to close
the door properly, but they still recognised that a modification
was required. They came up with something Convair described as
a "Band-Aid" fix which did not solve the inherent problem.

In essence, the fix to the door involved linkages that went
through so many bends and angles that they were more flexible
than they should have been. The result was that you could still
close the door, and believe it to be fully locked, when it wasn't.

All this was stated in an unusual document called the *Applegate
Memorandum*, which Convair's top engineering expert wrote two
weeks after a cargo door came off the American Airlines DC-10
over Windsor, Ontario, on 12 June 1972. Applegate wrote, "It is
only [by] chance that the airplane was not lost."

Captain Bryce McCormick, who was flying the Windsor DC-
10, had plenty of luck, but he must have used it all up that day.
When his cargo door blew off at 12,000 feet he lost control of the
tail engine, the rudder and the stabilisers, but had limited control
of the elevators, and the ailerons were working. In other words,
not all the hydraulic lines had severed, as was almost certainly the
case at Paris two years later. The Windsor plane was also lightly
laden, with only 56 passengers, compared with 346 on the
Turkish plane.

The cockpit voice recorder of McCormick's flight after the loss
of the cargo door has since been used as a model of how pilots
should behave when faced with an emergency. Showing exemplary
coolness, the crew managed to control the plane successfully
enough to land at Detroit. One stewardess was nearly expelled
from the plane when the floor collapsed near the cargo door, and
a couple of passengers suffered broken bones during the emergency
evacuation after the plane had stopped.

Applegate's memorandum said that after Windsor McDonnell
Douglas was still looking at further "Band-Aids" to the cargo
door, and described the final solution which was adopted – to
install a peephole near the bottom of the door through which the
position of the locking pins could be checked – in this way. The
peephole was an absurd solution. The door was fifteen feet off the

ground, the window could be obscured by dirt or condensation, and final responsibility for this critical safety factor was left with baggage handlers.

Applegate reserved his main criticism for the design of the cabin floor. Irrespective of how idiot-proof the door was, holes open up in planes for other reasons, like bombs, mid-air collisions or flying debris from engine failures. Applegate complained that after the May 1970 pressure-test experience, McDonnell Douglas did nothing. "It seems to me inevitable that, in the 20 years ahead of us, DC-10 cargo doors will come open and I would expect this to usually result in the loss of the airplane," his memo continued. The cabin floor could not resist explosive decompression and when it collapsed all hydraulics and the controls of the tail engine would be lost.

Applegate's main concern in writing the memo was with Convair's possible future legal liability in the event of a crash, and the memo went neither to the FAA nor McDonnell Douglas. The latter wanted Convair to pay for the post-Windsor improvements to the door, while Convair said it was the manufacturers' responsibility. They batted financial responsibility to and fro without the safety considerations taking front seat or emerging from the inter-company correspondence.

Everyone knew that the door should be fixed, but the real reason the FAA did not compel McDonnell Douglas by law to fix the door was because the Nixon administration was going through one of those phases of American governance in which "big government" had become the enemy. Instead of regulatory zeal, the Nixon administration held that "voluntary compliance" would be the best way of working with industry on matters like this.

Accordingly, what became known as the "gentlemen's agreement" was reached between the FAA and McDonnell Douglas, under which the company would take its own sweet time to address the problem. This was done very gradually, but not in time to save the lives of the people on the Turkish plane. The practice of "voluntary compliance" by the FAA went out of the window just weeks after the Paris catastrophe.

The British air-accident investigator Eric Newton had a similar view of the DC-10 to Mr Applegate. He had been called on to pick through the ghastly wreckage of the Turkish plane because of his expertise in bombs exploding on aircraft, a possible cause that had to be ruled out early on. Once Newton, in conjunction with American and French investigators, realised no bomb was responsible, he resisted the media's obsession with the door to the exclusion of other factors. "The door was one thing," he says, "but the floor was the critical problem. Nobody had very seriously considered the size effect of the vastly increased volume of air in a wide-bodied plane. If you double the volume of a plane, you cube the quantity of air in it, and this is what's trying to escape through any hole. And yet the hole that the planes needed to be able to cope with was the same size for the jumbos as for the narrow-bodied planes."[5]

A hole that appeared in the fuselage of a narrow-bodied plane, like a Boeing 707, could easily be coped with by the airframe, and that generation of jets was designed so that no explosive decompression could cause any catastrophic failures, or jettison rows of seats. For the wide-bodied jets, however, this safety feature was abandoned. For certification purposes the then-new wide-bodied jets only had to deal with a hole the same size as their more narrow-bodied cousins.

Certification requirements, however, also state that the aircraft's structure must be able to maintain its integrity in an explosive decompression. In the UK these requirements are absolute, and clearly the DC-10 and, as we shall see shortly, the Boeing 747 fail to meet them. In the United States, however, there is a loophole. The manufacturers can show that if the likelihood of the catastrophic event happening is "extremely remote", they do not have to satisfy these requirements.

The most likely way for a hole to appear in a jet is for a door to come off. Despite the much more serious consequences of a door coming off a wide-bodied jet, nobody thought to specify that they should be safer. As a result the accidents keep happening.

One of the more recent befell a United Boeing 747, flight UAL 811, on 24 February 1989 with 355 people on board. It had left Los Angeles for Sydney by way of Honolulu and Auckland, New

Zealand. It had taken off normally from Honolulu when the crew
spotted thunderstorms on their weather radar, so they requested
and were given permission to deviate from their course and climb
further. As they were climbing above 22,000 feet the crew heard
a thump followed by a "tremendous explosion", in the captain's
words.[6]

They had suffered an explosive decompression because the
forward cargo door had blown off. Almost instantaneously, the
cabin floor collapsed and nine passengers seated closest to the hole
shot out of the plane together with their seats, just like the
passengers sucked out of the DC-10 near Paris. Debris, probably
including some passengers, was sucked into the engines on that
wing causing them to fail. No bodies were recovered. The flight-
crew had to exercise great skill to control the aircraft with only
two engines operating on one side, but they did so and landed
safely at Honolulu.

The investigators soon experienced *déjà vu*. The cargo door
was of a similar, electrically operated, design to the DC-10's, but
fortunately for the rest of the passengers on the flight from
Honolulu, the 747's hydraulic lines run through the roof of the
fuselage and the floor collapse had not affected them or other
flight-critical systems. The US NTSB closely examined the
accident. The following quote from the official report exemplifies
the deliberately dry tone of these findings, but between the lines
can be seen ingredients that would have enraged the travelling
public had they received wider attention.

> *Contributing to the cause of the accident was a deficiency in the
> design of the cargo door locking mechanisms, which made
> them susceptible to deformation, allowing the door to become
> unlatched after being properly latched and locked.*[7]

Consider the NTSB's determination of the probable cause of the
accident to Bryce McCormick's DC-10 in June 1972, seventeen
years beforehand: "The design characteristics of the door latching
mechanism permitted the door to be apparently closed, when, in
fact, the latches were not fully engaged."

The French official report on the 1974 Paris disaster used almost identical language. Electrically operated, outward-opening cargo doors presented a hazard to planes that were not there before, and yet few were making the connections, and nobody was attempting to correct them. The NTSB report into the UAL 811 accident was well aware of the similarity of problems in the DC-10 cargo door and the 747 forward cargo door. It noted, merely, "The revisions to the DC-10 cargo door mechanisms mandated after that accident [the Paris DC-10 disaster of 1974] apparently were not examined and carried over to the design of the B-747 cargo doors." They may not have been examined, but it would have been extremely strange if Boeing had not realised that the 747's cargo doors were prone to problems similar to the DC-10's. Their inaction, therefore, seems all the more surprising.

The NTSB chose not to slap Boeing and the FAA on the wrist for not doing something about the poor door-design. The UAL 811 report did say, however, "Also contributing to the accident was a lack of timely corrective actions by Boeing and the FAA following a 1987 cargo door opening incident on a Pan Am B-747."

When passenger aircraft were first pressurised in the 1940s, the type of door used was called a plug door, like those which you see in the passenger cabin of a plane. The door closes, and the edges of it are angled so that when the aircraft becomes pressurised, the pressure keeps the door shut, like the way in which water in a bath keeps the plug in the plughole. Unlike bath-plugs, plug doors cannot be opened by any means, deliberate or accidental, so long as the cabin is pressurised.

Such doors, however, must open inward and that takes up space. So engineers at Boeing and McDonnell Douglas were asked to design doors that open outwards when dealing with the cargo bays. Cargo is an immensely valuable revenue earner for airlines and every cubic foot of space inside the fuselage that can be devoted to cargo increases the profitability of the plane. At first, they came up with hydraulically operated outward-opening cargo doors.

The advantage of hydraulic operation is that pressure is

continuously applied to the door. If it is improperly closed the door will ease open as the cabin pressure increases. An electrically operated door, however, that is improperly closed may simply burst open. It is like the difference between a pane of glass and a sheet of perspex. Under continuous pressure one will bend a long way before shattering, while the other will shatter faster.

Despite their dreadful record, electrically operated non-plug cargo doors are still with us, and are very unlikely to be changed unless many more people are killed.

If the type of door was a compromise, then other standards were also under pressure when the wide-bodied jet came along in the late 1960s. Eric Newton had pointed out in the aftermath of Paris that floors are integral parts of the plane structure. The US and British regulations governing airworthiness unequivocally state that all parts of the plane's structure must be able to resist explosive decompression.

Neither the DC-10 nor the Boeing 747 could meet this requirement, which invites the question as to how they got their airworthiness certificates. The answer is that both plane-makers were able to show that the likelihood of a door coming off was "extremely remote". This meant that it would not come off more than once in every billion flights. As happens all too often, citing the remoteness of the possibility of a failure has been a cover for unsafe design.

Safety specialists have never been happy with this method of calculating safety. As Newton and others had already pointed out, the regulators were letting McDonnell Douglas off the hook by accepting their calculations of how remote the possibility of a door coming off might be. That calculation never even considered the fact that errant engine blades, or a bomb or other problems could cause a hole to appear in the fuselage, with the same explosive decompression resulting, along with the same potential for catastrophe.

Despite the importance of non-fatal precedents, and the need to pick up the lessons from them before they turn into catastrophes, there are many instances where lessons have not even been learned from the fatal crashes.

The worst accident to result from an explosive decompression had nothing to do with doors, cargo or otherwise. Vital lessons could have been learned from it, and were not, because although the engineering principles were the same, the type of aircraft was different. Again, this involved the DC-10 and the Boeing 747. In this case even the "Tombstone Imperative" failed.

The disaster in question occurred when a Japan Airlines 747 crashed in August 1985. It was the worst crash involving a single plane, claiming 520 lives. The tragedy resulted from an extraordinary set of circumstances.

JAL use 747s in a unique way. Mostly, they fly very short flights, rarely more than thirty or forty minutes, on domestic routes. The short routes are viable for these huge jets because Japan is so mountainous that travel by road and rail is difficult. As a result, the planes are pressurised many times more frequently than the average 747. This type of 747 was specifically designed for these frequent pressurisations, often ten flights a day, and had never suffered any problems.

However, the plane that crashed on to the mountain in 1985 had suffered a tail-strike, as it is known in the jargon, when the rear end of the fuselage was heavily damaged on landing at Osaka in June 1978. The rear-pressure bulkhead was damaged and had to be repaired by Boeing. This structure looks like a giant umbrella at the end of the fuselage, separating the pressurised part of the plane from the tail assembly, which is not. The "umbrella" was incorrectly repaired, giving it insufficient strength to meet the expected number of pressurisation cycles that would follow.

Seven years after that botched job, the chickens came home to roost. A few minutes after take-off from Tokyo on 12 August 1985 the rear pressure bulkhead failed and a huge hole allowed the pressurised air to surge into the tail. Effectively, the air rushing into the tail inflated it like a giant balloon, and burst it apart.[8] The pilots would probably have been able to cope with flying the plane with no tail-fin, but when it separated from the plane it severed all the hydraulic lines.

The 747 has four separate hydraulic systems running around the aircraft. One would be enough to operate all the control surfaces of this or any other jet, but if it failed the plane would crash, as the hydraulics are an indispensable part of what gives the pilots the means to control the plane. As a result, in the case of the 747, the hydraulics are separated into four independent systems for redundancy.

However, all four hydraulic lines converge in the tail, so when the tail-fin came off the JAL jet, it took all the hydraulic lines with it. This was thought so remote a possibility it was not even considered as the cause of the crash until the physical evidence of the wreckage left no other explanation.

After this event the 747's fate was sealed. The hydraulic fluid drained out into the sky and the crew only had control of the engines. The plane wandered about the sky like a dead leaf being blown on a 200-knot breeze for an extraordinary thirty-two minutes before it struck the remote mountain.

To prevent a recurrence, Boeing installed valves on all other 747 hydraulic systems. Even in the almost unbelievably unlikely event of all four lines being severed in another accident, the valves would prevent the hydraulic fluid draining away and the pilots would retain control of the plane. This design improvement was implemented on all 747s in operation, not just those constructed from that time on.

Curiously, this lesson was not applied to any other aircraft, even though all passenger jets use hydraulics and most would crash without them. Different manufacturers' aircraft vary in many respects, but not in hydraulics. They have between two and four hydraulic systems for redundancy, and with the improvements to the 747 a further level of safety was added.

It simply did not occur to the NTSB, the FAA or any of the other regulatory or investigative authorities that if these valves could turn out to be life-savers on a 747 then they ought to do the same job on any other jet with hydraulics. The Tombstone Imperative, in this case, was only operating for 747s, and not for other aircraft.

The airlines and the manufacturers have conditioned the aviation regulatory authorities not to add to their costs with new safety measures unless absolutely necessary. Whether this thinking lay behind the decision not to require all passenger jets to install valves in their hydraulic systems, or whether nobody thought of it, is not known. Given the history of safety regulation, however, the former is the more probable, even though installing such valves is not expensive.

The gap in this reasoning was fully exposed on 19 July 1989, in the course of one of the most dramatic air crashes of the post-war era, an event a Hollywood scriptwriter would probably have had rejected as too implausible. A United DC-10 was at 30,000 feet over the plains of the US midwest in cruise, usually the most relaxed part of the flight for the crew, when the huge rotor disc – the part you can see when looking at the front of a jet engine – span off the tail-mounted engine, flinging fan blades in all directions at incredible speeds. Losing the engine was an emergency, perhaps, but no disaster. The plane had two left, so no more than a diversion to the nearest airport was thought to be the likely outcome – at first.

Some of the errant fan blades from the disintegrating engine, however, had sliced through not one but all three of the aircraft's hydraulic lines. Although their professionalism never deserted them, it was with increasing alarm that the crew saw that their hydraulic pressure was disappearing. The pilots managed to keep the plane going, using some of the lessons about controlling the plane with use of the engines alone that Bryce McCormick had brought to prominence when he and his co-pilot were saving his DC-10 seventeen years beforehand.

The crew contacted their headquarters for advice about what to do. The engineers at base consulted all their manuals. Losing all hydraulics had never been imagined, for the simple reason that without them the plane ought to have been uncontrollable. The engineers had no advice for the pilots because, by rights, they should have been dead already.

Here, perhaps, the gremlins had for once decided to help the DC-10 overcome its appalling reputation. Despite the fact that it ought not to be flying, it was. Eventually, in a display of extraordinary courage and coolness under fire, the pilots brought the plane in to Sioux City airport. Unfortunately, it crashed on the runway, and although most survived the impact, a fire broke out. Of the 296 people on board, 112 died, about half from fire-related injuries.

However, had the lessons of the JAL jumbo four years beforehand been applied to the DC-10 and all other passenger jets, and valves installed in the hydraulic system, they would probably have carried out a safe emergency landing and never achieved fame.[9] Special valves were belatedly installed in the hydraulic systems of DC-10s after the Sioux City crash.

Rudy Kapustin shows his frustration with the way the system works in cases like this. "Airplanes and helicopters crash, crew members and passengers are killed, horrendous liability and damage litigation and unbelievable grief and suffering continues because, for whatever reason, there is still insufficient feedback, open exchange of technical information on a worldwide basis, thorough investigation of seemingly minor operational occurrences or mechanical anomalies."

We have already seen how concerns about proprietary information, or fear of government action can prevent information being shared, but Kapustin's anger is mainly directed at the fact that "preventing accidents" is not the guiding principle of the regulatory authorities.

There are myriad conflicts between airlines' operational demands and maintaining safety. If there is not always a conflict, there is certainly a balance to be struck. People frequently question airlines as to why they do not adopt, say, a water-sprinkler system for the passenger cabin to put out fires. If he or she cannot duck the question, the airline representative will always end up by asking whether you want the price of your ticket to double. This is disingenuous in the extreme. British Airways spent an estimated £60 million "rebranding" the airline, including repainting the fleet, in 1998 after spending millions on market research. Later it proved a failure and another livery change was required. And yet the issue of increasing the price of tickets only seems to be brought up in the context of new safety standards.

The reasons are simple. The rebranding was intended to increase BA's revenue, but the new safety technology that can make more profits has not yet been invented. Such is not the case for technology that increases profits by reducing operational costs.

Probably the most important area in the last twenty years for such innovation has been fly-by-wire operation and the computerisation of flight. Although all innovations in new technology have to be demonstrated as safe, it is inevitable that since cost-reduction is driving the whole process, safety has been compromised along the way. New technology always has teething troubles, and these usually involve loss of life. The human casualties sustained while getting FBW and computerisation right have run into hundreds.

FBW alone has only very rarely been associated with causing civil accidents, much less frequently than it has been accused. Where an FBW problem did arise on a Boeing 767 it caused a catastrophe and showed that its designers had not thought to reproduce the failsafe reliability of the system it replaced.

The plane in question was the pride of former Formula One world champion Niki Lauda's small fleet of planes. Lauda Air's *Wolfgang Amadeus Mozart* Boeing 767-300 ER was climbing out of Bangkok airport at 25,000 feet with engines on maximum power on 26 May 1991 when one of the two vast Pratt & Whitney PW 4000 engines went into reverse thrust. Within six seconds the plane was out of control, cartwheeling earthwards with no possibility of recovery, breaking up as it went. All 223 on board died.

No plane had been lost in this way before. It is an unfortunate theme of FBW and computerisation that, while eliminating types of accident that had happened to older-technology planes, they introduced hitherto unknown ways of crashing. Such is our concept of the march of progress, however, that when tried and trusted methods are replaced by new ones which result in accidents, the regulators never order the airlines and manufacturers back to the old technology, even when the cost implications are very small.

Although a very advanced jet, the Boeing 767 does not have FBW for the control surfaces, but it does for the engines. It is called fully automated digital engine control (FADEC). This is like cruise control on a car and keeps the engines doing what the pilots want by FBW links. It also enables the flight computers to vary thrust automatically. To supplement this system, Boeing installed an electronic system controlling the thrust reversers to replace the mechanical linkages in the cockpit. The electronic system would save weight, and would enable the thrust reversers to be controlled by the computerised system.

Thrust reversers are metal casings that slide across the plume of the engine's exhaust, directing it forward, so as to help the plane brake on landing. They must never deploy in flight and a series of failsafes prevented them from doing so before the new system came in. The casing that redirected the engine exhaust plume on the 767 was, at first, locked mechanically, and the lever controlling it in the cockpit was connected to it by a cable. The lever was set in such a way that it was physically impossible to move so long as the throttles on the engines were being used in forward motion.

The replacement, FBW system was not capable of such a failsafe device because it was electronic. However, it had a new safety device called an auto-restow. Should the auto-restow sense the casing sliding into the reverse position it would automatically stow it back in its proper position by electronically ordering the hydraulic system to do it.

The hydraulic system was designed to open or close the thrust reverser casing. On that flight out of Bangkok, the auto-restow evidently ordered the hydraulic system into action successfully a couple of times. However, when the hydraulic system, almost certainly owing to chafed and faulty wiring, moved to the position to deploy the thrust reverser, the auto-restow did not "know" it. So when it operated the hydraulic system to stow the casing back in its proper position, it was in fact ordering it into the wrong position, thrust reversal. The auto-restow, which was only there as a safety device, in fact caused the accident.[10]

Subsequent examination showed that 90 per cent of similar Boeing 767s had the potential for the same fault. Cost reduction drove this "improvement" and thus played a part in the deaths of over 200 tourists, flight attendants and pilots.

In early 1995 the FAA was in the midst of testing Boeing's new 777 for its airworthiness certificate. Boeing admitted straight away that in the event of an accidental thrust reversal the aircraft would not be controllable. Of course, that does not alter the rules, under which a flight test of such an event is mandatory. Nevertheless, Boeing managed to convince the FAA that the possibility of an in-flight thrust reversal was too remote to consider. The FAA accordingly granted Boeing a waiver on this part of the certificate. How much less remote was this eventuality on the Lauda Air 767?

CHAPTER 10

How to decide where not to go and how not to get there

SOME OF THE most common questions posed by travellers concerned about safety are the following: are there planes, places or airlines to avoid? The answer to most of these questions is yes, but there are many provisos to the statistics. And other information that could help us towards making informed decisions is often secret.

As a general rule, there are areas of the world to avoid flying in, and airlines too, and these differences are much more important than anything that separates different types of aircraft.

The first and easiest question to answer deals with aircraft. In the civil aviation world, size matters. The larger the category of aircraft, the safer it is. Helicopters are the most dangerous kinds of aircraft, followed by small private planes, then commuter aircraft, carrying fifty passengers or so, which are approximately half as safe as the safest aircraft, large commercial jets.

They become safer as they become bigger for a variety of reasons. Unfortunately, pilot pay is linked to the size of the aircraft they are flying, which is more a reflection of the responsibility on the crew's shoulders than the actual skills involved. This is a historical accident, together with the fact that aircrew are paid by seniority. Be that as it may, it means that bigger jets have more experienced crew.

Other points in favour of the greater safety of larger jets include the fact that they have a wider variety of safety equipment and navigational aids, and use the largest and thus most modern airports with the best equipment to help landing and take-off. They also normally cruise at between 25,000 and 40,000 feet, and higher up the air is generally less turbulent. And on top of all that the aircraft are maintained and inspected more strictly than smaller planes, and are governed by stricter safety regulations.

The smaller passenger aircraft like turboprops, with up to fifty or so passengers, have greater safety problems because they operate in a more hostile weather environment, as we saw with the commuter aircraft and their icing problems (*see* Chapter 9). The air is rougher between 10,000 and 25,000 feet, and the planes do more journeys than jet aircraft in a typical day. Their crews are also less experienced, even though they have to do far more hands-on piloting than their more experienced and older colleagues on jets. Furthermore, they fly into smaller airports with less sophisticated landing aids.

Some people believe that such aircraft are less safe than larger planes because they are driven by propellers. This is not the case. Turboprops are simply jet engines with propellers attached to the turbine shaft instead of fan-blades. Overall, turboprops have approximately double the accident rate of larger jets.[1] If you have a choice it would, obviously, be preferable to use the jet rather than the turboprop. Choice, however, is not normally an option if considerable delay and expense is to be avoided. There is another statistical caveat: an ageing, less well-maintained jet belonging to an airline in financial trouble will probably be more risky than a two-year-old turboprop being operated by a large, sophisticated airline.

When one tries to consider the relative safety of different types of aircraft, a statistical minefield begins to appear. Although one might permit oneself a comparison of the aircraft with the very best record against that with the very worst, there is very little in the crash record to tell us how to make up our minds. Indeed, Airclaims, the aviation insurance loss adjusters, who publish the most comprehensive data on aircraft accidents, introduce their statistical digest, *Airliner Loss Rates*, with this preamble.

> *Although a review of the* Airliner Loss Rates *will show that for a particular period, certain aircraft may have "better" or "worse" loss rates, this is not and should not be considered as necessarily an indication that one aircraft is "more safe" than another.* Airliner Loss Rates *does not attempt to look at or compare the "safety record" of different aircraft types. "Safety" is a different concept which cannot be quantified by the relatively simplistic determination of loss rates.*[2]

Airclaims publishes this as an "explanatory note", not a disclaimer. It is not simply a sop to airliner manufacturers who might feel they have been badly treated in the figures. The entire world fleet of passenger jets stands at only about 12,000, with a further 5000 or so turboprops. The rates at which they have fatal accidents vary between 0.1 per million flights to 5 per million, which means that the fleet of aircraft is simply not big enough for the crashes that do happen to be statistically meaningful.

Some aircraft with apparently poor safety records have been unfortunate to be worse hit by terrorism, for example, than others. The 747-100 (the earliest of the jumbos), for instance, has one of the worst statistical crash records but it has had an unusual share of terrorism to deal with and even one shootdown (KAL 007). The most recent jumbo, the 747-400, has a much better record than its predecessor, but that may have nothing to do with one machine being safer than the other.

Some aircraft, however, get reputations, no matter how many statistical caveats are offered. The McDonnell Douglas DC-10 has laboured longest under a black shadow. It is unique in its unpopularity, even in the aviation community. In the public mind it became associated with disaster, and passengers have often shunned it as a result.

At the time it took place, the DC-10 crash near Paris in March 1974 was the world's worst aviation disaster, and the public has rarely been as shocked as it was by the revelations about the history of decisions over the design of the cargo door. Long after all those problems were in the past, the reputation persisted. In the summer of 1996 panicked passengers boycotted an Excalibur Airlines DC-10, which proved to be the *coup de grâce* for the financially ailing operator, when smoke was seen in the cabin. It was a minor technical problem, but when it was resolved hardly anyone wanted to go back on board.

As mentioned previously, McDonnell Douglas abandoned the "DC" prefix as a result of the disastrous PR years of the 1970s, and later versions of the DC-9 became the MD-80, while subsequent versions of the DC-10 were named MD-11.[3] Despite this dreadful reputation among passengers, however, many pilots love the immensely responsive flying qualities of the aircraft. It also proved itself, in the Sioux City crash of 1989, for example, capable of performing beyond its design expectations. Finally, the statistical record shows that DC-10 crashes became less frequent as the fleet aged, while, normally, the opposite is the case.

Apparent safety can be deceptive in other ways. The Concorde, the Vickers VC-10, the Airbus A-340 and the Boeing 777, to mention but a few, are all large jets which have had no fatal accidents whatsoever. This, however, is illusory because the fleets are so small: there are only thirteen Concordes flying, sixty or so A-340s and so on. In theory, it would be possible for a very unsafe aircraft produced in small numbers not to have as many crashes as a much safer plane which has a large fleet.

Statistics can be unhelpful in other ways. Many of today's jets are more modern versions of old designs. Not only can individual aircraft last for thirty years or so, but the designs will last longer still. By the time the last descendant of the original Boeing 737 has finished flying, the design will probably have been airborne for well over sixty years. Each major variant, however, is considered a different aircraft for statistical purposes. The figures indicate that the 737-100 has a poorer record than 737-400 and later variants, but few passengers would know the differences between them.

A measure of some of the difficulties in using the statistics can be shown by looking at a number of individual cases. According to the Airclaims data, the Fokker F-28 had on average 131,000 flights for every fatal accident in 1976. (The figure for each year is a rolling five-year average.) By 1980, the figures suggest it was nearly three times "safer". In 1988 it then became about two and a half times "safer" than it was in 1980. But in 1995 its figures slumped, fetching up only slightly "safer" than it was in 1980. The swings and roundabouts are simply too violent to draw any real conclusions.

Another example of the difficulties inherent in attempting comparisons is shown with the 1960s-era McDonnell Douglas DC-9 and its more modern descendant, the MD-80, which came into service in 1981. In 1976 the DC-9 boasted a five-year average of one fatal accident for every 1.3 million flights. The more modern MD-80 needed to be in service for four years before it approached the same level. The positions have now reversed and in 1995 the MD-80 made 4.56 million flights for every fatal accident, against 2.4 million for the DC-9.

While we are at it, we may as well mention another factor. All new aircraft have higher accident rates in their first three years of service than they do subsequently. Generally speaking, all aircraft start badly and then level off. With the oldest aircraft the crash rate started to rise again after twenty years or so. That, however, may have as much to do with the nature of the aircraft operator as any inherent problems in the machine's age. Older aircraft are sold on to smaller airlines, whose finances and maintenance practices may not be as good as those of the owners of the brand-new plane.

Perhaps, then, we can afford comparisons between the generations of jet. Airclaims provides data on four classes of large passenger jet, class one covering the first generation of jets, like the Comet and the 707, through to class four, covering the most modern, like the A-320 and the B-777.

Even here, however, the figures do not offer much in the way of conclusions. The class-one jets are simply too few in number now to make comparisons, although during the 1980s they were approximately half as safe as the class-two jets. The differences were so consistent that it would be fair to say that comparison is valid, but because there are so few first-generation jets still flying, the information is of little use to us.

The third-generation jets – comprising the Airbus A-300, Boeing 747, Lockheed L-1011, Concorde and the DC-10 – is statistically the safest of all, outranking even the fourth-generation jets, although the latter may not have been flying for long enough to be statistically significant. Before, however, you decide only to fly in third-generation jets, bear in mind that which aircraft are included in which generation can significantly alter the statistical results.

The record, in other words, is not a safe source of judgements. The Boeing 757, for example, was running an accident rate almost second to none among modern aircraft flying in appreciable numbers, having had no fatal crashes despite being in service for ten years. Then came the American Airlines disaster at Cali in December 1995, followed by two further 757 disasters in the next ten months. Because those crashes came so close together, the aircraft's five-year average will have looked appalling just after the third crash, but that, of course, does not tell you the whole story.

In the First World War, soldiers sometimes leapt into newly formed shell holes on the principle that lightning never strikes in the same place twice. By this token, the safest way to get from New York to Paris on the day after the TWA 800 disaster would have been to fly on a TWA jumbo.

This brings us to the relative safety of the airlines. These are much more important determinants of the safety of the average flight than the design, age, history, technical excellence or otherwise of the aircraft.

Airlines

The fact that human error is involved in the vast majority of crashes means that airline managements are the most important determinants of aviation safety. They employ the pilots, the maintenance, safety and cabin personnel, set the atmosphere in the company and determine, whether consciously or unconsciously, how much safety will rule their operations.

Statistics for airline safety have some problems in common with those governing aircraft model safety. First, calculating the number of fatalities against the number of flights will only give misleading data. Pure happenstance can easily intervene to turn such a rate into a nonsense. The Turkish airline THY, for example, would have had a much better rate of fatalities versus flights after the crash near Paris in 1974, which killed 346, had it not been for British trade unionists.

The flight that was to crash only had about 150 people booked on board. However, there was an engineers' strike at Heathrow, meaning that some 200 passengers scheduled to leave Paris on British airlines transferred to the Turkish flight. When the plane crashed, the fatality rate for THY was thus much higher than if there had been no strike at Heathrow. The anomaly was not noticed by the *Sunday Times* journalists who wrote the book *Destination Disaster*, concerning the story of the DC-10.[4] They produced a league table of airline safety in one of the appendices which suffered from this problem.

Just plotting the number of fatalities against the number of passengers carried creates another problem. Some fatal accidents have one or two deaths, and others 300 or more. As a result, airlines which have had large numbers of crashes but not many deaths could be judged safer than airlines which have had fewer crashes but many more dead. The most sensible thing to do, therefore, is to plot the number of fatal accidents against the number of flights.

This approach has pitfalls too, especially if the airline is small. One crash will be a higher proportion of the flights of a small airline than a big one. Its figures will therefore look very bad on such a rating system and, because it does not make many flights, it would take it a long time to recover, statistically, from the crash. It is frequently misleadingly stated, for example, that 16 per cent of the airlines have 70 per cent of the accidents, which is often used to imply that there are a few rogue operators out there messing things up for everybody else.

This is another statistical trap. The largest airlines have the most aircraft, and therefore will have the most accidents, despite the fact that they are the safest airlines. If an airline had a theoretical fatal accident rate of, say, one per million departures, and made 10 million departures, then it could be expected on average to have ten accidents. If an airline with a rate of ten accidents per million departures only flies 1 million flights, it would only have one accident. It might be tempting, therefore, to assume that the airline with the lower number of accidents is the safer.

The other problem with aircraft safety ratings is the bald fact that the past is not necessarily a guide to the future. For example, is Qantas a good choice to fly with because it has not had a fatal event for so long, or a poor one for the same reason? One person might argue that Qantas is unlikely to have a bad crash because it has not had one for decades, while another could say that as time passes the odds of Qantas suffering a fatal event must be increasing.

As US studies have shown, even taking airline safety figures over a ten-year period does not get you very far. One report took eight American airlines and ranked them by flights versus accidents, producing three tables for ten-year periods, starting respectively in 1974, 1979 and 1984. Depending on what year you start with, you end up with completely different rankings. The reason for this is that one crash, particularly to a low-volume carrier, can send it from the safest ranking to the most dangerous in an instant.[5]

There are individuals, however, who have attempted to provide some kind of more precise information on this topic. The biggest boost to this work was given by the US Department of Defense after the crash of a chartered Arrow Air DC-8 on 12 December 1985 at Gander, Newfoundland, killing 256 – most of them US military personnel returning home for Christmas from Lebanon.

The US Congress set up a commission to study what could be done to allow the Pentagon's Air Mobility Command to choose safer airlines when chartering aircraft for its immense require-

ments, to move large numbers of military personnel around the
United States and the world. It set up the DoD Air Carrier Survey
and Analysis Office, whose job it was to find indicators of the
likely safety of an airline. Mindful of the pitfalls in the data, the
experts had to come up with indicators of possible future crashes,
instead of just relying on past data.

They devised a system called Air Carrier Analysis which
assessed the safety of an airline on five broad criteria: accidents
and incidents, operations, maintenance, service quality and
finances.[6] Using data from a wide variety of sources the
information is kept up to date and then crunched, using a complex
series of algorithms, into a table giving a ranking from 1 (very
good) to 5 (very bad).

In principle the system works well. The different types of data
are weighted for their relative importance. A series of incidents to
aircraft, for example, would be a larger input to the system than,
say, financial strength. However, all these factors are important,
and when they are correctly combined the potential is there for a
good way to assess safety.

The people who developed this system then took it to the US
FAA who promptly gave it another acronym, Safety Performance
Analysis System, and have been trying unsuccessfully to get it up
and running since 1991. The FAA wants to use the system as an
automated method of identifying potential problem airlines to
help focus its enforcement and inspection efforts. If it were
working, there is no real reason why the public could not have
access to the data as well.

Unfortunately, the data collection has to be ongoing and intensive for the system to work properly, and the FAA does not have
the good-quality data to put into the system. That is why it is not
up and running. In its absence the FAA has had difficulty focusing
its inspection efforts. In late 1997 the US government watchdog of
public bodies, the General Accounting Office, published a critical
report on the FAA's inspection of new airlines.[7]

Over a five-year period, the GAO found, new airlines,
especially the low-cost "lean and mean" airlines, had significantly
worse accident and incident rates than more established airlines.

And yet the FAA treated them in exactly the same way in terms of enforcement action and inspections. It would seem only common sense to speculate that a new airline, no matter how many experienced airline personnel it hires, will not be able to make as good a fist of safety and all operational matters as a well-established one. It seems the FAA did not agree.

However, the GAO endorsed the US Congress's initiative to investigate the provision of safety rankings to the public, and although the FAA is moving very slowly, it is likely that, one day, airline safety rankings will be made public. Whether they will be sophisticated enough to permit comparison, for instance, between small, "unsafe" airlines that have as yet had no crashes and large, much safer airlines which have had crashes, remains to be seen.[8] There is also a problem in that, if the system is truly predictive of crashes, then it would effectively prevent them because people would intervene. If they did then the relationship between the indicators and the outcomes would be broken.

A special problem, however, lies in the FAA's closeness to the aviation industry. If successful criteria are established for ranking airlines by their safety, the airlines will deploy their utmost power and lobbying strength to prevent it happening.

How to decide?

It is unrealistic to expect passengers to do their own research on the safety of airlines, but there are general indicators. Here are a few.

The airline's financial strength. Poor airlines or "cheap and cheerful" ones are riskier than rich ones, by and large. A good indication of possible operating problems stemming from financial ones would be if the airline looks as though it is having a special drive to lower costs. Training and maintenance may well be compromised in order to save money.

Avoid low-cost airlines. To those of us who can afford it, flying on more expensive airlines is safer than on "no-frills" airlines. These operations depend on low costs to offer cheap fares and they are most likely to be "just legal" (*see* Chapter 5). Beggars cannot be choosers, however. This makes it all the more important for the travelling public to apply pressure for standards to rise across the board.

The state of industrial relations. Bad morale among pilots or engineers owing to poor pay, increased duty time, redundancies and so on has been identified by the NTSB study of accident causes as a contributory factor in several crashes.

The country of origin of the airline. There may well be Nigerian airlines that are superior in safety terms to German ones, but it is unlikely, and if faced with a choice between the two, the German one would be the better choice.

The airline's reputation. We have seen that the DC-10 had an undeserved reputation. The same can go for airlines. US Airways found itself, for a time, in just such a position in the USA, although there was nothing substantially different about their safety practices. They had merely suffered a string of crashes coming fairly close to each other, in the manner of the Boeing 757 that went ten years without a serious crash before three very bad ones in the space of ten months. However, some airlines seem to crash with regularity and for similar reasons. These ones should be avoided.

Maintenance: in or out? Airlines which do their own maintenance are likely, on the balance of probabilities and judging from the trend towards increasing maintenance-related accidents, to be safer than those that do not.

Size again. The larger the airline, the more likely it is to be safe. When they operate large numbers of the same aircraft and have a large pilot establishment, trouble-shooting and comparing notes on the aircraft become easier. A large fleet also makes for better economics for safety processes by spreading the cost. Analysing data recorders on aircraft in normal operation is an excellent way of nipping problems in the bud, but an airline with only five aircraft will not want this kind of expense.

Scary skies

Having said all this, there are certain airlines which stand out for poor safety records. One crash may give an airline an undeservedly low safety rating but when a middle-sized airline loses seven aircraft in as many years, it may be time to shop elsewhere. That was Korean Air's record when one of its 747s crashed at Guam in August 1997. At the time it was the third 747 that the airline had lost. In August 1998 it neatly marked the anniversary of the Guam crash by comprehensively smashing up another 747 when it skidded off a runway while landing in bad weather.[9] The airline has also lost two DC-10s and three 707s in less than thirty years of operations, and suffers an appalling reputation in the pilot community.

Even if you can afford to pay more and change your schedule to avoid airlines like this, it is not always possible to do so. Increasingly, the world airline market is being controlled by a series of alliances, mergers effectively, between different airlines on certain routes. If you book with a major Western airline you may well find that you are flying on the aircraft of the junior partner in the merger, possibly a Third World airline with a poor safety record.

The practice is called code-sharing, meaning the airlines share their international recognition code, whichever partner airline is actually operating the flight. British Airways and American Airlines plan a large-scale transatlantic code-sharing alliance under which passengers will not know which airline is actually flying the flight in question. Passengers need not be concerned if the choice is between American and BA, but this is not always the case, especially outside Europe and the United States.

Korean Air's code-sharing partner is the huge US airline, Delta.

The bigger brother, looking at its partner's predilection for bending aircraft, proposed a complete overhaul of its flight operations, hiring more pilots, cutting duty hours and replacing the flight management staff. Delta initiated the programme, which included a confidential pilot reporting system and a better pay structure for crews. So seriously has Korean Air's management finally decided to take its problems that it sacked a number of managers and quickly ordered enhanced ground proximity warning systems for the vast majority of its fleet, even though these are not compulsory. Enhanced GPWS is the most advanced terrain warning system and offers the longest warning possible of terrain in the flight path.[10] As pointed out in Chapter 1, technical answers to controlled flight into terrain are not enough. Prodded by its senior partner and by its record to date, it can be hoped that the worst of Korean Air's mishaps are behind it.

Code-sharing, however, will continue as a major headache for the large airlines, if they do not want to be tarred with the brush of their naughtier juniors. This problem was highlighted in April 1998 when an Air France flight leaving Bogota, Colombia, for Quito, Ecuador, crashed into a mountain three minutes after take-off, killing all sixty-one on board. However, it was an Air France flight only in name; the twenty-seven-year-old Boeing 727 was operated by the Ecuadorian airline TAME. No detailed information about the cause of the crash was available at the time of going to press, but on the face of it the apparent error was not the kind of mistake that would be likely from aircrew trained by Air France.

Just after take-off from Bogota from the runway in question, a sharp right turn is required to avoid mountains. Apparently, the TAME plane did not turn at all, with obvious consequences.[11] Those who booked their flight to Quito with Air France in Paris, however, may never have known that Air France was not operating the whole route.

As this book was going to press, Garuda Indonesia, that nation's flag-carrier, was negotiating code-sharing agreements with KLM, Lufthansa and Qantas in the wake of a massive retrenchment precipitated by the general economic crisis in Asia.[12] While these measures make economic sense for all concerned,

Garuda can hardly be described as an airline which meets the same standards as those of its would-be code-sharing partners. Between March and June 1997 three wide-bodied Garuda jets suffered potentially disastrous landing incidents, in which nobody was injured, all less than a year after three people were killed in a Garuda DC-10 during a rejected take-off from Fukuoka, Japan.

In August 1997, *Flight International*, in a rare article that "named names" headlined "Indonesian air safety goes into decline", cited the landing incidents and detailed three fatal domestic airline crashes that year. Call it prescience or bad luck, but on 26 September, less than two months after the article appeared, a Garuda Indonesia Airbus A-300 crashed into a hillside near Medan, Indonesia, killing all 234 people on board.

Nobody would wish a massive economic crisis on any country, but in the cases of some countries in the Far East, it could be saving air travellers' lives. One rough calculation, made in April 1998, showed that 1029 people had been killed in fourteen air crashes in the countries of the Pacific Rim in the preceding twelve months. As 1200 or so is the average number of commercial aviation fatalities every year, the area is clocking up more than its fair share.

One airline in particular, however, seems determined to break all records for delivering passengers to their maker rather than their destination. China Airlines, which is a Taiwanese company, suffered a massive loss of customer confidence after it crashed an Airbus A-300 on 26 April 1994, killing all but 7 of the 271 people on board. Then, on 18 February 1998, another China Airlines A-300 crashed, this time at Taipei, killing 196 on the plane and 6 on the ground. Although full details were not available, the 1998 crash had many of the hallmarks of the 1994 disaster, both involving a stall after a "go-around" was initiated. It is easy to see how China Airlines A-300s might be difficult to fill. The president of the company resigned after the Taipei crash, and was followed by the Taiwanese transport minister.

Flight International reported that the airline was deferring aircraft orders because there had been a 10 to 15 per cent drop in passengers booking flights with them. The airline suffered a similar drop in trade following the 1994 disaster which lasted eight months. It was massively discounting tickets in order to try to persuade people not to follow their better judgement.

As if this weren't bad enough, China Airlines' domestic subsidiary, Formosa Airlines, managed to have the bad manners to crash a Saab 340 commuter plane, killing all nineteen on board on a domestic flight in Taiwan a month after the Airbus crash at Taipei. The same airline had managed to crash three planes, all the same make and model, in the space of five years, killing thirty. Shocked by this catalogue of disaster, Taiwan set up a new accident investigation body in May 1998, spurred as much, in all probability, by the 20 per cent increase in domestic travel by rail at air's expense as by any desire to save lives. Ironically, China Airlines had taken over Formosa Airlines in 1996 not only for commercial reasons, but, *Flight International* said, "with the aim of improving Formosa's safety record".[13]

Where not to fly

Where you are flying can be much more important than the type of aircraft you travel on or the airline you choose. Taiwan's poor safety record may have had something to do with a chaotic, deregulated market with massive overprovision of air services on many routes, and the probability that many corners were being cut in order to lower costs and maintain competitiveness. While that situation has eased in Taiwan, countries where civil aviation may be growing rapidly, especially in an unregulated environment, are also worth looking at carefully from the safety point of view.

The most dangerous place in the world to fly is Africa, which has an accident rate of thirteen hull-losses per million departures compared with 0.5 in North America (*see* Table 1). The statistics are collected by region, which can result in some distortions. The Asian sub-continent is grouped together with South-East Asian countries, so it is impossible to judge if one is much safer than the other and pulling up the average.

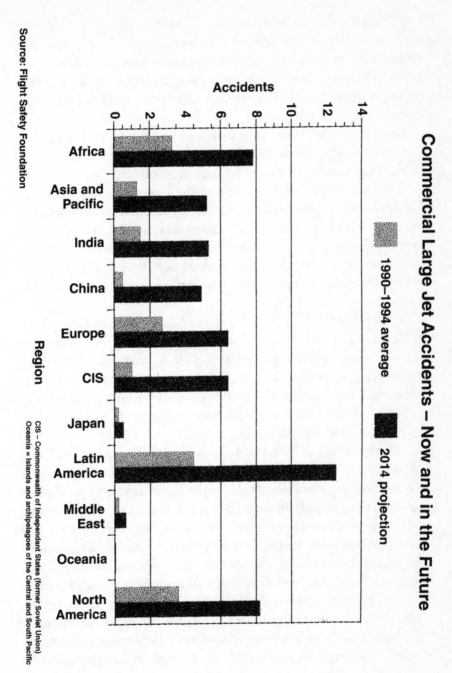

Commercial Large Jet Accidents – Now and in the Future

Source: Flight Safety Foundation

1990–1994 average

2014 projection

Accidents

Region

CIS – Commonwealth of Independant States (former Soviet Union)
Oceania = Islands and archipelagoes of the Central and South Pacific

The reason why Africa has such a poor record is not simply down to its airlines. As befits the poorest region of the world, the airport infrastructure is much poorer than elsewhere. Since the vast majority of crashes occur on landing and take-off there could well be a major correlation between this factor and the danger of flying in the continent.

Africa's air traffic control system also leaves a lot to be desired. Both this and the low quality of airport services increase threats to all aircraft, not simply the locally operated ones.

In an attempt to address some of the issues, the International Civil Aviation Organisation, to which all aviation nations belong, began in 1997 to carry out inspections of the standards in member-countries. To be a member of the ICAO you are supposed to observe certain minimum standards, but the ICAO is most reluctant to carry out any enforcement action on its members.

In October 1997, however, it published its concerns about some of its members after inspecting forty-five of them, but without naming any. It admitted that it had found "serious deficiencies at dozens of national aviation authorities". These concerned the training and qualifications of their personnel, the supervision of aviation in their country and the legal framework for enforcement and surveillance.[14]

What worried the ICAO most was the absence of qualified personnel. It is a typical Third World problem: if somebody is trained to the correct standards for the job of airline inspection he or she is very unlikely to want to work in a badly paid government job when they can do much better in the private sector. The ICAO revealed that only 40 per cent of the countries had a system to certificate airlines, only 24 per cent had a system of inspection, and only 9 per cent of them had drawn up an inspectors' checklist.

Overall, they painted a picture of an extremely lax or totally absent regulatory environment, extreme shortages of qualified personnel, and a significant proportion of authorities without any proper legal standing. Only 31 per cent of them had the authority to prevent airlines or aircraft from flying. What is now going to be done with this information is difficult to discern. What is certain, however, is that it will take a very long time indeed, and nobody will be named in the process. As it was, the inspections were all voluntary, and heavily restricted in their terms of reference.

Much of the impetus behind the ICAO campaign came from the US FAA, which started its own International Safety Assessment Program in 1992 after carrying out inspections of aviation authorities in countries which had applied to start aviation services to the United States. A similar European effort has started and it will probably be helping the ICAO carry out its inspections.

While the FAA may generally be reluctant to point the finger at any airline, it performs a useful service by giving a guide to the safety of certain countries by applying the principles of the ICAO. Few other countries use ICAO principles to inspect airlines and aircrew but it is perfectly within their powers to do so. They may not be able to ground aircraft, but "naming and shaming" should have some effect.

When the FAA inspected the countries, it found a catalogue of horrors, most of which it listed as follows:

- inadequate and in some cases non-existent regulatory legislation;
- lack of advisory documentation;
- shortage of experienced airworthiness staff;
- lack of control on important airworthiness related items such as issuance and enforcement of Airworthiness Directives, Minimum Equipment Lists, investigation of Service Difficulty Reports, etc.;
- lack of adequate technical data;
- absence of Air Operator Certification (AOC) systems;
- non-conformance to the requirements of the AOC system;
- lack or shortage of adequately trained flight operations inspectors, including a lack of type ratings;
- lack of updated company manuals for the use of airmen;
- inadequate proficiency check procedures; and
- inadequately trained cabin attendants.[15]

This led the agency to provide the public with a table of the countries it had inspected (*see* Table 2). Countries with a score of 1 comply with ICAO rules, those with 2 do not but the FAA is talking to them about raising their game, and those with 3 have got a lot of work to do. (This list is revised frequently and can be visited on the Internet.)

TABLE 2

FAA Flight Standards Service International Aviation Safety Assessment Program (IASA)

Number	Country	Category	Number	Country	Category
1	Argentina	1	28	France	1
2	Aruba	1	29	Fiji	1
3	Australia	1	30	Federal Republic of Yugoslavia (Serbia and Montenegro)	1
4	Austria	1			
5	Bahamas	1			
6	Bangladesh	2	31	Gambia	3
7	Belgium	1	32	Germany	1
8	Belize	3	33	Ghana	1
9	Bermuda	1	34	Guatemala	2
10	Bolivia	2	35	Guyana	1A
11	Brazil	1	36	Haiti	3
12	Brunei Darussalam	1	37	Honduras	3
13	Bulgaria	1	38	Hong Kong	1
14	Canada	1	39	Hungary	1
15	Cayman Islands	1	40	Iceland	1
16	Chile	1	41	Ireland	1
17	Colombia	2	42	India	1
18	Costa Rica	1	43	Indonesia	1
19	Côte D'Ivoire	2	44	Israel	1
20	Czech Republic	1	45	Italy	1
21	Denmark	1	46	Jamaica	1
22	Dominican Republic	3	47	Jordan	1
23	Ecuador	2	48	Kiribati	3
24	Egypt	1	49	Kuwait	1
25	El Salvador	1	50	Marshall Islands	1A
26	Ethiopia	1	51	Malta	3
27	Finland	1	52	Malaysia	1
			53	Mexico	1
			54	Morocco	1

55	Nauru	2		69	Portugal	1
56	Netherlands	1		70	Romania	1
57	Netherlands			71	Saudi Arabia	1
	Antilles: Curacau,			72	Singapore	1
	St Martin,			73	South Africa	1
	Bonaire, Saba,			74	South Korea,	
	(St Eustatius)	1			Republic of	1
58	New Zealand	1		75	Spain	1
59	Nicaragua	3		76	Suriname	3
60	Norway	1		77	Swaziland	3
61	Oman	1		78	Sweden	1
62	Organisation of			79	Switzerland	1
	Eastern Caribbean			80	Taiwan	1
	States (OECS):			81	Thailand	1
	Anguilla, Antigua &			82	Trinidad	
	Barbuda, Dominica,				& Tobago	1
	Grenada, Montserrat,			83	Turkey	1
	St Lucia, St Vincent			84	Turks & Caicos	2
	and The Grenadines,			85	Ukraine	1
	St Kitts & Nevis	2		86	United Kingdom	1
63	Pakistan	2		87	Uruguay	3
64	Panama	1		88	Uzbekistan	1
65	Paraguay	3		89	Venezuela	2
66	Peru	1		90	Western Samoa	1
67	Philippines	1		91	Zaire	3
68	Poland	1		92	Zimbabwe	3

Category 1 Meets ICAO Standards
Category 2 Does Not Meet ICAO Standards (Conditional)
Category 3 Does Not Meet ICAO Standards

Another useful aid can be the leaks that occasionally find their way out of the International Federation of Airline Pilots' Associations' meetings. The organisation groups together nationally based trade unions for pilots, and a feature of its activity is the exchange of information on the state of airports worldwide. In August 1998 the *Sunday Times* of London obtained a copy of the report and published extracts.[16]

The report said that San Francisco International airport was the most deficient of all the airports in the world. Fifteen airports were listed as having "critical safety deficiencies" and another 150 had "major safety problems". The others named were:

- Nice, France
- Wellington, New Zealand
- Fornebu, Oslo, Norway
- Suva, Fiji
- Buenos Aires, Argentina
- Leticia, Rio Negro and San Andres, Colombia
- Maiquetia, Venezuela
- Nauru, a Pacific island
- Lagos and Port Harcourt, Nigeria
- Kabul, Afghanistan
- Schiphol, Amsterdam, The Netherlands[17]

In later public statements the IFALPA backtracked somewhat, anxious, as most civil aviation organisations are, to maintain a united front and keep all problems "in the family". "If airports and airspaces are listed, it means they have serious deficiencies, not that they are unsafe," the *Sunday Times* quoted IFALPA executive director Cathy Bill as saying. "There are potential dangers, but there are potential dangers when you get in any plane," she said.

Many of the pilots' concerns here deal with the problem of non-precision approaches and the absence of instrument landing systems. Although this is such an important factor in accidents, it still receives scant attention.

The IFALPA report also listed potentially dangerous airspace. It included thousands of square miles over Africa, China and South America. The North Sea found a special mention because of the heavy military traffic using the English and Scottish bombing ranges, and the enormous amount of civil traffic working for the oil industry below 10,000 feet.

Even if the information on the safety of airlines, aircraft and places to fly were readily available, as passengers we have little choice, not only between airlines and aircraft, but even between transport modes. If you do not want to fly to a dangerous Greek airport, say, you will either spend days driving there or a fortune on sailing.

What it all implies is that we should be pushing much harder as passengers to raise levels of safety throughout the aviation business all over the world. Pressure brings change. Lobbying for it and then getting it will mean we don't have to worry about not having choices. It is likely to be a long road.

Glossary

AAIB Air Accident Investigation Branch. The UK's official aviation accident investigation body.

ABS Automatic braking system. Developed for use on aircraft landing gear long before it went into cars.

ACAP Aviation Consumer Action Project. US-based lobbying organisation for passenger rights and better commercial aviation safety founded by Ralph Nader.

AD Airworthiness Directive issued by the US FAA. Like the "Airworthiness Notice" in the UK, this signifies an order to carry out a fix to an aircraft type which must be accomplished immediately.

Airway A "shipping lane" for aircraft.

ALPA Airline Pilots' Association. The largest US trade union representing commercial pilots.

APU Auxiliary power unit. This is a jet turbine separate from the engines, usually located in the tail (the APU's exhaust can be seen as a hole at the extreme end of the fuselage) which generates electrical power and is used most when the aircraft is on the ground.

ASRS Aviation Safety Reporting System. The US system for the anonymous reporting of aviation incidents, run by NASA.

ATA Air Transport Association. Principle US organisation representing airlines.

ATC Air traffic control.

BALPA British Airline Pilots' Association. Main UK pilots' trade union.

BCAR British Civil Aviation Regulation. Name for the specifications and rules that all British-registered aircraft in the appropriate categories have to meet.

BEA Either Bureau Enquêtes Accidents, France's air-accident investigating body, or British European Airlines, the now defunct airline which merged with BOAC to form British Airways.

Black box Interchangeable term for the CVR or the FDR. They are orange to enable easy location in wreckage.

BOAC British Overseas Airways Corporation. Merged with BEA to form British Airways.

CAA Civil Aviation Authority. The UK's official aviation regulator, rule-maker and airworthiness authority.

CAT Clear-air turbulence.

Centreline The line running down the middle of the runway. The "extended centreline" is the imaginary straight line on the same axis.

CFIT Controlled flight into terrain. Industry euphemism for planes hitting the ground because the pilots did not know where they were.

Check captain A senior pilot making an assessment of a pilot or pilots flying a normal flight.

Check flight One on which the pilot/s are under supervision and assessment.

CHIRP Confidential Human Factors Incident Reporting. The UK's system for anonymous reporting of incidents relating to all aspects of aircraft operation. Equivalent to the United States' ASRS.

CRM Cockpit resource management. Psychologists' term for how the flight-crew interact with each other.

CVR Cockpit voice recorder. Records all noises on the flight-deck for thirty minutes on a loop-tape.

DFDR Digital flight data recorder. The more modern type of FDR.

DGAC Direction Générale de l'Aviation Civile, France's equivalent of the CAA and FAA.

DME Distance measuring equipment (*see* VOR). Method of using a radio beam to determine the aircraft's distance from the airport.

EFIS Electronic flight instrumentation system. Another word for "glass cockpit".

EGPWS Enhanced GPWS. The latest version of GPWS using GPS to give greater warning of terrain in the flight-path.

ETOPS Extended twin-engined operations. Twin-engined aircraft used not to be allowed to operate more than ninety minutes' flying time from an airfield. ETOPS rules define how a twin must be operated to be permitted to go beyond that time.

FAA Federal Aviation Administration. The United States' official aviation regulator, rule-maker and airworthiness authority.

FADEC Fully automated digital engine control. Electronic control for engines.

FAR Federal Aviation Regulation. Name for the specifications and rules that all US-registered aircraft in the appropriate categories have to meet.

FBW Fly-by-wire. Whereby the pilots' commands to the control surfaces and engines are transmitted electrically rather than by hydraulic lines.

FCS Flight control system. Term normally used to denote the computer package controlling the aircraft's FBW systems.

FDR Flight data recorder. Records from four to five hundred or so "parameters" of the aircraft's state and movements, e.g. airspeed, heading, altitude, vertical and horizontal acceleration.

FMC Flight management computer. The hardware behind the FMS.

FMS Flight management system. The computerised navigation system. Pilots enter the co-ordinates of where they want to go and the FMS controls the aircraft's engines and control surfaces to get them there.

FOD Foreign object damage. Usually refers to jet engines which have sucked something into the intakes.

FSF Flight Safety Foundation. The premier industry safety organisation.

Glass cockpit A modern aircraft in which mechanically operated dial instruments with needles and watch-type faces have been replaced by TV-style monitors displaying the same information graphically.

Glideslope The vertical component of ILS. A radio beacon allows an instrument in the cockpit to tell the pilot whether he or she is approaching the runway at the correct descent angle.

Go-around When the pilots break off a landing. They then go around at a pre-defined altitude and try again.

GPS Global positioning system. Highly accurate satellite-based position-fixing system finding increasing use in aviation.

GPWS Ground-proximity warning system. Warns crew with a variety of audible warnings when they are descending too fast or when there is terrain ahead.

IAPA International Airline Passengers' Association. Lobbying organisation for greater aviation safety, better airline standards, and passengers' rights.

IATA International Air Travel Association. Principal international organisation representing most airlines.

ICAO International Civil Aviation Organisation. United Nations treaty organisation with nominal authority over aspects of international commercial aviation.

IFALPA International Federation of Airline Pilots' Associations. International body grouping national pilots' trade unions.

IFE In-flight entertainment.

IFR Instrument flight rules. Those which apply under IMC.

ILS Instrument landing system. Generic term for the wide variety of aids available to pilots to help them land safely, which is normally composed of the glideslope and localiser.

IMC Instrument meteorological conditions. The state of the weather meaning that you must fly on instruments, or IFR.

JAA Joint Aviation Authorities. Europe-wide regulatory body.

NASA National Aeronautics and Space Administration of the United States. Everyone knows about the "space" part, but it also carries out extensive aeronautical research.

NTSB National Transportation Safety Board. The official US accident investigation organisation.

Localiser The horizontal element of ILS. A radio beacon enables an instrument in the cockpit to tell the pilot whether he or she is on, or to the right or left, of an imaginary line running down the middle of the target runway.

NPA   Non-precision approach. A landing undertaken without ILS.

Pax   Passengers.

PF   Pilot flying.

PIC   Pilot in command.

PNF   Pilot not flying.

RTO   Rejected take-off. When take-off is abandoned during the take-off run.

SRG   Safety Regulation Group. Body within the UK CAA which is responsible for deciding on safety matters.

TCAS   Traffic alert and collision avoidance system. A radar-based system which warns pilots of other aircraft that may be closing with them.

Turboprop   A jet engine with a propeller attached instead of a large fan.

V1   The speed beyond which an aircraft must continue take-off, even if an engine fails.

VR   The speed at which the aircraft rotates, or gets the nosewheel off the ground.

V2   The speed which the aircraft is aiming for after rotating.

VOR   VHF omnidirectional range. A radio beacon often used in combination with an aircraft's DME for navigation when landing. Hence "a VOR/DME approach".

Windshear   A type of severe downdraft usually associated with thunderstorm activity which can upset a commercial jet on take-off or landing.

Notes

Introduction

1. When referring to aviation and aircraft I will, unless otherwise stated, be referring to chartered and scheduled commercial passenger transport operations by jet and smaller turboprop aircraft. Light aircraft, private flying, and helicopters, all of which are much more dangerous than the first category, are excluded.
2. Flight Safety Digest 1/94
3. A note to Boeing's tables reads, "Rates: In general, this expression is a measure of accidents per million departures. Departures are used as baseline for rates because accidents statistically correlate much better to departures (or cycles) than to flight hours" ("Statistical summary of commercial jetplane accidents, 1959-1996", *Airplane Safety Engineering*, Boeing Commercial Airplane Group, Seattle, Washington 98124, USA, June 1997, p. 5). The company does not publish the accident rates of other transport modes.
4. Figures from *The Economist*, "How Safe Is Your Airline", 11 January 1997. It may be worth noting that the figures are British. Britain has a road casualty fatality rate that is one of the lowest in the world, and about half that of the USA.

5. The former Soviet bloc is excluded, quite possibly for no better reason than to keep the global figures down.

6. 'Civil Air Transport Safety: Accident Causes and a Proposal for Focused Regulatory Targets', paper given to the Flight Safety Foundation and International Federation of Airworthiness 47th International Air Safety Seminar, Lisbon, 31 October 1994; updated and amended January 1996 by Ronald Ashford, aviation and safety consultant.

7. "FSF CEO Says Industry Must Change, Use All Its Tools, Help Third World Air Carriers or Accidents Will Increase", FSF press release, 18 December 1996.

8. National Civil Aviation Review Committee, opening remarks, 8 October 1997. See http://www.house.gov/transportation/aviation/aviation.htm

9. A "hull-loss" is the industry's term for the writing off of an aircraft, whether or not any injuries resulted.

10. Conversation, 8 May 1996.

Chapter 1 – Why planes crash

1. *Flight Safety Digest*, January 1996, citing Statistical Summary of Commercial Jet Aircraft Accidents: *Worldwide Operations 1959–94*, published by Boeing Commercial Airplane Group. The category "weather" cannot, as I remarked above, be cited as any reason for a crash. Flying into weather that is too bad for the aircraft to handle is a human error, be it by the pilot, poor aircraft design or erroneous weather reports. The weather couldn't help it. The same goes for the category of "mechanical defects", which can only have human origins.

2. *See* Chapter 5. Official reports will blame the crew for incorrect actions, even if the emergency began with a failure for which the crew bore no responsibility. Almost every case of "pilot error", therefore, is only a part of the accident causation. Some experts believe that the role of pilots is often extended by aircraft manufacturers to include compensating for faults in design.

3. After the crash another airport, Reina Sofia, was built further

south on the island at a better location and this is where most flights now arrive. Los Rodeos, the airport where the disaster took place, is now called Tenerife North.

4. Those listening to the CVR could not tell whether he said that or "We are at take-off". The impression they gained, however, was that he felt unable further to question the captain's judgement but felt the need to tell someone what they were doing. (Source: conversations with the retired NTSB investigator who worked on the Tenerife report, Doug Dreifus.)

5. From an interview by Bob Bragg with Darlow-Smithson Productions, June 1996.

6. Ironically, KLM was one of the first in this field and had hired a British psychologist called Tony Dawkins, who argued against the traditional hierarchical, military-style command structure of the cockpit only shortly before the crash. His programme had not yet had time to take effect. Unfortunately for the cause of learning lessons from such tragedies, the official Dutch investigators withdrew from the formal investigation, which was completed by the USA and Spain, and the civil aviation ministry never officially admitted Captain Van Zanten's error, preferring to blame poor communications between cockpit and tower for the tragedy. It remains a sore point within Dutch civil aviation and is still capable of causing severe embarrassment, as I found when I failed to get anyone from KLM, the Dutch pilots' union, or the aviation ministry, retired or serving, to go on the record about it during my research in 1996.

7. Earl Wiener, cited in an edited version of "An analysis of CFIT accidents of commercial operators: 1988 through 1994", Netherlands National Aerospace Laboratory, *Flight Safety Digest*, April–May 1996.

8. *Flight International*, 9–15 October 1996, quoted in "Controlled flight into terrain, what is being done?", by Peter B. Ladkin on his excellent website "Computer-related Incidents with Commercial Aircraft" (http://www.rvs.uni-bielefeld.de/~ladkin/Incidents/FBW.html).

9. *Flight International* supplement, 4–10 March 1998, p. 29.

10. *Flight International*, 21–27 January 1998, p. 5.

11. *Flight Safety Foundation News*: press release dated 27 February 1998, "Flight Safety Foundation receives Flight International Aerospace Industry Award for CFIT accident-reduction campaign".

12. *Flight International*, 21-27 January 1998, pp. 35–46, *Airline Safety Review*. The two worst, which are probably the ones that the FSF could not avoid in its statistics, were the crashes of a Korean Air 747 at Guam on 6 August 1997, killing 228, and of a Garuda Indonesia Airbus A-300 near Medan, Indonesia, taking 234 lives, on 26 September 1997.

13. AA965 Cali Accident Report, by Aeronautica Civil of the Republic of Colombia, as obtained from Peter Ladkin's website, op. cit.

14. Ibid.

15. Ibid.

16. *Airline Pilots Magazine*, 1996. As obtained from their website: http://www.webcom.com/terps/alpamag/alpainfo/02APR96/

17. The ICAO made them compulsory for all aircraft over 30,000 kgs and carrying more than thirty passengers in 1979, and the US FAA made them compulsory for such aircraft in US air space in 1974. Although most of them have it anyway, no purely domestic airline is obliged by the treaty to have it.

18. Netherlands National Aerospace Laboratory, op cit.

19. John Savage, in *ICAO Journal*, March 1997.

20. FSF Safety Alert, November 1996.

21. Airbus is allegedly thinking of incorporating this feature into its new aircraft equipped with the latest GPWS system, EGPWS.

22. The NTSB said that if he had maintained the angle where the stall-warning started they would have cleared the ridge. He was not properly instructed in how the stall-warning operates, and was thus in all likelihood unaware that he could have climbed at a slightly steeper angle than he did.

23. As this book went to press the US FAA was about to mandate the installation of EGPWS in all aircraft of the appropriate size.

24. *Aviation Week and Space Technology* made installation of EGPWS on all commercial transports one of its "top ten safety priorities" in an editorial, 2 June 1997.

25. Roberts quoted in Ladkin, op. cit.

26. FSF press release, 19 August 1997.

27. To the resounding sound of stable doors slamming after horses have bolted, the FAA, which is responsible for Guam airport, has rectified the fault on the MSAW and forbidden non-precision approaches into Agana airport.

28. See MacArthur Job, *Air Disaster*, vol. 2 (Australia, Aerospace Publications).

29. McDonnell Douglas attracted some criticism, too, on designing the pylon attach points in such a way that they were prone to damage unless extremely sensitively handled.

Chapter 2 – What happens to a plane in a crash

1. Garuda and Indonesia's Aircraft Accident Investigation Commission backed their pilot's decision against the verdict of the Japanese authorities. See *Flight International*, 10–16 December 1997, p. 14.

2. All information on this incident is taken from *Accident Prevention*, vol. 53, no. 10, published by Flight Safety Foundation, which is based on the official government accident Report No. A95H0015, by the Transportation Safety Board of Canada.

3. The biggest difference between the Garuda and CAI events is that the Garuda plane was already in the air.

4. See Robert O. Besco, *Surviving Anomalies at Lift-off*, B/CA feature story, *Aviation Week* online, Safety Resource Center, February 1998.

5. The FAA has historically had a dual remit, both to promote aviation and to legislate for safety. The conflict this results in has attracted increasing criticism. *See* Chapter 8.

6. The pilot was anonymous. *See* Ralph Nader and Wesley J. Smith, *Collision Course: the Truth about Airline Safety* (Pennsylvania, Tab Books, 1994).

7. Op. Cit., p. 244.

8. 2 February 1998, 63 FR 8298. Federal Aviation Administration,

14 CFR Parts 1, 25, 91, 121 and 135 [Docket No. 25471; Amendment Nos. 1-48, 25-92, 91-256, 121-268, 135-71], RIN 2120-AB17, *Improved Standards for Determining Rejected Takeoff and Landing Performance*. Ironically, trade relations were just as involved in the change as safety. European manufacturers had complained to the United States that competition between US and European aircraft was being affected by the fact that European aircraft had safer and more restrictive V1 requirements to meet than American aircraft, meaning the US-made planes had a competitive advantage because of the extra fuel or payload they could carry.

9. A further complication arises from the fact that the de-icing mixture used, very similar to the anti-freeze used in cars, can itself reduce the lift of an aircraft's wing because it is viscous and can leave a film over the wing surface.

10. From "Oprah", 11 March 1997, dealing with survivors of disasters.

11. Besco, cit.

12. After the September 1989 crash, 25 were killed in a USAir 737 at Colorado Springs in 1991, then came the F-28 accident, and in September 1994 another USAir 737 crashed killing 132. In both the LaGuardia crashes the crew were blamed to some extent, but the other two remain unsolved. Nobody has suggested that USAir, which has now changed its name (probably because of their accident record) to US Airways, was doing anything wrong, or is any less safe than other American airlines.

13. This woman's account, and the one that follows, are from a study of airline accident survivors by Carolyn V. Coarsey-Rader, part of which was published in *Flight Safety Digest*, "Survivors of US Airline Accidents Shed Light on Post-accident Trauma", October 1993. Her doctoral dissertation for the University of New Mexico, Albuquerque, in 1992 was entitled "Psychological aftermath of air disaster: what can be learned for training?" A former airline employee, Dr Coarsey-Rader now acts as a consultant to airlines on their post-accident action plans.

14. Having learned the hard way, not only in this accident but from public reactions to its equally appalling treatment of relatives of the Pittsburgh crash victims in September 1994, USAir

became a leader in the field of post-crash contingency planning. As said earlier, it also changed its name, policy adopted by several airlines. After losing much business following its May 1996 DC-9 crash, ValuJet first acquired the operators AirTran and then decided to trade under that name.

15. This point was made by Peter Ladkin on his website, op. cit. Although this crash was computer-related and the A-320 is a highly automated aircraft, the system of using squat switches is also used on non-automated Boeings.

16. Runway 13 at LaGuardia is 7000 feet long, much shorter than an international airport's runway. London City Airport's is less than 4000 feet long but is only intended for use by smaller aircraft than use LaGuardia.

17. AAIB Bulletin No.: 8/97, Ref EW/C96/11/7 Category 1.1. Owing to a curious convention borne, one suspects, out of a desire to please the airlines, the AAIB, unlike the NTSB, never identifies the airline involved in incidents or crashes in its reports. It gives the registration number of the aircraft, though, so that anyone who is interested can look it up and see what airline or leasing company it belongs to.

18. Mary Schiavo with Sabra Chartrand, *Flying Blind, Flying Safe* (New York, Avon Books, 1997), p. 286. She lists the airports "pilots do not like" in the United States as: Boston-Logan, Washington National, San Diego, LaGuardia, Juneau and Sun Valley in Idaho.

19. Nader and Smith, op. cit., p. 241.

20. NTSB Report No. NTSB/AAR-91/08, published 22 October 1991.

21. *Aviation Daily*, 21 July 1997.

22. Evidence to US House of Representatives Transport & Infrastructure Committee, sub-committee on aviation, 13 November 1997.

23. See Job, op. cit., vol. 1, p. 79.

24. A 1990 study by the National Oceanic and Atmospheric Administration cited in Bruce Landsberg, "Beware the unseen wake", *AOPA Pilot*, 1994.

25. Patrick R. Veillette and Rand Decker, "Handling Horizontal

Tornados", *Aviation Safety*, July 1993.

26. Hugh De Haven, a pioneer of car safety, wrote a seminal paper, "Accident Survival – airplane and passenger automobile", for the Society of Automotive Engineers symposium in January 1952. Ironically, after remarking on the extraordinary life-saving properties of the pilot's harness, he had this to say about the seat-belt: "But use of shoulder harness – and safety belts – in automobiles, because of psychological problems, is not even on the horizon as a means of increasing automotive safety."

27. As if to illustrate the nearly random distribution of large commercial aircraft disasters, there had been none in the UK since 1985. Then came the destruction of the PanAm 747 over Lockerbie in December 1988, with Kegworth following less than a month later.

28. A 16 g seat is designed to withstand a shock sixteen times greater than the force of gravity.

29. Most of the following information is from Aircraft Accident Report 4/90, report on the accident to Boeing 737-400 G-OBME near Kegworth, Leicestershire, on 8 January 1989, HMSO, London, 1990. The crew may have been mistaken in shutting down the wrong engine, but there was more to it than that. The sequence of events is analysed in Chapter 5.

30. The vast cutting containing the M1 is in the midst of the approach lights for the runway. The cutting and road were later reconstructed as part of plans that had nothing to do with the crash. However, the embankments are now much steeper and if the 737 had crashed into the new M1 cutting it seems unlikely anyone could have survived. It is odd that a new hazard should be installed in a place that has already had a crash.

31. The last man to be removed from the plane had obviously been saving up his bad luck. He was returning home after breaking a leg skiing and was wearing a large plaster cast.

32. Phone conversation with one of the doctors involved, who wished to remain anonymous, on 28 June 1996. The wording in the report is, "Although the injury evidence did not indicate the degree of injury attributable to the bins, it is evident that they can cause additional injuries as well as hampering escape and rescue"

(p. 140). I understand Boeing made strong representations when the report was in draft to tone down the implied criticisms of the bin design.

33. Canada's Transportation Safety Board, "A safety study of evacuations of large, passenger-carrying aircraft", Report No. SA9501, TSB Canada 1995.

34. FAR 25-64 and JAR 25.561 and 25.562.

35. It depends on the plane. The US FAA has specified that all general aviation (private planes) aircraft must have seats that can withstand 25 g. Admittedly, private aircraft are much more likely to crash than large passenger jets, but a standard is a standard and 25 g seats would considerably increase survivability in commercial jet crashes.

36. Aircraft Accident Digest (ICAO) Circular 107-AN/81, pp. 5–27.

37. Quoted in Laurie Taylor, *Air Travel: How Safe Is It?* (Oxford, Blackwell Science, 1988), p. 137. Captain Taylor added his own comment: "The Board's studies . . . showed that many lives lost could have been saved if the aircraft equipment, including seats, had not failed on impact." The book was published before Kegworth.

38. Having a three-point safety harness is an alternative, but the problems of what to attach it to are overwhelming. If you attach it to the ceiling, the loose straps could get in the way during an evacuation and if you attached them to the seat back, it would have to be made rigid, thus preventing people from going over the seats on their way to an exit during an evacuation.

39. Quoted in Taylor, op. cit., p. 137.

40. Edited from Mr Desmond's letter to the UK House of Commons Transport Committee, and published in its "Aircraft Cabin Safety", vol. 1, (London, HMSO, 1990), p. 27. Mr Desmond was backing calls for better cabin safety, and also argued for measures that would prevent seats becoming detached from the floor, clearing rows of seats from in front of the overwing exits, and compulsory provision of smoke-hoods.

Chapter 3 – Fire and survival

1. Robert L. Koenig, "US reports examine new tools aimed at improving survival rates in aircraft fires", *Flight Safety Digest*, September/October 1995. On the percentage of fire deaths he is citing a study by the US General Accounting Office, and on the totals over twenty-six years UK CAA paper No. 93012.
2. From Al Siebert, "Thrivenet Oprah Stories In-Depth" quoting from "Oprah", of 11 March 1997, dealing with survivors of disasters.
3. Air accident investigators have pointed out that permitting changes by airlines to the aircraft operating manuals is pointless and dangerous. See Richard L. Gross, "Why flight-crew procedures fail", ISASI Forum, October/December 1997. Among other things, Gross says that adherence to an altered flight manual can actually *cause* an accident.
4. AAIB Aircraft Accident Report 8/88, Department of Transport, Crown Copyright. The report was published in March 1989 because of the enormous amount of research that went into it. However, the CAA was kept informed about the progress of the investigation on a regular basis, and initiatives and action were taken before the official publication.
5. Contractors were then in the process of adding a new water main to improve water pressure in the hydrants. To do this, they had to turn off the hydrants from time to time. The airport had a procedure whereby the senior fire officer would be informed, and the shut-off only performed by airport personnel. The system, however, had broken down, fire personnel were not informed and the hydrants were being shut down by the contractors. When the contractors arrived for work that morning they saw firemen trying to use the hydrants, and went over and switched them on for them.
6. Because of the importance of not hindering anyone trying to leave the crowded and narrow space inside an airliner, airport fire-fighters are not allowed to enter an aircraft while the evacuation is ongoing.
7. The gases were: carbon monoxide, hydrogen cyanide, nitrogen

dioxide, hydrogen fluoride, hydrogen cyanide, sulphur dioxide, ammonia, acrolein, aromatic hydrocarbons, aliphatic hydrocarbons and acetaldehyde.

8. An article in the New Zealand newspaper *The Press* on 31 July 1998 reported that a local aviation safety consultancy, Oldfield & Associates, found that alcohol vapours from smashed duty-free bottles could have worsened the fire that consumed the Boeing 747 that crashed at Guam on 6 August 1997. The report said it probably caused a minor flashover and recommended that the New Zealand CAA take a lead in pushing for duty-free alcohol to be bought at the destination.

9. AAIB Aircraft Accident Report 8/88.

10. Koenig, op. cit, quoting "Aircraft fires, smoke toxicity, and survival: an overview", by Arvind K. Chaturvedi and Donald C. Sanders, of the CAMI, Report No. DOT/FAA/AM – 95/8, February 1995. No criticism is intended of the work of these scientists.

11. Boeing recognised there was still a problem, however, and in 1977 issued new guidelines on toxic-gas emission. Airbus Industrie followed suit, and so did other aircraft manufacturers. But the amount of heat used to combust the materials was still, the AAIB believed, unrealistically low.

12. Some, Americans especially, have expressed fears that an airline or smoke-hood manufacturer could be sued if, by some mischance, somebody suffocated from using the device incorrectly.

13. "Smoke-hoods: net safety benefit analysis", CAA paper 87017, November 1987.

14. Quoted in "Getting out alive – would smoke hoods save airline passengers or put them at risk?", editorial staff report in Flight Safety Foundation, *Cabin Crew Safety*, double issue, November/December 1993 and January/February 1994.

15. The NTSB also repeated its long-standing recommendation that smoke detectors be installed in toilets. This time action was taken, leading to a curious anomaly. Now there are smoke detectors in all toilets, but not in all cargo holds.

16. Telephone conversation, 18 December 1996.

17. "Airline safety: special report", *Consumer's Digest*,

July/August 1997.

18. Quoted in Frances Barthorpe, "Divided on the lessons of Manchester", *Professional Engineering*, 6 September 1995.

19. Ibid.

20. There was another argument that regulators chose to employ in rejecting smoke-hoods. Most of the dead at Manchester and in other fire accidents had in their bloodstream lethal levels of carboxyhaemoglobin, which is the product of the blood's haemoglobin mixing with carbon monoxide. Carbon monoxide, the gas which kills people whose gas fires or boilers have blocked flues, is produced in every fire and thus cannot be avoided. But the crucial question is whether the aircraft-fire victims were incapacitated by the carbon monoxide, which needs high concentrations and relatively long exposure, or by hydrogen cyanide and the other poisonous fire products. The AAIB supported the generally accepted thesis that the cyanide knocked out the passengers, who were then killed while unconscious by the carbon monoxide. The CAA chose to say that as it could not be proved beyond a shadow of a doubt that carbon monoxide had not incapacitated the passengers directly, there was little point in attempting to control the output of toxic gases by burning cabin materials.

21. From Harro Ranter, "Aviation Safety Web Pages", citing *Flight International*, 17 April 1976, http://web.inter.nl.net/users/ H.Ranter/accreps.htm

22. Quoted in "Getting out alive", op. cit.

23. NTSB report AAR-91/08, published 22 October 1991.

24. From David H. Koch, "Recollections of my Survival of an Airplane Crash", quoted in Nader and Smith, op. cit., p. 183.

25. A.F. Taylor, *Aviation Fuels* (Cranfield Aviation Safety Centre), Appendix 1.

26. See "Aviation Fuels", by A.F. Taylor, Cranfield Aviation Safety Centre.

27. See Chapter 8.

Chapter 4 – Survivors

1. Many such guides have been produced in the past and all agree with some differences in emphasis and priorities. Examples include the *ACAP Passengers' Guide*. Some of the advice may not be applicable to first-class configurations.

2. All airline crew are also covered by the Warsaw Convention, whether the flight was domestic or not. As extremely frequent flyers, and probably trade union members too, many of them are likely to have paid out already for comprehensive insurance. In October 1995, the International Air Travel Association, which represents most airlines, announced members were waiving the $75,000 upper limit. Adherence to the fact has been extremely patchy and some airlines, like Ethiopian Airlines, are even still sticking with the 1929 upper limit for compensation for death – $20,000.

3. US House of Representatives Committee on Transportation and Infrastructure, sub-committee on aviation, hearing, 11 June 1998.

4. The Association of Asia Pacific Airlines announced in January 1998 a policy of restricting passengers' carry-on items to one piece of baggage no longer in any dimension than 115 centimetres and weighing no more than 7 kg (15 lbs) (Reuters World Report, 23 January 1998.

5. See Albert Helfrick, "Avionics & portable electronics: trouble in the air?", *Avionics News*, September 1996.

6. There were some post-crash fires, but fire was not an issue here. The destruction of the cabin was so total that there was precious little for fire to get a hold of. In any case, as often happens in a crash this severe, most of the fuel on board would have been thrown forward and out of the wings before igniting as a vapour when clear of the wreckage.

7. This was translated from Yoshioka, *Summer of the Crash* (Shincho-Sha, 1985).

8. Dutch roll is a term for an aeronautical phenomenon affecting all swept-wing aircraft whereby the aircraft tends gently to bank to the left and then to the right. This aircraft was also affected by

phugoid motion at the same time, involving the plane pitching down and then up. See Captain Haynes's account of his efforts to control his DC-10 in July 1989 against phugoid motion in Chapter 5.

9. In Japanese legend a Samurai who was captured and tied up, unable to move, committed suicide by biting off his tongue and bleeding to death.

10. Around the tenth anniversary of the crash it emerged that a US military helicopter had found the crash site. Although it was ready to land and offer assistance, the crew was told the Japanese authorities were aware of it and were coming, and so to return to base. Assuming, perhaps, there were no survivors, and as the crash occurred almost exactly at dusk, no helicopters or search parties reached the remote, mountainous area until the next morning. Given the sounds that Ms Ochiai heard while she awaited rescue, it is by no means unlikely that more lives could have been saved if rescue parties had reached the site that night.

11. The haphazard nature of the relatively greater safety of sitting at the rear is illustrated by the fact that in aircraft where the engines are mounted on the rear of the fuselage, like the DC-9 family, the Boeing 727, DC-10 and Lockeed L-1011, an engine could loose a fan-blade into the cabin. On the other hand, the rear of such planes is structurally stronger than in other aircraft because of the need to bear the additional weight of the engines. Swings and roundabouts, perhaps.

12. Canada's Transportation Safety Board, "A safety study of evacuations of large, passenger-carrying aircraft", Report No. SA9501, TSB Canada 1995. It was citing a 1989 survey of Canadian passengers.

13. The seat-belt on aircraft is as it is because it is a very old design and because little thought has been put into it. It would be better if it resembled car belts more, not only to avoid the unfastening problem, but to minimise injury. Car belts no longer have buckles in the centre because they can cause serious internal injuries in a strong impact.

14. Reasons for and against were aired at the US House of Representatives Transport and Infrastructure Committee,

subcommittee on aviation, 1 August 1996. See http://www. house.gov/transportation/aviation/aviation.htm.

15. See Job, op. cit., vol. 1, chapter 13.

16. *Consumer Digest*, July/August 1997, p. 25.

17. *The Times*, 30 December 1997.

18. Retired American Airlines captain William J. Sheriff wrote a letter to the NTSB investigator into the United CAT accident on 28 December 1997. Dated 16 February 1998 and published later in *Aviation Week & Space Technology*, the letter argues that the negative g forces which probably caused most of the injuries were most likely caused by the pilot's pushing forward on the control column in response to the original CAT encounter which pushed the aircraft up.

19. See Arthur Job, op. cit., vol. 1, chapter 6. They may not have intended to fly into this weather, but whether it was the pilots' decision, common or even company practice, it was also a clear example of safety being compromised for operational reasons.

20. *AirSafe Journal*, 28 November 1996.

21. See Job, op. cit., vol. 1, chapter 8.

22. See Job, op. cit., vol. 2, p. 163. Boeing had warned Aloha about corrosion and fatigue problems on its 737s and the official report heavily criticised the airline's failure adequately to maintain this aircraft.

23. Quoted in Nader and Smith, op. cit., p. 334.

24. Ibid., p. 333..

25. MacArthur Job covers this tragedy in exceptional detail in Job, op. cit., vol 2, chapter 9. Again, the severity of the fire does not seem to have impressed the regulators on the question of toxic emissions. The plane was carrying only forty-three passengers. Had it been fully loaded the death toll would have been much higher.

26. The flight-crew filed a Mandatory Occurrence Report, the formal name for a report on an incident that may have given cause for concern without resulting in injury or damage. Curiously, the AAIB did not investigate. No reasons were given and the public was offered no explanation of what had gone wrong then or later. See *The Independent* 14 February 1996.

Chapter 5 – Don't shoot the pilot: The human factor in flight

1. "Safety and statistics: what the numbers tell us about aviation safety at the end of the 20th century", *Flight Safety Digest*, vol. 16, no. 12, December 1997.
2. From *CHIRP Feedback*, no. 44, October 1997.
3. The source for this information was one of the lawyers representing the crash victims who noted the difference between the draft report and the published version. Further proof of the clubbish nature of civil aviation is evidenced by the fact that the AAIB's draft reports are submitted for comment, and possible alteration, by parties whose reputations might be affected. Those whose lives have been affected get no such privileges of right.
4. L. Taylor, op. cit., p. 79. It was ruefully remarked in the British aviation industry that the mistakes of the Comet were what made Boeing's airliners successful.
5. Thain's and Foote's stories are told in Nicholas Faith, *Black Box*, p. 157, and Job, op. cit., vol. 1.
6. *Flight International*, 24 February 1993; *The Times* 22 November 1989.
7. L. Taylor, op. cit., p. 194. Captain Leppard was using this example to explain why he was opposed to the use of video cameras supplementing the CVR at the 1983 meeting of the International Society of Air Safety Investigators.
8. See Chapter 10 for a discussion of Australia's aviation safety record and prospects.
9. The first Australian CVRs were crude, clumsy and barely crash-survivable. The CVR's passage into use in the rest of the world was eased by the addition of a "bulk erase" button to the tape recorder. On the uneventful completion of a flight, a crew suspicious that the CVR might have been used by management to spy on them can erase the tape.
10. Source: Macarthur Job, personal conversations, December 1996.
11. Byron Acohido, "Pittsburgh Disaster Adds to 737 Doubts", third part of five-part report in the *Seattle Times*, 29 October

1996. The newspaper's aerospace correspondent, Acohido won a Pulitzer Prize for his "beat" reporting on the 737 rudder saga, which involved one other major crash and a series of incidents. Full copies of the whole series may still be available on the *Seattle Times*'s website, http://www.seatimes.com.

12. "A Review of Flightcrew-involved, Major Accidents of US Air Carriers, 1978 through 1990", Safety Study NTSB/SS-94/01, Notation 6241, National Transportation Safety Board, Washington, DC, 1994.

13. I am using CRM in its generic sense. At United it is called CLRT, cockpit leadership and resource training.

14. But not, as usual, entirely unforeseeable. In 1972 the FAA studied the effects of an "uncontained engine failure" in the tail engine. The damage pattern was pretty much what VA 232 suffered. But the possibility that all three hydraulic lines might be severed seems not to have been considered.

15. Edited from a lecture given by Captain Haynes at NASA Ames Research Center on 24 May 1991. Copyright Al Haynes 1991. Quoted by permission.

16. NASA's Dryden Flight Research Center has invented and demonstrated a system called Propulsion Controlled Aircraft as a back-up in case hydraulics should fail. With help from McDonnell Douglas the engineers devised a way of translating the pilot's inputs into subtle changes in the power settings on the engines that would control the aircraft's movements in the event that no control surfaces (ailerons, rudder, elevator, etc.) were available. This takes all the guesswork out of controlling the plane by throttles alone manually, and makes possible manoeuvres that could not be achieved manually without an enormous amount of practice. It was successfully tested on 29 August 1995 on an MD-11, the DC-10's younger, more computerised brother. The beauty of the idea is that it only uses software, not hardware, and is therefore extremely cheap. NASA engineer Bill Burcham said, "Now that the technology is proven, I hope to see it incorporated into future aircraft designs. I also hope it never has to be used." Take-up by manufacturers and airlines, however, has been poor. But since the system is so cheap there is precious little reason why

it should not be mandated for use in currently flying commercial aircraft, not just new ones and those being designed now. Details on the NASA Dryden website at http://www.dfrc.nasa.gov/projects/pca/index.html.

17. Explored more fully by Ashleigh Merritt, NASA/University of Texas, "The Influence of National & Organizational Culture on Human Performance", *The CRM Advocate*, October 1993.

18. Dr Robert L. Helmreich, NASA/University of Texas, "Commission of Inquiry into the Air Ontario Crash at Dryden, Ontario", *The CRM Advocate*, January 1995. No CVR was available for analysis in this crash, leading some to argue that the investigation might not have been as thorough as it should have been.

19. Air Accident Investigation Branch, Accident Report 4/73. The report is not a normal investigation report, but the report of the public inquiry, chaired by a judge, into the disaster.

20. John K. Lauber, "Putting Professionalism in the Cockpit", *The CRM Advocate*, January 1995.

21. NTSB report NTSB/AAR-94/04, on American International Airways Flight 808, Douglas DC-8, 18 August 1993.

22. Passenger aircraft are used much more intensively than cargo planes. One calculation was that a twenty-five-year old jumbo jet will, on average, have been in operation for eight and a half hours every day of those twenty-five years, including time taken out for overhauls and major maintenance work. When an ageing passenger plane approaches the point where major refurbishment will be required in the next two years, say, it becomes more economical to replace it. An exclusive cargo carrier, however, would use the aircraft much less frequently, so the two years before the overhaul becomes essential could be stretched to seven years or more. When the major work cannot be put off any longer, the plane will be sold on once more, possibly for rehabilitation, or retired and sold for parts.

23. Guantanamo Bay is a corner of Cuba which houses the Leeward Point Air Station US Navy aerodrome and a US Navy base. It has been there since well before the 1959 revolution and despite all the tensions and conflict between Cuba and the USA

President Castro has made no effort to invade it or demand its return.

24. The US Navy subsequently forbade any civilian aircraft to land on this runway. But this crash was not enough, strangely. It took a DC-10 landing with one set of landing gear off the runway only two months after the DC-8 crash to prompt the action.

25. *CHIRP Feedback*, no. 44, October 1997. The CHIRP operators have to identify the people who make the reports, to verify the facts and confirm they are who they say they are. But this information is protected from disclosure to any other party.

26. Quoted in Aviation Week Group Forum, 1996. All were anonymous.

27. NTSB AAR, "Controlled collision with terrain Express Airlines, inc./Northwest Airlink Flight 5719 Jetstream BA3100, N334PX, Hibbing, Minnesota, December 1, 1993".

28. An Associated Press report quoted in *Aviation Safety Institute Monitor*, March 1994. The August 1994 edition of the *ASI Monitor* also reported the Hibbing crash.

Chapter 6 – Who needs pilots?

1. Airbus Industrie is a consortium of British Aerospace, MBB of Germany, CASA of Spain and Aérospatiale of France. But Frenchmen started it and are by far the most important members of the consortium. Its main base is at Toulouse.

2. Airbus calls it the flight management and guidance computer because it does not want to use the same terminology as Boeing. FMC, however, is the generally accepted generic term for the computer.

3. See David M. North's editorial in *Aviation Week & Space Technology*, 23 February 1998. Describing a ride on an Airbus A-330 he commented, "The speedbrakes were automatically retracted by the logic that a pilot did not want them extended if he were asking for full power. That feature might have saved the American Airlines Boeing 757, which crashed near Cali, Columbia in late 1995."

4. Many pilots did not like the idea of being managed by a machine in this way, and cited cases where pilots had been obliged to carry out unauthorised manoeuvres in order to get the plane out of a potentially disastrous situation. The answer from Airbus was: a) the aircraft's programs would not permit you to get into such a dangerous situation in the first place; and b) if by some chance it did, pilots can disable the automatic systems and fly the plane in "direct law", whereby it will accept any input from the pilot.

5. As is well known, Boeing's scare was short-lived. The Comet's designers had not fully accounted for the effects of frequent pressurisation and the weakened fuselage split apart in flight on several occasions, destroying the aircraft and all on board. By the time the cause of the mysterious crashes had been determined it was too late for the Comet to regain lost ground.

6. There is no proof that this is what happened, but the accident investigators, the investigating magistrate and all interested parties accept it as the most probable scenario.

7. Federal Aviation Administration Human Factors Team Report, "The Interfaces between Flightcrews and Modern Flight Deck Systems", 18 June 1996, Appendix D.

8. Daniel John, "New crash places focus on in-flight Airbus computers", The *Guardian*, 22 January 1992, p. 10

9. *Flight International*, July and August 1994, passim.

10. Although not having GPWS apears a gross dereliction of the airline's duty of care towards its passengers, there have been doubts that it would necessarily have saved the A-320's passengers that night in January. The type of GPWS available at the time did give some false warnings, and Commandant De Gaullier, for example, is one of those who believes that the approach to Strasbourg airport is just the kind where, had GPWS been installed, the pilots' normal instructions may well have been to ignore terrain warnings on final approach. François Guichard, the judge investigating the disaster, however, caused a demonstration flight to be made in which the approach was repeated as it was on that January night but in an A-320 with GPWS installed. He firmly believes that GPWS could have saved the aircraft.

11. Stuart Matthews, "Safety and Statistics: what the numbers tell us about aviation safety at the end of the 20th century", *Flight Safety Digest*, December 1997, fig. 10, p. 7, shows the trend. The graph shows that for the newest type of aircraft, Boeing 757, 767, 777 and Airbus A-320 and family, for example, the initial accident rate was 3.2 per million departures, falling to less than one PMD after about five years. Statistically, however, the A-330 crash did not count in the figures because it was not in revenue operation.

12. Translated from the French by the author from an interview with Mr Châtre in Lyon in May 1996 for Darlow-Smithson Productions and used with permission.

13. Mr Châtre had been wearing his seat-belt loosely. When the impact occurred he was thrown out of his seat. His feet caught the seat-belt, which broke his ankles and ripped off his shoes, before his momentum propelled him through a gap in the broken fuselage. He underwent dozens of operations to repair his ankles and graft skin to where he had been burned.

14. Despite being so near a major city, as well as being in the midst of France's most militarily sensitive area, hundreds of soldiers, air force personnel, gendarmes and police officers could not manage to locate the wreckage. It was snowing and pitch dark, but the military, police and emergency services were much embarrassed by the fact that a local TV reporter and his cameraman were first on the scene. They summoned help by mobile telephone.

15. One of many sources on this is Peter Ladkin, "An early incident to a China Air B747 on a transpacific flight, 19 February 1985", on his website, op. cit. Also NTSB/AAR-86/03.

16. Information from Harro Ranter, "Aviation Safety Web Pages", http://web.inter.nl.net/users/H.Ranter/specials/SAS751/sas.htm

17. FAA Human Factors Team Report, op. cit.

18. Ibid., p. 3.

19. Nadine B. Sarter and David D. Woods, "'Strong Silent, and out of the Loop': properties of advanced (cockpit) automation and their impact on human–automation interaction", Cognitive Systems Engineering Laboratory, Ohio State University,

Columbus, Ohio, CSEL Report 95-TR-01, February 1995.
20. FAA Human Factors Team Report op. cit., p. 3.
21. Charles Billings, "Advanced Automation and Human Performance", ISASI Forum, January–March 1998, p. 20.
22. FAA Human Factors Team Report, p. 3.
23. Peter Mellor, "Computer-aided Disaster", 13 July 1994, Centre for Software Reliability, City University, London.
24. Ibid.
25. Ibid.
26. Details on this incident from AAIB Bulletin 3/95.
27. An Airworthiness Directive was subsequently issued on this problem.
28. Such problems have been suffered on Boeings too. Although the 767 is not a fly-by-wire plane, it has a sophisticated FMS.
29. In the ASRS pilots are normally reporting a safety-related problem. The idea behind the system, which operates in many other countries, is that pilots can confess, anonymously, to a mistake. Thus, more mistakes come to light, and other pilots can learn from them. There is one small exception, which tends to skew ASRS reports: in the USA, failure to obey a federal official in the pursuit of his duty is a federal offence, and this includes the instruction from an air traffic controller, who is employed by the FAA, to a flight-crew to maintain a certain altitude. If a pilot commits an altitude deviation it is thus a federal offence. The error, of course, is immediately detectable by ATC's radar. The law in the USA states that if a pilot reports his altitude deviation to ASRS no legal action will be taken. As a result, ASRS reports include far more reports on altitude deviations than just about anything else.

Chapter 7 – Other humans' errors

1. *CHIRP Feedback*, no. 44, October 1997.
2. June 1996 edition of *Aerospace*, quoted by David King, "Incidents: the route to human factors in engineering?", 1996 ISASI seminar proceedings. King is a principal inspector of air

accidents (engineering) with the UK AAIB.

3. AAIB AAR 3/96 and Press Association articles of 25 July 1996.

4. Under an agreement with the FAA the airline had half the fine suspended so long as it observed an agreement on how it carries out its maintenance in future (*Aviation Daily*, 16 July 1998).

5. King, article cit.

6. NTSB AAR 4/84.

7. Taylor, op. cit., p 155.

8. *CHIRP Feedback*, no. 47, July 1998. Presumably, CHIRP considered the incident so serious that it was worth risking the probable identification of the aircraft involved to convey the appalling implications of what could have happened. There is no mention of whether anybody was dismissed over the incident. Oddly, probably because of crown immunity or privilege, the Queen's aircraft do not need an airworthiness certificate!

9. Eric Newton, "Some lessons learned from aircraft accidents – the engineering aspects", *Aircraft Engineering*, February 1978.

10. An NTSB study and a General Electric study cited by Wayne Glover, "Testing for failure, not success", ISASI Forum, July–September 1997.

11. Quoted in Laurie Taylor, op. cit., p. 142.

Chapter 8 – Investigators and regulators

1. The basic air-crash investigation code of practice is set out in the ICAO Annex 13.

2. Dr Carolyn V. Coarsey-Rader, who compiled a report on the experiences of survivors of air crashes (*see* Chapter 1, note 13) also studied the effects of crash scenes on the investigators. In a 1995 study, "Effects of investigation of a fatal air crash on 13 government investigators", she found that three of them, or 23 per cent, were suffering from post-traumatic stress disorder. They were attending the scene of the crash of a USAir DC-9 in Charlotte, North Carolina, on 2 July 1994, which claimed thirty-eight lives, at the time of the study. The investigators were both from the FAA and the NTSB. Each had investigated an average of

four fatal crashes in the year before they came to the Charlotte crash site.

3. From Thomas Farrier, Chief, Flight Safety Issues, Office of the Chief of Safety Headquarters, United States Air Force, "Adding Value to Aviation Operations: New Directions for the 21st Century Investigator", proceedings of 1996 seminar of International Society of Air Safety Investigators.

4. Quoted in CNN "US News", 7 May 1997, citing a USA Today article of the same day.

5. Quoted in Aviation Week & Space Technology special report on air safety regulation, 18 August 1997.

6. In the USA the NTSB was created in 1974 under new legislation which ensured its independence. The pressure to have the law adopted arose out of alleged political interference in the regulatory process by officials appointed by President Nixon. It was generally believed that this interference had allowed McDonnell Douglas to get away with not taking immediate action on the DC-10 cargo door, which in turn failed to prevent the Paris disaster in 1974, then the world's worst air crash.

7. See note 8, Chapter 9.

8. Cockpit voice recorders are designed in various ways. Some have just one "area" microphone recording all noise in the cockpit, while more modern versions have "hot mikes" recording directly from the headsets of the pilots in addition to the area mike. They record for thirty minutes on a loop-tape, so that when power is lost, as it would be during a crash, the last thirty minutes of conversation and noise in the cockpit is available to investigators.

9. Telephone conversation with Bill Tench, 18 December 1996. It was first known as the AIB, Accidents Investigation Branch, before the name was changed to AAIB, Aircraft Accidents Investigation Branch, in 1987. I have used the latter set of initials for the sake of simplicity.

10. FDRs record at least four parameters of the aircraft's behaviour – acceleration, airspeed, heading and time – and the most modern can record up to 500 parameters.

11. First the stick-shaker shakes the control column to alert the

pilot to the danger. Should no action be taken, the stick-push automatically pushes the control column forward to drop the nose and increase air speed.

12. Aircraft Accident Report 4/73.

13. Exceptions have been made in certain cases due to the intervention of responsible ministers.

14. In a reply to my queries about this on 20 March 1996, the CAA said that the AAIB's recommendation on rear-facing seats and upper torso restraint "was answered together with four other recommendations by one response. The response anticipates the co-ordinated research programme (it cited here a study by Mr Ray Cherry for the Joint Aviation Authorities Research Committee, but without mentioning its proposals on rear-facing seats, if any). The response does not, apart from brace position, mention any specific technical proposals or solution." Referring on to international organisations and other researchers is one way of deflecting safety recommendations, not to mention being vague.

15. Schiavo, op. cit., p. 13. Defenders of the aviation industry pounced with delight on some factual inaccuracies in Schiavo's book, allowing them to avoid answering the difficult questions which remained.

16. Mary Schiavo's statement to the US House of Representatives Committee on Transportation and Infrastructure, mid-1996. She was speaking on behalf of the Office of Inspector General, Department of Transportation, before she left her job.

17. Schiavo is not the only critic. Anonymous inspectors have written to the US trade magazine, *Aviation Week & Space Technology*, complaining that safety is frequently compromised by politics. An FAA aircraft inspector testified anonymously before a committee of Congress, saying that inadequate training was jeopardising safety.

18. See C.O. Miller, "Down with probable cause", paper presented to ISASI International Seminar, 7 November 1991.

19. Joseph O'Connell, "Remarks before the Air Line Pilots' Association Annual Safety Seminar", Seattle, Washington, 9 July 1968, quoted in C.O. Miller, "'Probable Cause': the correct legal test in civil aircraft accident investigations?" 23 April 1992,

published in library archive of Center for Aerospace Safety Education, Embry-Riddle Aeronautical University, http://www.pr. erau.edu/~case/library/.

20. Ibid.

21. Ira J. Rimson's "Investigating 'causes'", presented at the ISASI International Seminar, Barcelona, 20 October 1998.

22. An enormous amount of speculation centred on the possibility either of a bomb having been planted or a missile having struck it. High explosive leaves distinct traces because it explodes much more violently than any other material. Fragments propelled by a bomb will be found all over the wreckage and inside bodies, the mass of the small particles together with marks on where they were embedded showing how fast they were going. No such fragments were found. The missile theory falls down for the above reason, as well the fact that no parts of any missile have been found. Neither has a point of entry for a missile been found in the fuselage, or even fragments of missile shrapnel, in case the missile exploded close to the plane rather than inside it. Among the 95 per cent of the 747 which has been recovered from the sea-bed is not one iota of evidence to support sabotage or a shootdown. The persistence of these theories and the deter-mination with which many of them were expounded, complete with allegations of US Navy and FBI cover-ups, may well have been at least partly influenced by the fact that it took over a year before the NTSB could come up with an explanation. At first, they were strongly inclined towards the bomb theory, but the physical evidence would not support it. Speculation has continued unabated, including one offering on electro-magnetic interference providing the ignition source by the Cabot Professor of Aesthetics and the General Theory of Value, Elaine Scarry, which was published in the unofficial house magazine of the US intelligentsia, *New York Review of Books*, on 9 April 1998. The only plausible conspiracy theory on TWA 800 I have heard states that Boeing has secretly been encouraging sabotage and shootdown con-spiracy theories. In the event of a design or manufacturing-related fault being proved to be responsible for the crash, Boeing would become liable for damages. No such fascination has been

evidenced in the crash of the Korean Air jumbo which hit a hill on Guam in August 1997, despite the causes still being unknown and the number of dead being about the same.

23. Quoted in "Fuel Tank Explosions", *Aviation Week & Space Technology*, 14 July 1997.

24. Interview with Dr Loeb, "Panorama: The Fall of Flight 800", BBC1, 7 July 1997.

25. An Imperial Iranian Air Force B-747 freighter exploded in mid-air on 9 May 1976 near Madrid, lightning being suspected as having ignited vapour in the tank. Intriguingly and tantalisingly, this jet was a sister plane of TWA 800 and had been sold to Iran by TWA. Although doubts were expressed about lightning having been the cause, there was not enough physical evidence to conclude otherwise or on which to compare notes with the TWA 800 crash. On 11 May 1990 a Philippines Airlines B-737 central fuel tank exploded on the ground as it was taxiing, full of passengers. In the fire and evacuation that followed seven passengers died.

26. *Flight International*, 29 July–4 August 1998, p. 9.

27. Tom McSweeny in Avsig forum Compuserve.

28. See Nader and Smith, op. cit., p. 36.

29. The seminar was organised by the Parliamentary Advisory Committee on Transport Safety (PACTS) in July 1988. The CAA report was criticised by PACTS in its submission to the UK House of Commons Transport Committee (Transport Committee report, "Aircraft Cabin Safety", p. 33 (London, HMSO, 1990)).

30. *Flight International*, 29 July–4 August 1998 p. 9.

31. Conversation, 8 May 1996.

32. The same was the case with the mechanical lock-out system on the hydraulically operated slats of the DC-10. One thing, too remote to be worth guarding against, led to another and a disaster ensued at Chicago in 1979. The FAA's airworthiness regulations say that the aircraft should maintain its structural integrity in the event of an explosive decompression ". . . unless it is shown that the probability of failure or penetration is extremely remote". Interestingly, the British regulations contain no such let-out. The DC-10, therefore – and probably the Boeing 747 – is in breach of

the regulations. This point was made by Frank Taylor in his "Airworthiness requirements: accidents investigation and safety recommendations." ISASI seminar, Barcelona, October 1998.

33. Formally charging a body with a criminal offence is a judges' investigative device by dint of which they can collect evidence and carry out interrogations. Checks and balances may be few in France, but under the Napoleonic judicial code, as in Italy, Spain and elsewhere, investigating judges take prominent roles. In France and Italy, for example, the government produces an administrative report on the investigation and causes of an air crash, which is then followed by a judicial investigation. Like the British and US investigations, the French and Italian government investigator reports have no legal standing. The judicial inquiries can, however, take many years.

34. There is a problem in certifying software, too (see Chapter 6). Basically, it cannot be done. Software can go wrong in too many ways for success to be guaranteed. The best that regulators, and others in the field of safety-critical software, can do is to require that certain processes be followed in the designing and supervising of software. This was done in the case of the 777, but there was still a problem. Airbus Industrie had duplicated software code on different computers, and the duplicate code was written by a separate team of software designers using a different code system. That way, no faults common to the ways of writing code would turn up. Boeing used just one code-writing team and thus omitted one level of redundancy.

35. According to Schiavo, op. cit., pp. 184–6.

36. In the case of the Boeing 767's thrust reversers honesty and credibility both appeared to be lacking. See Chapter 9 on the fate of Lauda Air's 767.

37. Airbus and Boeing have been locked in bitter trade disputes for several years, the fights being staged mainly on their behalf by politicians and trade officials of the US government on the one hand and the European Union on the other. Boeing's supporters usually claim that Airbus competes unfairly by using government subsidies, and the pro-Airbus party normally responds by pointing to the enormous value of US military contracts to Boeing.

38. Schiavo, op. cit., p. 189.

39. ETOPS is extended twin-engine operations. In the piston-engine era there was a tendency for twin-engined aircraft in particular to suffer total engine failure if one engine failed. Often the additional strain on the second engine following the failure of the first was enough to cause it to fail too, and a serious crash usually resulted. Consequently, the rule was made that no twin-engined aircraft should be more than ninety minutes' flying time from a suitable airport. So long as the long-distance aircraft were 747s, 707s and the like there was no problem, but new jet-engine technology of the 1970s created twin-engined aircraft capable of flying immense distances, the Airbus 300 being the first of them. ETOPS are the exceptions to these rules, recognising the greater reliability of the modern jet engine. Over the years, manufacturers and airlines have lobbied successfully to extend the maximum permissible time from a suitable airport to the point where some aircraft, including the 777, may be up to four hours' flying time from a suitable airport. ETOPS rules also govern aspects of piloting and the maintenance regime for the aircraft. Waggish pilots have been known to label ETOPS "Engines Turn Or Passengers Swim".

40. NTSB AAR 96/01, vol. 1: "Safety Board Report"; vol. 2: "Response of Bureau Enquêtes Accidents to Safety Board's Draft Report (AAR 96/02)". The report was adopted and published on 9 July 1996.

41. The USA operates a so-called hub system. If you want to fly between major cities, you can get a direct flight. If your destination is not a major city, you will have to get there in two legs. First you fly to the "hub", where the airline operating your destination flight is based, and then fly out from there to your destination. Because your destination is relatively small, the second leg is often operated with smaller, so-called commuter aircraft like the ATR.

42. The NTSB cited five incidents before the Roselawn crash as precursors, specifically excluding the 1987 crash in Italy. C.O. Miller, however, who was hired as a consultant by one of the parties involved in the Italian crash investigation, says that it bore

a remarkable resemblance to the crash in Italy. Don Mullin, a former chief test pilot for McDonnell Douglas aircraft, who was also hired in connection with that investigation, agreed.

43. Vortex generators were added to the top of the wing. These small tooth-like objects sticking up from the wing, about half the size of a business card, break up the airflow over the wing and prevent the vacuum from forming over it until the angle of attack is higher than was the case previously.

44. ATR, or Avions de Transports Regionaux, has now been renamed AIR, Aero International (Regional).

45. One of the many paradoxes of the aviation system is that the more senior and experienced you become as a pilot, the less skill you are required to use. Newly qualified airline pilots start their careers in the more taxing environment of commuter aircraft before graduating, if they are lucky, to large jets, which have more automation as well as flying in less hostile conditions.

46. *Cincinnati Enquirer*, 10 July 1998.

47. Don Phillips, "Board says '97 Crash Was Partly FAA's Fault", *Washington Post*, 28 August 1998, p. F01.

48. It added, regarding the crew's and the airline's responsibility, "Contributing to the accident were the flightcrew's decision to operate in icing conditions near the lower margin of the operating airspeed envelope (with flaps retracted), and Comair's failure to establish and adequately disseminate unambiguous minimum airspeed values for flap configurations and for flight in icing conditions." From "Abstract of the Final Report", "In-Flight Icing Encounter and Uncontrolled Collision with Terrain, Comair Flight 3272, Embraer EMB-120RT, N265CA, Monroe, Michigan, January 9, 1997," presented at an NTSB public meeting, 27 August 1998.

49. Graham R. Braithwaite, "Air Safety in Australia: What Makes it so Good?", ISASI Forum, January–March 1997.

Chapter 9 – The Tombstone Imperative

1. Rudy Kapustin's paper on "How to effectively prevent major accidents". Paper given at Embry Riddle Air Law Symposium, 1994.
2. Aircraft Incident Report, "Airbus A 310-304 near Moscow February 11, 1991" (English version), p. 29. File No: 6 X 002-0/91, "Flugunfalluntersuchungstelle beim Luftfahrt-Bundesamt".
3. "ICAO grasps global safety-oversight", *Flight International*, 26 November–2 December 1997, p. 8.
4. No doubt McDonnell Douglas would have claimed that the change in designation was intended to reflect the fact that the MD-11 was a "glass cockpit", more fully automated aircraft, and that the same applied to the MD-80. Nobody was really fooled. Since the merger of McDonnell Douglas and Boeing the MD-80 family are now Boeings. The latest descendant of the DC-9 is called the Boeing 717.
5. Newton showed me a letter he had written to the head of the AAIB on 14 March, less than two weeks after the Paris disaster. He wrote, "this accident was one that should not have occurred. The warning was clear in 1972 and obviously the lessons from that accident were not learned . . . This is not a technical accident, this is a human failure accident."
6. NTSB AAR 92/02, "Report on United Airlines Flight 811, Boeing 747-122, N4713U, Honolulu, Hawaii, Feb 24, 1989".
7. The NTSB had issued one report in 1990, which laid much heavier blame for the accident on the door design, with which many safety experts have never been happy. But after an extraordinary search, the cargo door which had parted in-flight was recovered from 14,200 feet of water. This enabled the investigators to show that improper actuation of the electric motor due to frayed wires had been the reason the door was ajar.
8. This would make the aircraft illegal in Britain. Section 2.1.3 of the British Civil Aviation Regulations states: "Where a pressurised cabin is separated into two or more compartments by bulkheads or floors, the primary structure shall be designed to withstand any pressure differences which might exist between compartments

and, in particular, to withstand the effects of sudden release of pressure in any compartment having external doors which open outwards, or windows." This is quoted in Frank Taylor's paper, cited below. He goes on to say, "Note that in BCARs there was no let-out clause, the requirement implied that a door that opened outwards would, sooner or later, come open in flight and that the necessary safeguards must be in place to prevent this from becoming catastrophic. Since such safeguards were not present then clearly the DC-10 did not comply with BCARs." So, the DC-10 would still appear to be unlawful. The CAA has never explained why it has not enforced its own regulations. "Airworthiness requirements: accidents investigation & safety recommendations" by A. Frank Taylor, Barcelona ISASI seminar October 1998. The importance of this was brought fully home just as the DC-10 was coming into service. A British Vanguard aircraft crashed in October 1971 in Belgium after the rear-pressure bulkhead failed and resulted in loss of the tailplane, followed by that of all lives on board.

9. See Chapter 5.

10. Such planes are meant to be able to cope with accidental thrust reversal in flight anyway, so why total loss of control should have been experienced so suddenly was not known at first. The FAA accepted Boeing's implication that the pilots ought to have been able to handle it. However, the NTSB questioned Boeing's data on how the plane behaved when thrust reversal occurred on one engine. Under their pressure new tests were done and it was shown that the loss of lift on the relevant wing was two and a half times greater than the figure Boeing had given the FAA. The FAA had simply taken that figure on trust when giving the plane its airworthiness certificate. Far from the sixty seconds or so Boeing said the pilots had to correct the problem, they only had five seconds in reality, and it was not a situation anybody had ever been trained for.

Chapter 10 – How to decide where not to go and how not to get there

1. The only problem about calculating the relative safety of jets and turboprops is that the figures for the number of flights for turboprops is incomplete. The comparison is therefore made on the basis of the number of fatal accidents against the age of the fleet.

2. *Airliner Loss Rates 1996*, published by Airclaims Ltd, Cardinal Point, Newall Rd, Heathrow Airport, London TW6 2AS. All figures for aircraft accident rates hereafter are taken from this report.

3. What would have become the MD-95, the latest and largest member of the DC-9 family, was inherited by Boeing when it merged with McDonnell Douglas. It is now known at the Boeing 717.

4. Paul Eddy, Elaine Potter and Bruce Page (of the *Sunday Times* Insight Team), *Destination Disaster*, London, (Hart-Davis, MacGibbon, 1976).

5. Arnold Barnett, "How Numbers Are Tricking You", *MIT Technical Review*, October 1994. Professor Barnett was taking the International Airline Passengers' Association to task for ranking airlines on safety in this fashion. He also performed a public service by trashing "on-time" performance tables. He showed that the airlines with the best records for punctuality were the ones that operated in the best weather conditions.

6. From "Cross-Modal Work Helps OMC Improve the Safety of Commercial Transportation", *Volpe Center Journal*, Spring 1997. Because of the inclusion of "service quality", which itself includes on-time performance, the system is, strictly speaking, not solely oriented towards safety.

7. *Aviation Safety: New Airlines Illustrate Long-standing Problems in FAA's Inspection Program* General Accounting Office, Washington, DC (Letter Report, 17 October 1996, GAO/RCED-97-2).

8. *Aviation Safety – Measuring How Safely Individual Airlines Operate*, General Accounting Office, Washington, DC, March

1988 (GAO/RCED-88-61.)

9. JACDEC database. The accident happened on 5 August 1998 at Kimpo airport, South Korea. Fortunately, no one was hurt.

10. *Flight International*, 17–23 June 1998.

11. *Flight International*, 29 April–5 May 1998, p. 11.

12. *Flight International*, September 1998.

13. Cynics might call this a case of removing someone else's mote before you have tackled your own beam (*Flight International*, 8-14 April 1998, p. 35.

14. *Aviation Week & Space Technology*, 20 October 1997.

15. Overview of the FAA Flight Standards Service International Aviation Safety Assessment Program; http://www.faa.gov/avr/iasabr15.htm.

16. *Sunday Times*, 9 August 1998.

17. Schiphol was included because pilots allege that noise restrictions force aircraft into a region of high crosswinds.

Index

Permissions

Many thanks to the following for the kind use of their photographs:

Paris, 1974 © Associated Press
DC-10 rear cargo door © Andrew Weir
Riyadh, 1980 © Associated Press
Cincinnati, 1983 © Associated Press
Manchester, 1985 © Associated Press
Los angeles, 1991 © Associated Press
Japan, 1985 © Associated Press
Honolulu, 1989 © Associated Press
ATR-72 © Quadrant Picture Library
New York, 1989 © Associated Press
Thai Airways Airbus A330 © Quadrant Picture Library
Stockholm, 1991 © Associated Press
Guam, 1997 © Associated Press
Kegworth, 1989 © PA News
Guam, 1997 © PA News
France, 1992 © Rex Features